PRAISE FOR
Brian Francis Slattery and *Spaceman Blues*

"One of the most original novels of the year. . . . The end of the world was never so fun."
—Ain't It Cool News

"For Fans Of: the surreal odyssey of Ralph Ellison's *Invisible Man; Plan 9 from Outer Space* . . . For all its colorful characters and gonzo thrills, Slattery's debut is first and foremost a moving portrait of Wendell's griefs."
—*Entertainment Weekly (Grade: A-)*

"Slattery's debut is a kaleidoscopic celebration of the immigrant experience. . . . Pynchon crossed with Steinbeck, painted by Dali: impossible to summarize, swinging from the surreal to the hyper-real, a brilliantly handled, tumultuous yarn."
—*Kirkus Reviews*

"The flaming exclamation point that begins every subsection of each chapter is one of the first signs of the intensity and passion that pervade Brian Francis Slattery's debut novel, *Spaceman Blues*, . . . perhaps best summed up as a love song for New York City and for life, with the volume turned up six notches higher than usual."
—*Rain Taxi Review of Books*

"The book jacket describes *Spaceman Blues* as a 'literary retro-pulp science-fiction-mystery-superhero novel,' and it not only lives up to the hype, but may include a genre or two more besides. . . . The book weaves a mixture of gritty war elements with hard-boiled Hammett-like detective mystery, poetic romance reminiscent of Isabel Allende, and science fiction that brings Stanislaw Lem to mind—into something that seems fresh and compelling."
—*School Library Journal*

"*Spaceman Blues* is a welcome Band-Aid for those still mourning the loss of Kurt Vonnegut and his uniquely wacky, satirical brand of sci-fi. There's also a touch of Paul Auster's flair for genre blending and New York mythologizing. . . . A strange and whimsical mash note to the city, Slattery's apocalyptome proves that this newcomer is as thoughtful and irreverent as doomsayers come."
—*Time Out New York*

"What a breathless, mad tornado of words! When it shakes itself awake the earth trembles and the helpless reader is dragged gladly into its light. I haven't had this much fun with a book in years."
—*Harlan Ellison®*

BOOKS BY BRIAN FRANCIS SLATTERY

Spaceman Blues
Liberation

LIBERATION

BEING ★THE★ ADVENTURES OF THE SLICK SIX

AFTER THE COLLAPSE of the UNITED STATES of AMERICA

BRIAN FRANCIS SLATTERY

TOR®

A Tom Doherty Associates Book

New York

LIBERATION: BEING THE ADVENTURES OF THE SLICK SIX AFTER THE COLLAPSE OF THE UNITED STATES OF AMERICA

Copyright © 2008 by Brian Francis Slattery

Edited by Liz Gorinsky

A Tor Book
Published by Tom Doherty Associates, LLC
175 Fifth Avenue
New York, NY 10010

www.tor-forge.com

Tor® is a registered trademark of Tom Doherty Associates, LLC.

ISBN-13: 978-0-7653-2046-9
ISBN-10: 0-7653-2046-0

First Edition: October 2008

Printed in the United States of America

0 9 8 7 6 5 4 3 2 1

PART ONE

★ GREETINGS AND ★ HALLUCINATIONS

The way of the world, man, it's moving fast, toward either utopia or hell. Only trouble is, there's no way to tell which one's which.

· DOCTOR SAN DIEGO OF THE AMERICOIDS ·

CHAPTER I.

A PRISON SHIP; the resurgence of slavery;
life after economic collapse.

The former American prison ship *Rosalita* has been at sea for six years, and wears its history on its skin. The hull is weak with patches and dents, long streaks of rust that eat the ship's name off the metal; near the prow is a wide, eye-shaped wrinkle from collision, some of the inmates say, with another ship, a derelict clipper. No. A dead mine from World War I. No. The jutting mast of a sunken galleon hanging off a spur of rock at the edge of an abyss, filled with the corpses of slaves, rum and sugar, the stuff that drove the world mad. A narwhal, say others, or no, no, a creature the size of an island that rose beneath the ship one night and dove again, leaving the *Rosalita* wounded and the ocean churning and swirling around her. All they have to go on are bangs and shudders, screeches across the metal, the sounds of invisible catastrophe.

The ship rises and falls under the glaring subarctic sun; the bow tilts forward and back, growing a pelt of salt and ice that glistens the rails, slicks the deck. Stiffens the American flag above the tower. Two of the flag's stripes are missing; they're part of the patchwork umbrella stabbed into the snow on the deck, cocked away from the sun to part the wind around Maggot Boy Johnson, who lies in his pants and boots on a lawn chair bolted down in front of the bridge, sunglasses over his closed eyes. His shirt is in the snow next to him, folded over three times so he can put the radio on it. Only one speaker works, and it plays nothing but early Frank Zappa. Maggot Boy Johnson hated it at first, but he and Uncle Meat have come to an understanding. He tans into burning while the opening fanfare to "Peaches en Regalia" flows over him, the bugle call for a hippie army that marched at the peak of the American parabola, that moment when physics held its breath to allow levitation, a small reward before the descent. The hippies knew it then, Maggot Boy Johnson thinks; they couldn't build it into words but they could feel it; a floating in the stomach as history shifted direction. They stopped, hey, what's that sound, and knew that the spiny skyscrapers reflected in the river, the chasms of concrete, the wide streets and sidewalks, the power lines cutting into the hills and mountains above missile silos, the highways drawing lines across the blank plains under enormous skies, the pupil of God's eye, would be the ruins that their grandchildren wandered among, the reminders that once there was always water in the faucet, there was electricity all the time, and America was prying off the shackles of its past. The vision opened up to them and winked out again, and those it blinded staggered through their lives unable to see anything else, while the rest of them wondered if they had only dreamed it.

For the first twenty minutes of Maggot Boy Johnson's stay in the sun, there is only the snow melting on the metal, the water sliding underneath the ice to trickle down the stairs, through the hallways and bunks, the galley. But then he can see the water pooling in the hold, nourishing the seeds of vines that strayed onto the ship in Malaysia. In twelve years, when the ship runs aground on the coast of Mozambique, the stones will put a hole in the hull, sun will stream into the dank air, and the vines will crawl out to spill across the sand, fingers joining ship to earth. Hello, Africa; it's Malaysia. With the help of the Vibe, Maggot Boy Johnson can see that the

Rosalita will be covered in graffiti by then. He wonders how that paint will get all over the ship; wonders if he'll be around to find out.

Marco Angelo Oliveira jumps out of the sky, lands on the deck without a sound, spear in one hand; he runs his free hand over his slicked-back hair. At first, Maggot Boy Johnson doesn't even know he's there. Marco surveys the gray ocean with a hand angled across his brow, hoping for the first peak of an island, a sliver of shore, but the ocean does not comply. He sighs.

"Are we going home?" Marco says.

"Yes," Maggot Boy Johnson says, without opening his eyes.

"Then why isn't it getting any warmer?"

"It is. You just can't feel it yet. What do you call that thing you're holding?"

"An assegai."

"Ass a what?"

"Are those the warden's sunglasses?" Marco says.

"Yep. But that's nothing. These are Malloy's pants."

Most of the warden—his name is James Patrick Callahan, though the inmates never knew that—is now southwest of Reykjavik at a depth of 4,002 meters, his bones snagged in the rigging of a fishing boat listing to starboard, strands of skin and clothes unfurling into the current. The first amphipods found him by smell, but when they started eating, the sound of the chewing drew more for leagues around; it took the crustaceans weeks to eat the annoyance off his face. He was annoyed going into the water, annoyed even as he drowned. It wasn't that he should die before he had a chance to retire, or see America again, that he shouldn't have gone pulling brine into his lungs. He understood that the sea was a lethal thing; if it couldn't get down your throat, it would take your heat away. They were sailing on mercury, liquid nitrogen, hydrochloric acid, the warden thought, and he accepted it, forgave the ocean, which hadn't asked for it. He would have forgiven the inmates, too, if they were the ones who had tied him to a broken generator, then heaved it over the rail and let him slide along the deck after it, swing through the air, tumble into the water. They were like the sea to him, fatal and unreadable, a surface of changing faces, their calmness roiling into sudden storms, the eye of their fury turned on him.

No, he was annoyed because it was his guards who had tied his ankles, pushed the generator over, as if what was happening on the mainland could excuse it. There were riots in Los Angeles, riots in New York. Mexicans fleeing back across the border. The big factories—the ones with high walls and wired windows that you could drive by at seventy miles an hour, car windows rolled down and a Dead bootleg from 1974 on the stereo, and still be driving by it when Jerry finished his solo—the factories were going under, the workers sitting in their cars in the gigantic parking lots, smoking bad cigarettes, wondering what they were going to do now, while eight miles away on the other side of the compound, a man was clipping a door into the cyclone fence, peeling back the wires to let his family squat in the derelict buildings while he stationed himself on the roof with a rifle and sixty-two bags of salt-and-vinegar potato chips. There were killings out on the Midwestern farms, criminals roaring from town to town, borne on a caravan of rusted cars, a trail of food and gasoline, burning houses, leaving corpses chewed by shotguns in ditches. It was like that for a year, and first they could see it on the television, a newscaster in a yellow jacket standing in the rain, holding a gray microphone under the camera's glare, barking out what he was seeing when the flames behind him were plain enough. Speeches from a nervous president, sitting against the backdrop of a flag in an undisclosed location that the inmates joked was really in Canada. Then, one by one, the television stations stopped working. No news out of Washington at all, as if its mouth had been filled with dirt. The letters stopped coming, the paychecks stopped coming, and the Office of Maritime Penitentiaries couldn't be raised. Another month passed; they hailed other ships asking what was going down. One of the guards said he heard something about how there was no such thing as a dollar anymore. He opened his wallet, pulled out a five, waved it above his dinner in the fluorescence of the mess hall. If this isn't money, then what is it?

"Don't you get it?" the warden said. "America's gone."

"Sure it is, Chief," said Club Malloy. He wasn't the highest-ranking guard, but they all took orders from him anyway. It was the blear in his right eye, his hints that he had the same kind of history that the inmates did; he talked about his wife all the time, but never in the present tense.

"I'm telling you the truth," the warden said.

"The only thing that tells the truth is the dollar," said Club Malloy.

"The dollar doesn't mean anything anymore."

"Well that's too bad for you, then, isn't it."

So the inmates stood in a cluster on the deck while the warden slid off it; they heard him shout when the generator hit the waves, a small, bovine yelp when the water took him in. Then Club Malloy smiled wider and wider; just when it seemed his face couldn't make a bigger grin, the lips stretched a little farther.

We're in huge trouble, Maggot Boy Johnson thought.

That was four years ago. The guards declared martial law, shot the oldest prisoner, seventy-two-year-old Amos Straw, in the back of his head while he was reaching across the table in the mess hall for a salt shaker. Just making a point, Malloy said, though nobody knew what he was trying to say. In almost ten years on the *Rosalita*—he'd been put away for forgery fifteen years before, sent to Leavenworth, and then, when all the prisons got too crowded, sent out to sea on the new prison ships—Amos had never lost a card game. You could almost beat him at hearts, but at gin rummy he pummeled your ass. Poker was a filthy slaughter.

Four months later, thirty-nine inmates charged the guards' quarters, garroted one of them with a radio antenna before Club Malloy put the revolt down himself with a machine gun he kept next to his bed. He ran into the blocks, sweet and stinking with fresh blood, and shot the first two inmates he saw, strung up the bodies on steel cables on the deck. A warning, he said. We have thousands of bullets. The bodies hung in the sun until the next storm, when a gigantic wave, an exploding mountain of brine and ice, took them down.

The food on the ship dwindled, was traded for knives, cigarettes. Then food was currency. The guards locked the inmates in the hull and talked on deck amongst themselves. They hailed more passing ships, traded off spare parts, fan belts, electric switches, rubber seals. Then they stopped selling things; the inmates could hear one of the guards at the radio trying to hail the same ship a few times, one ship in particular. A conversation about the cargo still being alive. A week went by when everyone started starving. Then at sunrise another ship approached them, a black-and-green freighter flying a flag of a Roman warrior with sword and spear, his foot on the chest of a man sprawled at his feet. A broken crown. Something in crap Latin: *Labos te liberat.* The inmates read the faces of the crew, knew that look; they'd all had it themselves once, the nervous elation that comes with doing something you've never done before. Committing a new crime.

The guards picked out the five biggest inmates and lined them up in a row while the freighter captain, who had the name DIAMOND SAM stitched in rude letters on the back of his coat, paced in front of them, his eyes moving over the lengths of their bodies. He stopped in front of Piston Beauvoir, car thief, cardsharp, occasional bookie, who until the televisions died still took bets on games, fights, elections, whether it would rain in San Antonio, whether there'd be anchovies with dinner. Even made money on the flash floods in Tennessee.

"Open your mouth."

He did; Diamond Sam jammed two fingers into it, raked his nails against the gums.

"This one's rotten," he said.

But he found the other four whole. James Szspanski, who'd opened his brother's head with a sledgehammer when he found out the man had been sleeping with his wife. He'd played third base for six different teams in the minor leagues, eight years, before a torn ligament put him out. Alan Green, who'd stolen ten thousand in cash from a wire service, shot a security guard who tried to stop him. He said later it was for his daughter. Nobody knew what Henry Holloway had done to be put on board; in seven years, he'd never said a word to anyone, spent his days on the deck doing handstands, eyes closed, legs at a perfect vertical, even as the boat moved beneath him. Carlos Rivera had always said he was innocent, and everyone believed him after he lost a toe in a fight and didn't fight back. Diamond Sam took them all, shook hands with the guards, nodded to his crew, who hauled thirteen crates of potatoes and salted fish onto the deck. And history swung in front of Maggot Boy Johnson, lashed him to its pendulum. There were noises to port, a bell, creaking wood, murmuring voices; then a spectral ship sailed through theirs, the crew in the transparent hold throwing dice against casks of deep brown rum. It ate its own wake back to Massachusetts, sailed back along the malarial coast of the South to Barbados, where the rum turned to molasses, the molasses into sugar, the sugar into cane that men replanted with upward strokes of machetes in hazy green fields. Some of the men were walked backward, stripped naked, lain on dirt floors among corpses. Then all were forced to their feet. Racked by fever, covered in offal, they shuffled backward onto a fat, splintery boat, lay down again in tight rows among flies; then all was dark, dark and screaming until the doors opened again, and they were on Gorée Island off the coast of Dakar, looking out of a stone doorway to the greasy slave ship tilting on the ravenous water, and beyond, the ocean burning blue under a bleaching sky, with no land in sight.

That was when talk began of mutiny aboard the *Rosalita*, of orchestrating a coup. Inmates approached Maggot Boy Johnson at the ends of dark hallways, in corners of the hull. You better mean what you say about knowing how to drive a ship, they said. At first the strategy was a general uprising, of beating the guards down with the butts of their own rifles. There would be bullet holes and drownings, a man brained against the oven in the galley. They'd torture Club Malloy on the deck, sell the rest of the guards into slavery.

"The uprising is a bad idea," Marco said. "Too many of you will die."

"Better death than slavery," Big Mother said.

Marco just shook his head. "Make some noise tomorrow night. Then let me take care of it."

At midnight everyone rattled the bars of their cells, howled at the ceiling, a gorgeous choir of dissonance in the blackness of the block. They didn't even hear the guards come in. The lamps flashed on for three seconds, flashed off, and in the interval of brightness the inmates could see four guards dead in the middle of the floor, a fifth standing at the light switch in shock, Marco dropping from the ceiling on top of him. Seven minutes later a buzzer the inmates had never heard before screamed across the ship, the locks on their cells shunted open all at once, and they were free. They found the guards holding keys, headphones, toothbrushes, pants half on, shirts half off, lying on their beds, liberated from their lives. Marco wasn't even sweating. So the inmates knew the rumors were true, that Marco really was one of the Slick Six—the ones who pulled off impossible crimes, who stole houses from those who lived in them, drew millions upon millions out of the margin of error in the currency market, spirited jewels and paintings out of vaults and museums and into the black market, where money flew huge and invisible through the ether. They were wanted in over a hundred countries but partied in public in all of them: There was never enough evidence to put them away; their lawyer was too good. But Marco was the one who'd really gotten things done. The man who could hide in your shadow, in a coffee cup. The bringer of violence, who strung a chain of ghosts—men, women, and children—across five continents. The one who'd been sent away so the rest of the Slick Six could go free.

The inmates convened on the deck under a drizzling Antarctic sky, shifted from foot to foot to keep warm.

"What do we do now?" Helga Ramstead said.

"Go back to America," Sylvester Sylvester said.

"There's nothing there anymore," Ramstead said.

"There's just nothing on TV. Don't confuse the two."

"Shut the fuck up."

"I'm just saying there's got to be something there."

"No there doesn't."

They still couldn't see it; it was too much at once. They tried to use the dollars that some of the guards had stowed away in pots and pans after the food ran out, but the traders on other boats put up their hands and frowned. Haven't you heard? they said. Keep it. Show your grandkids. Tell them you remember the states united, and they'll shake their heads and laugh, tell you to stop lying. Then they started listening harder to the news that strained through the radio, crackled on computer screens, seeped out of the casual talk of the crews of other ships. More riots in Chicago and Los Angeles, big ones, over food. A hole in the roof of the Capitol. Millions of people missing. Dying cities, drying prairies. Slaves in the south again. Slaves all over. The Federation of New England.

"I think we should go back," said Big Mother. "Do you hear what they're saying? No more government. Which means there's no such thing as criminals anymore."

"That means no right and wrong either," said Piston Beauvoir. "Which means chaos."

"The law's got nothing to do with right and wrong," Big Mother said. "They're two separate things. Take away the law, it doesn't mean everyone burns everything down, does it?"

"You tell me."

They fought about it for three years. Maggot Boy Johnson walloped the *Rosalita* around Cape Horn in a shrieking thunderstorm that sank nine other ships; he smiled every time he saw lightning lance into the ocean, every time a wall of water jumped off the bow. They got into shipping off Eurasia, hid from pirates armed with machine guns piloting dented boats of tin and balsa on the windward side of a flock of rocks jutting off Indonesia. They sailed to Pulau Tengah, nine miles off the Malay coast, to drop off thirty crates of Sandeman port and several hundred pounds of Guatemalan coffee beans, and wound up staying for fourteen months. The island had been uninhabited for decades, until seven former oil executives and their Malay wives built a tiny town there in the ruins of the old Vietnamese refugee camp. They called it New Elysia, said they'd live there until the polar ice caps were gone, then let their wives and children go while they stayed to meet the tide; they deserved it, they said, for what they'd done. Every morning the seven men walked down to the beach, along the lacy line of foam where the waves drew lines in the sand, and there they lay down and let the waves surround them, fill their clothes, flow into their ears. They were listening for news, they said. Someday the sea will tell us when it's coming for us.

New Elysia grew to a hundred people who made their living running a resort for the lords of global commerce who vacationed on the western side of the island; everyone else partied on the eastern side. There were roads to be cleared, trees to fell. But it was days of shrimp and mangoes, nights of zapin, while the lights of the fishing village on the Malay shore painted wavering orange ribbons over the blue water. Four of the inmates married local girls in one ceremony, and the party lasted a week, until all the port was gone and the road to the resort needed clearing again. It wouldn't be so bad to die here, Marco thought, wavering through the forest at dawn. Not so bad to trip and fall into the ground, arms out, mouth open, let the planet swallow me whole. But then the Vibe, invisible, tugged on him, and he brought his assegai out from underneath his bed when he got home, began to sharpen its edges. The Vibe studied Marco's face, its eyes turning darker in concentration, then moved through New Elysia and found Maggot Boy Johnson still in slumber, walked into his head. Maggot Boy Johnson was dreaming that he was in an infinite supermarket, surrounded by vegetables as far as he could see, weighing a piece of broccoli on a tin scale, when the influence of the Vibe set in; the fluorescent lights bent down from the ceiling, formed a set of neon lips, and spoke with the voice of history. This Marco, the Vibe said. See how I will make him my servant, him and the rest of you. Please don't, Maggot Boy Johnson said. We've been through enough already. The fluorescent lights tried to laugh, but shattered instead; and the next day, they all found themselves standing in front of the *Rosalita,* looking at the rusting hull, at each other. They boarded one by one without even having to talk to each other, explain why they were going back, Malaysian seeds stowed away on the soles of their shoes.

Months later they are at the edge of the Arctic Ocean, moving away from Lithuania. It has been almost five years since America winked out of existence, but now news is escaping again, and the inmates want to know. Where's the girl I was with in the days before they put me away? She had pink plastic sandals, a gap between her front teeth. We posted bail, climbed into a 1976 Gremlin with the top sawed off, bought some fake IDs, and turned onto the first curve of a two-week bender through the motels, roadside bars, and convenience stores between Dickson, Tennessee, and Monroeville, Alabama. When there were storms on the highway, she wrapped her head in plastic so she could drive through the rain while I leaned back, spread my arms along the backseat, and closed my eyes, soaking up every drop I could. In front of the courthouse, she got up on her toes and kissed me, her hands on my back, and said she'd wait for me. No you won't, I said, thinking I was tough when I was just being stupid. The memory of it has only sharpened; it cuts me when I get too close. Where are my parents? Are they still ashamed of me? Where is my dog? I gave him a collar of red leather, and somehow he chewed it off. He chased the bus when it drove off from the jail; when the ship angled away from the shore, I kept watching the pier, thinking he would show up, legs in a blur, mouth open, tongue hanging to the side, his new blue collar already half gone. I was going to tell him not to swim, because we'd just have to turn him back again.

They know they've turned south when the water gets warmer. They can feel it through the hull, a glow of heat rising around them, slow tendrils of warmth twining between the bunks and chairs, the chipped tables. The water sloshing on the floor grows plankton. Ice breaks off the deck, drops into the ocean in deep splashes that sound like animals barking. One night, on Piston Beauvoir's watch, the black North Atlantic brine turns phosphorescent, and a pod of dolphins surrounds the ship, dark outlines in the glowing water; then they leap ahead of the prow, rise and dive, sending out fans of light with every splash, liquid fire in the air. The inmates start a betting pool on what America will be like when they get back. It'll all be destroyed, some say, black ruins, unburied bodies lying in broken glass in the street, the countryside all ravaged crops and abandoned towns, kids shooting themselves under rotting bridges. Naw, man, others say. It'll be like nothing ever happened. The lights'll still be on, the plumbing'll still work. Hot cups of coffee and toast with margarine, baked beans and bacon. Your girl in nothing but a tank top and underwear, watching a color television under the shadow of power lines, heaven in your living room. No way, the hippies say. Everything'll be green now, you'll see. Skyscrapers covered in vines with white flowers, sidewalks of velvety grass, rows of corn on the tops of buildings. Mountain lions sunning themselves on rooftops above streets turned to streams swarming with trout, and we'll take off our shoes on the moss at their banks, sit on the curb, and dip our feet in the water. The end of industry, the end of the rush, and as the last light-bulbs burn out and the kerosene runs dry, the universe will return to the North American sky; the stars we haven't seen since there were cities, when we thought they were sparks scattered by the gods.

A dark stripe of land climbs over the horizon, separating the gray sea from its cloudy twin. At the helm, Maggot Boy Johnson takes the *Rosalita* through a series of long sweeps in the water; he is the victim of an explosive chain of collective memories, of Norsemen in salt-crusted furs and leathers heading toward the distant shore, spied on by natives with bone earrings and arrows; of squat Basque ships rocking in an ocean boiling with fish, throwing out their nets and pulling them in again and again until the deck riots with cod; of fisherman out from the Bay of Fundy in those same waters, bobbing on silent seas, the last fish far below; and Maggot Boy Johnson doesn't know whether they're there in the water, or only there, in his head. As they follow the coast down, against the flow of the current, real ships join the phantasms. A fishing boat with five men on it who look like they've been at sea for eight months, their laundry strung out in tan-and-plaid flags from pilot-house to stern. Freighters parade away from the shore, another herd bearing down.

Near New York they're swarmed by a flock of scrap metal junks that parts around the *Rosalita*. A few sail up close enough that four men from the smaller ships can lean over the rail, touch the prison boat's hull, appraising it; they nod to each other, and a woman in pigtails runs to a siren mounted under the sail, cranks it up until it sends a caterwaul across the water, back into New York Harbor, where a curtain of brown-and-white smoke has been pulled over the buildings, over all of them save for a craggy spire that none of the inmates can remember being there. The sun is a raging fire over the hills by the time they reach the city. Maggot Boy Johnson pushes the prow through the tangled town of houseboats that rings Manhattan, a colony of barges, motorboats, and sailboats gutted and built up again with salvaged timber and corrugated metal, hooked to the harbor floor by cinderblocks on chains, lashed to each other by walkways of pallets, inner tubes, and ropes, detached to let the *Rosalita* pass. The boats teem with people moving among the rails and rigging; there are wraiths of music, the rubbery plunk and smack of homemade instruments under ululating voices, fires in charcoal pits on the roofs, plucked and spitted animals roasting over them, fattening the sky. The boats get so thick near the island that they hide the shoreline. Sixteen men and woman jump from boat to boat, holler and point, guiding Maggot Boy Johnson to a rickety pier bowing in four places under the weight of the throng upon it, aflame with oily light and noise. The dark blocks of the buildings rise behind them, serene monoliths, and it's then that the inmates see that all of the lights are out but one: a piercing searchlight slices down from the top of that tower, which everyone knows wasn't there before. The building's a tall tapered thing, hairy around the edges, its walls a jumble of brick and plastic, concrete and glass, jutting I-beams, as if the tower were built by the horde of birds that swarm around it, as if the birds were following humans in their quest for heaven, tearing down the buildings all around it and rearing the tower from their ruins.

The *Rosalita* ties to the pier, and the crowd's white noise begins to resolve into a polyrhythmic, atonal frenzy. In the setting sun's violent orange light, a dark-haired boy swathed in scarves of many-colored rags runs up the swaying ramp to meet Piston Beauvoir at the top, shouting at him in a language he doesn't recognize. The boy has a plastic bottle that's been cut in half, and he dances with it, rattling out insistent syllables. He mimes drinking, then being drunk; then Piston Beauvoir gets it. It can be a cup, this bottle, the boy is saying. A bowl. A shovel. A cage for insects, pet or invasive. A cover for candles when the roof leaks. Piston Beauvoir plays along, offers the boy his shoes, his belt, his government-issue shirt. But for the boy it's serious business; he stops talking, looks the convict over, from his overgrown hair to his worn soles, frowns, and spits. Piston Beauvoir has nothing he wants. He turns and flies back down the ramp, yelling and waving the bottle over his head, the sunlight setting him on fire while three dozen men and women rush to the edge of the pier with long ladders of metal and bamboo, angle them toward the ship; the ladders clatter against the *Rosalita*'s rails, and people climb over the kerosene water of the harbor, shout as they leap aboard, eviscerate the pilothouse, taking compass, radio, the leather chair bolted to the floor, navigation equipment dangling entrails of cut wires. Within seconds they've popped out windows and portholes with crowbars, collected the bent rivets in bags, hammered doors off their hinges and dissected the hinges with screwdrivers, whistling. They take every other step in the stairwells, seventeen chairs, four tables, a pile of guards' uniforms, three washing machines; eight men rip the stove and oven out of the galley, drag it to the deck, hoist it over their heads and soft-shoe back down the ladder to the pier with it. The ship is stripped in seven minutes, and a portly man wearing nine layers of clothes, three hats, one inside the other, approaches Marco Oliveira smiling, flings a brown envelope that Marco catches in two fingers.

"Fair is fair," the man says. Inside the envelope is a thicket of money in multiple denominations, but Marco has never seen the currency. He gets lost in the symbols, birds and Victrolas, buildings drawn at dizzying angles, as if by someone falling from a balloon, but recognizes the man framed in the middle at once; turns the bill over, sees how the silhouette on the paper matches the spire with its light sweeping over the city, the all-seeing eye, already brighter than the dying sun. His face changes, and the portly man laughs.

"Nerve thought you might react that way," the man says. "He says he wants to talk to you."

"Feeling's mutual," Marco says. Maggot Boy Johnson watches Marco's gaze rise to the tower, and the Vibe leans on Maggot Boy's shoulder. See what I told you?

Don't, says Maggot Boy Johnson.

Too late, the Vibe says. It's already started.

The streets around the docks are mobbed with people and stalls, lit by lamps of oil and animal fat, bonfires of old window frames and newspapers; people with electric signs wired to their heads and stores on their backs: locksmiths, jewelers, cell phone salesmen, shoemakers calling out for customers in a mash of English, Spanish, and Chinese, the new language of money. A band in factory uniforms tears through "La Morena" on banjo, requinto, harp, and washtub, rocking out on a muscular three, all sharp turns between frenzied runs and singing curling high with passion, a man next to them selling cured pig haunches covered with flies, smelling of salt and decay. Less than fifty feet away, somewhere in the alley between the mosque and the club, a duo of oud and djembe slide along a loping, driving beat; he's not selling any alibis, they sing, and five swaying couples stomp their feet to rattle the hardware shack next to them in time with the music. In the shack, a woman selling colanders and metal files, long twisted pieces of steel salvaged from car wrecks, while a man next to her with severe burns on his face sells stereo equipment and satellite dishes. There's a fight in front of the empty slave market, two men waving pistols at each other; maybe this baby'll do my talking for me, each of them keeps trying to say, but they're too drunk to enunciate, too gone to hear. A smoking aisle of rickety stalls is walled with calls for laundry, noodles, organ doning, trips to China, a tiny man with an erhu jamming with a large woman on an upright bass on the changes to "Babylon System," both of them singing in piercing, flat harmony. They're a couple, but she looks like she could eat him. A truck howls and backfires, blares an air horn. Four men are standing around an unconscious woman, arguing about motor lubrication while blood seeps out of her ear. A currency trader barks from the back of a van surrounded by roasting meat and rotting vegetables, spices and lighter fluid; the bills of a dozen countries are in his hands. On the broken sidewalk behind a slaughterhouse that used to be a church a woman saws into a dead dog's stomach, reaches in and pulls out a watch, her husband's. She's got his name etched into her front teeth, flashes it wherever she goes, though he died in the mass starvations four years ago. A circus has taken down a stoplight, raised a striped tent that hunches between the buildings; they have animals and trapeze artists, bleachers filling with people eating fried tripe and popcorn, an organ player blasting out music of deafening cheer while two women on stationary bicycles power the bellows. The crowd is tidal, swaying and flowing back and forth, until a huge freighter, solar panels hanging off of it, blasts its entrance into the harbor, and there is a rush forward toward the water, shouts and cackles, waving arms, ladders swinging toward the rails again. The money is already changing hands, a rattle of coins, a rustle of bills, as children dart across the space hanging high above the pier with hammers and blowtorches, welcoming the ship to the new America.

The inmates stand frozen in the whirling market. Sometime in the last six years, early in the morning, picking burnt gristle off a pan, or alone in a hallway, seawater raging on the other side of the steel under their hand, each of them accepted that the *Rosalita,* the ocean's simmering chaos, the other aging inmates, would be everything they'd have for decades. Now, here, amid the commerce and carnival, the yelps of numbers and sea lions, the buzz of bad wiring, girls skipping bottle caps off gasoline cans, eight of the inmates realize they don't want anything else. They turn toward the *Rosalita* and its rust, its creaks and its shudders, the new holes in the walls, and see themselves again in its halls and stairways, the wide riveted courtyards of the blocks, stewing fish on the deck over the coals from burning broken furniture. They could be citizens of their own country now, sovereigns of the rest of their years. They look at each other then, and because they've lived with each other for so long, they just nod, stride as one through the crowds, up the gangplank, and back to the *Rosalita,* as free as they have ever been in their lives. But Marco Angelo Oliveira is shocked by the feeling of his years on the ship sliding off him, flowing out and away from him, filtering into the ether to join the history circling the world. He has been sleeping, and his dream self has been busy, reading the words in the northern lights, listening to the whispers in the water, writing down the signals that appeared in the guts of fish, the scattering of teeth across the cell block floor, the sunlight bending through the portholes. Now that he's waking up, the Vibe taps him and he rises, a slow ascent into the air, between the buildings near the teeming market, above the city, the people below him flowing into a shimmer of movement on the shores of the half-dead city. Then the tops of the buildings are below him, even the spire spiked into the city's heart with its angry eye, and Marco can see the planet curve away beneath him, the Atlantic a rippling sheet of silk, the land a cresting sea of concrete breaking against forests and hills that have come to reclaim it. He follows the veins and vines of highways and train tracks, the speed made solid on thousands of miles of rail and pavement shooting lines across Appalachia, the deserts of Texas and Arizona, the fields of California, the blank plains of Kansas, and he knows with the clarity of childhood that the sound of a bell that was struck in his head the day he boarded the *Rosalita* will not stop ringing; and if he ever wants to be happy again, he must find the Slick Six, his family, his home.

CHAPTER II.

A reunion of ACQUAINTANCES; a brief
HISTORY of Zeke HEZEKIAH and the
AARDVARK; a jailbreak.

Nerve, a trader, occupied a warehouse near the Queensboro
Bridge a day after the dollar went south and the riots began. It was so easy; he threw a brick through a ground-floor
window, destroyed the shrieking alarm with a pair of pliers,
congratulated himself for guessing that the police wouldn't
respond anyway. He climbed to the roof, looked out over the
smokestacks, the high-rises on Roosevelt Island, the angled
glass on the towers on the other side of the river. Feathers of
tan smoke rustled in the wind above them, the work of chaos
and arsonists, but Nerve couldn't so much see the collapse as
feel it in the roughening of the air, hear it in the car horns
breeding car horns sliding together into a long, dense drone,
and weaving through it, the roar of a stadium, of millions of
people screaming and stomping their feet at once, everywhere,
all around him. His phone rang. It was a business associate in
Morocco; she had heard the news. What is it like? she asked,
and he held his phone to the mouth of the city, broadcasting the
sound of panic, so much like the sound of celebration.

He put five locks on the warehouse door, gave three boys
lodging on the first floor a steady supply of food and drugs to
patrol the place with guns. So he and Kuala Lumpur, a counterfeiter, have lived for five years. They saw the starved bodies

dumped into the river in piles; heard about the Aardvark's coup from repurposed police vans squawking the news up and down Queens Boulevard; saw the skeletal scaffolding of the Aardvark's tower shudder into the skyline, harried by crows; watched specks of workers give it flesh. They were on the roof again the first night the searchlight flared on, began its sweep of the buildings around it. They were pretty sure the light didn't do anything, but as a symbol, it was enough; it kept them from going outside during the day for the next three months.

Nerve lives on the top floor of the warehouse, sleeps in a bed hung by chains from the ceiling, lost in a maze of his stock: tools, engine parts, assorted pharmaceuticals, bullets, a small platoon of generators and refrigerators, furniture, crates of canned goods. He does a good business, has the accounts in Beijing enumerated in yuan to prove it. It is not a bad life, he thinks; it's easier than before, in some ways. No more need for fake identities, front organizations, and bribes, though the Aardvark demands as much paperwork as ever to move any-thing on or off the island of Manhattan. Forms, stamps, signa-tures, verbal permissions. All signs of the Aardvark's paranoia, Nerve thinks. All easy to fake, thanks to Kuala Lumpur, though it still slows him down. Also, if the Queensboro Bridge collapses, either by bombing or negligence, nobody's going to fix it, and his location will become problematic. And he doesn't know where his man is, hasn't seen him since the last fireworks of the last Fourth of July, when they could already see what was coming. I'll be back soon, he'd said; I'm just going to Ver-mont and back. I just need to get my brother. That was over five years ago, and Nerve still thinks he sees him in the back of another at least once a day.

Nerve's hand twitches when he sees Marco coming; it re-members the first time they met, how Marco bent the hand behind Nerve's back, closed a fist around one of its pinkies, showing the place where he could snap it off. Just crack that bone in two, Marco said. The skin and muscle give up a lot easier than you think they do. Nerve's brain forgave Marco after the Silk Road job, helping a Japanese fishing magnate with Chinese ceramics trade with a Saudi prince with Iranian rugs. Neither would say where they'd acquired their pieces, though three museums seemed to be missing inventory, four people had disappeared. There was a whiff of subterfuge about the deal from the beginning, and it became clear, as the plans became more intricate, that the trade was itself a cover for a larger and much more criminal transaction that Nerve suspected involved drugs for people, or parts of people. But Nerve said nothing, and got six figures for his silence; afterward, he and Marco had bottle after bottle of shiroka melnishka loza in a Bulgarian café at the end of a Tokyo alley damp from a week of rain. The memory of the wine graces Nerve's lips again, and they smile. But the hand still remembers.

"Nice place," Marco says.

"Tell me what you really think," Nerve says.

"Looks like it's falling apart."

"That's funny," says Nerve, though he doesn't laugh. "I was thinking the same thing about you. I thought they'd sent you up the river."

"Out to sea," Marco says.

"That's funny," Nerve says, though again he doesn't laugh. "How is it that you're back?"

"Civil disobedience."

"You're not looking for a job, are you? I could use a man like you. Business is as brisk as ever. But there are sometimes revenue issues. One finds oneself collecting unusual collateral. About three and a half hours north of here is an emu farm that I am now part owner of. The eggs make good trade, though sometimes I let a few hatch, then go up there and eat the birds before they get old and tough."

"Do they taste like chicken?"

"You'd think so. But I had one that tasted much more like beef. I suppose it all depends on what you feed them."

"So what do you feed them?"

"I don't feed the emus. There's a sign that says I shouldn't. The caretaker does it."

"And what does *he* feed them?"

"Other emus."

"So what do *they* taste like?"

"I'm so glad the prison ship didn't blunt your humor. I was afraid incarceration would make you jaded."

"Just cold."

"That's funny," Nerve says, though once again he isn't laughing. This is a family thing. Neither of Nerve's parents has ever laughed. What passes for laughter is a crinkling of the face, a silent shaking that makes them look like they've been insulted, so they say they like the joke even though the lack of laughter always makes them sound sarcastic. Nerve has wondered if his inability to laugh is congenital or social, though he knows the distinction isn't important now that he's in his thirties and doesn't really care if he laughs or not. People often look and sound their worst when they're laughing. The things that happen to their faces, the sounds that come out of them. Appalling.

"I'm looking for the Slick Six," Marco says.

"I figured. I believe they're all over the place now. What kind of plan are you hatching?" He still has the emus on his mind.

"It's a secret."

The secret is that Marco doesn't have a plan, not yet, but it's not a good idea to tell Nerve this. The suit Marco's wearing he stole from an apartment twelve blocks away less than an hour ago; this and his reputation as a man who can do things are all he has.

"Knowing you, it won't be a secret for long. I remember, oh, eight years ago now—"

"—Is that who I think it is?" The voice comes from behind a crate of life preservers; when its bearer sees Marco, she breaks into a sprint, leaps like a long jumper, and latches herself to Marco's torso, arms around his shoulders, legs around his waist.

"You've gotten bigger," she says. "And you're so tan."

"And you don't look a day older than when I saw you last. No, I take that back. You look older and it suits you."

"Only you could get away with saying that. And I lied. You look horrible. Pale as hell."

"Does that mean you'll tell me your real name now? I've been on a prison ship. I deserve it."

"Nobody deserves it, Marco."

She claims that she goes by the name of Kuala Lumpur because, not being able to read English at the time, she filled out her immigration forms wrong, didn't realize it until her papers arrived. Marco has never believed this story, even though he saw the documents. Kuala is, after all, a gifted counterfeiter. She takes personal responsibility for the devaluation and subsequent redesign of several minor currencies in the decade before the dollar's collapse. They have pictures of me in central banks and police stations all over Africa, she says. A poster of me at the Zimbabwe-Zambia border. I get to look at Victoria Falls all day, all night, until the telephone pole falls over or the Zambezi runs dry. She also does IDs, government documents, diplomas, land deeds. The Slick Six, who at the time were engaged in speculative real estate deals in Argentina, Costa Rica, and Venezuela, hired her for this, but it didn't take long for her and Marco to start flirting every time they talked to each other. Seven months later, the Slick Six invited her to join them; they could even still alliterate, Zeke said, and by the way, will you marry me? She rejected them all. You people are way too serious for me, she said. But she kept working for them all the same, works for Nerve to this day. She can draw up the papers to bring a hundred elephants across the East

River by barge, get a batch of anthrax to the docks to be traded for a fictional castle in Addis Ababa. There's not a signature she can't forge, though she's afraid to do the Aardvark's too often.

"I haven't heard from Hideo or Carolyn since they went to LA," Nerve says. "Word was they went legit. Something insane like that."

"Johanna went south," Kuala Lumpur says. "As in North Carolina. Asheville, the last free place in the old US of A."

"Funny place for a good Connecticut girl," Marco says.

"Well, you sure spoiled her, didn't you—"

Nerve is waving his hands in the air. "— Okay, okay, will the two of you please just "

"—Sorry," Kuala Lumpur says.

"Don't do it again," Nerve says.

"I won't," she says.

"I mean it."

Kuala turns to Marco. "Dayneesha's famous in Fort Worth. She's the new news."

"What about Zeke?" Marco says. "Do you know where he is?"

"Of course I do," she says. "So does Nerve." Her brow crinkles, the corners of her mouth tighten, and the Vibe visits her head. Say it, it says, and grants her a glimpse of a horse rearing in the middle of Madison Avenue, the rider firing a rifle in the air. Smoke turning the sky black.

"What?" Marco says.

When Zeke Hezekiah was eleven years old, a berry aneurysm on the internal carotid artery at the base of his brain popped, and he found himself in a coma. His earthly vessel was riding a bicycle at the time, and it continued on its course halfway down the block before the bicycle's tires grated against the curb and threw bike and rider across the sidewalk. When he woke up, it was January and he was fifteen, postpubescent and sickly, lashed to a respirator and an IV, alone under a humming green bulb. His parents' movement, the noises they made, disoriented him; for a tiny moment, he wished himself back into oblivion, but it didn't work.

Then it was months of therapy, learning to walk, to eat, to lift things. Two of his best friends had moved away, one to Seattle, another to Andorra. A third had gone to a juvenile detention center for four counts of rape, two of armed robbery, one of assaulting a police officer. Zeke spooked the ones who were left; they had closed the holes he had left in their lives, and they didn't want to reopen them. The size of his loss bore down on him at the end of August, as he waded across a stream to fetch a football. He felt it as a tidal wave roaring up behind him, gathering him up, tossing him into the air, throwing him onto sharp stones, dragging him into churning water. His sister told him later she found him screaming in the stream bed; all he remembers is clinging to the rocks.

He excelled in school, graduated early, finished college at twenty. Soccer and track, a hurdler. He played bassoon in the orchestra, trombone in a soul band that gigged in clubs with chicken wire around the stage, and guitar by himself at home, where he could slip between the strings and crawl inside it. His parents and friends saw determination—zest for life, his father called it—but the truth is that Zeke Hezekiah was driven by fear. He knew that it hadn't been the crash that put him down, but something in his own head; it was still there, scabbed over and inoperable; it or another aneurysm could pop again at any second, send him off for good. Seventeen years later, it hasn't happened, and the drive has mellowed into a serenity, an acceptance of the fragility of his existence that people mistake for Buddhism. Sitting now in a cell of what used to be a city jail, he believes that he was prepared well for the last decade, in which he has been a fool to fortune in a medieval way. He spent his twenty-second birthday strapped to a bed in a state hospital in the Republic of Georgia, after they found him in a drainage pipe in Tbilisi shuddering through heroin withdrawal, his American passport shivering in his back pocket.

Eight years later, he was in splendid exile looking out over cool blue water in what passed for an unassuming house in Monaco, with bank accounts in Liberia and Vanuatu, a house for his parents near the ocean in Andalucía, where they'd honeymooned long ago and where his mother had said she wanted to retire. About a third of his wealth was legitimate, amassed through a supernatural gift for currency trading. But the real money, he knew, was thanks to the Slick Six.

He saw the crisis coming long before it broke. The evidence was all around him, pulled from newspapers, from clips of politicians and businessmen speaking into bouquets of microphones, casual words from his brokers, conversations in hotel lobbies. Asia and Europe are far more vibrant than the United States these days. Far more opportunities for investment. The national debt of the United States may prove to be unserviceable; that slipping dollar isn't helping, either. Foreign ministers met with the secretary of commerce. The secretary was fired, replaced by another secretary, who was also fired. A strong statement from the chairman of the Federal Reserve that everyone knew was a plea to the governments of the world, the lords of global commerce: Please come back. Please let us have your money. We'll make it worth your while. We promise.

Zeke called Hideo in Los Angeles.

"Hideo. It's Zeke."

"Yes?"

"How much of your money is in dollars these days?"

"What is this about?"

"I don't need a number, just a percentage."

"I do not know."

"Guess."

"I do not know. Seventy-five percent?"

"That's a lot."

"Zeke. I live in America. Of course most of my money is in dollars."

"Well, get it out of dollars and into something else. Buy

Chinese bonds, a house in Europe, a factory in India. Whatever."

"Why?"

"Because the United States is going under."

"Maybe you are high?"

"I'm serious."

"America's economy cannot just collapse, Zeke. It is very different from a small country, a poor country."

"Not anymore, it's not."

It was all in the numbers. Foreign clients selling their dollars away, walking away whistling. Just act natural, they said. Act like nothing's wrong, and then sell everything. The Last Wave, a tribe of financial speculators and extreme surfers, were interviewed from helicopters, riding giant breakers off of Fiji. This is going to be the big one, they said through their suntan lotion. This is going to be what we named ourselves after. The money was jittery, ready to flee. It only needed to be startled.

Zeke called Johanna in Connecticut.

"Have you been watching the news?" Zeke said.

"It depends on what you mean by that," Johanna said.

"About your economy."

"My personal finances are in the news?"

"Look, Johanna. Get all your money out of the bank as soon as you can and convert it to something else."

"Why?"

"Because the dollar's going to fail."

"What?"

"I'm serious. It's right out of a textbook. Big debt. Creditors get nervous, start asking for their money back. We don't have it. Dollar goes south. Creditors get more nervous. Some of them take their money and run. Dollar goes further south. Feedback loop. Pow."

"You're sure we're not talking about my personal finances?"

"It's the same idea. Get everything and get out. Because

this hasn't happened to America in a long time and I don't know what's going to happen. If we're ready for it."

Planets were aligning, the moon pulling closer, asteroids winging toward major cities, the bombs already falling. At last, it was in the street, signs plastered to boarded windows, lines outside government offices. A store on fire. Small wars between crowds and soldiers, then just crowds. Zeke Hezekiah watched accounts in American dollars shrivel and vanish within a month. How could it be otherwise? The water was rising over the wall, the bombs exploding, buildings tumbling, the dollar lying in the road, bent at dead angles, bleeding itself out.

He took the last plane from Paris to New York before the strikes started, and while the shadow of his airplane slipped over the spine of the Atlantic Ocean, the American dollar died. In Washington, in front of thousands of cameras, the chairman of the Federal Reserve tilted his head toward the ceiling, let the lenses of his glasses catch fire in the spotlights, and explained the situation in a way that only economists could understand. Then he controlled himself and said, "For the foreseeable future the dollar is no more, but we are all still here and must do what we can in the chaotic times that are sure to come." He apologized, resigned, apologized again to the United States of America and to the world. As a man who treasured precision in a way that maddened all who knew him, this was how the chairman split the difference between what he thought people wanted to hear and what he was thinking. Were he speaking to his own people, an audience of rationalists gleaming with a lack of emotion, he would have said that this was a bad day for humans, but that history has seen many currencies come and go. We are not the first or the last. Everyone should relish the interesting times we live in, the changing of an epoch, the chance to start over. In the mountains, mere hours from where we stand, bears kill for food under trees pointing at the sky; off the coast of Chile, whales swim through cool water; on the ocean floor, tectonic plates shift apart and the seam bleeds magma that boils seawater and scabs into stone. These things the death of the dollar can never touch.

Zeke's plane dipped toward an airport the pilot almost couldn't see, landed on the end of a darkened runway, far from the terminal. The airplane's crew deployed the stairs meant for emergencies and ran off into a light rain while the passengers gathered around the plane's wheels. Nobody knew how to open the luggage compartment. Someone from first class was trying to form a committee when three vans, license plates torn off, horns blaring, the words CHARLENE'S PEOPLE-MOVING MACHINES sprayed across the sides, raced from the terminal across the tarmac, pulled up to the aircraft. A large woman in the driver's seat rolled down the window, throwing out a gigantic smile and a blast of old Wilson Pickett from the radio. Don't let. The green grass fool ya.

"Hiya, everybody," she said. "I'm Charlene Duchamp, and I'm here to make sure you get to your final destinations."

"What's going on?" Zeke said.

"All the stuff that happens when there's no such thing as money all of a sudden, that's what. Now are you planning on standing around on this runway for the next thirty years, or do you want a ride?"

"Our luggage—"

"—is being taken care of." One of the other vans was parked under the plane, and two men in pink jumpsuits were slamming sledgehammers into the luggage compartment's hatch.

"Relax," Charlene said. "We've done this a dozen times already today, and we're quick studies." From the speakers, Wilson Pickett screamed as only he could.

At the terminal, Zeke Hezekiah traded two pairs of pants for a ride from Charlene into the city in the back of a pickup truck, the cab radio screeching about how the sun's not yellow, it's chicken. All along the avenues, there were people with shopping carts full of canned goods, loaves of bread, jugs of water. A city getting ready to starve. But his place was as he had left it: a bed, a nightstand, a lamp, a phone. A Sufi rug, embroidered paths showing the mystic's road to Allah, an ascent into dissolution; at least that was what the man who sold it to him had said. Zeke picked up the phone, wondered why it was still working. Who was running the system?

"Zeke!" Kuala Lumpur answered on the seventh ring; Zeke could smell the pot on the other end.

"Hello, darling."

"Um. Are you in town?"

"Yes."

"Why did you leave Monaco?"

"You should see Monaco, Kuala. You can't pass a streetlight without a suicide hanging from it." That was the thing about economies collapsing. The more you had, the more you lost. The pensions, the bonds, the savings accounts, the money put aside from decades of work, all gone in two days; the collapse was a tsunami, and all of us and the American dream had been on the beach, eyes closed, chairs angled at the sun, too close to the water to get away.

"But why did you come here? You could have at least gone somewhere warmer."

"..."

"Oh. Oh, Zeke."

"I thought . . ."

"..."

"..."

"I'm sorry you thought that," Kuala Lumpur said.

"No, no. No. Don't be sorry. You didn't ask me to come."

"..."

"It was stupid of me, really," Zeke said, "assuming that just because the world as we know it was starting to come apart, that you'd decide you wanted somebody serious."

"Oh, honey."

". . ."

"Please take care of yourself?" Kuala Lumpur said. "Please?"

Kuala Lumpur rubs her temples with a thumb and middle finger. She doesn't tell Marco about this part of the conversation, what Zeke said to her, what she said back, but it blooms across her face, rises and falls in her lungs, agitates her fingers. Marco can see it all. This is why I can never do business, she thinks. I was born to mimic and to party. I'm useless for everything else.

"Where is he?" Marco says.

"In jail."

"That's nothing."

"It's not nothing, Marco, because the jail isn't the jail anymore. The Aardvark runs it, like he runs the city, the slave trade, everything. He didn't even have to charge Zeke with anything. Once he knew Zeke was in town, he just picked him up one day and threw him in a cell. Who was going to stop him? His face is on the goddamn money. That's how much it's not nothing."

"How did he get so strong?" Marco says. "How did that happen?"

When the United States was still the United States, the Aardvark was the financier of the largest illicit trade network in the country, the vortex of a spiral of people, food, drugs, money by the billions, but only seventeen of his employees had ever seen him, or heard his rumbling, rambling voice. In port cities up and down both coasts, in the safe houses of El Paso, the flophouses of Nogales, in ice-driven lodges along the Canadian border, they'd heard of him, but debated his existence; the idea that one man could have so much, control so much, without the government knowing was too improbable. On the northern border of Guatemala, in the coca fields in Bolivia, the poppy fields in Afghanistan, they knew him by different names, hadn't heard of him at all, cared only that the dollars came from New York and didn't ask why. He was a major target for several law enforcement agencies for over ten years; most of the information on him suggested that he moved to a different country every few months. There were rumors that he lived on a boat, a freighter tricked out to be a marbled mansion within, fed with the fruits of four continents, furnished with pieces from blackmailed Russian officials with palaces on the Black Sea, Syrian businessmen who disappeared whenever cars exploded in Damascus. These were all lies. The truth is that he never left Manhattan, lived on two floors of an office building in midtown that the elevators skipped unless he spoke his birth name, in his glottal voice, into the emergency phone. He lives in New York still, though it's no longer secret, not after he knocked down a city block and built his tower. He's given out floors to his vast extended family, which runs berserk from the twisting elevator shaft to the scratched windows; he lives by himself in its teetering peak. He controls most of New York by proxy, oversees a swath of Manhattan himself, from the southern end of the island up through the east side of Central Park, where squatters and homesteaders with small gardens and a few animals wage wars with clippers and axes against the rebelling vegetation. He makes speeches in Union Square, gesticulating from a podium while his voice booms from huge speakers. There can be no recovery without rules, he says. They are starting to call him the Emperor of New York; a man, you might say, with whom one does not fuck.

Yet fucked with him the Slick Six had, for years before the collapse, until Marco was incarcerated and the other five exiled themselves. By Zeke's calculations, the Six siphoned almost 270 million dollars off of the Aardvark's operations, on the California border, in a truck jouncing across Missouri, on a copper wire flashing transactions from bank to bank, leaving the Aardvark with empty crates, men and women shrugging shoulders, unbalanced numbers. It took the Aardvark seven months of sifting through his enterprise to understand how much he was losing, nine more months of questions and torture to find out who was taking it. Jeannette Winderhoek, his first lieutenant and lawyer, pleaded with him not to pursue them, though she knew better.

"It's not worth it," Winderhoek said. "They're mosquitoes."

"Mosquitoes cause malaria," the Aardvark said. "And Marco Oliveira is no mosquito." A twinge in his voice, an echo of pining, for an errant son, a utopia lost.

So the Aardvark began his hunt for the Slick Six, kept it up for almost a decade and even now isn't satisfied, though the Six are scattered or under his thumb, the money is gone, and the world is much changed. His third wife, a square woman with biceps like watermelons, is unsurprised. She knows how, in the earliest days, when the Aardvark was a local thug just developing a reputation, one of his associates, a man who went by the name of Bing Ling, lost four hundred dollars to him on a horse race, refused to pay, and ran off to Brazil. Fourteen years later, when the Aardvark's operations leaked into Rio de Janeiro, one day the Aardvark made his driver take a long swerve off the highway and into a favela. He directed the driver as if following a scent, squinted out the window, barking commands, and stopped at last in front of a tire shop where Bing Ling, missing an arm and an eye, slumped sleeping in a wooden chair against the painted plaster wall. The Aardvark didn't even wake him up before he shot him through the top of his head.

"Why isn't Zeke dead yet?" Marco says.

"I don't know," Nerve says.

"I'm getting him out of there."

"When?"

"Tonight."

"And after that?"

"We go south, I guess. To Johanna. Then Dayneesha. Then . . . wherever Hideo and Carolyn are."

"Will you say good-bye before you leave?"

"If I have time."

Kuala Lumpur smiles and looks at the floor. "See you in a few years, Marco," she says, but after he's gone, she lingers at the door.

"Do you think they'll be happy to see him?" Nerve says.

"Zeke will," Kuala Lumpur says.

"What about the rest of them? You remember them after Marco was shipped out. Remember the things they said? The way they talked about him?"

"They had money then, Nerve," Kuala Lumpur says. "Take it away, and what's left?"

Marco built his house eleven years ago on the roof of a Brooklyn warehouse, designing it to look like the top of a stairwell; a nine-by-nine floor, a door, a skylight, one angled wall sloping into the building's roof. The house is now covered in soot and pigeon guano. Nine winters have eaten the lock; he cracks it with the palm of his hand. A colony of mice has occupied his sleeping mat, oppressing the insects that rode in on them. His two changes of clothes are brittle, ready to dissolve. But he smiles when he sees his weapons, the oil varnishing their blades, the cloth binding them behind glass cabinets. He thought they would be preserved for a month, maybe three, and in the first year of his sentence he imagined how the rust was killing them. By the second year he gave them up for dead, thought this would be a salvage operation. But they shine as though he left days ago, as though they survived across the months of frost and heat sustained by the faith that his hand would return. Marco takes them out one by one, wipes them down, holds them across his lap. It's the reunion of parent and children.

He waits then until dark, sitting on the roof's edge cross-legged as the city undulates beneath him, the tarred tops of buildings falling away down the hill to dive into the harbor, heaving up again into rising spikes that push through the city of houseboats around them. The searchlight on the tower crackles on; other lights follow in patches, in Brooklyn, in Queens. The electric companies are gone; it's all local now, and some are better at making light than others. The streets sprout homemade poles thick with bundled wires, pirates of power stations, riding the old grid, the arteries of a fossilized giant. Marco catches himself wondering about the water system, those underground canals that drain reservoirs a hundred miles upstate. Who's running them now? Who will fix them when they break? In the years of the Slick Six, before his incarceration, Marco would have taken for granted that we're all seconds from mayhem, nail bombs in backpacks, buses careening down hills without brakes, comets curling around the sun to intercept us. He made sure that he could carry everything that mattered to him. When the firestorm comes, he thought, I am ready to run. When the giant alien insects invade, I am prepared to resist. His imprisonment was easy: His cell was bigger than the places where he was used to sleeping. Being one boiler explosion away from drowning didn't bother him: It was better than how he'd grown up, in slug-ridden barracks ripe with the butchering of enemies, the bouts of dengue, of Chagas' disease, fights with amoebas and tapeworms for dominion of his stomach. But in the bucking and swaying of the prison ship, he began to change. His asceticism uncurled into dissatisfaction, and he began to want. Not things he could name, not yet, but he wanted, and so he started planning, where he would be, who he would see, in the first four months of his freedom, the next six, within two years. It was a good plan, and under the pink Malaysian sky, he entertained himself by chasing down its details. He would land in New York, call the Slick Six together. I'm free, the message would say. Come and join me. But now Zeke is in jail, Johanna and Dayneesha far away, Hideo and Carolyn vanished for years. This world is not made for plans, he thinks, and leaves it at that, or thinks he has. Were he a man who looked back, he might draw out the irony that the person he once was—the child soldier, the assassin—would have been much more suited to the world as it is; that the person he is was better for the world that was. He might never have seen the inside of the *Rosalita*. He might turn that over in his head until he laughed or cried. But Marco is a man who does things, believes he can bang his past and future into any shape he wants to, through simple force of will.

He floats over the East River under a black hang glider, past the rusting stacks of the Domino sugar refinery, over the greasy water, the crowd of boats with their sails of salvaged tarps and half-broken solar panels creaking in the night breeze, the captains and merchants calling out what they've got in the plastic crates tied down on their deck: some near-soured milk, bottles of aspirin, a coil of telephone cord. They're looking for codeine, some lemons, a battery-powered radio. The hang glider wings between the darkened buildings, weaving through the shadows of the old projects and over the leaping span of the Manhattan Bridge, until Marco is passing over the tenements of Chinatown, and the windowless hulk of the city jail sketches its pitch corners in the sky, erasing the stars behind it. He spirals down onto the roof, disarms two guards without thinking much about it; but flitting downstairs into the cell blocks, melting into walls and ceilings whenever other guards drift by waving flashlight beams, Marco remembers why he did this kind of work, feels the old surge in his limbs, the lights going on in the primitive parts of his brain. I am a wolf; I am a ghost. He finds Zeke in three minutes, stands in front of his cell and shifts his foot on the floor just so, sending a vibration through the floor that wakes Zeke up in the reverse of the way a perfect drink puts you to sleep. Zeke's eyes open with lazy purpose, and he does a languid roll in his bed to face the shadow of the man in the hall.

"I was thinking you'd find your way here," Zeke says. "It's the—"

Marco puts a finger to his own lips.

"—logical place to start," Zeke finishes.

The cell door swings in. Zeke has no idea how Marco opened it, but is no longer impressed; Marco has performed too many stunts in front of him, spoiled him for all but miracles and blasphemies, the raising of the dead, cold fusion, a baby star burning on the surface of the Earth.

"How are you?" Marco says.

"Fine, fine. Can't complain. How was prison?"

"Can't complain."

Each of them hears the other smile. They were always the closest to each other in the Slick Six, believed they'd found in each other a soul in kind, though they never talked about it; that would have ruined it.

"I thought you would be tanner," Zeke says, "being on a boat for a few years and all."

"You can't see me. How do you know I'm not tan?"

"You don't smell tan. People who are tan, they smell different. I think it's the whiff of cooked flesh, like what a human pot roast would smell like."

"You disgust me."

"I know."

Their smiles get wider, and each wants to tell the other how much they've been missed, about the party in Cell Block Three with a jug of ethanol cut with limes and Tang, the fight with rugby players outside a beer garden in Stuttgart, the duel with chisels on a tanker off Mauritius. For Zeke, the girl in Montenegro who lived in a Zastava 10; they drove it up and down the Adriatic coast four times, the crags and cliffs falling into electric blue water all around them; they almost married in Budva on the third trip, but then said too much too fast, and she left him at the Croatian border. He never saw her again. A box of fruit floating in the South China Sea. The way his time in the Aardvark's jail has seemed like penance, though he knows it isn't. If they could distill the years into a few perfect syllables that would collapse it all into the present, right now, they would; instead, Marco just extends his hand, Zeke takes it, and the past remains where it is, waiting, the fuse lit.

They're about to go when another voice lifts itself from a nearby cell, quieter, more ragged than Marco remembers, but unmistakable. It says his name, first curling it up into a question, then forcing it into a plea, then spitting it out in a surprise that leans toward command. Zeke doesn't need to be told what to do. He paralyzes his limbs in midstep, a martial artist preparing to spin into the air, thinking about how he will destroy his enemies with his toenails, even though he knows he's just a currency trader. Marco is frozen against the wall; his already faint outline beginning to disappear.

"You have mistaken me for another," Marco says in a voice that isn't his.

"No, I haven't," the voice says. "I can smell you."

Marco looks at Zeke. Even through the dark, Zeke's eyes say: You should have worked on your tan. Marco points a long finger at him: Don't even start.

The woman in the cell is Andrea Maria Romanescu, also known as Maria Lista Sandinista. A militant anarchist raised by militant anarchist parents, she was throwing Molotov cocktails into squadrons of shielded policemen before most boys her age had thrown a baseball. Her father was a gifted mathematician, her mother a poet who turned her pen to writing manifestoes. They schooled her from the back of their yellow van, her father squeaking calculus equations across a chalkboard while her mother sweated behind the steering wheel, trying to lose the police; her mother read Victorian novels to her in the tornado shelter of a rest stop outside Kansas City while her father was in the bathroom, wiring up a car bomb. They taught her how to change her identity, what to say to the authorities when they had you in cuffs, how to break up and start riots with castanets. The FBI caught up to them at last when Maria was fourteen. They made her a ward of the state, extradited her parents to the countries of their births, where each was wanted for crimes against the state. She never saw them again. To this day, she imagines them in work camps, being forced to write anthems to the glory of the ruling party or assemble low-grade wristwatches, though part of her knows that this is a delusion.

Maria Lista Sandinista was the last person to see Marco before he boarded the prison ship, the only person he knew who saw it leave the pier in Baltimore. The Slick Six were scattered by then. Zeke Hezekiah had been in Monaco for almost four months, Johanna in Connecticut drinking 1866 cognac by the bottle, Hideo and Carolyn in LA, saying good-bye to crime, good-bye to those fine times.

"I'm not angry," Marco said on the dock, his ankles in chains.

"You should be," Maria said. "You were so loyal to them, and this is what they give you. A decade in prison, the best years of your life."

"They didn't abandon me."

"Oh really? I don't see anyone else in the Slick Six getting on the boat with you."

"You don't have the whole story."

"Then why don't you tell it to me?"

This was the root rotting under the soil, the way they poisoned each other. Even when he had come back with bandages, splints, thousands in cash, a large set of keys, a fake ID, he told her nothing about where he'd gone, what he'd done while he was away from her, and she couldn't leave it alone. She needed to know; the bomb thrower in her wanted to do these things, too. His silence was an acid in her head, eating into her thoughts, and neither his unbroken attention to her when he was there nor the obvious lust she felt for him could soothe it.

After the ship left, she arranged for a long residence in Nicaragua as the fictional niece of a prominent business family; under the name of Lupita Santiago, she would make a legitimate and very comfortable living as an exporter before the wobbling dollar destroyed the Salvadoran economy as if a nuclear bomb had hit it, and kidnappers—all under the Aardvark's payroll, though they didn't know this—invaded the house that bore her name. They thought she must still have something squirreled away, bars of gold taped to the attic ceiling, bolts of fine silk lining closet walls. They found an empty house overrun by spiders, birds nesting in the courtyard. But they found her in Chicago behind a pair of pink sunglasses, escorted her to her cell in New York, guilty of charges of conspiracy against the new empire. They say it's because of what she did as Lupita Santiago, but she knows it's because of the Slick Six, because she bothered to be there when the prison ship pulled away from the pier, while the rest of them ran.

"There's no time now," Marco said then, "but I'll tell you someday. I promise you."

"You never told me anything, Marco," she says to him now, in the dark. "You kept it from me all those years." She raises her voice as if she can't help it, as if the past is pushing the air out of her, and Marco winces, thinks about killing her; but it doesn't matter now. Someone shuffles in the dark two cells down, clears his throat.

"Who never told you anything?" a voice says.

"She says Marco never told her . . ." another voice chimed in.

"Marco never said . . ."

The voices are rising around them, a flash of news moving from cell to cell, carried across the stale air, and Zeke closes his eyes, for among this crowd, the Slick Six are famous. Being one of them kept him alive; but it won't let him make a quiet exit.

"Marco? Marco who?"

"One of the Slick Six was named Marco, right? Went to sea years ago . . ."

"What's he doing here now?"

"'Gone to sea, gone to sea, silver buckles on his knee. He'll come back and marry me . . .'"

"—doing here now, the man who can do things?"

"Zeke, is Marco getting you out? Take me with you."

"Yeah, man, get us all out of here, get us all out . . ."

Zeke hears Marco unsheathe something, move toward the bars where Maria Lista Sandinista's voice came from.

"I'm sorry—" she says.

"—You might have just killed us," Marco says. "Do you understand now? Why I kept it from you? This is why. Listen. This is why."

Marco, Marco, the syllables float from block to block, crawling into the ears of sleepers, writhing through their jaws until the mute lips are shaping them. The words warp dreams, make the prisoners think of games with water pistols, of days in public swimming pools. Marco, Polo. The weedy water of warm ponds and cold rivers, snapping turtles in the depths. Italians crossing Asia, wandering from the caravan to die facedown in a flock of mushrooms; nomads find the dried cadavers decades later, take the metal from their clothes to melt down, grind the bones to sell for medicine that lets you see into the future. In a few hours, Marco knows, the inmates will stitch the story of how he freed Zeke into their suffering, see the threads of light and shadow that form their faces, and they won't be able to stop talking about it, the night Marco came back from the ocean and stole Zeke Hezekiah like he stole the Aardvark's best paintings, his house on the western shore of Bermuda. The words will travel up through the guards to the warden, up to the city administrators, who will get into knife fights to decide who gets to tell the Aardvark. So will the Aardvark learn of what has happened, how he has been cheated again; so will Marco's escape become a chase.

"Can you at least let me out of here?" Maria Lista Sandinista says, in a voice like a six-year-old. But Marco and Zeke are already gone. The alarms go off from cell block to cell block;

red emergency lights spark off the cinderblock walls; inmates shout into the halls; guards holler at everyone to settle the fuck down. And Maria Lista Sandinista's parents speak to her through the ether, of timers, batteries, insulated wires, of putty that can tear down buildings. Be our daughter, they say. Do what we never could, because the van kept breaking down, because we paid for vegetables with nickels and dimes, and the FBI put a tap on our velour purse. Write your anger on the surface of the world in letters of fire, and let them rage until the words have destroyed everything.

CHAPTER III.

A lawyer's IDENTITY CRISIS; a drive
south; DOCTOR SAN DIEGO and the
AMERICOIDS; the betrayal and REVENGE
of the Inuit; a riot; visions of history.

Jeannette Winderhoek stands at the wide expanse of glass at
the top of the Aardvark's tower among a forest of statues
and bonsai, frescos and bas-reliefs pulled from ruins, tap-
estries depicting the usurping of kings by their underlings,
usurped in turn. The vines planted in a pot near the stairs have
crawled everywhere, fingers of leaves pulling at the elevator
doors, stuttering across the mahogany slab of the Aardvark's
desk, throwing an odor into the room that speaks of the trop-
ics, of Central America, Bolivia. From this height, Jeannette
Winderhoek is the eye of the city. She can see everything, the
outline of the island of Manhattan etched into the metallic
sheen of the harbor, Long Island and the mainland falling
away, the buildings spread out before her, the back of a concrete porcupine. Everything and nothing. The millions of windows are dark, impenetrable, the street so far below her that
the movement on them blurs near stillness. They say they control the city now, yet it is as much a mystery as ever; they don't
even feel the air it breathes until it grows into a hurricane.

She walks to the brass telescope mounted on a table, angles
it and gazes down the row of derelict office buildings on Madison Avenue, fastens onto the corner of the public library, the

outside of which is being cleaned by volunteers. The building and all of its books are still intact, she knows; the employees of the library made a spontaneous pact to defend it as soon as the police force stopped working, and now they just live in the building. They hauled beds into the offices and corners of the huge reading rooms, put plaid couches against the marble walls. An army of cats patrols the halls, has litters on the stairs. She imagines that some of the librarians are fulfilling a long-cherished fantasy. It's just them and the books now, the stamped serifs, the margins smudged with fingerprints. You can still go to the library, to the yards of windows casting long stripes of light across the stone floor, the long tables, the wood paneling, the paintings on the walls. You can still go and read the books. Except for the large firearms that the librarians carry, it's like nothing happened, as if every noon, businessmen are still eating their lunches under the lions.

Jeannette Winderhoek envies the librarians, that they should be able to carve their old vocations out of the new world. Her firm shut itself down the day before the courts closed and the riots began; by then, all of the other partners had left for Europe and Japan. She worked through the last day, a case involving a copyright dispute, folded her briefcase closed in an empty office. Her hand turned off the light, flipped the lock on the office door, a habit turned absurd. She shook the hands of her assistant and a junior lawyer, who wept. The American president tried to declare martial law to push back against the riots, but he'd already been given a vote of no confidence. Then a shooting in the Capitol took three dozen congressmen with it, and just like that, the government sighed out of existence. Jeannette Winderhoek still can't accept it. The law is real, isn't it? It's still there in the way people behave, the way they govern themselves. Cars on the right side of the road, look both ways before you cross the street, no killing your neighbor or taking his things without asking. It's in her law books, those giant brown-and-tan tomes with gold letters. The words in them are real, and they describe the law; depending on the school of legal thought, they *are* the law. The law was never more than that, right? Words on paper? Its greatest strength and most damning weakness. If it isn't real now, then it never was. But no one would argue that it never was. It had power, august and undeniable; it could move billions of dollars and send people to prison. It was real then, so it must be real now. Which means Jeannette Winderhoek is still a lawyer. It's not what she does, not anymore. But it can still be who she is.

Ah, but you forget, says the prosecution—Jeannette Winderhoek doesn't know how to argue just one side of a case anymore—the Code of Hammurabi was a book of laws once; now it's history, senseless outside of Babylon, the divine wisdom falling from Anu the Sublime, now unworshipped, the subject of archeology. All of those laws written in the books in the library of Alexandria, they'd be historical documents now if they'd survived the fire, the nomadic centuries. The law needs a government, a society to govern, doesn't it? The creaky debates of legislators giving it flesh, a judiciary kicking it in the stomach, installing teeth. But the Capitol is abandoned now; there's a hole in the roof. A family of twelve is living in the Chamber of the Supreme Court; they've piled bags and boxes on the Spanish and Italian marble; they sleep in a row behind the mahogany bench and do not dream of laws. So Jeannette Winderhoek, standing at the spyglass, is transformed from lawyer to legal historian, practitioner to academic, and the things in her head wither from profitable to arcane.

Then there's the slavery. First it was a rumor, people were selling themselves, selling their children. A rural thing. A farmer dismantling his house. A deal between two men: a girl pushed from one to the other, a bag of pharmaceuticals handed over. Both men looking over their shoulders. Then the specter crawled out of the South, followed the tracks of the Underground

Railroad, hot for revenge; and all at once, it was in New Mexico, Philadelphia, the South Bronx. The Aardvark sent Jeannette Winderhoek to see the markets for him; he didn't believe the stories were true, but they were. An auction block hauled onto a playground looking over the Harlem River, people caged in the basketball court. Currency traders in trucks, sorting foreign denominations into bins; four men with machine guns standing around, chewing gum. The auctioneer shouting across the asphalt through a bullhorn, a throng of buyers gathered, a larger crowd of spectators. Two men cheering. A woman wailing with an ancient Funkadelic T-shirt on: AMERICA EATS ITS YOUNG. An old man in a wool suit with an acid-eaten copy of *What to the Slave Is the Fourth of July?* in his hand, shaking his head and crying. Jeannette Winderhoek regarded it all, watched several dozen human beings shackled by their new owners, and as the crowd thinned and they carried away the block, she walked up to the auctioneer, told him who her employer was, and asked, with the politeness of a golden needle of cyanide, for a cut. The auctioneer agreed. He knew what the Aardvark could do. When the first returns came in, the Aardvark put two fingers to his mouth; his eyes dilated. He was putting it together.

"Aren't there laws against this?" the Aardvark said. She sighs when she thinks of it now.

"Good question," she said then. "But even if there are laws, nobody's enforcing them." De jure and de facto, she thought.

"It's an interesting social experiment, don't you think?" the Aardvark says. "Take away the laws and regulations but leave the capitalism. What do you get?"

Jeannette Winderhoek imagines herself on the plains of Kansas, a fallow, whistling desert of burnt corn stalks, the line of the horizon melted by mirage, broken by lines of telephone poles, the posts of grain silos, distant churches. Oil derricks rear back and bow, siphoning off the rocks' blood. The sky above an unblinking eye. Then, one by one, the signs of human intervention disappear; the power lines, the skeletal irrigation equipment, the houses huddled at the intersections of pebbly roads, the roads themselves; as though the camera keeps stopping and starting and things are taken away during its blindness. Soon it is just Jeannette, the wind, and the sky, and she feels herself slipping, understands why people might go to church more out here; it's so easy to be a victim of God's wrath. Were His gigantic hand to descend from the firmament to pluck you from the planet, there would no buildings, no valleys, no trees to impede its approach, no mark on the ground to signal your disappearance. Just a spiral upward into the atmosphere as the hand passes, pulling up dust into a wispy finger of soil, a tornado in reverse, until the wind carries it off.

Then a clot appears on the horizon, hissing out a metallic din that separates into the clash of parade instruments, the fanfare of an out-of-tune brass band. The shape grows into a multitude of people carrying a boxing ring over their heads; with a collective yawp they drop it in front of Jeannette Winderhoek and encircle her. The band's music is loud now, loud and decayed into aggressive dissonance, dismembering marches and pep rallies, as a man in a three-piece suit, silk hat, and tails enters the ring, paper deeds to stock and real estate spilling from every seam. His teeth beam in impossible whiteness, and he throws his arms open, a call to challengers. The band blats out a fat, rotting chord that flips stomachs, and another man ducks under the ropes, puts up his dukes, hair and beard down to his waist, braided and beaded, a leather vest, a faded shirt with a one-eyed smiley face on it, ripped pants, no shoes, rolling papers and tabs falling from his pockets. A bell rings from the sky, and the men bare their teeth and lunge; the crowd surges forward on a wave of shouts and trills, and the two fighters dissolve in a cloud of blood and paper, a whipping tangle of beads and tails, nails shredding clothes and digging into skin until both are opened from forehead to navel, opened and dying where they stand, prizefighting for the soul of America.

"You think I'm a pompous ass," the Aardvark says, and

Jeannette Winderhoek is back in the office, in front of the tele-scope.

"No, no," she says. "I would never say that."

"Okay then," he said, "how might we tap into and perhaps organize this emerging market?"

"Call Inu Kimura. And ask for the biggest loan of your life."

The Aardvark waited until three in the morning, so that he'd catch Kimura after lunch. The phone line crackled with the in-terference of the atmosphere; the signal sparked up to a satellite that threw it over the horizon to Osaka, where Inu Kimura picked it up, his fingers sticky with the juice of a dozen peaches.

"I have to make a very large request of you," the Aardvark said.

"Tell me the scale before we talk anymore," Inu Kimura said.

The Aardvark told him.

"A very, very large amount of money," Kimura said. "Why do you think that I have it?"

"Because you're a god among animals, Inu Kimura," the Aardvark said. "Because you control five major banks, and you and the president of Japan decide who the minister of fi-nance is."

"These are rumors," Kimura said.

"I happen to believe that the rumors are true," the Aard-vark said, "and I know that you didn't start them. Which means that your power is greater still."

"You exaggerate, Mr. Aardvark. But I do have the money. What do you want to use it for?"

"Slavery."

"That is illegal according to both Japanese and interna-tional law."

"The words 'legal' and 'illegal' have lost much of their im-portance here, Mr. Kimura. And you're just giving me a loan. You can't be held responsible for the things I do with it."

"Which are?"

"Taking advantage of economies of scale, Mr. Kimura. Big farms and factories sit idle all across America, lacking only a compulsory labor force to be revived and compete in the world market. Obtaining these properties requires no more than capital."

"Are there enough slaves?"

"Oh, yes. We just need the money to begin feeding them, buy equipment. Their indenture and the profits will sustain the operation once it's running."

"You are talking about startup costs only."

"Precisely."

"At the amount that you suggest."

"Yes."

For three seconds, the hiss of the phone line, a singsong elevator chime. Then: "My interest rate begins at five percent, held for the first six months, after which it will rise each month to be capped at eleven percent. I would not mind becoming more wealthy, but I do not want to make a slave out of you, either. Do we have a deal?"

Our peculiar institution is everywhere now. The slave markets are social events, with electricity, strings of Christmas lights, girls dressed in a hundred and five colors; bands made of junting guitars, spitting horns, skittering drums; carts with yellow umbrellas selling curried mutton and green beans, tamales with chiles; horses clapping their hooves against the ground, sweating in the heat while clowns on stilts with pump accordions let a flock of balloons escape into the sky. Jeannette Winderhoek is appalled. They should have gone through the proper procedures. They should have had the debates, covered the contingencies, resettled the uninhabited territory between individual and property rights. Hundreds, perhaps thousands of legal questions scream to be answered, and they'll keep screaming for Jeannette Winderhoek until she strangles the law inside her and burns the corpse.

Through the spyglass, Jeannette Winderhoek watches the blunt shape of an armored car growling down Madison Avenue; a flash, black smoke, and the armored car is flipped on its back, wheels spinning. Six kids with submachine guns rush the vehicle; one of them shoots the back open, and ten thousand tropical birds fly out of it, funnel away from the car in a rising cone of red, green, and yellow feathers that disperses high over the city while the kids dispatch the driver, then argue about how to flip the car back over.

"I just want to say this one more time," she says to the Aardvark. "The Slick Six aren't a threat to you anymore. I don't see any reason for this."

"You know that my respect for you could not be greater," the Aardvark says. "But my disagreement with you is fundamental."

"The game they played with you, sir, was about the law and money. Both of those things are gone now. There's nothing left they can hurt you with."

"This is the precise place where I disagree with you, Miss Winderhoek. You think I ever gave a fuck about the money or the law? They come and they go. This is about reputation. I owned a bank, twelve holding companies; I bent the law to my designs, because of my reputation as a man of righteousness and perfect vengeance."

"Well, having a good lawyer helped too, sir."

"Touché, Miss Winderhoek. But the essential point remains. Those six individuals, and Marco in particular"—she sees that twinge again, the shard of glass in his spleen—"are blemishes on a record of twenty years. Because they are famous, and because they were too proud to keep their mouths shut, they must be punished. It is not enough that they have been scattered across the country like a cursed people. I thought it was, but then in sweeps Marco like a—a—"

Jeannette Winderhoek watches the shard turn, the Aardvark's knees quiver with it.

"—a fucking superhero," he says, "and takes Zeke with him, who knows far too much about what goes on around here now. They must be destroyed, and the word must spread of their destruction, before I rest."

It must be the speeches in the parks, Jeannette Winderhoek thinks. She remembers him only a few years ago, all monosyllables, hand gestures, meaningful frowns. During Marco's trial he said only twelve words: He and his friends stole from me, and they will all pay. She could afford to be afraid of him then.

"When is he supposed to get here?" she says.

"I'm already here," the assassin says. He's sitting in a yellow leather chair near the Aardvark's desk, legs crossed, arms folded, his expression too blank to even be neutral. The plants around him shrink back, as if he is a place of no light, barren soil. She doesn't know how he got into the room; there was no bell from the elevator, no creak from the stair door. But he's been there for five minutes, and has been staring off into the middle distance, as though he's in a room with a million people or none at all.

"Do you know where they might have gone?" the assassin says.

"I like this one," the Aardvark says to Jeannette. "All practicality. See how businesslike he is?"

"He's saying he doesn't know," Jeannette Winderhoek says.

The assassin tilts his head to the right, looks toward the ceiling. "I'll find them," he says.

"For how much?" the Aardvark says.

"We'll discuss it when I return. Expenses can vary, and I foresee complications."

"Of course. When do you start going after them?"

"I'm already gone," the assassin says, and the yellow chair is empty again, the door to the stairwell closing; Jeannette Winderhoek never saw it open.

"Where did you find him?" she says.

"He's one of Kimura's. Four heads of state, he says, without anyone even knowing. Their constituents think they're still in power."

"Is he better than Marco?"

Before the Slick Six had Marco, they were nothing to the Aardvark; but Marco Oliveira, free agent, was his first call. His best man, the Aardvark said. In the rare times when the Aardvark reminisces, his brain revisits the first assignment he gave Marco, to convince two Algerian businessmen who were late in paying him for money laundering services to settle up. Give me five hours, Marco said, and three hours later, the Algerians were calling the Aardvark terrified, wiring him more than they owed—a premium, they said, if he'd just call off his man.

"What did you do to them?" the Aardvark said.

"What you asked."

He hung up the phone then and turned to Jeannette Winderhoek. I love that man already, he said, and Jeannette Winderhoek realized she'd never heard him say that word about anything, understood later why the trial hurt him so much—though in the courtroom, with the Slick Six parading before a judge he'd already paid for, he never stopped smiling.

"You don't think there's a conflict of interest?" she says.

"You suggested I mortgage my life away to this man, and over this you think there might be a conflict of interest?"

"This is more direct."

"Kimura's interest is in his interest, all eleven percent of it," the Aardvark says. "Hideo was his disciple a lifetime ago. They haven't spoken in years."

"Does he know where Hideo is? Or what you did with him?"

"I don't think he cares, Miss Winderhoek."

Jeannette Winderhoek returns to the window, the spyglass. The car is already gone, and three of the Aardvark's policemen are wandering around the blast site like blind pigeons. She imagines the boys joyriding the armored car through the old buildings at the edge of Brooklyn, getting it up on two wheels on the corners, sending bullets into the wall of a collapsed bank. We used to be those boys, she thinks; now we're in our tower with our security and ammunition, our pronouncements and public hangings, letting them know how much we fear them every time a body drops through a trapdoor.

Marco and Zeke are in a 1963 Aston Martin DB4 convertible, sliding along the curves of the Blue Ridge Parkway. The October afternoon is aging into evening; orange sun throws sheets of light over the road; the trees rustle in the warm drafts from the valley, setting free the first leaves of fall. Raptors soar in the thermals. Now and again the rocks and trees give way to a small field of honeyed grass, a few sparse crops, a warping clapboard house, a wooden barn with a balding roof, its shingles on the ground around it; the sun flashes back from the windows as they pass, and then the woods return. They have the top down, and the music from the radio strains through the whipping wind; don't the moon look good, mama, shining through the trees. Seven milk jugs full of gasoline roll in the footwell behind them on every curve. The assegai lies across the backseat, its blade yellow in the wavering light. Zeke is driving, his left arm hanging over the door, right hand gripping the wheel at twelve o'clock, and he can't stop smiling. Driving along the Blue Ridge Parkway in a convertible: It's another thing he swore he'd never do when he was an angry man in his early twenties, before he'd heard of the Slick Six and his speech was spiced with nevers. I will never eat an animal's testicles. I will never date her. He knows now that saying he will never do something guarantees that he will do it within ten years; and each time his life shows him how foolish he has been, Zeke wishes for time to fold over on itself, cut him off from history, his finger moving away from the trigger as the elk stumbles and folds its knees, lists into the snow. His mouth to her ear as her neck arches, her hand on his thigh. Rising from freezing water amid shorebound ice floes in a bathing suit and cap, other swimmers hopping around him, voices pitched like girls in languages he doesn't know, a twenty-two-foot bonfire encircled by towels warming on the beach. Driving down this road, in this car, with his friend.

Marco is asleep in the passenger seat, and the beat of the curves in the road brings him back to the prison ship. He is there in his cell, the door open to the block, and he can tell by the way the other inmates avert their eyes that it's past the three-month mark, after the fight that established him as a man who did not fuck around. It was him versus two larger men; they had a sharpened scrap of metal and a shard of glass, he had his left arm in a sling from a fall during a storm. It ended with the metal growing out of one man's throat and the glass driven into the other's eye, and Marco wiping the blood off the soles of his shoes, annoyed that it had spotted the cuffs of his jumper. In his dream, he leaves the cell and looks down onto the block floor, where Maggot Boy Johnson is playing Ping-Pong with Abraham Lincoln and arguing about history. If you knew it would come out like this, Maggot Boy Johnson is saying, you wouldn't have bothered to fight the Civil War, for the Union is no more. I was a man of my time, Lincoln is saying, and thank God for that. If I had seen into the future, I would have done nothing at all. It would have seemed so futile. We must live in the present if we are to make what we will of history. Maggot Boy Johnson pounds the ball over the net. That's nine to two, Abe.

The sun sets, pulls its light off the land, and the wind snaps in coldly. Zeke closes the convertible roof, wakes up Marco when the rising window jostles his foot.

"Sorry," Zeke says.

"Where are we?" Marco says.

"Virginia."

"The Old Dominion."

"They're calling it the New Dominion now. I hear they're planning to invade Maryland."

"What about Washington?"

"Not enough left to invade, I guess."

There are small fires in the woods just off the road, six people roasting a mammal, a child lazing a stick back and forth through the flames. A pickup truck on its side, the roof tattered with shotgun blasts. The hood hangs from its hinges; it is obvious even in passing that they attacked it just to pillage the engine.

"Did they steal the Bellows?" Marco says.

"The what?"

"The George Bellows from the National Art Gallery. The boxers."

"I don't know."

"That seems like something you would have known."

"It does, doesn't it?" Zeke says. "But information isn't what it used to be. If we were going to start over, you know, build a racket, that'd be an interesting angle to look into. Everyone still wants to know what's going on."

"Dayneesha already does that," Marco says.

"Really?"

"Yup. I saw it at Nerve's before I came to get you. People from all over the country send her what's going on around them, and she organizes it, sends it back out. You get paid if she uses what you send. Other people pay to read it."

"That's smart," Zeke says.

"If you do say so yourself," Marco says.

"I do."

"I know."

"You seem to know a lot these days, smart guy. So what's your plan?" Zeke says.

"For getting us all together? If I tell you, it'll ruin it," Marco says.

" . . . "

" . . . "

"You don't have a plan, do you," Zeke says.

"Nope."

"I thought so."

". . ."

"It would help," Zeke says, "if you had a job for us to do. Something big."

"Well, I don't."

There is a strain in Marco's voice, the push of a child's whine. Zeke knows what Marco wants to say: I just need to get us all back together again. I need this or I'll be in prison the rest of my life, the metal walls around me, the fields far away. I need this. He wants to say it, but Zeke knows he won't, and doesn't make him.

"You going to turn around now?" Marco says.

"No. We're closer to Asheville than New York by now. Besides, something will come to you. Or maybe me. I like the general idea. And I owe you."

"For the jailbreak? You would have done the same thing."

"No I wouldn't. In fact, I didn't. And now that we're talking about it, we should really, you know, talk about it. Because I'm sorry for what happened to you. We should have done more to stop it."

"We didn't have a choice. Somebody had to take the blame."

"It didn't have to be you. Or, at least, not just you. It could have been you and Hideo. Or you and Johanna—"

"—Look. Zeke. I don't want to talk about it."

"You mean not now."

"Not ever."

"Because it's in the past."

"Yes."

"But it still affects you, doesn't it?" Zeke says.

"So you want to talk about it?"

"Not as such."

". . ."

". . ."

"That's why we always got along best," Marco says.

"You think?"

"Yes. But I thought saying something about it would fuck it up."

"Me too," Zeke says.

"Did we just fuck it up?"

"I don't think so."

They roll toward North Carolina in the dark. And Maggot Boy Johnson, sitting in a bar in a basement on the burned edges of Chinatown, is assaulted by another vision. It repaints the room around him, erases the people, turns the bar into black smoke that soaks into the ceiling. He is in a room with a giant, coal-burning stove. Four German boys are huddled in the corner with bruises around their mouths. Two Italian boys are standing over them, speaking English spurred by accents from the slums of Rome.

"Where is the money?" one of the Italian boys says.

The Germans speak German to each other.

"Where is the money?" the boy says again.

It's clear to Maggot Boy Johnson that the Germans have no idea what the Italian boy is saying, but their instincts are right. One of them reaches down his pants, digs out a roll of brown bills. The Italian boy takes it, unrolls the top bill. His nose wrinkles.

"This is German money, you yutz," the Italian boy says.

"Your money doesn't work here," the other Italian boy says. "You're in another country now. Nobody will take these bills."

"We have the same problem," Maggot Boy Johnson says. One of the German boys looks right at him.

"Mind your own business and stay in your own time," he says, in a perfect imitation of his Midwestern descendants. Then the bar returns, Maggot Boy Johnson has a new stale beer in his hand, and the bartender is looking at him like he wants something. Maggot Boy Johnson gives him the leather belt he's wearing. The bartender takes it, appraises it, gives him three shoelaces. I need to learn Chinese if I'm going to get anywhere, Maggot Boy Johnson thinks.

At almost five in the morning, the Aston Martin drinks the last of its gas. Zeke feels the engine's death cough as they're cresting a hill, and he shifts into neutral; they glide down the slope and cross a rusted bridge in silence. Then Zeke pulls the car into the gravel on the shoulder, stops it, puts on the parking brake. He feels stupid watching his hand take the keys out of the ignition, another case of habit trumping reason. Like the people still trying to go to the bank after the dollar collapsed. They peered in the windows, punched the buttons of the automatic tellers. Still believing they could make things happen just by wanting them, still acting like Americans, though America was gone.

"Where are we?" Marco says.

"I don't know. Maybe we should have stayed on the highway."

"You know what we really should have done? Not taken an ancient car that runs on gas."

"Well, we're here now," Zeke says, and giggles. Marco stares at him. Trying to wave away Marco's attention only makes it worse. Inside his skull, Zeke's brain is in hysterics. I will never run out of gas in the middle of nowhere. He hasn't been this happy in years.

They sit down, lean their backs against the car; Zeke wishes for a deck of cards, while Marco realizes that he hasn't played cards since his thousand-and-twelfth game of gin rummy a year and a half ago in the Baltic Sea. There's so much to talk about—they haven't seen each other in years—but they lapse into the pattern of their friendship and say nothing; neither of them thinks that they have to speak.

They're in the miniature valley of a creek that winds and bubbles over rocks, then plunges into pools; under the bridge, the water is calm, a deep warm brown that catfish hide in when they want to live to be a hundred. Morning fog blurs the thick green slopes to either side. Fences run across the hills, swerve out of sight, where livestock bellow, wary, sliding toward panic; there are no signs of people anywhere, as if the farmers were abducted, pulled into the sky or led away in trucks, the cows still in the pasture, the tractor halfway out of the barn, coffee weaving threads of steam in the kitchen.

"You know," Zeke says, "if we needed any more proof that things are different now, this is it right here. Four years ago, the two of us wouldn't have been left alone on this road so long. Somebody would have come along either to pick us up or shoot us."

"About that," Marco says. "Why did the Aardvark put you in jail? Why didn't he just shoot you?"

"I made myself valuable to him. Gave him some advice, made him some money. He even started to trust me a little. But I didn't think I'd ever get out, Marco."

"I didn't think I'd ever get out, either," Marco says.

". . ."

"Someone might be coming to shoot us," Marco says.

"If they are, they're taking their sweet time about it."

"Have you seen any of the others since—"

"Since you went to prison? No."

". . ."

"Is it really that surprising? It's not like we could do business anymore."

"But apart from business."

"Was there an 'apart from business'?"

"If there wasn't, then why did you go to New York?"

". . ."

"Ah. I'm sorry."

"It was never me she wanted anyway," Zeke says. He's looking straight at Marco now, and has stopped tapping his foot against the rocks. "Don't worry, I don't hold it against you. After all, it was nothing you did. Just like it was nothing she did to hook me. Sometimes I think that at any given point, you could connect half the world like that. There was a woman in Monaco, the wife of a textiles magnate, who wanted me; I don't know why. And a man who lived on a yellow sailboat wanted her. And no doubt somewhere in the Mediterranean someone wanted him; some poor woman, or a man, in Alexandria, or Beirut, maybe. Her to that sailor, to the wife of the textiles magnate, to me, to Kuala Lumpur, to you. And on and on, until the chain loops back on itself, connects up again. A big ring of desperation around the planet. But for us, it's just the people we want, and the people who want us."

"Are you asking me about anyone in particular?"

"No, no. Just thinking in the abstract."

". . ."

"Is there? Anyone in particular?" Zeke says.

". . ."

Three hours later, the ground vibrates; from the north, there is a clamor of voices, the squall of an electric guitar, grinding and wavering, growing louder and louder, a shuddering engine of rust and oil. A tour bus yowls over the top of the hill, snaking three trailers behind it, all painted with swirls of pink and lime green, festooned with stickers and graffiti, dogs and birds, dancing figures melting into starbursts and sunlight. People hang out the windows, people are piled on the roof, pitching and swaying, whooping as the bus wobbles down the hill; whoever's driving it isn't sure how to control it, and the bus veers to one side, crosses into the other lane, then swerves back, the trailers whiplashing along the same path, groaning and screeching, picking up speed as the caravan growls down-hill. The people riding on the top yell and wave their hands; a few of them dangle over the edge, are pulled up by the others as bottles and packages slide off and break open in the road. Zeke and Marco leap up, at first pretend that it's coincidental, but soon their mistrust gets the better of them and they're off the shoulder, crouching in the weeds, wondering if they should push the car into the trees. But as the bus crosses the bridge, it eases, shudders to a stop, and the door opens in front of them, releases a miasma of jaunting drums and Mary Jane, unwashed hair and ragged, happy voices that flow onto the gravel, over their feet, into the earth and the creek below the bridge, where the fish hear it and mellow, the rocks feel it and soften, and the water slides toward the sea.

"Hey, you two," the driver says. "I got something to ask you. You got any gas?"

"No," Zeke says.

"Motherfucker," the driver says. Then he just sits there.

"What?" Zeke says.

"Nice ride. Is it yours?"

"It is now."

The driver laughs. "Totally," he says. "But you're out of gas."

"Yes."

"Drag." He leans back, talks to someone behind him that Zeke and Marco can't see. Then he looks back at them.

"Hey," he says. "Today the gods of circumstance smile upon you. Doctor San Diego has authorized me to extend an invitation to both of you fine gentlemen to join our merry party, the Americoids."

Marco knows who Doctor San Diego is. Before the Slick Six were slick, Doctor San Diego and his right-hand woman, Keira Shamu, were the major conduit for natural hallucinogens from South U.S. into the United States, a minor conduit for U.S. currency into South America. If all of the stories about Doctor San Diego are true, he is over one hundred and ten years old; Marco has always believed that the name has been passed down at least once, like the Americoids are pirates, pirates or revolutionaries. Or perhaps there is no such person; the emaciated, bearded vehicle of joy is a legend created to make the business friendlier. Doctor San Diego restricts himself to pot and other natural psychotropics because, he says, they are emissaries of nonviolence. I am in the trade of bliss, he says. I am a servant of the Big Now, turning the bummer inside-out wherever it is found. He allows transactions on credit, takes IOUs, lets customers pay him in rutabagas, turnips, massages, prayer. Good karma is my true profit, he says. Yet he was also one of the richest people in California, until the ATF stormed his mansion near Eureka, a solar-powered bamboo-and-hemp compound guarded by redwoods observing the Pacific. But the feds found the doctor gone and the house empty, no furniture, no carpets, lightbulbs taken. Now he's the richest nomad in the Americas, from the Hudson Bay tundra line to the Uruguayan shore. He has partied with decommissioned troops in Colombia, generations of families who live in the junkyards of Guatemala City; once he split a spliff with the man who had commanded Marco when the boy was not yet ten, though neither of them knew the connection. The man was trying to put his war years away, sink them in the well, and Doctor San Diego did not ask. My bus runs on good times, Doctor San Diego says. That and gasoline, the driver thinks.

"Who are the Americoids?" Zeke says.

"We are all Americoids," the bus driver says. "Most of us just don't know it yet. Come aboard, brothers. The name's Felix Purple, and I will be conducting you to your destination posthaste. What *is* your destination, by the way?"

"Asheville."

"Everyone's going to Asheville. As if there were only one way to be free." He salutes the convertible. "Good-bye, beautiful ride."

The smell wraps around them first, a musk of herb and sweet sweat; then shapes emerge, people lying on the floor near the windows, huddled together, standing in tight circles, holding on to leather straps that have been bolted and welded to the ceiling by bulbs of metal. The bus floor is covered in a patchwork of mattresses and blankets; the Americoids took the seats out years ago, gave them to a village in Ecuador that they thought needed chairs; *silla, silla,* they kept saying, when the villagers were just trying to say good-bye. Everyone is talking at once; dozens of names and places collide in the air: the things he did, the things she did to him, have you heard this album? They swear they're never going back. They all jolt together as the bus kicks forward again, lean in unison toward the front as it angles up the hill. Someone calls to turn up the radio, though it's already playing "Willie the Pimp" as loud as it can, all bass rumble, hissing high-hat, clicking gears, a violin like a buzz saw, Captain Beefheart's hooting hellion blues, Zappa's guitar tumbling and soaring, since Felix Purple's calling the playlist.

"Where are you going?" Zeke says to a man huddled near an electric heater, which appears not to be plugged in.

"I don't know," the man says. "Assville? Something like that."

"I think you mean Asheville," Zeke says.

"That's what I said. What did you think I said, Assville?"

"You *did* say Assville."

"Wait, *what* did I say?" the man says.

"Assville," Zeke says.

"Man, it's not Assville, it's Asheville."

"I know that."

"Then why did you say Assville?" the man says.

"I only said Assville because you did," Zeke says.

"But I only . . . oh, shit." The man's eyes widen with panic, and he spends the next few seconds staring at his watch. Then he sighs, relaxes.

"What?" Zeke says.

"Just wanted to make sure we weren't, like, replaying the same couple of seconds over and over. It's happened to me before. You just go around and around, and never get there."

"Get where?" Zeke says.

"Assville."

"There. You said it."

"No, man, *I* said Asheville. *You* said—oh shit." He looks at his watch again, sighs, relaxes.

"Stop teasing him," Marco says.

"But it's so much fun," Zeke says.

"That's because you've only gone around twice," says a girl in jeans and a fringed leather jacket with the words BORN TO SCALP painted in white on the back. "You go around more times, and you stop laughing and start believing. Once I saw the Mayan calendar painted on the side of a school in southern Mexico. It was wheels within wheels, gears within gears." She widens her eyes, wiggles wizardy fingers at him. "The innermost circle was for days. You could see all of that one. The next for weeks, then months, then years. Out and out, to centuries, millennia, who knows what. The school wasn't big enough for that outermost wheel. It was almost a straight line. Get it? Whenever you think you're going in a straight line, it's just because the wheel's really big. You could go to the moon and not feel the curve, but it's still a circle. You just have to get far enough away to see it."

"And you are?" Zeke says.

"Asia Sherman. Pleased to meet you."

"You Mayan?"

"Nope. Sioux."

"New Sioux, she means," says the man who's going to Assville. "She's our talisman, warding off marauders."

"He means, as long as I'm on the bus," Asia Sherman says, "the New Sioux won't touch us."

"Why's that?" Zeke says.

"Because I'm the chief's daughter."

"Why aren't you out marauding, then?"

"I'm not into that kind of thing."

"You ever heard of the New Sioux?" says the man.

"No," Zeke says.

"You will."

A rope ladder swings from the emergency exit hatch in the

ceiling, and Marco and Zeke climb to the roof, where people sit in a tangle of limbs and torsos, pushing against the railings, shouting at each other while their belongings fly upward into the vehicle's velocity, an airborne wake of clothes and old newspapers. Three men and a woman are burning through five pounds of opium, arguing whether the universe began as a singularity, or is just expanding after a big contraction trillions of years ago. To the extent that measurements of time are meaningful in such a discussion, since time itself shifts, they are quick to qualify. Big Bang or Big Squeeze?

"Bang!" the first two men say.

"Squeeze!" the third man and the woman say.

"You look like you're looking for someone in particular," says a woman in a blue smock, seven months pregnant; she can't remember who the father is, but knows with complete certainty that her unborn daughter will one day found a religion by accident, as profundities drop like grapes from her lips, cool and tart, and her believers run to catch them.

"Keira Shamu," Marco says.

The woman points behind her to the walkways of hemp and two-by-fours between the trailers, Americoids hanging out on them, leaning out as far as they can over the pavement, bleary with speed. *Look! I'm walking on snakes!* someone shouts. A triangular entrance has been pushed into the top of the last trailer, as if by a giant can opener, and Marco and Zeke slide down the bent metal into a soup of hashish and apples, the jiving push of an Afrobeat record, percussion shuffling over staggering horns, a man barking into a microphone, mocking and angry with the vision of a better world than the one he's in. People sit and stand around tables riveted to the trailer floor, shouting at each other over the roar of the road, throwing dice that ring with the clarity of bones, snapping down cards. They lean forward and sweep their arms through the game; they lean back to the hookah to put pipe in mouth, faces collapsing as if playing the oboe, then relaxing to let smoke slither out.

Four voices rise with chattering emotion, are put down with violent hushes, until the axles groan under the labor of a hill and the whole room pitches upward, angles downward again, cards, dice, and all roll and skate off the tables to slosh across the floor, and everyone puts up their hands and squeals; they're on a roller coaster that turns the last two minutes into ancient history. When the floor levels again, they put down their hands and blink, can't remember what game they were playing, don't care; they know only that they love the people sitting across from them, their fellow humans, and they pick up cards and dice to play again and again.

The Keira Shamu they seek sits at a table with a pad and paper, her feet in a washtub full of bottle caps, the casino's chips.

"Hello, Keira," Marco says. "Remember me?"

"Of course," Keira says, through glazed eyes. "The last time I saw you, you should have been on fire."

Keira Shamu has been working for Doctor San Diego for almost twenty years, is considered to be one of his most focused operatives, more logical when she's stoned. She and Marco met when Doctor San Diego and the Slick Six's interests both happened to converge upon a fungus native to Greenland, off the radar of drug-enforcement authorities, appearing in the botanical literature only seven times, but well known among the Inuit and global connoisseurs as a world-class hallucinogen. Capable of surviving less than three days when removed from its habitat, it was at least a hundred times more valuable than gold by weight, depending on the vicissitudes of the commodities market, of course. Very little of it had ever been seen outside of Greenland until a ship captain, an engineer, and a biologist in Nuuk had a mountain-to-Mohammed idea. They created the ideal habitat inside the hull of a freighter, cultivated a quarter acre of the stuff, set a course that kept them north of forty-two degrees latitude, putting their closest port to the United States somewhere in the maritime provinces of Canada. They chose Digby, Nova Scotia, because of its relative seclusion, and because the engineer had always wanted to eat the scallops there. Doctor San Diego's high-end customers were very interested in the product, which would be broken up into much smaller acreage and each section sped by boat to ports south within forty-eight hours. At those ports, customers were waiting on docks, leaning against cars with tinted windows and chauffeurs, planning to take the stuff in the car, then be driven to the beach, the woods, a nightclub, a hotel room, a karaoke bar, the public toilet of a train station, the places they liked best to be altered. The monetary transactions, involving very large sums of euros and American and Canadian dollars, needed a presentable front to the port authorities of the United States and Canada and the foreign affairs office of Denmark; the Slick Six were thus called to work their mojo. For their trouble—three hours of work for Zeke and Carolyn on a Friday afternoon, with a quick assist from Kuala Lumpur—the Six would net $974,523, enough to send Marco, their man who could do things, to the piers of Digby to make sure that the handoffs of the product itself were smooth and easy.

They were not. Minutes after the freighter arrived, a thick fog ate the harbor; fishing boats left in a line, disappeared one after the other into the mist. The night before, the engineer had found the one bad scallop in Digby and eaten it, and he squatted at the edge of the pier to retch into the gray water. The Greenlander biologist and captain looked nervous; they were people with day jobs, regular hours, health benefits, wives and children, and as they looked over the people who they were dealing with now, with their missing digits and casual talk of human trafficking as they loaded the small boats, they understood that they were in the kind of trouble their grandparents had warned them about when they were children. Keira and Marco tried to calm them; everyone here's a professional, they said, and in two hours they wouldn't have to see any of them ever again if they didn't want to. It didn't help. Looking back, Keira is pretty sure that this was because the Greenlanders knew what was coming. It wasn't the sailors making the biologist and captain nervous, or the scallops that had made the engineer sick.

The freighter was half-emptied when a sound came out of the fog, first like seagulls, then like seals. Then like pigs. Then, it was clear, it was human voices throwing out ululating screams, like Marco had never heard. A dark boat pulled itself from the mist, headed for the pier at great speed.

Keira blinked at the accelerating vessel, pulled the joint from her mouth. "All our people are accounted for," she said, her voice all pinched surprise. "I hope these are friends of yours." She coughed.

"No," the biologist said. "They're not."

For the Inuit of northern Greenland, the people on the boat, the fungus was a secret treasure. For a few, it was a sacred instrument, a means of speaking to the gods; for others, a thing that set them apart from everyone else, for the good times they had with it were like no others. For the elders, it was an investment, a thing they could offer to the pharmaceutical industry when the forces of the global market threatened them with extinction at last. Take this and give us the patent, they would say. Give us enough money so that we can afford to be left alone. The elders had shared it with an anthropologist seven years before with great reluctance, because they weren't stupid, knew how academia was chained to commerce. The individual who had convinced the elders, a younger Inuit who called himself Herjulf, had vouched for the anthropologist's goodness, made a brash promise: that if the fungus was ever in danger of commercialization, he would do whatever was necessary to prevent it.

Sure enough, the anthropologist made a passing reference to the fungus in an article about marriage rituals and Inuit interpretations of dubbed television shows, noted the plant's

hallucinogenic properties. Two months later, psychedelia afi-
cionados were calling the anthropologist on the phone, arriving among the Inuit asking to speak with the gods, trying to be
sensitive because they didn't realize that many of the Inuit
took it just to get high. The elders gave Herjulf a sideways
glance. But the seekers turned out to be decent people, took the
drug as the elders instructed them to, thanked them for the experience later. Thus the elders lowered their guard just enough
to let another enterprising young Inuit smuggle a patch of the
fungus to Nuuk, where the engineer bought it, saved it for cul-
tivation, used just a little himself to see what the fuss was
about. When the elders discovered the youth's transgression,
they ostracized him, then turned to Herjulf. Remember what
you said you would do, the elders said, and Herjulf agreed to
honor his promise.

But his investigation was too slow. By the time he found out
what the engineer was doing with the fungus and where it was
going, the freighter had already left the harbor, bound for
Canada, and his choice was clear. He enlisted the suicidal captain of a small fishing boat with maybe two sails left in her,
barreled across the chop of the North Atlantic, around Yar-
mouth, up the Bay of Fundy, just in time to part the fog at
Digby Harbor. The boat's engine roared, frothing through the
water, and as his captain took another swig of tequila for courage, Herjulf started a bonfire on the deck. What he knew, and
what everyone on the pier was about to find out, was that the
same chemical that gave such a blissful high was also a firebomb, and there was still an eighteenth of an acre of it in the
freighter's hull, along with several full tanks of gasoline.

In the next few seconds, only two things mattered: where
on the pier you were, and how fast you could run. The biologist,
the engineer, and Keira and her joint were the closest to the
shore, and Keira had been a sprinter. She had time to dive behind a stack of tires, turn around, and watch as the boat
rammed the freighter and sent a widening sphere of writhing

orange fire across the surface of the bay, over the pier, changing transfixed men into ashen models of themselves, turning
gray and brittle where they stood. Marco was standing right
next to the freighter when it went up, and she swore she watched
the flames eat him; yet, the next day, he met her without a hair
singed in a used bookstore overlooking the water. As the police
wandered up and down the blackened pier trying to understand what had happened, the two of them split the advance
payments out of professional courtesy. The Slick Six came
away with $440,562—still not bad for three hours of work.

"I'm afraid," Keira says now, in the Americoids' trailer,
"that we have no work for you at this time. The bottom appears
to have fallen out of the high-end drug market."

Zeke's brain catches on this. If the bottom falls out of the
high end, where does it go? He chuckles a little—this is just the
kind of thing that he finds funny and nobody else does—and
the gamblers at the table next to him eye him, eye each other,
accuse each other of having sent signals through Zeke until the
dealer reminds them that they're playing for bottle caps, that
they're all best of friends.

"We're not looking for work," Marco says. "We're looking
for Johanna."

Keira Shamu starts singing the song, nails Dylan's whiny
swoop.

"She was named after that song, you know," Zeke says.

Keira rolls her eyes. "Who wasn't conceived to that song?"
She drifts into the next two verses while the table next to them
is pushed over, bottle caps flying off in a wave of pinging
metal. At last, she snaps back to attention.

"You want to know where she is, right?" she says.

"We heard Asheville."

"You heard right. But the place is just big enough that
knowing Asheville doesn't get you all that close. Within ten
miles, sure. But that's no good when you need to be within ten
feet. You know, when I was living in Milwaukee, I met a couple

who after they started dating realized that they'd gotten on and off at the same bus stop within five minutes of each other every weekday for three years. Like the Liza Minnelli song . . . how does it go? She met a Londoner first, but they did not hit it off, yah dat dat dah dah dat daah, daah, dah dat dat da . . . anyway, they only met after she switched jobs and moved to another neighborhood. Big kielbasa fans, those guys. When you're younger you can eat what you want, but as you get older those nitrates can start to catch up to you. Speaking of nitrates—"

"Keira," Marco says.

"What were we talking about?"

"Johanna."

"Right. Johanna is one of the easiest people to find in Asheville. The trick is that nobody there calls her Johanna. They call her the mayor. Because she's, like, the mayor. They elected her this July on the platform of making Asheville its own country."

"Isn't it a little small to be a . . ." Zeke says, "though Singapore pulled it off, didn't it." Now he can't help himself. "There's no good reason they couldn't do it, except for the issue of backing up their currency. They'll either need to start collecting things of intrinsic value—gold, silver, saffron, uranium, whatever—or start producing something"—here Zeke's head tilts, he eyes Keira—"very lucrative. You wouldn't happen to be involved in that particular aspect of Asheville's plans, would you?"

"Like I said, we have no business for you," Keira says.

"Is that a roundabout way of telling me to mind my own business?" Zeke says.

"Interpret it any way you like," Keira says. "Nobody's going to stop you. You have all the freedom in the world; you can do whatever you want. Paralyzing, isn't it? Now, Marco, honey, before I come down and my mind completely goes, can you tell me one thing?"

"What's that?" Marco says.

"How did you escape the explosion on Digby pier?"

"Trade secret."

"But I've always been so forthcoming with information. Come on."

Marco pauses for a second, then bends down and whispers in Keira's ear. Her eyebrows meet in concentration; she nods four times. Then, at last, she smiles.

"Ingenious, dear," she says.

The brakes scream; the trailer tilts forward, harder and faster than before; the back end lifts off the road and begins a vertiginous swing to the right. For a second, gravity flees, and ladies and gentlemen, we are in space; everything is aloft and moving: bottle caps, people, tables, cards, hookahs, and dice float through the air. Then the trailer lands, and everything splashes to the floor. The stereo coughs up its batteries and goes silent. I think my arm's, like, busted, someone says. Then a pair of hands bangs on the side of the trailer from the outside, a desperate voice screams to be let in before two shots cut it off. The sound of running feet, five more shots, cries for help. Marco looks at Zeke, who nods, and they both vault to the ladder, climb to the roof.

The Americoids' convoy is bent all over the road, the three trailers in a zigzag, the bus facing almost sideways. They at first see only hills and trees; a man scrambles out from under the trailer and disappears into the underbrush. A voice from behind is yelling at Felix Purple to move the fucking truck. More people run into the woods; shots follow. Marco and Zeke turn around. In front of them is a cleared valley boxed by razor wire, barred with barracks of corrugated metal, a cluster of rusting factories rising from the cracked earth, spouting small fires. In the fence running along the road is a wide hole, clipped and propped open by what is now the corpse of a woman with a large pair of pliers. Other corpses lie around the hole, but even more people are writhing through it, crawling under the trailers, vanishing into the woods. The man yelling at Felix Purple wears a blue jumpsuit and has a shotgun. Felix is squinting, yelling back, You going to shoot, go ahead and shoot, I don't give a damn. Other men in blue jumpsuits run along the fence; they follow the people in dirty clothes into the woods, and there are shots. Inside the compound, a last few are sprinting toward the hole in the fence, but a multitude—six or seven hundred—are being corralled by more men in jumpsuits, who fire into the air around them. One last man breaks off from the crowd and runs like mad for the perimeter. The guards do not hesitate. They shoot him in the legs, and while he wriggles on the valley floor, one of them walks over to him, hoists him up on his blasted feet, and slits his throat. It is this, killing a man like he was a pig, that makes Marco understand. He has seen it before, people killed like livestock: he was six and in Bolivia, and the fence was rustier, farther away; but there were barracks, a building on fire. Other children nearby, all of them with weapons; the adults with knives, whips, their voices. They were circled around Javier, a fourteen-year-old who knelt on the ground with burns on his hands, the product of a homemade bomb that went off too soon, took his best friend with it. They'd intended for it to explode when they went out on patrol, throw the training camp into disarray while they crashed through the jungle to the road to La Paz, climbed aboard a bus to the cinderblock neighborhoods around the capital and never pick up guns again. Instead, there Javier was in the middle of the camp, his friend in pieces in the bomb's ashes, his own hands unusable for the rest of his life, which he knew totaled about six minutes. So he spoke his mind, running a spittle-strewn string of curses toward the adults. Do your own killing. Fight your own fucking wars.

One of the adults nodded at Marco and smiled.

—*Hijo. Disparaste tan bien esta mañana. Vamos a ver si puedes acabar con el,* he said. You did so good at shooting this morning, son. Let's see if you can finish him.

Marco shook his head.

—*Has matado hombres muchas veces*, the adult said. You've shot men many times.

—*Jamás a un amigo*. Never a friend.

—*¿Cuál es la diferencia?* What's the difference?

Marco calculated, stepped into the circle with Javier, raised his machine gun.

—*Sabes que puedes dispararles a ellos en vez de a mí, Marco*, Javier said. You know you could shoot them instead of me.

Marco shook his head again.

—*Eres un esclavo*, Javier said. You're their slave.

—*¿Dónde lo quieres, Javier?* Marco said. Where do you want it?

—*Al cerebro. Y no erres*. In the brain. And don't miss.

Another fire blooms from the valley; black smoke boils into the yellow air. The wind shifts, spirals into a small cyclone, and the Vibe gathers itself out of the air to hover behind Marco, tap him on the shoulder. You have been bad, my man, the Vibe says, and by bad I do not mean badass, but bad.

I know, says Marco. I know that.

You must do something about this. This thing in front of you. This thing in you, the Vibe says.

What am I going to do? Marco says. It's history.

Later, you will know, says the Vibe, and undoes itself, drifts away on the curls of the breeze.

On the roof of the third trailer, beatific and oblivious, Doctor San Diego is asleep in the lotus position, a wide, tooth-flashing smile on his face. He has been through this part of the world seven times in the last four years, each time pulling a tighter circle across the continent to come back. He is in decaying orbit around Appalachia, and his smile gets even wider when his sleeping brain imagines his younger self, the one who believed in inexorable progress until a San Francisco earthquake sent his house into a gully while he crouched in the aisle of a supermarket, hands over his head, cans of soup racketing around him. He now understands that this expectation of progress applies only to young nations, for most of the planet lives among the ruins of dead empires: Angkor Wat, the Great Zimbabwe, Rome, the Mughal palaces. The plumbing in Lisbon, five hundred years old. The ancestral pyramids and roads in Central America and what the Spaniards did to them. Progress is a soothing lie, thinks Doctor San Diego's addled brain, and for over two centuries, all of North America lay swooning under its comfort. Except you, the doctor says to the South. You woke up over a century ago, in blood and fire. You have your rotting plantations, your mass graves. The thought that the best times are behind you is a spike in the skull. But it prepared you for this, the death of the Union, the last lowering of the flag. While the rest of us reel and clutch at the air, you know there is nothing to do but accept. You've already done it once.

And the ghosts of the South writhe in the ground, spit the dirt from their mouths to speak: No, doctor, you have it all wrong. We have been fighting for more than a hundred years, and we will keep fighting until our bones turn to earth, and the Earth falls into the sun.

CHAPTER IV.

This little ASSASSIN goes to market; a
REUNION with and brief history of JOHANNA
SALINGER; a prison ship transformed; how the
RIBBONS OF HISTORY make Johanna
vulnerable; a conversation at night.

The gas station at the Virginia border has been out of gas for three years. The pumps are gone, the building's glass removed, the lengths of rubber hose sectioned off and taken away. Weeds chew through the seams of the asphalt and concrete, spread fingers of green across the black-and-white surface. But everyone knows it as Georgia Pine's gas station, for the open-air market where people come to barter, the thick braid of cables running from the power lines along the road to two dozen outlets, the stalls clustered under the rusting canopy, fanning out toward the road, shooting out along the shoulder. People trade clothing and kitchen utensils; plastic buckets reinforced with duct tape; guitars glued together from the splintered shells of five other guitars; copper pipes; baked goods; pirated French cell phones, you can't read the screens, but you can still call. In the shade of the garage an old-time stringband, slicing fiddle, stabbing banjo, thumping bass, banging guitar, is raising a righteous ruckus on "Indian War Whoop," music born of sharecroppers and slaves, of sparks from the friction between Africa and poor Europe. The banjo player lost his fingers in a fire but glued nails to his hands, and now he smacks the banjo around with metal and thumbs. His startled voice scurries across the market, chased by the groove, which pulls words from him about Wounded Knee and smallpox; we should never have let them land. They run their sound through stacked speakers that take up two of the market's outlets, blast their rhythm into the hills. Georgia Pine herself handles security with a sawed-off shotgun and a smile, does small engine repair on the side. The older mechanics say she's only been at it for a few years; they can see it in the way she handles the tools. But they can't deny her skill, because she's putting them out of business. They watch her with a jealous eye as she opens up a chainsaw, works with screwdriver and pliers, bleeds out only three drops of oil before she stitches the wound, pats the engine good as new, walks off with a basket of vegetables and a box of lightbulbs. They can't figure out how she does it, bitch to each other over gumbo under the awning where the pumps used to be, now housing trays full of grits, pans of vinegar barbecue sauce, the beer someone's devoted his life to making; if he has to live without beer, he says, he's not going to bother.

In the days after the collapse, when the lights blinked out and the alarms went off, and police cars slept on their sides in the street, there was blood on the walls of their towns, men with rifles walking from house to house, whistling come on, come on, we won't hurt you, while the brewer and his neighbors crouched in a ditch, water up to their shoulders, hands over their children's mouths. They watched small wars break out and die, a man killing his boss with a chisel for sleeping with his sister, two families sharpshooting at each other through the windows of their houses over the unsettled lay of a property line. Two women knifed to death in the pink booth of a family restaurant; nobody ever knew why. A chain of exploding barns; machinery gutted and dismembered; the tension that law enforcement stifled, released at last, scraping across the county, peeling off years of progress. They slept in shifts, remembered to duck, taught their kids algebra, told each other to hang on. Now the wars are over and the apples are tart and sweet, the wells filled with clear water, and they shoot deer with arrows from the roof of their garage, hang the animals from their porches and invite fifteen people to share the meat. They throw parties in the winter that last for five days, hours of firewood and dancing, windows fogging with steam and smoke, a band doing their best James Brown with accordion and guitar, motor parts, an old trombone, and everyone shouting about getting on up, clapping their hands on the two and four until the rain stops and dawn comes. They ride horses home, cars rigged to run on batteries; they walk along the quiet, cracking highways with groggy children on their shoulders, tugging their hair, and think, this is what they survived for.

Georgia Pine's husband runs a local newspaper out of the auto garage's office, the *I-81 Bulletin,* he calls it, though it only covers the fifteen square miles around him, augmented with news from Dayneesha's feed. He was a reporter before the collapse, covered city hall, the police station, won a local award for a story about a war veteran who raised horses and hanged himself in the stalls when he learned he had pancreatic cancer. His paper folded after the collapse; the editor drove to Florida, said he wasn't coming back. Fine by me, said Georgia Pine's husband; I'm not leaving. So he edits the *Bulletin* now, has three reporters, does odd jobs fixing fences and shingling roofs. Four advertisers cover printing of five hundred copies, six pages of newsprint each. He stays up late on Tuesdays in the auto garage to get the paper out on Wednesdays, tells Georgia Pine he does it because someone has to keep the bad news coming. But people know him now, tell him stories hoping he'll cover them, get them in the paper. He harasses the mayor. It's like voting all the time. He has an interview with a former water tester for Fish and Wildlife, who says that maybe the collapse wasn't so bad after all, for those who survived it. The end of big industry; clear air, cleaner water. Maybe the planet won't be so angry at us now.

Agents of the lords of global commerce are set up on the other side of the road watching a laptop hooked up to a satellite dish by electrical wire and a coat hanger, exchanging baht for rupees, colones for a small commission. They're moving an undisclosed sum out of the New Dominion and into an account in Kyrgyzstan that carries the name of a man who does not exist. We'll put your money anywhere you want it, however you want it, the agents say. Who's going to tell us not to? The agents multiply in the unregulated landscape. The racketeers in Richmond remember a short, wiry woman with hair of blue and gold, who swore and spat and flipped them off before handing them a briefcase with the kind of cash in it that you can retire on if you're willing to move to Myanmar. A plastics manufacturer remembers a tall, dirty man with hair and beard jumbled to his waist, a long pipe curling away from his lips to dive toward the floor and curve back up again, green smoke weaving out of it to circle his head. An arms dealer recalls an old woman in a smock and bandanna, four teeth in her gums. Someone else, a child. But the agents are the closest thing anyone has to a bank; they wince, then hand over their yuan, watch it flying across the world, trailing transaction fees that the agents collect, take their living from. But at least people will get their money back when they ask for it. Most of it, anyway.

"I need this much in yuan," the assassin says. He hands an agent a roll of money in ten different currencies, tied in a purple ribbon. The agent weighs it in her hand, then unrolls the bills, passes her palm over each one.

"Sixteen of these bills are counterfeit," she says.

"Too counterfeit for you doesn't mean too counterfeit for Somalia."

The agent smiles. "They're usable, I think."

"So you'll exchange them."

"Minus a risk premium."

"Of course."

The assassin loiters on the edge of the market, eating a slice of cornbread that tastes like the baker's out of salt, though everyone says they like it better that way now. He's following the traces in the ether left by Zeke's and Marco's passage, a trick he learned in Zimbabwe a decade ago from a man who claimed he was the Last True Chief of the Shona, heir to the Great Zimbabwe. The assassin went through Harare just as the coup was starting, danced through machine-gun fire in front of Manny's Nightclub, got a bullet in the calf before he became invisible, just to get to a blasted, oil-soaked field near the burned-out airport, where the Last True Chief squatted in a paisley-painted Japanese van missing half of its windows, blasting Ghanaian funk, a trumpet and sax locked in combat in a spiky ring of percussion, everything on overdrive, no condition is permanent. There should be many wives at my feet, the chief said. Visitors from surrounding kingdoms bearing tribute in grains, animals living and dead.

"That man, he is crazy," said Thomas Sithole, Shona himself by descent, though he cared more about his job as a stationery salesman and owner of Manny's than his family ties; he still brought in the chimurenga bands, though there were .38-caliber holes in the sides of his speakers, streaks on the house electric guitar from mine blasts, cracks in the calabashes. "He is trouble. You hang out with him long enough, you get a machete in the neck or worse." He didn't see what the Last True Chief could see, what the assassin came to learn.

"Take this," the Last True Chief said, gave the assassin a plastic cup of acrid brown liquid. A helicopter burred overhead, and the chief looked up at it, waved his hand as if pushing it away.

"This smells like cleaning solution," the assassin said.

"It is gasoline," said the Last True Chief. "But not just gasoline."

The effects were at first euphoric, then nauseating. The Last True Chief laughed when the assassin vomited his chicken with garlic and milk onto the van's tires. For the next hour, the assassin had the deep and peaceful conviction that his stomach would crawl out of his throat and drag his liver with it, that he would die watching the two organs wrestle in the dust. Then all was clear, clearer than it had ever been in his life, as if the lenses in his eyes had been sharpened. The Last True Chief was squatting over him with an expectant look.

"Tell me if this appears different."

He waved his hand over the assassin's eyes, and streaks followed his fingers, made dull orange stripes and curls that persisted for a moment before fading, as if sinking into murky water. The Last True Chief rose, and his image smeared; he left a trail of light as he walked to the van to get beers.

"When things move, they blur," the assassin said. "I'm hallucinating. Or you've done something to my eyes."

"Not to your eyes. To your head. I have altered the way it understands time."

"What do you mean, altered?"

"You can see into the past. Only a few seconds into it now. But with discipline, you can stretch that into months."

"But if I see everyone's past at once, won't everything be a huge blur?"

"Discipline again. With practice, you will be able to decide what parts of the past to see and not see, and thus re-create history."

The assassin squints at the highway in front of Georgia Pine's now, and a horde of glowing ribbons of color stripe along its length, weaving and braiding around each other, the paths of refugees and those who preyed on them. He squints harder, and one by one the ribbons peel away and shrivel into the earth, until he finds the ones he's looking for. Zeke's is bright yellow, Marco's a dark red, and they shoot straight down the highway in parallel, an arm's length away from each other, getting brighter the farther south they go, until they're neon rays against the side of the rising hills, then lost in the mountains. The assassin blinks and the ribbons disappear. Nobody notices when he vanishes too, along with a truck with Virginia plates and a full tank of gas, the body of the driver flung into the ditch, staring at the sky, mouth open in protest.

The old green sign that gives the name of the town, Asheville, is still there, bent and rusting, but it is unnecessary now, for all around the border of the town is a blockade of stones and felled trees that turn the highway into a one-lane road guarded by three men, two with shotguns, one with a clipboard and a large hunting knife. As the Americoids approach, the man with the clipboard walks toward the cab; the guns hang back, level the barrels at the truck's grille, at Felix Purple's head, then pretend to look away. We do this all day, their faces say.

"Your name," the man with the clipboard says.

"Felix Purple of the Americoids."

"Your business."

"To spread good vibes wherever we go."

"Number in your party."

"Unclear, sir."

"Are you shitting me, Mister Purple?"

"No, sir. We pick up and drop off a lot of folks as we go our merry way."

"It's obvious this is your first time to the Free Township of Asheville and Black Mountain."

"Me personally? Yes, it is."

"You need to have a clear and straightforward reason for entering the township, or I can't let you in."

"Now you're shitting *me*."

"I am not shitting you, Mister Purple."

There is discussion among Felix, Keira, and Doctor San Diego himself, who gestures in the air as if waving away very slow flies. His vibe has been harshed. Twenty minutes later, the caravan has left seventeen people at Asheville's border and is turning around, growling away from the blockade. The music takes fifteen minutes to fade after the trailers are out of sight; Jimi has to finish what he was saying thirty years ago in Berlin, and Eddie Hazel is hot on his tail, for he has tasted the maggots in the mind of the universe. The smell will last for another four days, seep into the guards and mellow them without their consent. A week from now, they'll all show up late, late without excuses, after having slept better than they have in years.

The fifteen Americoids left at the gate declare themselves refugees and willing to work; they're given slips of green paper and pointed toward the town.

"We're here to see the mayor," Zeke says.

"Who are you?" the guard says.

"Tell her that two of the Slick Six are here."

The guards' eyebrows rise in unison, and soon Zeke and Marco are riding along Black Mountain Highway in a truck that turns off and up until it's on a dirt road that slinks into the hills above the city, ambles by fields gone to seed, a line of woods on the other side of the valley, the swell of a round peak spiked by a tilting radio tower.

"Name's Ralph Morrison," the deputy says. "Heard a lot about you."

"Good things, I hope," Zeke says.

"You could say that."

"This place is gorgeous."

"Yes, sir," Ralph says.

"You from around here?"

"Yes, sir, I am. Born liberated, and I'll die that way, Lord willing."

Ralph Morrison was running a supermarket near Black Mountain when the dollar fell; he saw the first shocks ripple across his store just a few days before it happened. Vegetables from Mexico, twice as much as they were the day before. Those fancy peppers from Holland, unattainable. He bought what he could, put it on the shelf with new stickers. Called his suppliers; the prices were different again, even higher.

"What the heck's going on with the broccoli?" a patron asked him. "They growing it in Beaujolais?"

"I don't know."

After a few days, he just took the price tags off; they didn't make sense anymore. He took a blackboard out of his stock, changed the numbers every few hours. People started coming in with pocketbooks full of bills, then shopping bags. Came out with seven cans of green beans, a carton of milk. A man in a greasy cap offered to fix Ralph's car for a frying pan and a gallon of cooking oil. Ralph Morrison agreed. A week later, he saw people across the street banging on the doors of the bank; more people running down the block, like in old movies, news from other countries. So that's why they call it a bank run, he thought. People really run. He closed his store a week later, walked into the police station.

"Afternoon, Mr. Morrison," they said. "What brings you here?"

"That depends," Ralph Morrison said. "You either give me a job—I'll take anything—or you lock me up now, because I either do a little B&E or nobody eats at my place tonight." He laughs about it now, but he was serious then.

They turn into the driveway of a collapsing farmhouse with a fence warping along its side, drive up to a barn with a fresh coat of red paint, new white shingles, a few windows, a phone line stapled to the outside and running through a window, because the mayor doesn't trust the cell and satellite services anymore. Johanna is standing in front of the house, arms folded across her chest. Marco smiles from inside the truck. Johanna catches it, but doesn't give it back.

"So it's true," she says.

"So what's true?" Zeke says.

"You two on the loose. Did you know that the Aardvark's

got a bounty out on both of you? We got the message this morning."

"How much?" Marco says.

"It's not how much. It's what, which in this case is a piece of Queens. A little piece, but a piece. I would collect the bounty myself, but he'd recognize me." She has yet to smile; her lips curl, eyes slide from Marco to Zeke and back again.

"You're screwing with us," Zeke says.

"Am I?" Johanna says.

When Marco saw her last, her back was to him, one hand crawling behind her head to worry the skin at the nape of her neck; she left her briefcase on the defendant's table; she was giving up, it was over. At the plaintiff's table, the Aardvark's lawyer, a woman with thick glasses and what looked like a chipped tooth, tapped her papers into a neat stack and bound them with a rubber band. The Aardvark himself sat back in his chair, hands clasped atop his belly, a giant grin on his wide face. He looked at Marco, passed his fingers along his throat, and hissed. As though he had beaten his and Marco's past to death with a shovel.

"I'm so sorry for what happened to you, Marco," Johanna says.

"It's not your fault," Marco says. "Everyone in that room but us had been bought."

I don't mean that, Johanna thinks. Since he was sent away, she has thought about him more often than is healthy. His scent. Remorse that she didn't try harder, that she let the trial proceed even when she knew the Aardvark had paid the judge, paid him and threatened his family, stocked the jury with his associates. There were motions she could have made, a whistle she could have blown. I denounce these proceedings. This is a lynching. Miscarriage of justice. In her dreams she closes her eyes and jumps into the sky, flies over the ocean to the prison ship, finds him in his salty cell and shrinks to the size of a strawberry seed, rolling into his ear to hear his thoughts, burnt by shock, stretching into resentment, then bursting into hatred at everyone else's freedom. In her dreams, he is coming to kill them; the police find her choked to death, pages of law books jammed into her mouth. Under her dress, she has a pistol taped to her inner thigh. She watches Marco's hands, his feet, for signals of attack. But they don't come, and for four seconds, she's confused. Then she understands.

"Come in," she says.

The barn's ceiling soars high inside. A blanket of darkness is draped over the rafters, hiding the animals that live there, eating, mating, nesting, raising their young, the report of their claws and wings tapping against timbers that spiral to the floor, where Oriental rugs unroll across uneven pine, surround a Buddha of a stove, scurry under rice-paper screens that hover around the bed. Seven lamps peer from behind salvaged couches, teeter on end tables with two legs nailed to the wall, hang down from unseen beams, but only two of them work; Johanna has only three lightbulbs, keeps switching them around and out, thinks they'll last longer that way. The mountains have already stolen the sun for today, and in the dimming light she pads across the piling to an iron kettle singing out a cone of steam, pours it into three cups to make tea. They all sit in front of the stove, for the weather has decided to turn cold; they cross their legs, hold their cups in both hands, pass looks around, cowboys in a standoff, each one daring the other to speak first.

"So why are you here?" Johanna says.

"I have a plan," Marco says, "to reunite the Slick Six."

"For what?"

His mouth opens, but no words emerge, and Johanna knows what he wants to say. She decides to be cruel, laughs at him before he can speak.

"The world has nothing to offer us anymore, Marco. It's only what you can make from it now."

"Wasn't it always that way?"

"No. Not like this. You've seen the slave camps, right? Half of those people put themselves up on the block. They're so desperate, they're starving. That's the difference now, Marco. When you fall, nobody catches you. Things break and stay broken. The lives we used to have, whatever they were, they're impossible now."

"I'm not saying I want it to be the same," Marco says.

"And I'm saying I'm not interested," Johanna says, and throws him a pause just long enough for him to feel the hurt, again, of having nothing to say.

"I thought . . ." Marco says.

"You thought what?"

". . ."

"What I have here is good. Good enough. I'm sorry you've driven so far for this, but I think you should go."

"But we just got here," Zeke says.

"Which is my point. You two, you need to keep moving if you enjoy the idea of not being shot at, or stabbed, or clubbed over the head."

"That's funny," Zeke says. "We were just talking about how much we missed that."

"I'm serious, Zeke. I'm not going to turn you in to the Aardvark, but when word gets out that you're here . . . really, you should go. Maybe you'll have better luck with Dayneesha. She always liked you better than I did. Besides, what do you need a lawyer for? Nobody cares about the law anymore."

Marco stares at her. What's wrong with you? Your story keeps changing.

No it doesn't, she thinks. It just gets more complicated.

The last time Marco and Johanna slept together, she said she couldn't be with him because she was afraid of him. They were in Laguna Beach, in a beaten brown bungalow sagging between two houses of gleaming pink and turquoise; below them, out the window, a sea set on fire by the sun surged against the sand, while silverware clanked in a neighbor's screened-in kitchen in rough rhythm with some early Skatalites, jaunting through Studio One static, a bleating guitar, fuzzy horns, a trombone solo from a man reconciled to hard times and taking a couple of hours off, having some beers, whistling at girls, moving his feet. Marco rubbed his eyes, stumbled out of bed into the next room. More rustling, the screen door smacking against its frame. She went to the window, watched him walk naked into the waves and start swimming. He was committing suicide, she thought; he would go until he was exhausted, then let himself drown. But he was back two hours later, briny and hardened with cold, said they should rejoin the others, who were already plotting their next job from a brownstone in Boston, a city Marco hated. His dive in the ocean, the length of his swim, was a measurement of his anger. If he had needed to, she thought, he could have kicked his way to Asia to spend it. But he didn't need to, and it pricks her now that it'd taken him only two hours to work her out of him, when years later, he is still with her, in the shadows of the rafters, behind the rice paper, watching her sleep.

Marco stands up. "Excuse me," he says, leaves the tea to freeze on the floor.

"Where is he going?" Zeke says.

"It doesn't matter," Johanna says. "He'll be back. I'd say within an hour."

Zeke says nothing. She wonders then if she has said too much, if inside Zeke's head, he's mocking her.

"Do you know what this is about?" Johanna says. "This plan of his?"

"No," Zeke says.

"But you think he has something in mind?"

"Sure."

"We're not on trial here, Zeke. You can answer with more than one word."

"Okay."

". . ."

". . ."

"So what do you think his plan is?" Johanna says.

"I don't know. I don't know if he knows yet. But I believe he's piecing it together."

"And what'll happen when he does?"

"I'll help him accomplish it."

"Just like that."

"Sure."

"How can you trust him like that?"

"Why can't you? Don't those years mean anything to you?"

"I'm glad you're leaving so soon," Johanna says.

Zeke laughs, hard, and Johanna doesn't know if it's because he thinks she's joking, or because he knows she's not and thinks that's funny. A sudden hate blooms in her: It's the same old shit, this complete inability to be serious. She has seen him laugh during gunfights; he laughed when he heard Marco's verdict.

They both finish the conversation in their heads in the next five seconds. You dumb fuck, she says, don't you see? He's trying to go home, like a kid hanging on to one too many balloons, floating over the fair. I wanna go home.

Do you really think that's all there is to it? Zeke says.

What else do you think it is?

He's trying to be good, Zeke says. Make his peace.

I know, she says. I'm not an idiot.

Then why won't you let him?

Johanna gives Zeke an angry look, leaves him inside, walks into the cricketing night, onto the road that goes down the mountain. Clouds haunt a moonless sky, the trees hang in close, but she finds Marco anyway, walking up the slope again, already coming back to the world. He stops moving when he sees her, his breathing stops, the edges around his shape blur and vanish, and for eight seconds, she's alone, the hairs rising on her neck, her other senses rushing to fill the space. Night birds click their claws on rocks and wood; insects rustle in the leaves. A faint scent of rot pulls a scarf across her face; the humidity pushes into her skin. Then his hand is on her stomach; she tilts back, lets her lips land on his cheek. Her breath curls around his ear. You son of a bitch, she says, turns, and is lifted up; she scales him; his hands are underneath her, and she hooks her feet around the back of his knees. They rock back and forth in the road, in the dark, until her hands dig into his back and she returns to the earth.

They don't come back together. Marco tells Zeke that Johanna's right, they should go. She gives them a yellow 1985 Mazda pickup with a spare tire bolted behind the passenger seat. The body's rusty but the engine is good, she says; when it breaks down, they can sell it for parts. It's amazing what people will do with them. Families of six live in the shells of station wagons, use the fuel injection to pump water into an irrigation system, fit the engine and axles with hoops of wood and metal to spin cotton.

She watches them turn down the driveway from the door of the barn, puts her hand up in a half wave. As they curve around the ruined house, Zeke's arm, hanging out the passenger window, rises and waves back. But Marco's head doesn't turn, his hands don't leave the wheel, and she shudders as her fear and her lust twist into pity.

She was born into a wealthy Connecticut family that owned a third of the town where she grew up; there's a graveyard on the village green, protected by ordinance, a plot marked for her already near casualties of the Revolutionary War, a town judge who died of pneumonia in 1826. Her girlhood was a parade of brunches in winged brick mansions overlooking golf courses and reservoirs; cocktails on the patios of spired homes clinging to the rocks of the Thimble Islands; birthday parties on the Sound's pebbly beaches, in riding stables in the foothills of the Berkshires. She hated it all, the propriety and position, the family's complicity in the bloody birth of America, the massacres across New England, the Pequot bones sunk into swamps, driven into the ground, paved over with shopping plazas and rest stops; their survivors enslaved three centuries earlier, sold down to the West Indies for rum, for sugar. She convinced herself that when she finished high school, she would abandon it all, take the train as far west as the money in her pocket would get her, then get a job where she stood. She would be a waitress, a short-order cook. A nanny. Join the park service fire crew, digging ditches in the woods to contain flames. She refused to apply to college, left the day after graduation on a bicycle careening toward the train station, shaking with dumb anger. Six days later she was broke and hanging on a pay phone in Detroit, begging her parents to buy her a plane ticket home; she applied to twelve colleges that fall. But in college and law school the old feelings returned, so she immolated herself with partying that frightened her classmates.

"Those people are dangerous," they said.

"They just know how to have a good time," she said.

She was the last to join the Slick Six, and it was Zeke who found her, at a party in San Francisco thrown by two record executives in a house perched on the side of a hill that the festivities were shaking loose from the bedrock. Zeke could see the floor warping, broken strings of pearls pooling along the baseboard. He had a photograph of Johanna in the palm of his hand, while the living version almost pitched herself off the balcony until one of the record executives, her boyfriend for the next four days, caught her by an arm.

"It's Johanna Salinger, right?" Zeke said. "Like the song, then the writer?"

"Yeah, very cute, like the song then the writer. What about it?" she said.

"I'm Zeke Hezekiah," he said.

"Oh my God, I'm sorry, I didn't mean—"

"No offense taken, Miss Salinger," Zeke said. "Your reputation precedes you, in every regard. I'd like to talk to you in private."

They wriggled through the party and out to the curling driveway. By the time they reached his car, she was sober. They drove down to the harbor, where ships trawled in from the bay to be unburdened by cranes and men in dark suits spoke in hand signals. It took Zeke three hours to explain it all to her, the legal representation they needed, the places they wanted to be able to hide between the laws. She didn't listen to a word he said, said yes anyway. They learned later that the party wrenched the house off the hillside two hours after they left—it tumbled onto its roof and crashed into the house below it—and Zeke saw in Johanna a wistfulness, as though she wished she'd been there. She remembers her years with the Slick Six as a procession of courtrooms, police stations, people in suits that cost more than cars, gleaming beads of parties in cities that lit the land to the horizon, the narrow hours of the night curled into the plunger of a syringe, then a club where people seduced each other in seventeen languages. Her name in the paper all the time, pictures of her on courthouse steps, the only one smiling, always looking right into the camera. See how much I can get away with? She never answered the phone if she knew it was her parents; they had to drive to Massachusetts, Rhode Island, call from a pay phone encrusted with stickers in a truck stop in Wyoming to trick her into picking up. She couldn't bring herself to hang up on them once they hooked her, endured an hour or so before she started fighting.

"You've always been ashamed of me," Johanna said.

"We're not ashamed of you," her father said. "We're worried about you. Can't you tell the difference?" They were dead a year later, a car accident in Montana, the remains sent back to Connecticut to be buried on the town green. She got the news weeks later after she finally returned her older brother's seventh message. She never called him back, but in the back of her brain, head tilted back as she sat in cars and cabs, helicopters battering over São Paulo, she talked to him all the time.

When Johanna lost the case against the Aardvark and Marco went to prison, she understood that she was done. She couldn't look at him when the police took him away, couldn't talk to any of the Six. Leave me alone, she said at last to Dayneesha, who was just trying to be friendly. It's over. No more. Other criminals approached her for representation and were spurned, kingpins and money launderers, men implicated in real estate fraud and tax evasion. She withdrew from the law altogether, flew to Hartford, turned off of 84 and onto the roads that ducked and swerved through the Connecticut hills, the trees overwhelmed by vines, the houses peeking out of gullies, hiding on rises of land squared off by stone walls, until she was back at her ancestral home. She sat on the wide sofa before the fireplace, thought only about what she would do next. A clothing store, a restaurant, a silent partner in a hotel. Anything with no history.

When the economy collapsed, it was a personal insult, for she had gone legit, leveraged capital against capital, the tottering mobile you build when you try to play the game fairly, balancing all the pieces and holding your breath. Why couldn't this have happened eight years ago, she thought. She would have thrown her head back, sawed off the heels of her shoes. Instead she watched the banks fold in on themselves, the big oil and gas companies shut down their plants, try to sell them. In the winter, she thought, the towns will start to freeze. She called up her brother; I'm going south, she said. He was already gone, talking to her from a satellite phone on a thirty-seven-foot sailboat parked forty-seven miles off the coast of Venezuela. Better hurry, he said, before they close 95 and you can't go anywhere.

She barreled down the highway, passed the looting along the Connecticut shore, the fires in the marinas, the mansions at the mouths of the rivers and bays emptying into the Sound, Darien, Noroton, Cos Cob. A commuter train streaming flames from its windows, still running north, leaving a trail of oily smoke. Grocery stores with broken windows in Mount Vernon, boxes of food scattered in the parking lot. Cars flipped over along the highway through Jersey and into Pennsylvania, ambulances screaming down the breakdown lanes. By nightfall, she was in southern Virginia. She pulled her car into a patch of trees on the side of the highway, turned off the engine and the lights, and then she could hear it: screams from the farms around her, the town nearby, gunshots, cars crashing, as if the whole country were thrashing itself to death. She crawled into the backseat, tucked her knees under her chin, jammed her shaking hands between her thighs, and sobbed until she couldn't breathe, for the Slick Six, for herself, for the family she'd forsaken, the land around her, cracking and bleeding, tornadoes destroying mountains, curtains of darkness drifting down from the sky. When she slept at last, she dreamed of traffic jams and taxes, electric bills, garbage day. Men doing road work in bright orange vests, cones along the double yellow line, a steamroller kicking up the stink of fresh asphalt. A man with a ponytail under a yellow hard hat, waving her on with one hand, holding a circular sign in the other. Slow.

The mayor of Asheville concerns herself now with food, the water supply, the bridges over the Swannanoa; people say pieces of them are falling in the water. She had no idea people could produce so much garbage. But it's the slavery ban, the town's concession to its hippie past, that crowds the place with refugees. They came first from neighboring towns, then Virginia and Georgia. Now they come from everywhere; they've heard that here they're allowed to be free. She doesn't know what to do with them all. There are shantytowns along the roads from Tennessee, disputes over where Asheville ends and slave country begins that start with shotgun blasts and end with knives, clubs, sharpened tools, people hauled into the backs of trucks who squirm away to jump under the tires. But they've elected her twice, shake her hand when they see her in front of the Grey

Eagle, in Jack of the Wood at the edge of a frantic pile of fiddles and banjos, a horde of booming guitars and chucking mandolins. You're a little Lincoln, they say, and she thinks of the Pequot at the bottom of the Mystic River, in the ocean off Barbados. If only you knew where I was from.

She doesn't know, as Maggot Boy Johnson does, how history is curling in on itself. One of her ancestors, a certain Jerrold O'Shaughnessy, became an agent on the Underground Railroad to harry his father, who owned 782 slaves on a plantation in South Carolina. Father and son raced against each other throughout the second half of the 1850s, the father buying slaves, the son freeing them. Every night Jerrold came home covered in dirt; his story was that he was a livestock trader, an occupation his father despised.

"How was wrestling hogs today, son?"

"Terrible," Jerrold said. "They keep getting away from me."

In July 1859, his father discovered Jerrold's betrayal, and then there was warfare. Jerrold ran from the house ducking curses and rifle bullets; on his next trip north, driving a wagon of runaways in barrels labeled as rye whiskey, he stayed, moved into Connecticut, set up a cotton-trading company, took the name of his betrothed, and married into Johanna's grand old family. As the glue fumes exit his brain, Maggot Boy Johnson traces the journey of Jerrold's genes, flitting from parents to children, parents to children, until Johanna writhes from her mother's womb, sprouts hair, gets curvy, heads south. Somewhere in Maryland, as she breaks from the New England cold, she passes Jerrold's wraith in his wagon, trundling north. He knows his kin and waves, but she can't see him.

Maggot Boy Johnson rises from his stupor and finds himself back in his cell on the *Rosalita*, the red shutters on the windows, a mural of the kitchen of the apartment in Cleveland where he grew up, his mother rolling out dough in her nightgown, a radio taped to the wall, a little Bobby Womack spiraling from the

speaker, she wanna know that she's not walking on shaky
ground. His books, a fading paperback of the Qur'an, a leather-
bound edition of *The Adventures of Huckleberry Finn,* mildewed library copies of books about the coelacanth, expeditions
to the poles, to Nepal. Laid-back hip-hop struts into his ears,
four women practicing their thing on the cell block floor, a
trumpet with a rag stuffed in it, bass, drum kit banged out
from trash can lids and a suitcase, the MC plucking out soul
licks on a banjo and working on flow, throwing her voice. They
moved onto the ship yesterday, them and a few dozen others,
and up and down the cells they're taking out the bars, putting
in doors and windows, luscious curtains stripped from theaters.
They're painting with enamel on the metal walls, a jungle of
letters and faces, a snapshot of now. We are here. Families with
animals came the day before yesterday—can we live here? is
there room?—and the children scatter like thrown seeds
throughout the hull, hiding and seeking among rat nests and
boiler fittings while chickens and goats roam the deck; every
evening, the galley air is thick with stewed meat and vegetables. Two of the women think they're pregnant already, and
Piston Beauvoir and Helga Ramstead are beating pieces of the
rail into cradles. Big Mother presides over it all, welcomes any
who want it, will do so until there's no room left. He's proud of
his ship, aware of the symbol they became within forty-eight
hours of reaching New York, when he told the Aardvark's harbor police to fuck off and they did, because Big Mother's name
is so apt, because he showed them without moving a muscle
what he'd been put away for. They flout the Aardvark's author-
ity just by being there; they're a knife cutting off the fingers of
his reach, the folk heroes of the new underground. Someone
hung a sign over the bow, THIS SPACE IS FREE, and there is
business conducted in the mess hall that Big Mother doesn't
need to know about, meetings that begin in suspicious stares
and forced eloquence and end in empty bottles of moonshined
sambuca, broken glasses, choking laughter, hands pounding

the metal table. Several have asked if the *Rosalita* is for sale, promise enough for Big Mother to move to a penthouse in Shanghai, swim in under the city's rising sun. But Big Mother isn't interested in commerce, and there among the livestock, watching the harbor's water darken with evening, Maggot Boy Johnson understands why. They all grew up fighting, behind schools, in apartments in the shadows of water treatment plants, in the parking lots of bars and factories, in the cafeterias of county jails. But they've put away their knives now, uncurled their fists; a peace they didn't know existed has fallen upon them, and everyone on the *Rosalita* knows it's here to stay, as long as they don't scare it away.

All along the Atlantic coast and creeping inland, the grays of night are chasing day into the ground. In Philadelphia and Baltimore, the power is on in patches; in the vast swathes of darkness around them, people grope through the streets with flashlights, lanterns, torches. In Washington there is no power at all, and on clear nights with a new moon, the galaxy unfurls above, its wan light seeing into the future, turning streetlights into trees, sidewalks into paths of rugged moss, buildings into cliffs where falcons dive. In thirty years the vegetation will flood out of the parks, break through the pavement, bore though roofs, climb up walls to claw them down. In 150 more, the forest will grow thick and dark over everything, re-create the swamp that engineers worked so hard to drain, preparing for the day when the earth warms up enough to bring malaria out of exile. It seems like an eternity to us, because we're young and impatient; the woods and the diseases can wait.

Johanna's first nights in the barn were sleepless. She lay there in the dark, twitching her eyes at every snapping twig, talking tree. She believed at first that it was her fear of being prey, then understood that it was the isolation itself. The animals moving around the barn at night smelled her inside and didn't care. The trees, the mountains didn't know she was there. A prelude to being dead, dead and forgotten. She moved her hands in front of her face and couldn't see them. It was as though she was gone already. But she has come to accept it now, and sleeps deeper than she has in her life. The fading chirps of birds, the insect orchestras, the crackles of rodents and their predators in the brush have become her ocean waves, the sounds that signal slumber. She doesn't know it, but her hearing is sharper, lets her know things that she remembers when she wakes up. She's not surprised anymore when there's blood on her doorstep, the last act of a battle between mouse and owl.

Even so, she doesn't hear the assassin's approach. He leaves his stolen truck at the bottom of the hill, flits up the road, down her driveway, in almost perfect silence. The first sign she has of him is a shape in the window, gone the moment she looks, but then he is in the room, moving toward her without a sound, as if the man himself is far away, and has sent his shadow to do the killing.

"Who are you?" she says.

"I was going to ask you the same question," the assassin says. His head turns from side to side, surveying the room. "I can see that they were here for a while. A few hours, maybe. Meaning that you were the purpose of their trip here, not just a stop on it."

"I asked you who you were—"

The assassin is within reach of her, one finger over her lips. His hand smells like mint.

"Are you Carolyn or Johanna?"

" . . . "

"Oh, you can tell me. I already think you're one or the other, and my employer would be just as interested to see you dead either way."

"I'd be pretty interested in that myself," she says.

The head tilts. "You must be Johanna. But it's irrelevant. The only thing I want to know is where they're going."

"Let me guess. If I don't tell you, you'll kill me."

". . ."

"I'm not telling."

The shape in front of her draws closer, puts his face up to hers. She can hear him draw breath through his nose, release it from his mouth. It smells like mustard, and she thinks of Marco swimming in California, his hands on her in the road hours ago. It wouldn't be so bad to be done in now. Not so bad. She blinks, and he's at the door.

"I'm not going to kill you," he says. "It would be unprofessional. But Johanna? Don't wish for death so hard. One day it will come, and I have news for you: It's never quiet."

He knows this because he can see how the ribbons of the dead end. They blur into flowers, balls of hazy light, the trails of thrashing limbs, convulsions, a soul rattling in its husk. They never want to go. The assassin has heard the things that people resuscitated on operating tables talk about; the bright corridors, the reunions with friends and relatives, the chance to give historical figures a piece of your mind. He doesn't know about that. From what he can see, even if there are sweet gardens beyond waiting for us, we still fight it all the way up to the gate.

CHAPTER V.

The last laugh on the ALAMO; old friends,
NEW SLAVES.

Two ghosts, Silas and Isaac, flicker in and out of sight, leave the lines of their clothes and bones trailing behind them in rags of light. Over a century ago, they drove cattle between Oklahoma and Mexico, picked up enough Spanish to move the cows, get the good tequila, the women who didn't mind talking to men who spoke like children, the peppers named after local gods that opened up their skin and dissolved them in their chairs. They killed seven Mexicans in the war of independence, took three bullets and a piece of shrapnel between them; Silas still has a stitch in his hip that sways him when he walks.

One night they slept on the rocks on the banks of the Brazos under a blanket of weeds and rushes and dreamed the same dream, of farmers tilling fields with elephants and purple plows, planting flowers that opened tendrils of petals and sprouted houses of red and yellow, all in a row, multiplying to cover the earth, until the river rose and pulled them in. They woke up just long enough to drown.

But their ghosts still follow the trails between Colorado and the Fort Worth stockyards, haven't even noticed the changes in the land, the cities jutting out of the ground, falling back in. They pass now, oblivious, pulling fish from their throats, right through Dayneesha's warehouse, the first floor piled with two-by-fours, signs for boots and Western wear, the yard in front mazed with junked cars. Nobody sees them come or go, though Dayneesha's cousin Ray, who hasn't spoken since he fled the Southwest, cocks his head toward the cyclone fence and sniffs, swears he catches the tang of chiles tickling the hairs of his nose. It takes him back to his touring days, a chipped electric guitar in his hand, a sweating microphone at his mouth. A club in Memphis off Elvis Presley Boulevard, posters of R. L. Burnside stapled to the walls, goin' with you babe, I'm goin' with you babe. Later, a haul across the country, and then a show in Socorro, New Mexico, walls of orange and blue, a girl spinning and shaking in front of him, then sliding a habanero into his mouth after he gets off the stage. Take a bite, she said, just one. He always said he'd go back and find her, and he did, but the new war in Mexico found her first; when he saw what it had done to her, all his words left him.

"I can't believe it's so green here," Ettie Duchamp says. "I thought Texas was supposed to be a desert."

"If it was a desert," Dayneesha says, "what would all the cattle have eaten? Sand?"

They are sitting on the second floor around a pressed wood table, the chorus of hums from the machines around them resolved into a flat seven, coffee in tin cans getting cold. Ettie Duchamp's lips purse in pursuit of a comeback. She'll think of one hours later, as she's falling asleep, another one a month from now, when she sees a baby stroller, a smoked ham hanging in a window. But right now she flounders in a miasma of associations that refuse to congeal. Her lips unpurse.

"We have people from down this way," she says.

"Whereabouts?"

"Shreveport."

"That's in Louisiana. We're in Texas. Big difference, sister."

"Honey," Ettie says, "when you're from New York, talking about the difference between Texas and Louisiana is like talking about the difference between Venus and Mars."

"I wish Mexico felt the same way," Dayneesha says.

History is playing a prank on Texas, always making it choose between independence and peace. The border skirmishes are now almost all north of the Rio Grande. There's been a stand at Corpus Christi, but fingers of the front flick at Houston, Austin, Dallas. In Fort Worth, they feel the report of falling rockets, see the long streaks in the sky. Every month or so the Dallas night is a lightning storm of artillery, the crumbling thunder of buildings breaking. The next day, the refugees arrive on the freeway, in wagons pulled by cows, cars with the engines ripped out to make room for aunts and uncles, harnessed to horses instead. They set up camps in the serpentine parks along the Trinity River, blue and green tarps stretched between PVC pipes, wash their clothes in the cocoa water under the Main Street Bridge and string them from the trees near the vast parking lot at the end of North Taylor Street, where kids kick a soccer ball skinned of its color, patched with duct tape, denim, and glue; they holler and hop while their parents squint at the sky, waiting for new streaks of cloud to be drawn there, arc down between the abandoned office buildings and disappear behind the tower of the Tarrant County Courthouse. For an agonizing instant the illusion of peace persists; then it grows into fire and withers in the heat. They know the shore of the river is next—it has to be—and some of them are already heading for Ranger, for Cisco, for Baird, places the war might pass over. But for now they just want the hours to stretch out wide across a huge afternoon, the ripples on the river to slow until they're like the unfurling of a warm blanket; the ball to rest at the peak of its flight, then laze to the ground, until yesterday and tomorrow are a hundred years away, and there's only this game on the dusky asphalt, children with bloody knees chasing the shadow of the patched sphere, looking up into the sun, taking so long to blink that it's like they're all sleeping. Perhaps when they wake up, America will be whole again.

"Here," Ettie says, and slides a coil of fiber-optic cable across the table. "I hope this is what you wanted. It took my sister an awful long time to get it."

Dayneesha smiles. "You don't have to sell it to me, babe. Everything's already agreed to. But Charlene wasn't lying. This is good stuff."

"The rest is in the truck. And this will give us coverage for—"

"Six months."

"How about we make it seven," Ettie says. "Like you said, it's good stuff. And you need us as bad as we need you."

Charlene Duchamp's People Movers have sprawled out of New York City to fling routes across the country from ocean to ocean, fuzzing the borders of Canada and Mexico. The Duchamps didn't think much about it at first; they just took people where they wanted to go, from New York to Baltimore; Baltimore to East St. Louis; East St. Louis to Memphis, Cheyenne, Sacramento. First it was couples with suitcases, men in sweaty suits, teenagers with duffel bags who insisted they weren't hungry even after two days on the road. Then it was families with clothing balled into nets, dragging animals in cages. People who were leaving and not coming back. Which meant the Duchamps weren't getting any return customers.

"We need information," Charlene said back then. "The places that are going under, places where people are trying to get out. Do you have that kind of thing?"

"Sure," Dayneesha said. "You follow the catastrophes and stay one step ahead of the slavers, and you'll have all the business you can handle."

Now the Duchamp People Movers are a continental network. They have satellite offices in Seattle and San Diego, a major hub in Miami. Their trucks drive into the holds of ships and everyone gets out, arranges their luggage into a pile they can sleep on. The refugees are going to Europe and Japan; they're going south of Mexico. They land on the coasts of

Guatemala, Belize, and Honduras, pray against malaria and Chagas, move into the mountains. They walk into Canada, follow roads into Osoyoos, Onefour, Coaticook, Grand Falls. Help me out, they say, I just came from the United States. It has all made Charlene Duchamp very wealthy. She has a small compound in southern New Jersey at the edge of the Pine Barrens, where the Aardvark cannot reach her. He once tried to buy her cooperation over sushi and sweet white wine on the deck of the Empire State Building. When she refused, he tried to have her thrown over the edge; she pulled a short knife from the sole of her shoe, hamstrung one of the Aardvark's boys, backed into the elevator. Your wine sucked, she said.

"Deal," Dayneesha says. "Seven months. I've had a good year. Just remember this when times get hard for me. And tell Charlene I miss her."

"She misses you too," Ettie says. "But she don't miss coming down here. Why are you down here anyway?"

Dayneesha nods toward her cousin Ray, who's upstairs cleaning the guns, tapping his foot in a mean shuffle.

"Family," she says.

"It's always family these days, isn't it?"

This exact phrase flits through Zeke's head several hours later as their headlights flit over the sign telling them they've left Louisiana. Come again soon! He'd seen pictures of Louisiana on television, documentaries about old accordion players, and had imagined the state as a vast swamp. He knew that was impossible, but he'd always wanted to see it: the smooth, dark water, the cypresses leaning over their mirror images, draped in Spanish moss; this place where land dissolves into water. There's an honesty in it. Put a rock in the stream and it dissolves into sand. Put a continent against the surge of the tide, and the ocean eats the coast, the land breaks in half, surfs across the world for ten thousand years to break against a far shore, push jagged peaks toward the sky, like crests of water themselves, just slower. In the Midwest, or up in the mountains, where you can compare the place you're standing to photographs of it from a century ago, it's easy to think things will stay and stay, but in the marshes you can see how the land and water trade off with each other. Once you move past the terror of it, Zeke thinks, it doesn't seem so bad.

But they cross Louisiana in the dark, and he doesn't see any of it. And Marco, behind the wheel, hands at ten and two, hasn't said anything for three hours. So Zeke thinks about Johanna; he could tell what she was thinking, and under her inquisition, there was a pang in his brain telling him that he'd involved himself in something stupid. This family thing. It was too much at first, more than Zeke had designed his detachment to bear. He almost didn't get in the truck, almost stayed with Johanna and risked it, getting his head shorn from his neck, sent to the Aardvark in a vacuum-sealed crate.

But now, in the Louisiana night, where the humidity is a hungry creature, he thinks it through, goes back to the beginning, to the day he first met Marco, when the Slick Six were not six. It was just Hideo, Dayneesha, and Carolyn, and they'd taken on Marco to do a bank vault next to a water main undergoing repair; they had uniforms from the city, hard hats, signed permits. They cleaned the vault out in three hours, but now the gold needed laundering. They knew they had to be smart about it; they also knew that between them, they didn't know enough to be anything but stupid.

They researched Zeke first: his tax returns, employment contracts, bank records. Observed him from the fire escape of the apartment across the street. Discovered he was very single; a monk, almost. He worked, ate almost every dinner in the expensive Peruvian restaurant around the corner. He read, did yoga, showered before bed. They watched him do this for almost a month, joked about what an unbelievable bore he was. Then Marco cut the pane out of the picture window in his bedroom, slipped the latch, and woke Zeke with a knife point pushed into the skin of his throat. Zeke opened his eyes, didn't wet the bed, didn't even jump.

"There's nothing here," he said. "Nothing worth anything."

"I know that," Marco said. "We have been watching you."

"What do you want, then?"

"You."

"My organs could get you five figures apiece, depending on the market, exchange rate, and transportation costs. Sometimes I smoke a cigarette socially, which I'm sure knocks a few thousand off of my lungs. I can get you much more if you keep me alive."

"I was hoping you'd say something like that."

The gold was dispersed across the world within a month, stationed in bank vaults across Africa and Latin America; melted down into haphazard shapes; planted in mines; made into wedding bands, hoop earrings, birthday presents, anniversary gifts. Dayneesha bought a house in Fort Worth for her grandparents, Hideo a place in Osaka for himself. Marco told nobody what he did with his cut, but a war orphanage near La Paz seemed at once to double its operating budget. They gave Zeke a commission for his trouble, thanked him, never expected to see him again; they didn't think he liked the work. Neither did he. But the next day he sat in his office and glowered. He now thought of the regulations he'd spent years learning and defending as obstacles that annoyed him. And they were so easy to avoid, it seemed to him: a false name here, some doctored photos there, a good paper trail for the feds to walk down and get lost on. He reminded himself that he was thinking like a criminal, that he didn't actually need the money, that it wasn't worth the risk; but months passed and there were no phone calls from banking commissions, no officers with warrants standing next to his doorman. He took three weeks' vacation, told everyone he knew that he was going to Vermont, charged a room outside of Montpelier to his credit card, and let someone else stay there while he flew to Paris, hired a professor of literature to take him to the house in Roussillon where Beckett lived during World War II; the white walls, the red shingles, the arched windows, the arms buried in the back yard, the leftovers from his aid to the French Resistance, the Boy Scout stuff, he used to say. At night they stayed up in the cafés and debated about the best North African guitar players. Ali Farka Touré, dammit, the professor argued, ears red with inebriation. I don't care how good everyone else was, before or since. He opened it all up. Zeke paid for the rooms, the bottles of wine, bought paintings, had them shipped back under an assumed name. The night before he went back to work, he sat in his apartment, drank *vin doux naturel* from Banyuls and looked at his art. He called Hideo the next day.

"I want in."

"You cannot have in."

"Let me in or I rat you out."

"Rat us out and you rat yourself out."

"Oh, just let me in already. You know someone like me can expand your operation. I don't have to tell you by how much. Your biggest problem is hiding the money you get. Let me in and that problem goes away."

"How far away?" Hideo said.

"Off this planet," Zeke said.

Then it was years of raves in the shells of oil tankers in India, electric guitar and drums in the Malian desert, Dayneesha doing ecstasy and dancing for three days in a club on a rotating disk at the top of a Hong Kong skyscraper, breakbeats pounding and skittering across the floor. Zeke, later, bleary with hashish at a ghazal dub show in Kurdistan, soaring Muslim melodies over a smoked-out Jamaican one drop, and everyone waving like kelp in a languid current, him with a girl in a long brown dress whose name he never knew. In Iceland, they ate the eyes of sharks, chased them down with aquavit that slid down their throats like mercury. On the sandy coast of Liberia they ate fish they couldn't recognize; twenty minutes before, a huge woman had caught them with her hands and grilled them over a pile of charcoal. The meat sashayed away from the bones, was butter on the tongue, and Zeke knew that fish would never taste better to him than it did then; it never did.

They got their subpoenas from the offices of Winderhoek and Associates, but they knew who was behind them. Johanna stood in her suit with her arms crossed, brow wrinkling and smoothing. Carolyn's hand spidered over her mouth; Hideo's eyes angled toward the door. Zeke lay on the couch, scratching his head. Dayneesha sat on the floor. Words stuttered out of them: Maybe we can, there's always a chance that, it doesn't mean that. But they couldn't; it did mean that. There was no chance.

"This is stupid," Marco said. He stood at the windows. "There's no reason for any of us to go to prison."

"You mean, other than the fact that we're guilty?" Zeke said.

"He has nothing hard on us, unless one of us talks," Marco said. "I won't turn any of you in. And none of you will turn me in."

But one of them did. Zeke has never found out who, though he remembers how persuasive the Aardvark could be. The man he sent to Zeke didn't talk about physical harm. He threatened financial destruction, the ruin of his reputation. He would make sure Zeke never worked again. Then he talked about Kuala Lumpur, how much of a shame it would be to drag her into this. The things that could be done to her.

"It's useless to do anything to anyone," Zeke said. "To me or to her."

The man smiled. "I forgot to mention how much I enjoy hurting people."

Zeke looks at Marco driving into Texas; his hands are still at ten and two and he wants to tell him: I never talked, Marco.

I didn't because I knew you wouldn't have. It was beyond trust. I just knew. You are a brother to me. But it would kill these things to say them.

"The stars at night," Zeke says, "are not big and bright."

"We're not deep in the heart of Texas yet," Marco says.

They pull into Fort Worth at dawn. The highway between Dallas and Forth Worth is thick with craters and metal carcasses, some from a long-ago shootout between separatists and the National Guard that nobody's had the energy to clear away, others dug by the rockets from the south. A colony of dogs lives inside the rusting body of an armored troop carrier. The streets of Fort Worth are strewn with papers of a dozen colors, signs for the missing, people sleeping in rows along the sidewalk. A few raise their heads as the truck passes, mouths open, still dreaming. They meander into a labyrinth of warehouses to what can only be Dayneesha's place: Spray-painted on the gate to the courtyard of a big brick building is the silhouette of a woman with an Afro as tall as her body, hip to the side, finger pointed out and away, FOR THE LOVE OF MONEY, PEOPLE splashed across her chest. They're pulling in, all smiles, until the truck trips an alarm, loses its tires to a low hail of darts and spikes. Zeke and Marco start crawling out of the windows and onto the hood when they see the long barrel of a military-grade sniper's rifle slide out of a window, aim in their direction.

"Don't come any—holy fuck, it's you!" Dayneesha yells. "Ray, don't shoot!"

The rifle slides back inside. Twenty-one seconds pass. Then the door to the building flips open, and Dayneesha is running across the parking lot with a shaved head and a gigantic smile that lets them see the gold stars planted on her canines.

"How the hell are you guys?" she says. "I'd apologize about the truck, but I know it's not yours."

"Johanna told us the tires were worth something," Zeke says. "You planning on reimbursing us?"

"I got tires; don't worry about it. Just come inside and tell me how you are. Tell me how the fuck you are."

The walls against the stairs to the second floor writhe with cables, the machines upstairs set the steps to thrumming beneath their feet. Upstairs, computers surround them; monitors bolted to the walls, resting on the floor, hanging from the rafters, leaning in to peer at the intruders, all of them busy at once with a roil of images, scrambling voices, a sparking wire of words: a twelve-pound baby born in Kirkmansville, Kentucky; Abe Turley fell off his roof in Sumatra, Montana, swears he was dead for three seconds but walked away with just a broken wrist; five hundred dead in Corpus Christi; pine bureau for sale in Nageezi, New Mexico, cheap; four boys for sale in Haverton, Pennsylvania, cheap; the town of Greenfield, Ohio, burned to the ground three days ago; Toyota pickup wanted in North Paris, Maine, runs on vegetable oil; three fine horses stolen from a yard in Meriden, Connecticut; fifty thousand half-starved refugees arriving in Willacoochee, Georgia, nobody knows where they're from; sneakers for sale in Wallowa, Oregon, best offer; woman for sale in Thornhope, Indiana, best offer; man survives stabbing, drowning, writes concerto for glockenspiel; dog wanted in Lamona, Washington, must be able to kill and eat snakes; man for sale in Excelsior Springs, Missouri, best offer; tornado strikes Waukomis, Oklahoma, town feared disappeared; woman in Shevlin, Minnesota, teaches her cat to paint—

"You really are the news," Zeke says.

Dayneesha laughs. "Sure. But did you ever hear that old reporter joke? You can either write the paper or read it? I don't even look at the screens anymore. I do search requests if someone's looking for somebody, or they want to know everything that's happening in South Dakota, I'll set them up. But Ray here does the daily feed. People think what I put out there is the most important news around the country that day, but it's really just whatever caught Ray's eye. I don't know if that makes me any different than papers before. But it makes me realize I never knew what was going on before, even when I thought I did. Now at least I know I don't know a damn thing. But I can find you a decent push-reel lawn mower for a not-bad price in no time."

"Or a slave," Zeke says.

"Yeah," Dayneesha says. "The slavers mention all the people they buy and sell, so nobody buys someone that someone else already owns. Big market right here in Fort Worth."

"You ever been?" Marco says, and she narrows her eyes, looks at him for too long.

"No. Every city's got one, though, a whole network set up, and our man the Aardvark is running the whole show from that tower of his. Thing's made out of human bones, I'm telling you."

"But you helped him build it."

"Yeah, I did," Dayneesha says. "Sometimes I try to defend that choice. I say, well, if I didn't keep the information coming, somebody else would. They're a big-time operation; they'd figure it out. That doesn't change the fact that it's me who's helping them, does it? But I got me, and Ray, and when I find the rest of my family, I'll have all of them too, and I can't bring down slavery all by myself. And, people: The money's too good."

"It was too good for me too, Day," Zeke says. They both look at Marco. We sold you out when we went to work for him, they want to say. Took the money and didn't even write; and there is a twinge in Dayneesha's brain, the lighting of a fuse. She doesn't know where to start, and if she does, how she'll ever stop.

"So how'd you get here?" Dayneesha says.

"Johanna lent us a car in Asheville and—"

"—No," Dayneesha says. "How'd you get here?"

She makes Marco begin on the prison ship, makes Zeke start with his flight to Monaco. Survival tactics in the North

Atlantic. The best espresso on the Mediterranean coast. Metal ladders and marble steps in morning light. A stew of Spanish and Chinese, a broth of European words. Then the shudder of collapse, a ripple against the ship's rudder, an earthquake on the shore. For Dayneesha, a ride from Chicago to Fort Worth on a bus packed with people and bags, yelping children and dogs, guns on the floor, every few hours the smell of vomit. She stood in the aisle, may have slept against those standing near her all the way through Kansas, but it's hard to remember. By Oklahoma, the bus was a swamp of stale sweat and diapers, the windows fogged with breath. The driver gave a boy four candy bars to wipe the windshield down every fifteen minutes with a pink towel. Then there was a holdup, the bus surrounded by men with machine guns on horseback who made them all get out, took everything they could from the white people. A man wearing camouflage pants protested; a look passed between two of the riders, and one of them put a bullet through the protestor's skull. He winced like he'd been beaned in the temple with a quarter, did a half spin, and spilled across the shoulder of the road.

"Anyone else want to fuck with the New Sioux?" the other rider said.

After she was off the bus, she smelled the clothes she'd been wearing and burned them. She regrets that now; she could have traded them for a stapler, a package of pens, 150 yen, maybe 600 yuan. Fort Worth looked like the tornado from 2000 had come back. Half the windows in the high-rises were gone. Plastic bottles scuttled in the street; a broken power line slithered against the side of a building. Pieces of masonry lay hulking on the sidewalk like asteroids; store awnings hung in tattered strips; letters from signs lay in the gutter. People walked across town with splotches on their clothes, days of grease in their hair. An old couple didn't leave their house for days; they'd heard about looters, gangs who stripped victims down to their skins, left them unconscious in the middle of the freeway. Their cat complained about the lack of canned salmon; the couple looked at each other and wondered when they might have to eat him. And Dayneesha's family, the ones she'd ridden the spine of the country to protect, were nowhere to be found. Just her cousin Ray, living in their grandparents' house with three chickens, a fattening pig, a .44. But he hasn't said anything since she found him. They've developed a sign language for simple things: lock the door, get the guns. Anything complicated he writes on a blackboard in the kitchen. But he won't tell her why his voice is gone; he doesn't want to talk about it.

"Joke's on me, right?" Dayneesha says.

"Why haven't you left, then?" Zeke says.

"I couldn't before. I had nothing. Nothing anyone wanted bad enough to give me a ride out of here. Nothing I wanted to give." There is a hurt in the way she says it that makes both men pause, not push any further.

"But you could leave now," Marco says.

"I got all my gear here."

"You could move it. People don't care where the news comes from. They just care that they get it."

"Marco, where am I going to go? I don't know where my family is. My name is all over the country, and they haven't called, you know: Here we are, come and join us. I'm in all fifty states, and it ain't happened yet, it ain't happened."

A shuddering thump pulses through the ground. Three more in staggered succession, flickering all the screens at once, peppering the voices from the speakers with static.

"They're bombing Dallas," she says. "Oh, all those people." That twinge in her head again—a truth has been spoken to her, but she's not ready to hear it.

"I have a plan to reunite the Slick Six," Marco says.

Dayneesha nods. "What did Johanna say?"

"Does it matter?" Marco says.

You poor bastard, Dayneesha thinks. "And do you know where Hideo and Carolyn are?" she says.

"No," Marco says.

"So you don't know what's happened to them, do you."

"No. Tell me."

"Marco, they're slaves."

". . ."

". . ."

"Where."

"California. Near Watsonville."

"How long have they been there?" Marco says.

"About eight months."

"How did it happen?"

"They sold themselves. I think they were starving."

"And you didn't help them?"

"Marco, I was just about starving myself. And I didn't know where they were until they sold themselves and got posted."

"How much would it cost to buy them?" Zeke says.

"They're not for sale," Dayneesha says. "The Aardvark will see to it that they're not."

"You said you had tires?" Marco says.

"You're going after them now?"

"Yes."

"I hate to point this out," Zeke says, "but we just got here, and I have car ass."

Marco looks at him. Don't fucking joke around.

I'm not joking around.

This is serious.

So am I.

"You can stay here if you want, but I'm going," Marco says.

"Just like that? What are you going to do when you find them?"

The Vibe slips in through a crack in the window and circles Marco's head. It's whispering something, but Marco can't hear it.

"I don't know," he says. "I have to see what's going on first."

He has his foot on the gas before Ray has finished tightening the last nut on the rear tire. Dayneesha watches them careen around the corner, hears the tires sing on the next one. She stands there for over a minute, watches a rocket trace an arch of smoke across the hazy blue, its stream ending somewhere east of her; the impact vibrates the soles of her shoes. She pulls the metal gate to the warehouse closed. Thinks of her grandparents' house, empty now. Her parents. Cups her hands and shouts to Ray, I'll be back in a little while. I have to see it for myself, she thinks. See what I've become a part of, what the world has fooled me into.

Downtown Fort Worth swarms with a new horde of refugees, children and babies screaming, parents shaking with terror and indignation, jabbering at the people who are already there. Don't you know how serious this is? And the people raise their skinny arms, point toward the river, nudge their chin in the same direction. Don't worry, honey. You'll get used to it. The burger and beer place is now a chicken joint called Rusty's Avian Clearinghouse, serving every part of the bird— if you'll eat it, we'll fry it, they say—along with shots of grain alcohol that you can cut with the sugar-water squatting in a plastic milk jug on the counter. An old city bus growls and shimmies in front, surging with passengers, dogs, and birds, benches soldered to the roof and covered with a tarp and strips of fencing, tires chewing on broken glass. She waves at the driver, who nods, and she climbs to the roof while the bus angles north, jostles onto the bridge over the Trinity amid a mass of people with bundles and baskets balanced on their heads, sharp squares of sheet metal, the merchants of the new economy. The crowd thickens as the bus lurches down Main Street; the driver lays down a blast from an air horn and the people part for ten seconds, then close in again. Four boys climb onto the side, giggling, fingers curled through an open window, toes latched to grooves in the bus's walls, hitching a ride, until the driver's son wades through the passengers on the inside, bangs at the boys' knuckles with a rubber mallet, and the boys jump off squealing and tumbling, roll on the pavement, flow back into the trunks and crates, scraping their feet. Then the bus turns onto Stockyard Boulevard with its stores duded up in wooden planks, split-rail sidewalks, long, meandering porches, ghost signs fading above the doorways. The places that used to sell stirrups, spurs, and license plates to tourists are now flophouses, whorehouses, stands selling heroin and whiskey in tiny increments. Men and women in dirty clothes, tattered cuffs, ragged hems, stand in a jagged line and wait for their fix, to call up their courage, blunt their terror at selling themselves into slavery. At the gate to the yards, currency traders holler out exchange rates from white wooden booths, start in small coins for the starving, work their way up to yen, yuan, and pounds sterling for the traders, going into denominations that most people will never see. The crowd is insane now, the street choked with howling trucks, yelping dogs, people roaring and pushing into the yards, buses with bars over the windows trundling people out. But even over the horns and hawkers, the men in sandwich boards selling binoculars, the woman festooned in colored foil yelling lollipops, cotton candy, tin toys for the children, Dayneesha can hear the stockyard barker, his high, nasal voice pumped into the air through two-story speakers mounted on the old weigh station, calling out numbers that rise on a swell of noise until one word—*sold*—shoots them down, as another rocket lands on Dallas and the multitude shudders with the wave that goes through the ground.

The bus stops just inside the gate, and people climb out the windows to avoid paying, swing down off the roof, chickens and canines biting and flapping. Dayneesha shoulders through the mob to the pens, where the spectators crowd around a block with a square of black earth around it, a man in red-and-white striped pants and a top hat standing beside it, calipers and a tiny hammer in his hand. The musicians that play between the rounds of bidding are churning through something Dayneesha can't recognize—it's all jangling strings yearning to break, a spastic drum, the bass player lost and inaudible, shouting out incomprehensibility as loud as he can; it's the end of words, the end of music. Then the man in the striped pants nods, the music stumbles and dies, and a beautiful man steps onto the block, scratches on his legs, a long scar on one hand, a constellation of tiny boils on a forearm, dreadlocks matted and coming undone, but still beautiful. The man in the striped pants puts down his calipers, pulls a pair of long shears from his top hat with a flourish, and cuts away the beautiful man's clothes; four quick strokes to the shirt, two longer drags on the seams of the pants. Then he gets a stepladder and cuts the man's hair; one by one the locks fall from his head, roll down his face and off his shoulders, catch in his fingers, gather at his feet like snow. It's then that the color of his eyes softens; he's pulling away from all this, departing from this place: good night everyone, don't wait up for me. The music is gone and the voices are withering away; all the sound is going out of the world. That was my great-grandfather, Dayneesha thinks, and his brothers and sisters. Her people, covered in grease and tar, limbs pinched and pricked, fingers forced into their mouths, their heads full of curses, entreaties, or nothing, nothing at all, because they killed themselves to bear it. They are chained together and drowning, staring up at me from the ocean floor, and they look at me and shake their heads. So this is what you used your freedom for.

My family is gone, she thinks. They are gone and they have left no message; the words aren't coming; the photographs will never arrive. Tonight, she thinks, I will take Ray and go, find Marco and Zeke under a blue-roofed gas station outside of ·south San Isidro, where there's only enough gas to fill the tank once but enough room for her, her only two friends, her last cousin.

But on the bus away from the slave market, the Vibe taps her on the shoulder. Something's wrong, it says, but she swats it away. As she approaches the warehouse, the Vibe insists, tickling her neck, running down her spine, and this time she sees the tire spikes tripped. Now she doesn't need the Vibe; her eyes can trace the recent history of death, someone zigzagging through the piles of junk, Ray shooting from a second-story window. More bullet holes on the side of the school bus up on blocks; she follows the lines in the air back to the window, open only a crack, enough to slide a rifle barrel through and still be able to aim; there's an angry hole in the glass, wood splintered from the frame. The zigzagger threw something, just one thing, and Ray stopped, the gun grew quiet. The lock on the front door lies snapped to pieces. Dayneesha doesn't need to see any more—the spike burrowed into Ray's skull, the assailant's shadow floating through the warehouse, her kitchen, her bedroom—to know that she has two seconds to decide what to do. Hours later, shrieking across the Sonora on a stolen motorcycle, the loss of her cousin will knife into her stomach and she'll have to stop, kneel in the sand by the side of the road, and wail into the headlights, high and primeval, for the last of her family is gone and she's alone in this world. But there in front of the warehouse, she just turns and walks away, doesn't look behind her. I'm coming, boys. Don't drive too fast; I'm coming.

Marco and Zeke are skimming across the Arizona desert, lizards and scrub as far as the headlights will let them see, a town with lights out, doors locked, windows smeared with sand, swimming pools filling with dust. The desert is taking the place back, dunes growing on the sides of schools and garages, blurring the lines of curbs, narrowing the highway to one swerving lane lined by tilting telephone poles; both of them watch the road, expect it to peter out into an expanse of earth, nascent cacti. Later, while they're skating through the light film of dirt that lines Interstate 8 between Casa Grande and Gila Bend, they pass through a cluster of ghosts from a troop of migrant Mexicans who had died trying to get to

Phoenix eight years ago. Because the migrants' last hours were hallucinatory, they awoke into their spirit lives confused, wandered among small birds and reptiles looking for human life, a sign to point them toward home. They've been walking along the highway for two years, their steps slow and heavy, and as the car passes through them, they cry out, ask for directions, a lift. Marco's ears tingle, he can almost hear them, but the buzz against his eardrum never resolves into words, and he doesn't even slow down.

CHAPTER VI.

Reconnaissance; the last DAYS OF ORDER
and the fields of CENTRAL CALIFORNIA;
the ghosts rise.

A re you awake?" Carolyn says.

"No. I am sleeping," Hideo says.

"How about now? Now are you awake?"

"I am still sleeping."

"You don't talk in your sleep. So you must be awake."

"Kari. What do you want."

"I saw Marco."

"He is in prison."

"But I saw him."

"What time is it."

"Two-thirty."

"In the morning."

"Yes."

"I am asleep at two-thirty in the morning."

"I'm telling you, I saw him."

"I believe that you think you saw him. But I must see him myself. In the daylight. Now, I am asleep."

They're risking too much by talking. It's bad enough that they're together, though they've done it dozens of times, creeping across the rows of strawberry plants in the hanging mist, taking an hour and a half to cover a distance that would take five minutes walking. But the punishment doesn't daunt them anymore. They've been whipped already, know it can't kill them unless they decide to give up halfway through. Even then, it wouldn't be so horrible; each of them has already decided what to do. If Hideo gives up, Carolyn will walk into the ocean, make no attempt to swim. If Carolyn gives up, Hideo will run for the edge of the fields, arms waving in the air, giving the guards the easiest shot possible. It surprises both of them, the way they've harnessed their lives together. In their years in the Slick Six, there was nothing between them but explanations of plans, corrections of English.

"At three thirty-six, you will go at the bank—"

"—in the bank."

"Go in the bank. Yes, yes."

She was charming, of course; it was why Hideo had chosen her. He and Dayneesha sent her to parties to dazzle crowds into blindness. A day later, when it was discovered that several rare paintings had been stolen upstairs while she entertained hosts and guests, the victims suspected her at once. But she was an abstract concept; nobody could remember the color of her dress, the shape of her nose, the brooch at her breast. A curator once recalled her eyes—they were sumptuous daggers, he said—but he couldn't draw the rest of the face around it. The security cameras in hotels, museums, and mansions caught only hat brims, the back of her head, blond, black, brown. They couldn't even guess the color of her skin. It was a rare gift, to enthrall and vanish, to make everyone fall in love with her and then forget everything about her.

Carolyn and Hideo began to talk only after Marco was sent away, at a dinner in New York for the five that remained. Zeke was getting on a plane for Paris in four hours, brought no luggage with him, toasted Marco twice and left before dinner was served. Johanna said nothing, left soon after Zeke on a cherry-scented commuter train up to Connecticut. Dayneesha put her elbows on the table, steepled her hands. She wanted to go out dancing, somewhere where a horn section leaned into the same microphone as the singer while the bass and drums laid down a serious strut, let her move against strangers, pass along some of what was leaving her, what she had been.

"I never liked Johanna's moods anyway," she said. "So, are you coming dancing with me or what?"

"No," Carolyn said. "I'm leaving early in the morning. And I'm exhausted."

"Where are you going?"

"LA."

"Me also," Hideo said.

"Me too," Carolyn said.

"Me too," Hideo said. "I am going to Los Angeles too."

They met first once a month, then once a week, coffee in Pasadena, gorditas and fish tacos in East LA. They went to Crystal Cove just north of Laguna, hiked down the bluff until the shopping malls and peach-colored developments were out of sight and there were only the curls of sand and wave, the immensity of the Pacific, a woman in a pink bathing suit and flippers riding the surf toward shore, descended from seals. Their friends assumed they were sleeping together, didn't understand that they were war veterans, that the panic in their blood was real, for the damage they'd done, the death they'd wrought. She worked in public relations for a major media conglomerate; he was a talent scout for a major record label. He signed a band that toured Asia. She massaged a divorce through the press.

"I feel like an asshole," she said.

"Me also," he said.

"People work for years to get what I have."

"Yes."

"Does missing being a criminal make me bad?"

"No," Hideo said. "Also, I do not see the difference between what you do now and what we did then. In money terms. What is it, siphoning? Siphoning money off the rich."

"What about moral terms?"

"Ah," he said. "After Marco joined us, the morality became complex," he said.

"Yes."

"There was too much death, I think."

"Yes."

But they still missed the life, now that it was over. They'd forgotten how they used to stare through the night, their arms and legs splayed out across their beds. Hideo had dreamt he was nestled in a pile of corpses, Carolyn that she was floating down a river of coagulating blood, and both wondered how they'd ever get out of it alive. She finished her coffee, looked out on the pastels and bright glass of the new Old Pasadena, the people clustering at the corners, good citizens waiting for the chirping crosswalk sign to tell them they could move, then swarming into the intersection, a gaggle of bright bags, T-shirts, sunglasses, singing cell phones, and whitened teeth, serene in the image of a long string of tomorrows not so different from today, avocados and air-conditioning punctuated by sex and smog alerts, a four-hour traffic jam from an accident on the I-5, the smoke from distant wildfires. It didn't seem like too much to ask for.

"I have to go," she said.

"Me too," he said.

"That's right. Too."

"You did not correct me before."

"I've given up trying to change you."

"I am hopeless."

"No. You're charming," she said. "Is it time for us to get married now? Have children?"

"I do not want to marry you."

"I didn't mean to each other."

"Oh. Good."

They watched the riots start on the televisions in their offices as though they were happening in another city thousands of miles away. Interviews with upset bank managers, people outside the bank who were even more upset. Where's my money now? they said. How do they think I'm going to eat? How am I going to feed my children? The art-deco tower of city hall wavering in the background. Panic writhing on the muted faces, the city talking about mayhem. You know something is happening here but you don't know what it is.

On South Grand Avenue downtown, a phalanx of police in black-and-silver riot gear barricaded the Mizuho Corporate Bank of California with an armored car, set their shields in a wide semicircle of plastic and metal, stuck their rifles like spears between them, yelled into the surging crowd: Would you please disperse, just please fucking disperse. The street was already cordoned off, more police were coming to clear the mob away, but the commanding sergeant, standing in front of the police truck with a bullhorn, could tell it was already too late. The people before the shields were angry and confused; they could feel how things were coming apart. It was a bad scene, even before the Red Hand of Anarchy showed up; when they did, with their crimson masks and black sweaters, the sergeant had a premonition that he had less than a half an hour to live. He put the bullhorn down, ducked into the serene lobby, and called his wife, told her to leave as fast as possible, and then said a few things he'd never quite gotten around to saying, though he'd thought them almost every day, while watching her step into the shower or squat in the garden, picking rosemary.

The Red Hand huddled as the mob grew around them; for twenty seconds, the sergeant couldn't see them at all. Then, all at once, they crested through the crowd, shouting and throwing punches, smashed themselves against the phalanx's shields, pummeling at heads and torsos with crowbars. The police responded with the butt ends of their rifles; there were eleven minutes of bruises and blood while the police pinned the Red Hand to the ground and the crowd whirled and contorted, trying to flee but not knowing how.

At last, the police hustled the Red Hand into the back of the truck, and the sergeant's mouth opened, incredulous; he was a kamikaze pilot left over at the war's end, his explosive-rigged plane still at bay in the hangar. Perhaps he wouldn't die after all, he thought. He was wrong: One of the Red Hand, grinning, pulled the theatrical move of opening his jacket to show them the plastique that lined it. Yes, this had been their plan all along, to get inside the truck and blow it up, take as many policemen with them as they could. We are servants of chaos, the bomber thought before he set himself off; and had time too, to think of Maria Lista Sandinista, whom he hadn't seen in years. Maria, someday you'll get to do this too.

A low boom thudded through the floor, and in Carolyn's office, heads turned to look out the window, where fire left its wavering mark over the tops of towers, throwing off a tail of black smoke. Then another explosion, farther away, blooming out of the soil of office buildings and palm trees. Swooping sirens formed a dissonant chord, rising and falling, that Carolyn had heard before, dozens of variations in dozens of countries, singing through the street as she and Marco hid beneath a Dumpster wrapped in plastic or swerved on a moped toward a helicopter waiting at the pier. She had seen the lights from police cars bounce off the sides of skyscrapers as she rose on a kite into the Dubai night; she had floated underwater in a drysuit while police boats trolled the bay in Cape Town. And she knew what to do now.

It took her six hours to get across the city, running, pedaling on stolen bicycles, hitching rides in the backs of pickups already spilling out people and luggage. She passed three men breaking into a jeep, putting it in neutral, pushing it away. A family of fifteen walking under the freeway with a set of living room furniture hoisted on their heads. A man dragging a red cooler full of batteries behind him, a large stuffed giraffe under his arm, for his daughter when he found her.

Hideo's house was a box of white panels and glass balanced

on the ridge of a hill in West Hollywood. Los Angeles was already eating the sun, pulling it under the horizon with a hand of smog. Something was wrong with the streetlights—they weren't coming on—and the roads were getting dark, gray thickened by shadow that smothered noise; she had never heard it so quiet. She rapped on the door, then kicked at it, called his name, was about to pick up a brick from the garden and throw it through a window when a ladder slid down from the roof.

"Climb," Hideo said. He was up there with a rifle and two pistols; she recognized them all from the days of the Slick Six, remembered them on hotel beds, in the bottoms of suitcases, on his lap in small planes. She couldn't remember ever having seen him use them.

"There has been no looting here yet," he said. "But, by the mall, it is beginning." From the valley below, shouts and whistles, breaking glass, a chorus of cheers.

"When we leave this place, we will have nothing," he said.

"Why did you stay?"

"I was waiting for you. I knew you would come. You always did."

It hit them, then, the enormity of their loss. Johanna nursing her wounds in Connecticut, Zeke detached in Monaco, Dayneesha back in Chicago. Marco in prison. It was walking without legs; and as they watched the fire spread below them, her hand crawled under his, his fingers closed around it. They fled Los Angeles in Hideo's car, got up the coast as far as Ventura before two tractor trailers in flames blocked the road. The stores in Ventura were all closed; it was just the rows of white, arched buildings and palm trees, the boardwalk along the beach, the high pier over the water, like it was early Sunday morning, but for a tent city growing from the sand, a child in mismatched clothes, holding one left shoe in his right hand. They ditched the car at the state park, collapsed onto the sand by the jetty, in the lee of the wind; sat close together without speaking, watching the smoke from the highway boil into the air above the hills and the heaving ocean. When it got dark, and there was only the sound of the surf and the wind through the rocks behind them, she straddled and kissed him while her hands scrambled to undo the buttons on his shirt.

Five months later, the shirt was stained with grease and sweat, flecks of blood from three weeks before when he and Kari had cornered a dog, slaughtered it, and eaten it after roasting it on a spit over a burning, hacked-up door. Carolyn sold herself for a sum she couldn't ever hope to pay; then Hideo stood on the auction block, his ribs ridging the skin on his chest while the auctioneer tapped his muscles with a cane. His tongue was dry in his mouth; he hoped only that they didn't check his teeth too well, because he knew one of them was ready to come out.

The slave camps at Watsonville are a vast enterprise, spiking fences into the ground across the strawberry fields and farmhouses that run from the edge of town to the teetering edge of the cliff that drops to the deserted beach, a long crescent of sand bending from Monterey to Santa Cruz. It's still strawberries here, strawberries and oranges, because the water's still coming from the north. Myra Jong, the slaver, has a satellite phone to the water barons; she tells them when the bandits are draining the pipeline. Her office is in Watsonville, in the shell of a purple diner; she sits in a booth near the window to show how unafraid she is, but everyone there is armed twice over. She eyes the new slaves, has her men beat the rebellious ones with metal pipes they tore out of the kitchen plumbing, shoots the ones who can't work anymore herself. She has them sit right across from her in the booth, asks them if they'd like something to eat, or a cigarette, which is a tease: Her pistol's already in her lap, aimed at their gut, and the cigarettes are long gone. When they open their mouth to respond, she puts a bullet in their stomach. Then she gets up, puts a second one in their left temple. What a waste, says Cesar Ramirez from behind the counter, using two bullets like that. And she laughs, because Ramirez is screwing with her; he's the one who suggested using two in the first place.

The slaves live in tents of mildewed burlap, dusty blankets, troughs of brown water and mess halls in orbit around Watsonville, circled by moons of sentries. The slaves have taken to walking to the outhouses with their hands in the air after one of them, sick with vomit and approaching diarrhea, ran for relief and was shot dead by two of the guards, who thought he was trying to escape. Sickness tears through the camp in waves: cholera, dysentery, typhoid, tuberculosis take more than the guards do. Myra Jong doesn't like sick slaves; they take food and water and give her nothing in return. It puts them more into debt, but after a few months it's clear to everyone that the size of the debt is a formality anyway. At a certain point, she just shoots them and buys more slaves. She's done the numbers, has a chart that shows when she feeds and when she shoots, but it's just a linear equation, simple algebra. A few months ago, Hideo figured out how to keep himself and anyone who would listen from being put down. Now he and a few dozen other slaves each smuggle food away from mess, hide it in their clothes, wrap it in plastic, and stash it in the roof of an outhouse so they can feed the sick more than their share without the slavers knowing. This shifts the curve on Jong's chart, puts a few more days between a feverish brain and a bullet's tip. When the slavers find out, many of the slaves will be whipped, and they'll stare at Jong while the skin is taken off their backs, forcing a smile onto their faces. Let her know they're onto her, that they're just waiting like the diseases once did.

"I saw Marco again," Carolyn says. Now they're in her tent, huddled together in the strawberry fields amid rows of women sharing gray and brown blankets, their collective breath merging into a dense fog.

Hideo nods. "I saw him myself. In daylight."

"So he's here."

"Maybe."

"What is he doing here?"

"I do not know."

The hope wings through them both that Marco is coming to get them out; behind it, on a leash of fire, the howling fear that he has come to kill them, for the way they left him behind.

"Where is he now?" she says.

"I do not know," he says.

Across the thousands of miles of the former United States of America, people are asking the same question. Where is Marco? the Aardvark rumbles. It's already dark in New York City, and the power's out in Jersey and Brooklyn again; they light fires on the tarred roofs to illuminate the streets below. He can tell through the spyglass that the city has been deconstructing the offices around him, taking a chair, a desk, a window, though he never sees it happen. His gigantic family is in riot on the floors below; if he hadn't taken away their guns a few weeks ago, they would be using them now. All told, the emperor is displeased, for his empire is unruly, always breaking, burning, falling down, and then there are lines to see him, to see Jeannette Winderhoek, who they know has his ear. Complete strangers ask his sister what can be done about the water on Roosevelt Island, as if they know better than he does how to use his family's politics to get to him. Kidnapping threats appear in the mailbox: fix the sewers or you lose a daughter. Others mewl at him, give him presents—cars, food, bolts of cloth that wind up heaped on the floor below his office—but even then, there are threats. It's written on their eyelids, on the palms of their hands. If you don't fix the broken things, I will break more things, and you can't stop me. In a flash of introspection, the Aardvark realizes why the authorities never caught him: not because he was so clever, or because they were too slow, as he had always thought. They just had so many other things to do. There were the bridges, the water, the garbage, the schools, fires in tenements, fires in apartments, fires in subway stations. Just holding the city together was so much work. Before collapse, he had been a fly in a tornado. And for two and a half seconds, the emperor of New York wishes he was a fly again.

Where is Marco? Maria Lista Sandinista says. The jail is getting crowded; inmates sleep in the hallways, under stairwells, push closer together until violence makes some of them into corpses that the Aardvark's men drop into the harbor. She has been revisiting her Bakunin again; she's reading about the bombs of more than a century ago, the ones that made the river of history jump its bed. She has already smuggled in a few parts, lengths of wire with alligator clips, a battery, a switch. She doesn't know quite what to do with them, or how big the weapon will be. But she can already see the flames, a small and furious sun rising inside the jail, bringing light to its dark walls, to the bars and locks, the stains on the stairs, the faces of the inmates stretched into wonder. For a brief second, everything will be clear; and then she will be free.

Where is Marco? Johanna lies in the dark in the Free Township of Asheville, and her eyes won't close, though the assassin is long gone. He's gliding across the Southwestern sands, following the ribbons of light along the highway. Dayneesha is roaring by the gated communities on the hem of Los Angeles, feels the guns follow her down the road. She's dying for orange groves, the truck stops in Bakersfield, strawberry fields forever. And Zeke follows the wooden steps down the dune at the edge of Myra Jong's camp, walking into the orange light that spills across the Pacific, soaks into the sand, rises up to the sky, until everything is touched by its soft fire. Marco is lying on the beach in wet clothes, laced by bladder wrack and seaweed, hair thick with salt, toes curled with cold. He looks dead, but he has only been swimming.

He was in the water for forty-five minutes, but he made it almost a mile out, his arms turning in slow circles into and out of the water, his legs scissoring back and forth; he rose and fell on the swells of the tide, his eyes looking down into the deep blue California water. The bottom dropped away fast, as fish flashed below him, ribbons of movement and color. Then there were only the rays of the sun lancing the depths, sparking the particles in the water to trace their descent. He stared into the water as though into space, into waves that had circled the planet for millennia, distracted by land. And the Vibe gathered itself from the dying light, swirled around the swimmer, humming to itself.

I thought you said I had to do something, Marco said.

You do, said the Vibe. But I need to show you something first.

Something moved beneath him, something big—a dolphin? a whale? No. A rock, a boulder of speckled granite was rising upward through the water toward the surface, a chain bound around it five times over, then angling into the dark, drawing itself out of the murk until it ended at a manacle, another, another; and captured inside them was a clot of fifteen slaves that had been pulled to the bottom of the ocean centuries ago, staring back at him now, their eyes accusatory, mouths open with anger. A watery cry escaped from one of them, and the ocean began to darken, shift, as three more boulders, six, twelve, a horde of them, like a school of giant jellyfish, pushed toward the light, thousands of slaves lashed to them in terror and rage, hands tied behind their backs, wrists tied to their ankles, rising upward all around him; a host of men and women ballooning with seawater, their eyes fixed on him, hands reaching out, all speaking at once, talking in a hundred languages but saying the same thing, how they'd been screwed, how they'd been cheated, how we all deserved better. The rocks breached the surface, strained to lift into the sky, and the drowned slaves surrounded him until their hands were upon his limbs and a dozen mouths were at his ear, and he was crying into the ocean, I'm so sorry, I'm so sorry for the things I did. And the world spoke back: You have to do better than that. Much better. The Vibe ripped through him then, showed him, for an instant, the wars of his childhood, the guns in the jungle, the roof of a post office in Malaysia, zapin in the street below. The time in prison, the time at sea. The slave camp in Virginia, bleeding black smoke, the refugees streaming across Texas, the fires behind them. The wounds in the land. And a rattling cackle passed through the water and the air as the years all careened together, and the living and the dead gathered in his head, revealed to him what must be accomplished before they would be ever be satisfied.

"I know what I'm going to do now," Marco says to Zeke, back on the beach. "I'm going to put the Aardvark away, and put us all back together. I'm going to set us all free."

"Hideo and Carolyn?"

"Them. And the rest of us. And the slaves. All of us."

Part Two

★ The Empty ★

Man

Morals? The Vibe does not concern itself with morals. It is concerned with history. And history is a slaughter.

· DOCTOR SAN DIEGO OF THE AMERICOIDS ·

CHAPTER VII.

The state of LOS ANGELES; confrontation;
revolting DEVELOPMENTS.

The freeways of Los Angeles, from the 210 shooting through the foothills of the San Gabriels to the 110 lancing through the air over Compton, are drifted with scurrying plastic and dust; glass bottles and tin cans; the shell of a car by an exit ramp, torqued and rusted, paint boiled away by fire, a vestige of riot. There's a hush over the highway now; its miles of quiet concrete, which curved through the metropolis with industrial grace until the pillars crumbled at their fault lines, are buckled and folded by the hand of an earthquake that took a third of the LA skyline two years ago: People standing in the street saw the ground flex, ripple like water, watched the city change its face. The places of white stone, shining metal, and glass are empty now, brushed over with fine sand, gray and brown, a signal of the buildings' decay, the desert's languid return. But all through the streets—the wide boulevards bordered by strip malls of blue and adobe, carnicerias and social clubs, gas stations that almost never have unleaded but always have diesel, hunching rows of brick stores with painted signs for tattoos and tires—the city of Los Angeles throngs with people. The stores are all dark and empty, powerless, a line of ovens baking rats and insects in the afternoon heat. But the stands in front of them are full; plaid shirts strung on clotheslines; bootleg CDs and counterfeit sneakers; a speaker spitting out Akwid so loud that the fuzz from the overdrive turns the trumpets into saxophones, Sergio and Francisco into carnival barkers coughing syllables toward stands selling tamales and carne asada. Smoke rises from grills and steamers wedged into the back of a van with one side cut off, powered by tatty solar panels and the vehicle's dying battery. The family that lives inside is having a good day; they're selling burritos as fast as they can wrap them. The middle sister dances out front, sings out *come on baby come on baby baby come on,* clapping and stamping out a dance hall beat while her mother does business in six currencies, knows the exchange rates, does the math without thinking. It's like this every day from the waning tail of the heat until midnight, sleeping pigs and peacocks screaming in aluminum cages, running through the crowd and attacking children, until a helicopter chatters overhead, and the men with wide hats tilt their brims upward and hiss, aim and discharge five greasy handguns, and everyone scatters screaming until the aircraft leaves for another boulevard of fallen palm trees: the Los Angeles River, reeds at its banks, reaching the ocean again.

The helicopter rises above the city, turns the people below into beetles, then specks of sand, as it dozes for four seconds in the air, wobbles in an updraft, and settles down atop the U.S. Bank tower's circular crown. Jeannette Winderhoek steps out of it, hunches under the wind of the blades, and runs toward the end of the landing pad, where three men in white suits wait for her, holding black briefcases in hands grazing their belt buckles. She recognizes one of them at once: Mr. Yamamura, first lieutenant to Inu Kimura. Yamamura nods.

"Welcome to Los Angeles," he says.

"Thank you for coming," Winderhoek says. "I know it's a long way for a meeting."

"It is nothing," Yamamura says. "Kimura has several business concerns in the area."

"I bet."

Now Yamamura's head cocks. "Not to worry. You are his largest and most important client."

"I should think so," Jeannette Winderhoek says, though she guesses he says that to everyone.

Her helicopter has left, but already another one is landing. The rich say the streets are not for them anymore; the news from satellite television teems with stories of couples ambushed and hijacked two miles from home, their cars and persons stripped of anything of value, then dumped into the surf. They all travel by helicopter now. The Angeleno sky fills with angry buzzing as they rise from mansion backyards and alight on the roofs of offices or the parking lots of restaurants that have turned salt cod and beef jerky into delicacies. So they are prisoners in their own city. The word among the rich is that the city is a ruin of derelict cars and graffiti, patrolled by half-feral gangs and packs of coyotes that come down from the hills to scavenge in ransacked supermarkets. They hear them howling in the hills, barking in the street, scratching at the windows as if they smell something good inside. But Jeannette Winderhoek, in a wide boardroom with tinted windows looking over the city that smooths out beneath her, is skeptical.

"It doesn't look that bad down there. Looks clean," she says.

"Maybe picked clean," Yamamura says. "They say some have become cannibals."

"Do you believe that?"

"I do not believe anything."

By the time the riots were over, Los Angeles had lost over half of its population, dispersed in a wide fan around the Southwest, dispatched on threads of ships that spun out from the bay, threw orphans across the world. They arrived in Tokyo and Osaka by the shipload, refugees streaked with rust and oil, fumbling for the introductory Japanese phrases they'd drilled into their brains as they heaved across the Pacific. Where is the toilet? I need a doctor. Can I live here? They worked in meat-canning plants in rubber aprons and galoshes, translated business deals, taught English to ambitious businessmen in corporate suites, decided to forget all about LA, never learned how the city gave itself to the ones who stayed. Vast families that had crammed themselves into three-room houses with backyards full of paint cans and gasoline-soaked carpets expanded to fill a block, tore out the fences between the lots, grew crops in the sunny corners, built playground equipment from furnaces and boilers, stacks of four-by-sixes, rafts of plywood with signs on one side saying OWN THE HOUSE YOU DESERVE. People left shacks next to railroad tracks for stucco houses on wide, winding streets; wandered from room to room; ran their fingers along furniture and televisions, netsuke, clothes hanging in closets; discovered that the suit jackets almost fit, they were just a little tight in the shoulders. They're now pulling corn out of the hills, gathering in the shipping yards along the coast, replacing the freighters with commandeered fishing boats that bring in yellowtail and snapper, raw barracuda stewed in oranges and lime. On Tuesdays and Fridays, there's a market in Long Beach, seafood in ice, shriveled vegetables, and every Angeleno who visits thinks back to the day they realized that this life is better than the one that came before it. They were sitting on the roof of a tienda and watched the sun go down over Santa Monica and slide into the sea. They were climbing up Mulholland Drive and heard a squirming guitar, a churning organ wriggling from a wood-sided house in Laurel Canyon. They were watching the Amberson and Gomez Flying Acrobat Family with their children in the parking lot of the farmer's market on Third and Fairfax, a galumphing brass band, gnarled contortionists, a woman on a camel lurching around the ring, showers of candy fanning from her sweeping arm. They were sitting at the shore among the long rows of cranes and saw one of them pop its moorings, tilt screaming and moaning into the water, lie there with its feet in the air, drinking from the ocean. The electricity's off and the water is bad. They cradle papayas and mangoes in their hands, apologize before hacking them to pieces. But their seven-year-old children can't even remember riding in cars, and the parents look at the dusty station wagon rotting in the driveway and understand that they don't miss any of it: spending hours in a hardened mass of cars on the freeway, pouring concrete for foundations on barren hillsides, driving down bolts and rebar; the linen suits, the calendar, the night shifts at diners and laundromats, the stench of soap under crackling neon. They can't recall what it was all for. A collective idyll has spread under the helicopters: Los Angeles has become their secret paradise, the dead power lines their jungle vines, the bulbs of streetlights their budding flowers. They do what they can to keep the city's reputation as a place of mayhem, start fires at random, chase away the hippies with shotguns, unloading them over their heads, cursing at them in Spanish. They plant stories about kidnappings that end in mutilation, of gun battles that leave dozens rotting in mall parking lots. They know it won't last, it can't—the hippies keep coming, the word that LA is groovy now passes among them, across the universe—but they're doing what they can to delay their inevitable expulsion.

Jeannette Winderhoek and Yamamura finish their meeting fast. "In closing," Yamamura is saying, "Mr. Kimura is quite pleased with his arrangement with the Aardvark, and thanks him for his dependable servicing of debt. He trusts that the terms aren't too constraining?"

"Oh, no," Jeannette Winderhoek says.

"Miss Winderhoek—between you and me—could the Aardvark pay it all off if he wanted to?"

"I'm not at liberty to say," Miss Winderhoek says.

"Then there is nothing more to discuss," Yamamura says. "Thank you again for your time."

Jeannette Winderhoek rises, closes her briefcase.

"It is so much money," Yamamura says. "Is it not, Miss Winderhoek?"

"Yes it is," Jeannette Winderhoek says. She turns to face him, and they share a look that each of them has kept private until now. The world is wrapped in a film of wealth and connections, and they skate across it while millions drown below. Their apartments are too big for them, thick with scrolls from China, figurines from Ghana, cloth from Peru; gifts at the end of lucrative transactions, talismans from the lords of global commerce. Yet sometimes both of them wish it could be simpler. A porch. Water. Coffee. Only the day ahead of them. The new Los Angeles whispers to them through the glass, come outside and join us, but it takes too long to say the words, and both are gone before it finishes its sentence.

The elevator carrying Jeannette Winderhoek comes to rest between two floors with such grace that she doesn't realize that she's stopped moving. Then the lights buzz, flicker out. She stands in the dark; her hand is moving to the stiletto stored in the side of her briefcase when something cold stops it.

"Don't pull it out. It's me."

The lights are restored, and the assassin is standing next to her. He lets go of her hand.

"Ms. Winderhoek," he says.

"Very suave."

"Suave is for soap and Casanovas, Ms. Winderhoek."

"I assume you have a reason for coming here."

"Oh yes. I'm here to tell you that you are speaking to a dead man. See?" He shows her the severe puncture wounds in his side, the wet glint of muscle, a hint of organ, no longer bleeding.

"Did it hurt?" she says.

He shrugs. "Not as much as other things I've lived through. Some professional courtesy on Marco's part, I think."

"How many did you kill before he killed you?"

"Of the Slick Six? Zero. Incidental to the mission? Six . . . ah, Miss Winderhoek, don't feign offense. We know that the market determines the price of a man now."

"Where did it happen?"

"Outside of Watsonville, on the beach. Three of the Slick Six had gone there, to the farms of Myra Jong—"

"I'm familiar with her operation," Jeannette Winderhoek says.

"I know," the assassin says. "I know, in fact, that you've seen the fields yourself. I also understand now that the Aardvark is part owner of two of the Slick Six."

"The most harmless ones, as they proved when they sold themselves into slavery."

The assassin smiles. "But now the others have joined them, and I think that Marco Oliveira is planning a catastrophe. Beyond mere crime, perhaps."

"Do you think he could do it?"

"Why couldn't he?"

"Where are you going with this?"

"Being dead," the assassin says, "has forced me to take a long view of things. You were wrong to say that the Slick Six could no longer threaten the Aardvark. They can, and they will. But they only can because the Aardvark himself has made it so. He did not have to jail Zeke. He did not have to buy Hideo and Carolyn. And he did not have to send me after them."

"But that would be admitting defeat, and you know he doesn't admit to anything."

"I know. But I am not sure you see the way he has allowed history to double back on itself. The circles are spinning again, the forms of the past returning to us."

"You're not making any sense at all."

"I'm just saying that if he had not done these things, the war would have been over years ago."

"This is a war now?"

"It might be."

"Does that make you its first casualty?"

"Maybe. My ribbon is cut."

Outside Bakersfield, the lights along the highway vanished, and there was only the splash of road fleeing the headlights, the eyes of stray animals blinking from ditches, branches from orange groves creeping toward the road. Nomads lived within them now, the assassin had heard, trolling the thousands of acres on foot in small caravans, catching rain in funnels tied to their heads. When two groups found each other amid the trees, there was violence, a skirmish over bread and fresh water, a corpse among falling fruit. The assassin ran across one group who dragged trees across the road to make him stop; after he killed them, he piled their bodies in a ditch and set the blockade on fire. He marveled at how Dayneesha's trail merged almost to perfection with Zeke and Marco's. Were his vision less acute, he might have thought that they were all in a convertible together, the boys in front with their arms hanging out of the windows, Dayneesha sitting behind the driver, head back, staring up into the night sky, a stash of weapons snug by her side. Three teenagers joyriding. But the Last True Chief's training had been too good, and the assassin could tell they'd left her behind in Texas, didn't even know she was following them.

He passed through Watsonville, took the road to the coast through the land patched with strawberry fields, past the tents of the slave camp, the flashlights on the guards' rifles throwing quivering beams into the mist at the end of the night; then the road angled through a field cut into lots ready for development—houses clinging to the ground in four of them, the rest wavering with weeds—and finally broke free and turned toward the shore. The salt air enveloped him, thickened his hair, and he settled into a calm. It wasn't just the nearness of his prey; it was the sea itself. For the assassin, it was almost religious, as if the waves carried a secret about the truth of the world that they told every time they broke, and though we couldn't understand what they said, when the ocean pulled us under and we swallowed it, breathed it into our lungs, we took in some of its meaning.

He found Marco, Zeke, and Dayneesha on the beach around

a withering fire, huddled together under a single blanket. The motorcycle that Dayneesha had stolen lay on its side, sand scouring the shine off the chrome. Dayneesha and Zeke were facing the coals, and their sleep was deep and obvious. Were Marco not there, the assassin could have killed the other two from where he stood, twenty yards away. With two knives, it would have been easy. If he changed his position, he might have been able to do it with just one, though that would be showing off, an unnecessary display of ego. And there was Marco to consider. His face was toward the assassin, his eyes closed, his mouth a little open, showing the tips of his teeth. It was an uncanny mimicry of sleep. But as the assassin got closer he could tell that Marco wasn't sleeping, for the Vibe was not right.

"How long have you been waiting for me?" the assassin whispered.

"It's okay to talk," Marco said, without moving or opening his eyes. "They won't wake up."

"Fine," the assassin said. "How long?"

"Two hours and thirty-nine minutes. Forty . . . seven seconds."

"Your legs must be cramped. A little sluggish."

"Before you move, I have something to tell you," said Marco. "I know your work."

"I know you too. From the Tunis job. Excellent work."

"Thank you."

"No, thank you. I learned a lot studying that job."

"As long as we're talking trade, what was it like training with the Last True Chief of the Shona?"

"It was hard," the assassin said. "Much more haphazard than I expected it to be. He kept making me drink this horrible alcohol all the time. He said it was the key to the training. I think he might have just been lonely."

"It wasn't like training with Ravi Gupta or Bai Dao. That was all discipline."

"Exactly," the assassin said.

"Even the Yanomami. That was discipline too. The chest-pounding duel. The scars on the head. Making curare."

"It's still the best poison I know of for arrowheads."

"Yes," Marco said. "But this skill you picked up from the Last Chief was worth the lack of discipline. It makes you much more efficient than I ever was. Some of your work is famous within the assassin community because of it, though I'm sure you know that. I have immense respect for your methods and the skill with which you perform them."

"The feeling is mutual," the assassin said. "Why didn't we ever work together?"

"I was always a little intimidated by you."

"Don't belittle yourself. I could never have done what you did with the kind of . . . flair you showed."

"Which is why," Marco said, "I hope you take what I am about to say as a sign of utmost respect."

"Of course."

"That when we start fighting, it will take me a little over six seconds to kill you."

"How do you figure?"

"You'll have to attack me first," Marco said.

"Not true," the assassin said. "I could kill one of the others first."

"Don't fuck with me. We both know how stupid that is."

". . ."

"So your first move is toward me," Marco said. "If it's coming straight in, then I lead with the Diamond Kick."

"And I counter with the Golden Scissors."

"Which opens the way for the Necronomist's Claw. You lose," Marco said.

"Perhaps. Let's fight it out."

"Not yet. Because your actual attack will be aerial."

". . ."

"Won't it?"

"Yes."

"The Soaring Raptor, which you learned from Red Kwon, my mentor, only three months before he died. He gave it to you and to no other, because you were his favorite student. To my knowledge, you've used it four times, each one lethal. The Soaring Raptor made you what you are today. I was so jealous that Red Kwon had favored you that I challenged him to a duel. I swore I would kill him. You can imagine his response."

"Yes."

"I recovered. But I've been studying. I visited the places where you used it. I followed the path you must have taken with my eyes. I even visited your victims before they were put in the ground. And I know how to beat it."

"How's that?"

"It's much simpler than you think. An old Xhosa trick."

"With an assegai?" the assassin said.

"That's right."

"But you don't have an assegai."

"Of course I do." He shifts to his left and there it is, the wooden shaft, the dark blade drawing a line of light in the sand. "I know what you're going to say—it's more like an iklwa than a standard assegai. But the trick is the same either way. I knew that if the Aardvark were to send anyone after us, it would be you. Because you're the best in the world, and nobody's ever beaten you. So I prepared. You could say I've been preparing for five years, because I thought you'd come for me on the ship."

"You smuggled an assegai into prison?"

"It wasn't easy. Then I thought you'd come for me in New York. I was wrong about the timing of it. But I knew you were coming. And I knew you'd never studied with the Xhosa."

"The Last True Chief of the Shona always said I should have," the assassin said. "He said they were motherfuckers."

"He was right."

" . . . "

"So, do we need to play this out?" Marco said.

"We might as well."

"Good."

"It is good," the assassin said, and smiled.

"I am sorry we never worked together. I would have liked that," Marco said.

"The Aardvark told me he always liked working with you best," the assassin said. "Said you broke his heart when you took up with these people. I understand why."

". . ."

"Well. Should we do this?"

"Let's," Marco said.

After the assassin died on the sand, he walked back up the long stairs in the dune until he reached the top, then turned and looked over the morning light angling into the Pacific, the waves heaving in from Hawaii, sons and daughters of distant tremors and the tug of the moon. His killing days rose from him, a flock of greasy birds that flapped and wheeled over the water, and he waved good-bye, let them fall away. The assassin was dead and at the gate, and he wanted to laugh, or cry, but he was too tired for either.

In her booth at the diner in Watsonville, the skin along Myra Jong's left arm tingles, as though a heart attack is brewing; it's the Vibe moving through her, alerting her to her part in a grand design, though the Vibe is prickly and won't tell her what it is. She becomes suspicious; her hands pull bullets out of her pocket, load her pistol, though there's nobody sitting across from her to shoot. In the last few days, her slaves seem to have become quiet. She doesn't have complete evidence of this; they still shout to one another in the fields, talk at meals. The usual level of mild insubordination, someone's head against a rifle. It's in their manner, their movements. They have become inscrutable to her, a cloudy sky concealing the invading spaceships above.

She keeps calling for news from the foreman, sends an agent into the camp masquerading as a slave, a trick she learned from another owner up north who'd ferreted out a would-be revolt leader, cut off his head, and hung it from a pole over the fields. But her agent has nothing to say. Nobody will talk to him, as though they know he's a spy, or it's too late to involve anyone else in their plans.

"Do you think there's something going on?" she says.

"Most definitely," the agent says.

"What?"

"I have no idea."

Weeks pass. The weather cools, grows foggy. Crops wane. One of the broken-down Victorian homes outside the town falls victim to a fire; master and slaves stand together in the fields to watch the walls lean in, the roof lift off from the heat. Then it all collapses in a sigh of thick smoke. The slaves are getting quieter and quieter. Her agent still has no information, and now he's cagey, as though he's been threatened.

"What's going on with you?" she says.

"Nothing."

"You know that if I shot you right here, nobody would care."

"I know."

She orders more guns from an arms dealer in San Jose. The only ones she can get her hands on are some Type 56s, Chinese copies of Kalashnikovs by way of Burma. A quarter of them rust in the middle of the Pacific Ocean, another eighth are skimmed off in San Jose, disappear into the landscape. She makes a big show of them when they arrive in Watsonville, has her boys unload the crates in front of the slaves, lets them watch while the rifles are given out and a volley of ammunition blows out the windows of a motel, gnaws pieces out of its wooden doors. She wants them to see it all, to understand that if she's going to be taken, it'll be in noise and fire. It never occurs to her how quiet it will be.

She wakes up with Marco's hand over her mouth. No. Most of his hand is over her mouth, but two fingers have slipped between her lips to pinch her tongue, stop the speech in her throat. He has both feet on the bed, crouches over her, his face very close to hers, so that his breath, cool and odorless, plays across her face.

"You're wondering where Cesar is," Marco says.

She nods.

"I wanted to give him the same choice I'm giving you, but he woke up before I could immobilize him. He's in the hallway now. Well, some of him is. If I take my fingers out of your mouth, will you promise not to yell?"

She nods.

"To whisper?"

She nods. His fingers float past her teeth, leave a slight taste of sugar.

"Two-thirds of your guards are taken care of already," he says. "Half of them gave in without any fight at all. They could be at the highway by now. The other half I had to kill myself, which, as you can imagine, wasn't very hard. Though I'm impressed: You inspired a lot of loyalty in your men. The pay must have been good. Or you treated them well."

"I did neither," Myra Jong says. "They were just so desperate for work that they thought they were happy."

From the west, the wind from the sea carries a flock of hollers, goaded by machine-gun fire. She can tell already how bad it is for her. Were her men fighting back, there would be long cascades from the guns, a wash of screams, the white noise of charging feet, the sound of a besieged few thinning the ranks of a mob. But it's all short and sporadic, the report of guards being shot where they stand or fleeing across fields, and the silent slaves sweeping toward the town, tracking her as if they can smell her in her bed.

"What's this choice you said you wanted to give to Cesar?" she says.

"I could get you out of this," Marco says. "Help you escape."

"So I can be your living messenger? No thanks."

"I could do you right here, then. Spare you what's coming."

"Oh, you can't save me from that. They're animals tonight. Do you think they'll leave Cesar's body alone? Now think of what they'll do to me. No. Let me control this, as much as I can."

"I won't let you hurt any of them," Marco says.

"You idiot. I know that."

By the time she gets outside, twenty of her former property have encircled her house. They have shotguns and semiautomatics, the Type 56s she paraded in front of them. Others have farm implements: scythes, shears, sharpened hoes. She looks at her empty hands. She was a teacher once, four battering years in a high school in Chicago; then she sold insurance policies—life, fire, and flood—had a knack for convincing people to take out bigger policies on their lives than they could afford on paper. You're worth it, she said. When the economy collapsed, she was running a stationery store. The power blinked out; then a trash can crashed through the front window and the sound of the orchestra of chaos tuning up in the street swirled through the darkened room. A dozen thieves were in and out of her store before she could speak. She remembers it like a haiku. Fire outside; it snows paper in here. I try to catch it; it melts.

The circle of slaves tightens. Two of them have ragged stripes of blood on their clothes already. They smile at her, and she makes a decision. She runs toward them, screaming the worst things she can think of. She is unsurprised when the first wave of bullets passes through her, a fan of hot poison that hits everything inside her; by the time she reaches the man with the scythe, she knows she's done. The man raises the blade, and she falls to her knees, holds up her head, makes it impossible to miss. On the other end of the scythe, his hands on the swinging handle, Tyrone Fly feels like a magician. The blade passing through the slave owner is the bullet passing through the apple, slow and shattering, the scythe fulfilling a destiny laid out for it by its maker in Kentucky, who crept into the factory by moonlight before the curved metal and the wooden shaft were joined, sprinkled them with whiskey from the still of his dead brother, waved his hands over it: And you shall set them free. For the next few seconds, everything is a wonder of color as Myra Jong folds to the earth. Then the smell hits him, of meat and tangy saltpeter, and Tyrone Fly understands what he has done. Thirty-four years ago, he was a child outside of Phoenix, Arizona, searching for red rocks on a reposed angle of quarry chips, heavy machinery operating above. Then he was a wrestler in Tucson wearing red trunks with yellow zigzags, a mask over his face, his hands on a towering trophy; then a truck driver hauling canned goods into Omaha through a hailstorm that cracked his windshield, thrashed the grass along the side of the road, broke the skulls of animals in their pens. Twice married, twice divorced. The second time, he and his ex-wife met in the Buttercup Motel outside Cincinnati right after the papers were signed, stayed there for three days until the manager called the police on account of the noise. She said she would keep in touch, but he never found her again. If she could see him now.

A ragged, rattling gasp claws out of Myra Jong's throat, and as she hits the ground, a unified shout of horror and exhilaration rises from the slaves, flutters the edges of the circle of men and women until it collapses and explodes outward, flying across the crops, out to the freeway, over the sea. Tyrone Fly is still holding the scythe, can't seem to let it go. The slaves riot around him, pass around eight-year-old six-packs of beer, plastic bottles of vodka and rum, send up cheers again and again while he stands there, looking over his work. At last he lifts his head and sees Marco moving away from the slave-owner's house, walking slower than anyone else, but gone before Tyrone knows it; and in that span of seconds, Tyrone Fly is visited by the Vibe for the first and only time in his life. His brain floods with premonition, of the ripples he created moving on far beyond the freeway, pouring north through the red-woods, south through Los Angeles and San Diego, east over the mountains; manifesting on the high plains as a rising wave of tools thrown down, gunshots, smoke rising from grain silos. But he won't be there to see it; no, the Vibe puts him in the air somewhere, on a rickety machine whipping its wings high above unrecognizable ground, and Marco coming for him in a cloud of steam and blood.

There are parties until dawn from the wire fences at the edge of town to the peak of the dune, the liberated tear the tents down, burn the oily fabric. Couples flit from the flames to bed down in the fields; the beach rages with shouts and dancing. Nobody can say where the instruments come from, but there's a band with an accordion and a cacophony of drums, the leader bellowing words across the sand, the crowd yelping and shrieking back. The desperation will come later, when they understand how the world has wrecked them, set them adrift; but tonight is all freedom and possibility, the next day ages away, the last few months, years ago, and receding into a gray distance beyond where the memories can reach. And so they forget how the revolution started, that it had begun weeks before, when Marco flew through the camp, took Hideo and Carolyn with him, and they all met at the edge of the surf, together for the first time in six years.

"Well," said Zeke, "we all look thinner."

"We look like hell," Dayneesha said.

They stood in the sand, shifted from foot to foot. Marco pulled at his lip and spat, and all at once, they were rushing forward, catching each other in their arms and crushing each other hard enough to empty lungs, break ribs. It's good to see you. It's so fucking good to see you, man. Then, they did what they do best: They began to plan. The revolt was easy, the sort of operation Marco had done since he was a kid. He could do half of it himself; the slaves, he was sure, would do the rest.

"But then what?" Dayneesha said. "We do this, and the Aardvark sends more than one man after us."

"We'll have to finish him too," Marco said.

"He is the center of the slave trade, the emperor of New York," Hideo said. "It will take an army. And something to pay them with. This is a . . . bigger thing than we have done in the past."

"Are you saying we shouldn't do it?" Dayneesha said.

"Maybe."

"You don't think we can come up with the money."

"No. I am talking about the violence it will create."

"Do you want to stay a slave?" Marco said.

"Of course not," Hideo said.

"Then what other choices do you have?"

Many, Hideo thought. Flee to Asia and never return. Change his face; change his name. Disperse again across the world. The end of him and Carolyn; they could both live as long as they never saw each other again. He in Tokyo, an accountant for a holding company, shoved by pushers into a train each morning, a wife and three children in a house with steep stairs, frayed tatami, a large gray spider that eats the flies. Carolyn in Halifax—she always said she liked it after the Digby job—running a clothing store, married to a second violinist in a string quartet, no children. They could be happy, both of them, in moderation, but neither could look at the ocean, the water that connected them, without thinking of the other, and the memory would be a razor, cutting them if they tried to get too close. Better than slavery, better than death. But Dayneesha was right; Marco was right. The Aardvark would never let them go. One day there would be a bomb in the train station set just for him. A massacre in his house, his wife lying on the stairs, facedown, feet pointing at the ceiling. A bomb on the ferry from Halifax to Dartmouth, on the boat's second run of the season, so the water would kill her if the flames didn't. And even if they escaped, they could never stop moving; never stay in the same bed for more than four days; never rest long enough to even think of the other again, except in visions that left them hungry.

But still, but still.

"What do we all say?" Hideo said.

"I say we do it," Dayneesha said.

"I'm in," Zeke said. Hideo looked at Carolyn, then at the dune, to the east. If Johanna were here, he thought, she'd split the vote.

"Fine," Hideo said. "I will go to Osaka to line up the funds."

"I think I know where to find the army," Dayneesha said. The bus holdup in Oklahoma, the protestor kinked in the gravel by the side of the highway. Anyone else want to fuck with the New Sioux?

"Do you think they'll do it?" Zeke said.

"I don't know."

"Do you even know how to find them?" Hideo said.

"We'll find them," Marco said. "Just get the money."

They all nodded at each other then; through the years in prison and exile, the houses corroding in the rain, the flesh burned off in flight, they could feel the old buzz coming back; for Hideo, the buzz and the fear, the tang of nausea, of being history's fool. And as they wondered where Johanna was, thought that she should be here with them, she lay writhing in her bed, in thrall to bad sleep. In her dream, she and Marco were struck by lightning at the same time; the electricity opened up their heads, and their memories rode the bolt into the atmosphere. They wandered through the next five years, while the burns on their faces healed into stains, but their pasts never returned. She slept on the moss of the Willowemoc as it wound through the pines of the Catskills; he leaned on a cyclone fence around a factory in Bridgeport, Connecticut, eating a sausage on a roll for the first time. In a cinder block bar near the airport outside Marshall, Arkansas, she and a mustached man slinked back and forth to a waltz keened out on a fiddle and electric guitar while the rain hammered the planet so hard that everyone spent the night, slept under the tables, in each other's arms, jackets folded under their heads. He fixed houses in Indiana, balancing fifty feet up, shingling the ridges of roofs with buckets of tar roped to the chimney; at night there were small parties with the local girls in Valparaiso, twenty-two cases of Warbird T-6, a man with six facial piercings stomping his feet and blaring a harmonica to the songs on the radio, making them better. They met at last in West Virginia outside a shack selling ice cream and live bait amid the flooded gorges, off a highway carved into the sides of mountains that reared up like breaking waves. They didn't know each other but they recognized each other's faces, the shadows that the lightning had left on their skin, and they walked up to each other, kissed before they spoke. Their memories were still in the air somewhere, gathering above them, trying to get back in, but they couldn't hear it, couldn't see it, didn't need to know.

CHAPTER VIII.

The NEW SIOUX in repose; seven days of light;
the crossing of the PACIFIC and the
PURCHASE of MANHATTAN.

The hills of Wisconsin push themselves out of the planet's hide
and break into crags that betray bedrock from the Driftless
Area to Devil's Lake. At the army plant five miles south of
Baraboo, generations of grasses are burying spent ammunition
under layers of their dead, already talking about winter, when
ice will freeze the lakes, bring down the limbs of trees, and paint
a slick skin on the scrap animals in Dr. Evermor's empire of
metal: hordes of iron insects stamping in the dirt; flocks of giant
birds with feathers made from scissors; an avian symphony of
aluminum and steel, with gargantuan basses that taper with
grace into the heads of auks, a battalion of beaks fluting into
trumpets, bodies swelling into timpani, splitting into harps, xylo-
phones, and strings, all led by a rusty bug-eyed ostrich conducting his brethren in a clanking, buzzing elegy for the end of
industry. All still standing, standing still, though the sculptor is
gone. The storm he'd been waiting for showed up at last almost a
year ago, a boiling darkness pregnant with electricity, and the
man kissed his wife, climbed into the tower of one of his cre-
ations, flung his arms wide, and waited; and lightning forked
from the sky, sparked around him, and carried him off.

Robert Blackfeather Sherman leans back in a wooden
chair in the patched, veiny shade of a tree that's lost half its

leaves; arms folded, smoking a long pipe that needles out from under his wide Stetson, sends threads of smoke into the branches above him. His horse, a mangy thing with bullet scars in its flanks, rips out grass to the roots with thick teeth; his gun, an antique M-16 for which he casts the bullets himself, angles within reach, a leather cap tied over the barrel to keep the dirt out. The sun is not yet down, but his wife is already sleeping in their tent, pitched under a tree that will fend off some of the rain when it comes. Soon his unborn son will wake up in her womb; he's convinced the fetus is nocturnal, that it sings to him from the uterus and affects his dreams. Sherman has a bit of Crazy Horse in him, his men say, the way he listens to what his sleeping brain tells him. But it hasn't led them astray yet. It was his dreams that told them to abandon the Pine Ridge Reservation, the vinyl-and-brick houses, the naked sheet rock, the graffiti and the gravestones. They saw the announcements that the government was going under on grainy televisions, partied in bars and in their homes, serious revelry that ended with houses on fire; chickens beheaded, plucked, and eaten; people dancing in the dust of the Dakota roads to radios skanking out Burning Spear while others lay on the ground laughing about just how Marcus Garvey's words had come to pass. That night Robert Blackfeather Sherman read his future in a mound of torn coats and old shoes piled at the place where Chief Big Foot had fallen after the white men shot him. His dreams drew his people together, they took the name Sioux—that slur, that desecration—and decided to own it again, because they'd be enemies, not friends. So Robert Blackfeather Sherman led them into the expanse of the Midwest, from the Canadian border into Oklahoma, raiding army depots for weapons, stealing horses from farms, becoming scourges of the landscape, living spirits of retribution. Robert Blackfeather Sherman is a legend now, and his people prosper; their tents cover the hill that slopes before him down to the river that flows into Sauk City; children play in the frigid water where bald eagles fish. His people are a movable city, and he its leader, without reserve.

His wife shifts and moans inside the tent, the hills smother the last of the sun, and Robert Blackfeather Sherman's pipe drops from his mouth as the skeletons of skyscrapers rise in his brain, Mohawk ironworkers dancing along I-beams hundreds of feet above the street. Then Dayneesha's face forms in Robert Blackfeather Sherman's head, an urgent expression on her face, mouthing the same phrase over and over. In Oklahoma, his hand had fallen upon her shoulder as she stood with feet far apart, her own hands on the side of the bus, eyes on the road beneath her. We're not going to hurt you, he wanted to say; when his nephew shot one of the passengers in the head, spat out a taunt, Robert Blackfeather Sherman was disappointed, angry. It was a waste of life, a waste of ammunition, and later he lectured the younger man. We can't kill without discrimination, he said; it muddies the message. They can't understand that we're exacting revenge, taking back what's ours, if they're dead. His nephew scowled, screwed his foot into the dust, shot back: You think they'll ever understand it anyway?

Dayneesha won't leave him. Her face is as urgent as ever, and now warping stripes of light rise around her, music ascends from an unseen depth, a rumbling beat climbs to the surface, getting louder and louder; then it all winks out, and he is back in Wisconsin, leaves scuttling at his feet, the next season sharpening the edge of the air. Who the hell is that? he thinks. And why am I thinking of her now?

Eighteen hundred miles away, in the desert outside of Las Vegas, a forty-foot neon cowboy, thumb hitched in the air, cigarette dangling from his mouth, is getting bent into the outline of a jellyfish smoking a cigar. The glass sculptors wiggle out a cloud rising from the lit end, turn the whole thing on, and the crowd goes mad; a stack of speakers the size of a restaurant throbs out a bass line that makes waves in the sand.

"I said," Dayneesha says, "she's one of the New Sioux!"

"We ran out of pork, like, a year ago," says a man dressed in multicolored tissue paper, a pink eyepatch over his right eye.

"Not moo shu! New Sioux!"

The man looks at the speakers, then cranes his head, looks behind him. "Excuse me," he says, "but it looks like my booty's shaking. I have to go."

Dayneesha narrows her eyes at him, trying to get him to stay; but he's gone already, and now spinning dancers pour around her in a tide of legs and frothing arms. She swims through them for ten minutes as the lake of revelers gets wider and wider, churning into a boil of hoots and screeches that slice into the spaces between the beats, fatten the groove, make everyone dance harder. By the time she reaches the edge of the festivities she's in a much darker and quieter place, where couples, small groups in red and pink and blue, steal into the scrub, arms around each other, heads leaning in to kiss.

"This is useless," she says. "I don't know why we thought this would be a good idea."

"One of them must know where she is," Marco says. Dayneesha doesn't even jump; doesn't know how she got used to it, knowing that Marco would appear as soon as she wanted to talk to him; could disappear whenever he wanted. He was never there; he was always there.

"Nobody here knows anything," she says. "At least for the next five days they don't."

In California nobody would talk to them about the New Sioux, or spent the next twenty minutes explaining that trying to find the New Sioux was a death wish; so they've come to the Seven Days of Light to find the Americoids, to find Asia Sherman, wheels within wheels. This approach is turning out to be more fun. Already the mob of dancers is forming tentacles that sweep away from the speakers, people pulsing against each other with their hands in the air; the music shifts from a pound to a sprint, a beat that's almost too fast to follow, and the people drop pills and quicken, throw out shouts that tell everyone else that they'll still be doing this when the sun goes down, comes back up again; they'll greet the next six tomorrows with feet moving, arms waving, chanting words in a language they won't understand later, though they can't speak anything else now.

Eight months after the collapse, Las Vegas ran dry; the people turned the faucet and got nothing, not even a shudder from the pipes to mourn the water system's demise. The rumors flew that the dam at Glen Canyon had gone and taken Hoover with it, piled up a five-hundred-foot wall of water and stone that scoured the Colorado, erased five dozen towns, turned the Imperial Valley into a vast lake of submerged cotton and drowned alfalfa, unleashed the algal blooms of the Salton Sea and diverted it into a greater ocean that stretched into Mexico, the foundation for a floating city of birds, a wilderness of fish. Las Vegas residents hiked up into the mountains to the sand flats of Lake Mead baked into cracking, expecting to see the basin empty, a bright white band beginning hundreds of feet up on the hills where the water had bleached the rocks; Hoover's shattered shell in the cleft of the valley; the river roiling far below, still chewing on its release. But the water was still there, chafed by the wind into whipping waves; it was the pumps that weren't working. The machinery had failed; something had gotten into the intake and wasn't coming back out. Nobody knew how to fix it, and as Las Vegas parched, people left in funereal droves, a line of cars like fluttering candles across the Nevada flat. The dancers, musicians, party promoters, cardsharps, booking agents, and restaurateurs watched them go, turned and looked at what their city had become, the silent giants of dead casinos, fountains flooded with sand, cascading rainbows of neon playing across empty concrete, blank stages, serene copses of slot machines and blackjack tables. And beyond the strip, the development that never happened: the barren earth cut into swirls and checkers of roads; street signs planted at the corners of paths beaten into the dirt; the bones of half-built houses growing out of empty lots; heat-split and straining, a wooden staircase dangling into space; the remains of the commerce of risk and dreams.

"What do we do now?" said a baccarat dealer, wrist in a sling from slapping cards for years, and a go-go dancer smiled, a spark in her eye.

"Well," she said, "we could throw a party."

They cut through the copper umbilical cords that fed the dying city; scrounged up an array of decaying solar panels and sound equipment; hauled it all out to the desert in electric golf carts and construction gear; festooned it with strings of bulbs and molded plastic, stripes of neon; deconstructed the unfinished houses and arrayed them into stranger shapes; draped them with scarves of shining fabric; built another city from the body of the old one; and got the word out that they were throwing the biggest party since the collapse of civilization. They flew in six DJs from Europe in small planes, set up rings of phosphorescence three miles wide, and waited to see if anyone would show up. They expected a few thousand, had nightmares of only a few hundred, starving, hoping to be fed, then destroying everything. Instead, four thousand people were there on the first day, circuit boys and party girls with silk streamers and delicate drugs who pitched a tent city in a fan around the towers but almost never inhabited it, for the party was too good; the signal went out on satellite phones and brought more partiers, a spiral of vendors with aluminum carts and propane tanks boiling chilis and stews, animals to be slaughtered and butchered, wagons of blankets and used clothes, fruit from California, bright blue tarps, amplifiers powered by hand cranks and treadmills, jingling bottles of alcohol, boxes of bandages, antiseptic, splints. The vendors set up in a ragged grid near the tent city and made a killing. The party grew to ten thousand on the fourth day; the promoters hauled out more lights from the desiccated strip, more speakers, thought they needed more music; but by the third day, the partiers had formed five bands with electric guitars and trash cans, dented horns and cracked violins, a bass built from a water tank, everyday people taking it higher, doing a full Sly set with ska instrumentals that skittered into the wide ditch of a groove left by the ghost of Fela Kuti; and the celebration burned for four more days until the batteries wore out and the lights faded. Then there was only the desert night, undiluted by surface light, and the partiers, the vendors, the cooks, the animals, slept under a moon huge in the sky, close enough to kiss the earth.

In the morning, a coalition of partiers approached the promoters.

"When's the next one?" they said.

The promoters looked at each other. "As soon as the batteries are full," one of them said, and the rest nodded.

"So there will be another Seven Days of Light," the partygoers said.

"Seven days of what?"

"That's what we've been calling it."

There have now been over forty of them, tens of thousands of people dancing under a sprawl of neon to music that shakes the sand as voices tangle together in a constant roar. From a distance, it's like everything's on fire and the multitudes are panicking, panicking in four-four time, but it's just people partying; there's a small town's worth of them who never leave. During the Seven Days, they cook, sell water, fix bandages, assist in births, bury the dead; they've started a graveyard a few miles away, marked the plots with wooden triangles covered in green paint that captures the sun during the day and frees it at night. They clean the place when the Seven

Days are done, burn the trash, wire the money they've made
to a cluster of bank accounts in Canada, Europe, and China.
At night, they have parties of their own around a tall bonfire,
a fallen spark of the heat in the heavens, music heavy with
drums. One hundred and sixteen children have been born to
them already; they'll grow up knowing only this cycle of
weeks of noise and joy, weeks of placid cool; and until they
hear the stories from the hordes that swarm them when the
juice is on, they'll believe that everyone in the world lives just
like they do.

"It's a good party," Dayneesha says. "Maybe the best I've
ever seen."

"Better than Hong Kong seven years ago?" Marco says.
"You loved it there."

"Those were good parties. But not like this."

"There are no Monday mornings now. This is what you
get."

"..."

"You want to get in there," Marco says.

"Yeah."

"Go. I'll look for someone who can help us."

"You're sure."

"Yes."

Dayneesha grabs his hand. "I know you'll able to find me
later. Just don't tell me how you do it. I've never wanted to
know." Years ago, this impulse saved her over and over again.
When she was a child in Chicago and discovered she could
manipulate numbers in her head, that was all that mattered;
the painted cinder blocks and stained plastic chairs of her
school, the bangs and screams in the apartment next door,
didn't distract her. When she was a teenager, accessing the
mainframes of banks and government agencies was a game, a
problem to be solved; she was doing it in her bedroom at 2:45
in the morning when her cousin was shot and dragged into the

living room, the secrets of the Department of Defense flickering on her screen as she screamed his name into his ear while the paramedics cut away his clothes, leveraged him onto a stretcher. She never saw him again. She didn't ask Hideo what her work was contributing to when he brought her on, didn't want to know who might be getting hurt. She bought her mother a car with the money from the first job, sent her brother to community college on the second. When the Slick Six were slick, and she was working twenty hours a day from a terminal in a tenement basement while maintaining her position as a silent partner in a land deal for a substantial part of a small African nation, she looked only at the data, names and photographs, a tilt of eyebrow, the cut of a jacket. She heard sounds through planted microphones, distorted, crackling, muffled. Saw shadows through grainy footage from security cameras. Never looked at news reports afterward. Marco appeared in the basement smeared and salty-smelling, showered in the next room under a loose fixture for a half an hour. She never asked.

The music pulls her away from him, and she drifts toward the light and sound, the jaunt that reggaeton put into rumba, until a wheeling arm of dancers wraps around her and takes her in. The speakers draw her close, the waves of bass realign the atoms in her, until she flexes with every pulse and they move through her, like warmth, like love; she's surrounded by hands, other bodies, bending to hers. A pill is between her fingers; she takes it without question, and the next six hours happen all at once, blurs of color that sharpen into the blue sole of a sneaker, the party from fifty feet in the air, three men slaughtering a piglet and roasting it over a water tank that's been cut in half and filled with coal. The crack of breaking bone, its marrow on her tongue. A plaid blanket. The mottled rubber inside the trunk of a car, words mumbling from the backseat; the smell of their roses does not remain. Then, revelers resting in a pile to stay warm, a round face with big eyes forcing a smile, a hand on Dayneesha's shoulder. A voice emanating from between the teeth.

"Are you Dayneesha?"

Dayneesha nods.

"The one looking for the Americoids?"

She nods again.

"I think I can help you."

"Do you know where they are?" Dayneesha says.

"No."

"Then how can you help?"

"I was one of them."

"Good for you, honey. Does your jacket say what I think it says?"

The mouth pauses. "Yes. But it was only what I was born to do. I've never actually done it."

"How nice," Dayneesha says, and at long last, loses consciousness. When she wakes up, the sun is raging above her and everything is quiet; the power ran out four hours ago and the partiers are going home. Dayneesha's arm is around Asia Sherman's waist, and for four seconds, in the bleary fog between sleeping and waking, she believes they're in love, and one of them is pregnant with the other's child.

"I was wondering when you'd wake up," Marco says, sitting cross-legged in the dust under a black plastic umbrella. "Is this who I think it is?".

Asia Sherman's eyelids snap open, and Marco can see the rims of blue around her irises, the marks of Robert Blackfeather Sherman's first wife; they said she got them from Custer himself, staining the people for generations later, dragging their history behind them on a chain. The Vibe dives into her eyes, swims into the turquoise until it runs into the water of the Pacific off of California, through which growls the *Mumbai Stinger*, a freighter out of San Jose that really is a slow boat to

China; its final port of call is Dongtan, where it will deposit the few miles of timber stacked in its hold and the last of its passengers, so long as they're willing to be brought ashore in a container.

"My traveling companion," Hideo says, in Malay. "Carolyn."

"It is an extreme pleasure to meet you, madam," the captain says.

"And you," Carolyn says.

"You speak Malay?" the captain says.

"A little. Just for you." She takes his hand and almost kisses it, smiles instead.

Zeke doesn't understand a word of this exchange, but it's easy to see that the captain is dazzled. A pulse of blood pushes through the captain's body, reminds him of when he was seventeen, on the shore in Kampong Bagan Jermal, attended by bobbing fishing boats under a hot moon, a hand on his girl's thigh, offering her anything if she would just take off her dress. He basks in the rush; his genitals stir; his eyes glaze. It's too much for the poor man. Later, when he rhapsodizes in an outdoor Afropop bar in the metal slums of Bangkok, the air heavy with grime and guitars, he'll realize that he can't remember Carolyn's name or face, only the feeling he got when her fingers hooked his hand. It'll make him stop in midsyllable; then he'll make up all the details for the boys around him because he's decided that the feeling was enough.

The captain heads for the door, jostles Zeke as though he were an end table.

"It's only because you don't speak the language," Carolyn says.

"It's because I'm not you," Zeke says. "Don't worry, I'm not offended. He hits me; he hits on you. What's the difference?"

They have been on the *Mumbai Stinger* for three days, and twice, the captain has found a way to hit Zeke, maybe because Zeke persists in asking him where the poop deck is. There is no poop deck on this ship, the captain says, bewildered and annoyed. We have no poop deck here. The first time the captain hit Zeke was in the mess, when the captain laughed so hard at a joke told in Malay that he tipped his chair back into Zeke and the bowl of canned clam chowder he was carrying, sent man and chowder sprawling onto the ridged metal floor. The second time was on the deck, when the captain, describing the length of God knows what, threw his arms wide and almost knocked Zeke over the rail. Knuckles white, body tilted at an unstable angle, Zeke looked into the purple water and did the math, figured that if he went overboard; it wouldn't be a straight shot into the waves; no, he would bounce first off a rusting protuberance in the hull that would either break his ankles or brain him, depending on how he spun. He was running the numbers on this, at the mercy of the ship's pitch; but just as he was sure it would be the ankles, the ship angled toward him, dropped him back on the deck where he had to duck to avoid being hit again by the captain, who was now describing, in a high chuckle, how wide some other godforsaken object was. Meanwhile, Carolyn needs only to dole out the smallest charm to keep the captain from checking the runaway slave roster, explains that they just need to get to Osaka and everything will be all right. The captain agrees; as long as he's talking to her, everything really is all right.

"Osaka it is," the captain says, and Hideo nods. We will go to Osaka and stay there, he thinks, if there's word that Marco and Dayneesha have failed. We'll call in a dozen favors so that Kimura will pay to alter our faces, begin again as children who have inherited knowledge from a previous life but are not beholden to it.

Four other passengers are on the freighter's deck with them. Two of them have just been married, or are acting like it; they stand at the rail along starboard necking and letting the wind tangle their hair. He has holes in the knees of his slacks, and the bottom of her dress frays into tatters. Two men stand at the stern, one's hands in the pockets of a gray canvas coat; he stares into the water while the other man kneels and fools with a shortwave radio. He hooks it up to a box with a crank and bright red wires, turns a switch on the back, and puts a pair of headphones on. The man in gray canvas sits on the deck and turns the crank while the man with headphones speaks into an antique receiver. Is there anyone out there? Can you hear us? They hear voices, humming tones, think it's the message they're looking for, but it turns out to be the first stanza of a Montenegrin pop song, a beautiful three-minute thing about girls and riding in cars.

That song is also talking to Maggot Boy Johnson, who's sitting in a Serbian prizefighting club on the piers of New York City. The song plays on the PA between matches, and half the spectators sing along amid crying of children, calls for fried dough, knife fights over unsettled debts. He's there to bet on Big Mother, because Big Mother has never lost a fight and never will. In a few months, frequent bettors and bookies will become aware of this and the club will ban Big Mother from the ring because the odds aren't enough to cover their losses, but for now, Maggot Boy and Big Mother are getting rich. They come home with bags of dozens of currencies slung over their backs, a pile of the new empires, walk to the rails of the cell blocks and empty them into the courtyards; and the citizens of the *Rosalita* buy wine and smoked pork, wool socks for children, and strings for the Portuguese guitar, so there can be fado from midnight until five in the pilothouse, the wailing melody, the chiming strings, the room filled with the stench and tar of cheap cigarettes. Big Mother is in the ring now, pulling his punches a little to make it look like a contest; he lets his opponent, a large Chinese sailor who he knows is more fat than muscle, land a few powerful shots on his jaw, a charade he maintains for three rounds. Then Big Mother starts fighting.

The sailor takes a hit that almost breaks his cheekbone, another that moves a rib closer to his lungs, realizes what's going on before anyone in the crowd does. It makes him howl and flail, throw punches that would do some damage if they could only connect. But Big Mother dodges them with ease; he leans back, steps aside, lets a few glance off his shoulders. Then he gives the sailor an uppercut that snaps his head back, two more that make him void his bowels, and the sailor spins to the floor in a hail of cheers and whistles while money moves through the stands in a rustling whisper.

Maggot Boy Johnson is humming across the ring to collect his winnings when a gong sounds in his head and four Dutchmen in leather britches and wool jackets pass through the roar, muskets cocked over their shoulders. They move through Big Mother and stride to the center of the ring; the leader turns and shouts, and a fifth man, his woolen jacket stripped off, enters drawing a cart of a dozen guns, a bag of guilders swinging from one barrel, the wheels of the cart uneven, lurching. The five of them stand in the ring, pacing the ground, sitting down, standing up, scanning the middle distance while the next fight scurries through them, as though each was a scrap of smoke, a fragrance; they're still waiting when the loser is carried out of the ring by his arms and legs, thrown at his horrified wife, who begged him not to fight for money. Halfway through the next match, as a spindly Sierra Leonean gives a bullock of a Cuban a bloody nose, five Lenni-Lenape in white shirts, deerskin pants, and bracelets around their arms glide in from the other end of the ring. As the Cuban topples onto his side, there are brief negotiations; the Dutchmen produce papers, a thin bottle of ink, a quill, ask the Lenni-Lenape to make their marks. They do, and just like that, they hand over the island of Manhattan, set history spinning on the wheel. The Dutchmen make a show of presenting cart, muskets, guilders, as though these things were obtained at great sacrifice. One of the Lenni-Lenape thanks them in stuttering

Dutch, tries to hold them there, form the Dutch words for the questions that are shooting between his friends—can we still live on the land, eat its game, catch its fish?—but the Dutchmen have already left the ring as a new fight starts, and a tooth, knocked out by a fist to the mouth, spins end over end toward the ceiling.

CHAPTER IX.

Messages; the SNAKE RIVER; the slow
boat to CHINA; the changing luck of
CAPTAIN BENGWE SALOON;
Tyrone Fly joins the circus.

The ghosts of America were quiet for four hundred years, the people who had been taken, taken away; the Iroquois with holes in their heads, holes in their chests, burns across their skin; the casualties of forgotten wars; the slaves with skulls fractured by shovels; immigrants dead of tuberculosis and polio; the Cherokee starved in the South; the Yoruba who broke from his shackles to sprint across the sand in Virginia and get shot down in the surf; the Poles who froze to death in Chicago basements. They passed through the barbed wire strung across dunes of snow, lines drawn across land that did not ask to be divided; scratched at the underside of the asphalt over the ground where they'd been massacred, now paved into a shopping center parking lot; they tapped at the copper pipes growing ice; floated just beneath the surfaces of rivers, faces up, fingers out. There were more of them than there were of the living, but as the country clawed its history into the planet's surface, manifesting the destiny it saw for itself, they never got a chance to say a word. Over the past few weeks, they've made some noise, pulling each other out of the ground, out of dark water. They see how America is descending from the firmament, dragged down by the weight of their collective demise. In the Midwest, they stalk the fields for stragglers, people in the long open spaces between towns, where there's nothing between them and the sky but frayed power lines. They rise out of the water in New York Harbor; Maggot Boy Johnson sees them scrambling up the hull of the *Rosalita,* meets them on the deck, asks them please to wait, just a little while longer. And they march into Asheville every night, a procession of slapping feet, corrosive brass, voices tearing free from invisible throats in aggressive disharmony, a mockery of the old order, a harbinger of the coming chaos. The guards at the gate shudder as the horde moves through them, look at each other, start telling each other jokes to drive the spooks away. But tonight it doesn't work, for on the heels of the dead, the first survivors from Watsonville come weaving down the road, their clothes hanging from their bones. Let us in, they say, please let us in. You don't know what we had to do to get here. The stories that fly out of them over the next three days are garbled, contradictory. In some, the slaves rise as if responding to a signal from space. In others, it's a coup, so fast that the guards just give up. Others speak of outside influence, sinister and righteous. But Johanna reads the truth behind the words, thinks she sees the shapes of her friends, her former lover, in the way that death came to the camp and set the slaves free.

"How many of you will be coming?" she says.

"I don't know. Hundreds, maybe. Thousands?"

"Watsonville wasn't that big, was it?"

"No. But there have already been more revolts."

"How many?"

"I don't know. Word got around about what had happened in Watsonville."

"How?"

"I don't know."

He could have just taken Hideo and Carolyn, Johanna thinks, taken them and vanished. It would have been so much easier, and then she could leave Laguna Beach at last, them lying together under a broken ceiling fan, salt on their clothes, as the water broke the rocks beneath the house. I can't be with you, the things I've seen you do. Then, on the road, on the mountain. Why are you here? Why are you fucking here? She felt his answer before she heard it in the rags of his breath. I want to deserve you.

"Oh yeah," one of the women from Watsonville says. "You're the mayor of this town, right?"

"That's right."

"Someone had a question for you. He wanted to know if he's good enough yet."

I can't go back, Johanna thinks. But that's only four words against the mountain outside Asheville, the Pacific off California, and she swoons as the parade of shades moves through her, impatient for the next pause at the top of the curve of history. It has to be coming soon; they can feel it.

Tyrone Fly's hands are bleeding. There are cuts along his wrists and fingers; the skin on his hands has rubbed open. Blood flows along the handle of the saw, jumps onto the teeth and spins off in droplets, onto his shirt, into the ground at the foot of the tree. The man at the other end of the saw groans: A callus broke, and now his hands are bleeding too. They're a third of the way through a redwood, and at the rate they're going, it'll take another four hours. Then another team will come to knock it over, hack off the limbs with axes. Inside the foreman's office, the slaveowners are talking with four Thai businessmen representing a chief executive officer who is building a palace for his third wife that must be a testament to his fortune. He started with mahogany, tore down what he'd built and started over when he heard that redwood was available again, and now he needs more of it, faster, his representatives say. The slaveowners wait, and the representatives hand over a briefcase of yuan. A few years ago, they might have used it to buy more equipment, power saws, trucks. But people are cheaper than gas these days. Once you use the gas, it's gone; you can always get another man.

Tyrone Fly managed to stay out of slavery a month and a half. The first week he hitchhiked from Watsonville to Santa Cruz, where there was no work; through San Francisco, which was blackened by fires. In Eureka, he worked as a short-order cook in a diner that fried eggs on strips of tin over open flames. Then the chickens died and they ran out of eggs, and the owner walked into the woods and shot himself. The two waitresses headed down the coast; we hear something interesting's happening in LA, they said. In the last week of his freedom, Tyrone Fly lived in the parking lot of a liquor store underneath garbage bags held together with duct tape, lashed over tree branches with twine. Eureka's slave market was a half a mile away; he could spot the ones who were on their way to sell themselves, boots worn to scraps, looking at nothing, willing themselves into blindness. He held out for a few days until it got to him that they looked better than he did.

The loggers had calipers for his arms and legs, the fat on the side of his hip. They didn't even check his teeth, didn't care if he lasted very long; they went through slaves like the slaves went through the wood. In the ocean at the base of a cliff, there was a pile of them with broken legs and crushed skulls, mangled torsos, tied up in burlap bags weighted with stones.

"You're not one of Myra Jong's, are you?" the auctioneer said. It was a trick, a trap, Tyrone Fly thought. They know the truth already; they'll kill me if I lie.

"Yes, I was, sir," he said.

"Did you have any active part in the revolt?"

The shudder along the scythe's handle. "I did not, sir," Tyrone Fly said, "unless you call running like hell active. I don't think anyone can blame me for running, sir."

The slave market had stitched together the particulars of the revolt from scraps of stained cloth exhumed from blood-darkened earth, the memories of the guards that survived, slaves who were caught and thought that telling would get them off easy; knew also that the folk version of the story was already taking on a tone of reckoning, a judgment passed upon sinners by the righteous. Jong and her men struck down by a force that flew from the ocean and killed them in their beds. A few of Jong's slaves were killed on the spot when they came back up on the block—a bit of retaliation—though word of that didn't get out the way the news of the revolt had.

"I can't blame you for running, Mr. Fly," the auctioneer said, and sold Tyrone Fly to a certain Simon Nightingale for a sum that would take him twenty years to work off, if nothing happened to him first. His blood slicks the blade of the saw now. Yesterday, he thinks, Boo Handle was driven into the Northern California earth like a railroad spike by a tree the size of an office building. Saved us the work of getting rid of him, Simon Nightingale said, loud enough to hear. He's trying to scare them, but everyone's heard of Watsonville, heard too about a revolt in the camp just south of them. Not so much a revolt as guerrilla warfare, less an uprising than an assault with local assistance. They say it started with rockets angling from the hills into the camp, a streak of steam and smoke, a mushroom of fire, men with machine guns running among the stumps of trees, the slaves dropping their tools to join them. Tyrone Fly turns to his partner on the other end of the saw, and they both nod, both know what's coming. When it does, in tracers darting among the trees, feet rustling through foliage, cries leaping from tent to tent, and searchlights snapping on and sweeping the grounds as the guards try to return fire, Tyrone Fly finds that he can't move, doesn't want to, can't quite figure out why until his partner finds him lying on the floor, ducking and covering, and stands over him with a pickax and a shovel, offering him first one, then the other, as a grenade howls through the forest, releases the screams of shredded timber, dismembers men behind him. Tyrone just shakes his head no, puts a look on his face that lets his partner read why: I don't want to kill anyone ever again. His partner nods, uncages a ragged yelp that says he's willing to try. Afterward, when Simon Nightingale is lying in a disassembled heap on the porch of the foreman's shack and the guerrillas are taking names, handing out weapons, swelling their ranks, his partner catches Tyrone again before he slips into the woods.

"You going with them?" Tyrone says.

"Yeah. We're going north, then east. Coordinating with other groups, they say."

"Others?"

"They say there's an army of us out there."

"You're a braver man than I," says Tyrone Fly, and as they extend their hands and shake, each one leaves his blood on the other. The Vibe draws a line from them that shoots due east, rearing up over the Klamath Mountains, the Warner and Toano Ranges, across the expanse of the Great Salt Lake Desert. It plunges into the water, climbs out to skip along the spine of the Uinta Mountains; jumps into Colorado, and at last descends onto a metal bridge spanning the Snake River as it winds through scraggled mountains, the caravan of Doctor San Diego and the Americoids lumbering over the shaking girders. An array of solar panels is bolted to the roof, angled toward the sun, but the bus is stalling anyway; several dozen of the Americoids are gathered at the back and front, pushing and pulling, trying to show the engine and axles how to do their jobs. Felix Purple is in the driver's seat, pumping the gas pedal; he doesn't know why, but it helped a day ago in Utah, let them avoid what he likes to call a Donner Party situation. At last, the engine grumbles to life, the bus shakes and rolls over the rest of the bridge, then idles on the road while the Americoids climb onto the trailers, fire up the stereo and sixteen bowls, and Bob's sneer rides a whooping slide, God told Abraham, kill me a son.

The solar panels are a new thing, just a few days old, bartered for after the Seven Days of Light were over. In return, the panel owners got a few of the trailers' speakers; a duffel bag of wrinkled euros in small denominations; and eight pairs of pants, which a few of the Americoids now regret having given away, seeing as how they're in Colorado in autumn in Hawaiian shorts. They're also still working out the solar panels' kinks. The big problem is that the panels take up space on the roof once occupied by Americoids, so the trailers are more crowded, it's harder to sleep, even harder to gamble, and dancing is out of the question. Some of the Americoids tried to hang out under the panels, the thinking at the time being that the panels would keep off sun and rain, let the Americoids surf the bus all the way across the country. But once the panels are fired up, the heat under them is intolerable, and nobody can figure out if that's what's supposed to happen or if they hooked them up wrong. All they know is that after a few hours, they can't take it anymore. Only Doctor San Diego stays on the roof. He seems immune to the radiation, or maybe he's using it, the Americoids say. He takes over a minute to fill his lungs, exhales over the next two, eyes closed, mouth grinning wide, face tilted toward the sky.

Marco, Dayneesha, and Asia Sherman are sitting on a mattress with six kids who are crawling over each other for their turn to sit next to the pretty ladies. Someone in the back is blaring a fat piece of Philly soul out of a one-speaker radio; even through the distortion, the speaker screaming for a break, you can hear the voices rising and falling, offering salvation or sex, though in the strings singing over that monster groove, the difference doesn't matter. Felix Purple is whistling another song in another key altogether, both hands on the wheel, pulling the trailers a little faster than usual. He's got a new honey in Limon, Colorado, a baby with a baby. They met last year when the Americoids broke down on I-70 heading into town, and she drove out in a red truck rattling with gas cans and whiskey bottles. They talked all night, watched the sun from the east shoot across the plains, the gnarled ranch fences, the low brush and sage, paint the tops of the hills beyond, then flood over the town until they were breathing in pink light. Then he was gone for two months. When he came back, she made him meet her at her house, wouldn't let him out for two days. When he came through the third time, she was round and out of breath, craggy from creating life. You don't have to be around for this, she said. I didn't mean to sign you up. Felix Purple took a long look at the road stretching to a point across the prairie outside of town, at the bus and trailers teeming with Americoids, his tribe since the collapse of the country, his people on wheels.

"What if I want to sign up?" he said.

"I won't stop you," she said.

It's been a long few months since then; the colors of the country seem paler now, drier. He spent the Seven Days of Light dead sober, danced a few steps, lit up a doob with some dudes he was tight with, but it had no effect. It wasn't that he didn't want to be there; he did, he did; but for the first time in his life, he wanted to save a piece of himself for later. And he kept thinking about the child. A girl with dirty braids, defiant teeth. A boy with gigantic glasses taped to his face, writing symbols in the sand. And her, her little wooden house in Limon, the giant trees shading the roof, the rotting porch, its three rooms; just a few hundred square feet of the world inside, but maybe enough to drive the rest of his days.

"You're hauling pretty fast," Dayneesha says.

"People to see, my man," Felix Purple says. "People to see. Where did you say you were headed again?"

"The plains," Marco says.

"Care to be more specific?"

"Kansas?" Marco says.

"That narrows it down."

"Moving target," Marco says.

Felix Purple eyes Asia Sherman through the rearview mirror. He squints, squints again. He knows that face, or parts of it, has seen them ever since she joined the Americoids. Now he reconstructs it at last, unsmiling at the butt of an M-16, the business end pointed at his throat while the New Sioux wheeled and fired in the air, tied the Americoids' clothes into bundles, siphoned off ten gallons of gas from the bus, lashed everything to their horses' flanks, raced into the South Dakota dawn. The Americoids have never been back there. Doctor San Diego says the place is a blight on the planet, for the evil mojo that transpired there, the killing of a race for land, the ravage of the land itself. Felix Purple doesn't want to go back either, doesn't even like crossing the plains. At the time, the gun at his neck, he kept his cool, even asked Robert Blackfeather Sherman to back off a little, because the metal against his skin was uncomfortable. But in his dreams, a burst from the rifle separates head from neck; the head rolls out the window, lands faceup on the side of the road, and his eyes watch his body jerk into motion, make the bus and trailers careen down the road while the Sioux send a volley after them that fills the Americoids with bullets. He's never thought much about it before, but it hits him now: She's more than just a talisman.

"You look just like him," Felix Purple says.

"Like who?" Asia Sherman says.

"You know who." He puts two fingers behind his head, wiggles them like feathers in the wind. "You related?"

"He's my father."

"So you're going home-like."

"You kidding?" Asia Sherman says. "I'm not going anywhere near them."

"So what are you two doing with her?" Felix Purple says to Marco and Dayneesha. "The New Sioux have no use for you."

"It's us that want to use them, sir," Marco says.

Now Felix Purple is starting to put it together. "What are you brewing?" he says.

"Nothing you need to know about," Marco says.

Felix Purple takes his eyes way off the road, to the children wrestling in the seat next to them.

"Stay away from these three, kids," he says. "They're some bad hombres y mujeres. Especially the hombre."

It's snowing east of the Snake, and the road, cracked and half-buried by a landslide, turns to muddy slush. Felix guns it for a few miles, then gives up.

"Denver'll have to wait for morning," he says to Doctor San Diego, under the solar panels.

"So mote it be," Doctor San Diego says, and smiles; and Felix Purple glories in his benevolence.

The fires of the Americoids cluster on the hillside around the caravan, baking the earth dry; they sit around the light and speak in the drawled, lilting dialect that's becoming theirs and nobody else's. Ten of them have written hymns to the Vibe in it, a rolling gospel in five-part harmony with percussion and baritone sax accompaniment. The music wheezes and bleats, an animal calling for its young. The sax is meandering through its verse; then it rushes forward, drags back; when the singers respond, it's as if they're following the rhythm laid down by the lungs of the hill they're standing on. The land breathes in, shakes in a long sigh, and the Americoids tap their feet in compliance. Soon they gather next to the trailers to sleep. Inside the second trailer, Marco, Dayneesha, and Asia Sherman are stretching out, just closing their eyes, when a lantern light swings across them.

"Keira?" Marco says.

"I'd heard you'd joined us again."

"Couldn't stay away."

"Is Zeke with you?"

"No," Marco says.

"Where is he?"

Marco props himself up on his elbows, looks toward the roof.

"Somewhere near Hawaii, maybe."

"Vacationing?" Keira says.

A bad joke. Everyone knows what happened in Hawaii after the food ran out, and the ships stopped coming, and there was no way to leave. Everyone but Marco, who wonders for a moment if Hideo, Zeke, and Carolyn are nestled in the sand somewhere, but the hint of betrayal never enters his mind.

"No," he says. "Just on his way to Asia."

"What about me?" Asia Sherman says.

"Not you, the continent."

"I am not incontinent," Asia Sherman says.

"I know."

"I am an island unto myself."

"Shhh," Marco says. "You're still asleep."

"Why is he going to Asia?" Keira says.

"Promise not to tell anyone?"

"Promise."

Keira kneels down, and in a soft voice, Marco tells her everything. His breath is cool, and the words stream out of his brain until Keira's mouth opens, her heart quickens.

"Wow," she says. "Do you think you can pull it off?"

Marco shrugs. "Think it's worth trying?"

"It'll change everything."

"That's the idea."

The drugs in Keira want to say more. This is more than dodging explosions in Digby, riding fire. You're bending back history. The next few weeks have singing strings fixed to their ends. But you cannot guide the arrows; you can't even say which way they'll fly.

"Quiet," Keira says to the drugs, and stands up again, shifts from foot to foot.

"When you see Zeke again, tell him I say hello." And her voice wrinkles; she thinks back to the way they all floated in the trailer in Virginia. How Zeke's body brushed against hers. After gravity reclaimed its domain, his eyes moved down and to the side to avoid her stare. He felt it too, she knows he did, so she sends out a signal now that vaults toward the moon, traces a parabola in the stratosphere, and descends over the dark Pacific waves. It pierces the deck above the room where Zeke lies in a hammock, reading a ten-year-old style magazine still suffused with the stench of perfume samples, rife with articles about the bank accounts of celebrities, tips for unusual sex positions, dozens of pages of ads for purses, suits, and footwear. The signal slows and turns, slithers up his leg and under his shirt, warms his skin, and Zeke responds, puts the magazine down, closes his eyes, though he can't say why.

On the deck, the two men have rigged the shortwave radio to emit a stream of long, soothing tones; on the horizon, a smaller ship receives them, and the captain, a Nigerian expatriate who goes by the name of Bengwe Saloon, smiles.

"The cargo is rather valuable," his first mate says, "at least to the one who's paying to ship it."

"Will he be willing to pay more?" Captain Saloon says.

"Perhaps. It depends on the extent of his vanity."

"And the crew and passengers?"

"They are interesting," the first mate says, and shows Captain Saloon the papers. Captain Saloon frowns.

"A complication," he says. "But possibly lucrative."

"Should we take them now?"

"No. The Pacific is wide. Let us cross a little more of it before we raise hell."

The first mate laughs, and Captain Bengwe Saloon smiles again. He's always smiling now, for the years after the collapse have been good to him. He used to believe he was a serious magnet for bad juju, as three houses and an apartment building burned down around him, two of them from lightning strikes. A car he stole from an ethnomusicologist popped both its axles as he was crossing the Ogun River out of Abeokuta and the vehicle heaved into the water; he swam out of the window, watched the car snuggle against the river bottom as he clung to the bridge's pylons. Twice he spent almost a year in the crumbling jail in Lagos for crimes he didn't commit. The first time, the man shown breaking into the ambassador's house in the security camera footage could have been his twin; even he admitted it. The second time, it was clear that the woman who identified him to the police was insane; she had seen something, something had been done to her in the civil war in the countryside, but the judge was uninterested in the technicalities of who had done it. Upon release, he discovered that, eight months before, the guards had confused him with another inmate who had died of yellow fever and sold off his few possessions. For the next two years, he scavenged food and metal on the road between Lagos and Cotonou, from behind the houses of oil barons with honorary posts in the ministry of commerce, private security guards who slept on their roofs with shotguns and flashlights.

Then the widening wave from the collapse of the United States of America washed over Nigeria, took half of the oil barons with it. Bengwe Saloon, leaning against a signpost, watched one of them leave, packing three-fifths of his family, sharp bundles of artwork, blue plastic suitcases of gold, into a rusting jeep, leaving seven kids to dissipate into Lagos's dust-filmed streets. The Vibe entered into Bengwe Saloon then, poured down on him from a great height and flowed through the arteries in his arms, the muscles in his legs, moved through his brain until words formed, unmistakable, irrefutable: It is your turn.

He walked to the front gate of the house and kicked it in, strolled across the lawn and through the front door, found the office at once, as though it was calling to him. Everything of immediate intrinsic value was gone, but papers remained, naturalization documents, records of transactions with Dutch and American oil concerns. And, in a brown envelope, the deed to a ship; a medium-sized fishing vessel that was built for coastal waters but could survive in the open ocean barring a hurricane. He loved it as soon as he saw the pictures. The black hull with a pink stripe at the top, ringing the deck. The name: *Lucky Sun*. It was registered in Liberia, and he almost wept imagining someone else occupying his boat as he sat there swooning over the photographs, until further papers explained that it was in port in Lagos. He put on a suit he found in the bedroom closet, took the papers, spent the day walking toward the water, the documents rolled up in his left hand. At the port, they nodded at him when he said he was a cousin of the owner. He smiled to himself, his first smile in years, since fooling them had been so easy; though the truth was that the oil baron had been lax in his bribes, so they didn't care anymore who took his ship.

The *Lucky Sun* has been good to him. He has traced figure eights across a map of the Earth, seen volcanoes erupting on islands off the coast of Indonesia, whales at play off Alaska, a long swirling color in the sky above the Azores. He has accounts now in six different countries under six different names, and none of the account managers even knows who he is. And he gets to marry his first mate, a Panamanian woman with a long, swinging braid who has never told him her name, though they don't love each other any less for it. In a collision with an iceberg off the coast of Antarctica, when the hold was filling with ice water, the cold flowed up through the metal, and he shivered under ten blankets, and her warm hands kept him alive.

He turns the *Lucky Sun* toward the freighter. The line between sea and sky is rimmed with ribbons of yellow and orange. A band of green arcs over the *Mumbai Stinger*; overhead, deep purple; and Bengwe Saloon thinks to himself, It's good to be here. For the next forty-seven minutes, everyone is asleep, Nerve and Kuala Lumpur in their warehouse near the East River on the leading edge of the light; the Aardvark and Jeannette Winderhoek in their high tower; the citizens of the *Rosalita* swaying on the small waves in the harbor; Johanna under the bats in Asheville; the New Sioux sprawled in tents in the scalloped fields outside Winnebago, Nebraska; Marco, Dayneesha, and the Americoids huddled against the Colorado cold; Inu Kimura drenched in Osaka's nocturnal light. The people of the *Mumbai Stinger* rocking on the Pacific, the crew of the *Lucky Sun* in pursuit. They dream of each other, a network of desire delayed and waylaid, chains buzzing with the promise of betrayal. One good pull and they all come together, fly apart; money scatters and pools in a wired frenzy; bullets flit through cold air shielded by hot streaks of friction; and tens of thousands of people are pulled with them: some dragged, yelling and stumbling, feet tripping over each other; some pointing and waving, sprinting for the door, rushing to begin again, wanting to remake the continent and themselves even though they know it's impossible. The past is the past. But the past is the past.

Tyrone Fly opens his eyes. He is lying on the easy slope of an exit ramp off I-70 in Kansas, the flat earth falling away around him. He's been unconscious for six hours; the red car he was thrown from lies on its back in a fire of yellow flowers, the driver crushed beneath it, the other two passengers severed and broken in front of a billboard advertising the world's largest prairie dog, only fifty miles to go. He doesn't see any of it, looks straight into the sky, wondering, How did I get here? How long has it been? The last few days wander back to him in fragments. The car burning across eastern Colorado, riding the long valleys. The driver leaning back into the upholstery, one foot hanging out the open window. The young couple in the back, she leaning in to kiss, sleeping in a question mark across the seats. Tyrone's thumb in the air, trying to hitchhike, twenty miles east of Eureka; they were going to Jersey, had no problem stopping in Cincinnati. He had this idea that if he could just get back to that motel—the pink doors, the tan furniture, the swimming pool surrounded by Astroturf in the parking lot—then he would know what to do. And maybe she would be there, leaning against a vending machine, spare change and souvenirs jangling in her pocket like they did when he found her last. Even if the city was burning around her, she would turn toward the car as he opened the door on the passenger side, fold her arms across her chest, and make him walk the final thirty yards. Where have you been? I've been waiting for you since forever. Not for twenty-six days, not for eighteen months, because she wouldn't be counting time anymore; too much would have happened since their first marriage for the things that killed it to matter now.

A shadow passes over him, a hunched shape blocks the sun. A sharp musk of earth, matted hair, and diesel crawls into his lungs. Tyrone Fly rocks his head, looks around. The leg of a rhinoceros is planted four feet from his head, the animal hauling a wheezing calliope wrenched from factory plumbing, all copper pipes, pistons, a bellows belching steam. Hippopotami on the other side of him shift from foot to foot, tilt the platform balanced on their backs, a canopy made from sheets and black umbrellas, a mass of gears and fan belts underneath it; long aluminum tubing bent into spirals, letting off streams of purple smoke, a machine running, serving an uncertain purpose. Horses and camels with contraptions strapped to their sides, chassis of steel, burst intestines made of wire. Then Tyrone Fly sees the men and women, painted all in white, black circles around their eyes, crawling over the machines, pulling taut the ropes of the circus tent mounted on six elephants, cackling and spitting at each other. One of them turns, pops his head toward Tyrone. His mouth cocks open when he sees that the sleeper is awake. He barks out an order, and then all the heads snap his way; all the mouths open at once. There are four seconds of silence before the screaming starts, a clanging din of percussion, violins of metal, glass-breaking quartertones from the calliope, the screamers answering back with a woozy, slithering chorus of dissonance, the sound of a marching band being disemboweled under the animals' roars. Now all the machines are clattering into motion, they shake and catch fire, throw off spinning pieces, stagger into the air like drunken carrion birds; and seventeen men descend upon Tyrone Fly to bear him aloft. The music swells around him in a lurching rise; the land around him warps into a swirling sea boiling away beneath his feet; and the animals speaking his name, the howling faces shrieking at the sky, the machines falling out of the air bleeding diesel and steam, are all there is.

CHAPTER X.

GRAPHOLOGY; the plain and the SEA are the same; a barter of INTANGIBLES; the iron road.

In the back room of a warehouse near the Queensboro Bridge in New York, Kuala Lumpur works under a fluorescent lamp with a fountain pen, practicing the same scribble over and over. A small stack of papers—permissions for trucks to enter the city, ships to dock there—is piled at the corner of the desk, emblazoned with the Aardvark's elaborate imagery, the curlicues on the currency of the empire run mad. Forging them was easy, the paper nothing a counterfeiter with connections couldn't procure, the fonts and stamps typical bureaucrat stuff. Ornate but lightweight; easy to replicate. A day with a fine chisel, a block of wood, pieces of rubber. The challenge is copying the Aardvark's signature. She could do it slow, let her pen explore every wobble in the line, the fractals that spin off when nib and paper collide, but that might not be good enough: it has to fool Jeannette Winderhoek's eye, the Aardvark's own, and to do that she has to sign as he would. The technical details: same pen, same ink, same strength and speed of hand; these are easy, the skill of her trade. She knows the angle of the pen, the load of the ink, the way the hand races over the curves, cuts turns, sits and lets the ink collect, as soon as she sees the signature's shape. But she also has to divine the Aardvark's brain, make his hand hers, know the things his fingers have done and put them into her own. She has documents bearing his signatures from the last two years to refer to. His writing has loosened since she last impersonated him. He must have to sign so many things now, a man who used to torture people in airplane hangars sitting at a desk for hours each day, writing over and over again—what? The Aardvark's signature is illegible, and for a couple of days, she was mystified, blinded by what everyone calls him, the moniker of his crime days, the name he used to sign. Then she got it: The Aardvark is signing his real name now, and though she doesn't know what it is, couldn't hope to glean it from the signature itself, she's nailed it a dozen times. And she understands the Aardvark's burden a little more, how much he hates running the city. I'm here, the scribble says, the true man, trapped in this tower, under a mile of papers and ink. Someone get me out, tell me I can leave. Somebody let me go.

"That's the Aardvark's signature," Nerve says.

"Yeah," Kuala Lumpur says.

"Bet you're making a pretty penny off that."

"Depends. It's on spec."

"It's not for the Slick Six, is it?"

"Dayneesha called just a few days ago. From somewhere in Nevada, I think. I couldn't trace her."

So Marco got Zeke out, Nerve thinks. "What are they planning?"

"Don't know. Whatever it is, it involves moving a whole bunch of something into town without anyone looking twice at it."

"Sounds . . . big," Nerve says.

"I think it's going to be."

". . ."

"Nerve," Kuala Lumpur says. "If what they're doing works, I'll make enough for us both to get out of here. I've been thinking Argentina."

"I don't want to go," Nerve says.

Your man is not coming back, she wants to say. He never

made it out of Vermont; he's there now, on the side of the road, half eaten by crows. Or he's in Canada; he found someone else. You should too.

"I know," she says.

"Their plan might not work," Nerve says.

"Maybe not," Kuala Lumpur says. "But they seem serious. As serious as ever."

In his dream, Zeke is an antelope bounding across a silver prairie, his head heavy with horns, hide bristling with fur, the taste of grass in his mouth. His herd is scattered, decimated by predators, dark things with lunging claws, though no scent of blood hangs in the air, no bones lie on the ground. A bell rings, a wide copper clanging, muffled at first; then the ground breaks open in front of him and a church sheathed in skin rises from the chasm. The bell is in its tower, its ring sharp and loud, music and voices rising from the pews inside. Antelope Zeke presses his cold nose to the church's veiny door, and it is warm, alive. If he bit it, poked at it with his horns, it would bleed.

Then he's upright in his bunk, eyes open, wondering what the fuck that was about, when he hears another clang from somewhere above him, voices sloughing through the ship's metal. The lights in his room are out; he shambles into the fluorescent hallway in his underwear, squints at his watch. It's 2:38 in the morning. Someone's running on the deck; someone else is shouting. The door at the top of the stairs screeches open, and Carolyn puts her hands on the rails and slides down the banister to land next to him in a sweaty panic.

"I am an antelope," Zeke says.

"Put some pants on," Carolyn says. "Now."

Something large and heavy crashes on the deck, skids across it to crash and break into pieces. Zeke's fly is still unzipped when they reach the aft stairs; the boat makes a mad swing to port as they're halfway up, and they slam against the wall, catch themselves, and vault to the top, where Hideo opens the door, gives them a look that tells them to be quiet, even though the deck is loud with shouts, screams, and what Zeke's pretty sure are gunshots.

The deck is amok with running and fighting, the captain and crew armed with fire axes and charging toward four men Zeke's never seen before with small machine guns, in clothes that have been on them for weeks. Another crew member wrestles a fifth stranger with a long, greasy ponytail. The honeymooners are already in half-nelsons, the woman screaming. The cracked remains of an upended lifeboat crinkle into the bow; every few seconds they take bullets from the men with guns, and it occurs to Zeke that maybe one of the passengers is behind the splintered craft. Who are these guys? Zeke thinks. Then there is another copper clang; a curled hook is being dragged along the deck by a rope that leads over the side and latches onto the railing, and three men clamber over it, run into the hold of the ship.

"Pirates!" Zeke says, as though he were four years old. "We're being boarded by—"

Hideo covers Zeke's mouth, but the pirates have already spotted them and are moving toward them, loading their weapons, shouting syllables none of them can understand. An old look passes between the three of them, a look they gave each other for the first time ten years ago, on the roof of a Communist-era office building in Kiev, when all the floors below were rolling flame; again a year and a half later in the snow in front of a diamond mine outside of Yellowknife, bullets sparking off the rocks. Again in an orange blimp crossing low over choppy waves in the Straits of Gibraltar. But not the day before Marco's trial.

Hideo nods. "Over together?" he says. Carolyn nods back. Zeke zips his fly. Then all three of them run for the edge of the deck, vault the railing, and launch themselves into the air. The freighter moves out from under them, and for a moment, Zeke is an albatross, floating southward toward Antarctica. Then the wake of the ship churns below them, and there's a shock of cold: needles, broken glass, electricity. This isn't the way I imagined going, Zeke thinks.

A hand grabs his ankle, fingers clamp around the bone, and he's hoisted from the water by a giant of a man with an oily rag wrapped around his forehead. The giant's free hand clutches Zeke's arm and throws him on the deck of the *Lucky Sun*, where Hideo and Carolyn shiver next to him; before any of them can speak, they hear laughter behind them.

"Thank you for making our job so much easier," says Captain Bengwe Saloon. "If only everyone would jump in the water, we would not have to climb up there to get you."

The giant picks up all three of them at once, bundles them under his arms, and takes them belowdeck. The bunks are metal shelves lined with thin rubber mattresses that smell as if they were stacked next to rotting onions. The giant strides out, closes the door, and pushes what sounds like a safe in front of it.

"Hey," Zeke says. "Where do you think the poop deck on this ship is?" But Hideo and Carolyn aren't in the mood; they're back in Watsonville, under the damp tents, crawling through strawberry patches while the guards shoot a runaway for sport.

"This is maybe not the worst place we have been," Hideo says. It's a game that they played when they were slaves.

"Was it worse in Mogadishu?" Carolyn says.

"Maybe it was worse there."

They listen as seven other people are dragged down the hall, confined. A loud bang and a shudder as a wave lifts the *Lucky Sun* into the freighter's hull. Voices murmur from the deck, a parry of disagreement, footsteps. Then the motor growls behind them, the jolt of the beginning of motion.

"Is this man a slaver?" Hideo says.

"I don't know," Zeke says. "It's hard to tell."

"If he is, it will be bad for us. Nobody will buy Kari and I."

"Kari and me, dear."

"Nobody will buy us," Hideo says. "There is too much history now. It will be better for him to leave us in the ocean."

"Unless we give him a cut," Zeke says.

"Of what?"

Zeke looks at him.

"We do not have that to give yet," Hideo says. "We will sound like insanities."

"Maniacs," Carolyn says.

"Yes, yes. Maniacs."

"What else do we have?" Zeke says.

A few hours later, the giant's wide feet sound in the hall. The heavy thing is pushed aside, the door swings open, and the giant is there with three empty bowls and a cauldron of simmering orange stew that swings from a pole laid across his shoulders. Squatting, he dips the bowls into the stew and scoops, puts the bowls on the floor.

"No spoons," he says. "Sorry."

"Hey," Zeke says. "Tell your captain we have something to offer him."

"Everyone offers something," the giant says.

"Our offer is big," Zeke says.

Captain Bengwe Saloon's smile is wide and generous, like he's tasted a peach for the first time. He extends his broad palm to each of them, clasps his other hand around theirs when they shake it.

"Before any of you speak," he says, "I should tell you that I know who you are. I know that you, Hideo Takahashi, and you, Carolyn Crowley, are slaves from the Watsonville compound, and the slave register believes that you are still at large. More important, I know that the two of you—and you, Zeke Hezekiah—were once members of the Slick Six. All three of you have bounties on your heads. Very large. And the Aardvark does not like those who stall his efforts, which I am doing by not handing you over today, this hour. So you are problems to me in ways that I do not believe I have to describe to you. It is all very troublesome. So what is this offer you have to make me?"

"What would you say to a piece of New York?" Carolyn says.

First the captain laughs. Then he's not laughing.

"How big?"

"Not prime real estate," Zeke says. "But big as you can grab, if you're there at the right time."

"The city is not yours to give away, Mister Hezekiah. It is the Aardvark's."

"That depends," Zeke says.

"Do you know of Inu Kimura?" Hideo says.

"Of course," Captain Bengwe Saloon says.

"That is who we are going to see," Hideo says.

"What are you planning?" says the captain.

Zeke tells him. The captain's eyes do not widen, but his scalp twitches. He crosses his arms, asks questions. Zeke answers, and the captain puts his hands on his hips. When Zeke finishes, he shakes his head.

"Your plan is insane," Saloon says. "It is very tempting to turn you over in Singapore. Or perhaps kill you all here, sail to New York, and collect the bounty myself, before I am accused of something. But I have heard of what you have done in the past. Stealing houses. Many ships. Hundreds of millions, from people that governments are afraid to touch. Those jobs were also insane, and you did them. And I would like an island in New York Harbor. Not a big one. But an island, enough for me and my people."

"So it's done, then?" Zeke says.

"No," the captain says. "First I must tell you that until I own my island, I own you. I reserve the rights to throw you overboard, or shoot you in the head, or turn you over to the Aardvark, if I do not believe my island is coming to me."

"How can we refuse?" says Carolyn.

The captain barks, a short laugh. "You cannot. Now. Where was the freighter taking you?"

"To Osaka. Kimura," Hideo says.

The captain nods. "We will be there in two days." He moves in close, pats Zeke on the back, then slaps him on the cheek, not soft.

"I own you," he says, and smiles his big, genuine smile, as though it has rained all his life, and now it's his first sunny day.

The captain returns them to a different cell, a bunked room below his own quarters; every night, the cot that the captain and his wife use rocks against the floor. The man himself is vocal, almost florid. They hear almost nothing from his wife until the end, when it's easy to imagine that her strength could destroy her husband. They screw in eight languages. The first night, Hideo, Zeke, and Carolyn are a little embarrassed. By night five, all sympathy is gone, and what humor they could draw from it—lip-synching, miming with the furniture, conducting—is also gone, and there's just annoyance, wishing that the captain and his wife would take just one night off.

"How do you think Dayneesha and Marco are doing?" Carolyn says.

"I don't know. Marco's never done anything like this before, has he?" Zeke says.

"I do not know," Hideo says. "Has he?"

This is the thing about Marco: They're all a little afraid of him. More than a little. Before the Slick Six were six, Hideo, Dayneesha, and Carolyn were in Miami, in sunglasses, suits of yellow linen; legs crossed in chrome chairs; pink-and-green cocktails under a white cloth umbrella; in front of them South Beach's brick boardwalk, palms, sea, and heat-lightened sand, passersby in a flashing stream of bikinis and sculpted shorts, unbuttoned shirts, the patter of European inflections. A boy in a red bathing suit digging in the sand with a plastic cup, his balding father calling to him in French, the boy shaking his head *non, non, non.*

"We need another man," Carolyn said.

"What would he do?" Hideo said.

"The physical stuff. Intimidation. Maybe incapacitation."

"Like your evil twin," Dayneesha said.

Carolyn laughed, and six men and three women turned their heads to stare at her, couldn't remember her face fifty yards later, though that night, their dreams were soft and sweet. "Right," she said. "My evil twin. With a man like that, we could double our profits."

"And maybe commit new crimes," Dayneesha said. Her eyes narrowed.

"What if one of them was manslaughter?" Hideo said.

It took less than a year. They were stealing proprietary information from the offices of a diamond company in Johannesburg. The company had never let the information become electronic; it was handwritten in a plastic-bound book, scattered throughout the brains of two dozen employees who had all memorized pieces of it. Hideo sent Marco in to get the book after Dayneesha had disabled one of the alarms from a laptop. They knew that another would go off soon, thought they would have enough time to get out. They didn't. Hideo was waiting across the street in a green sedan when two private security guards pulled up in an armored truck, came out with guns already drawn. Marco emerged, book in hand; he would be shot there, Hideo thought, sent to the morgue, dragging questions behind him. They should have stayed with fraud, counterfeiting, laundering. Then Marco moved, faster than Hideo had ever seen anyone do anything, and all the rigidity in the guards left them, their guns floated to earth, the guards themselves fell backward down the stairs without stumbling or trying to break their falls, and Hideo held his breath as the guards' souls swept past him, howled down the South African highway.

The alarm in the building started to shriek, but nobody else was coming. Marco walked across the street, passed the book through the window.

"Let's go," he said.

"Marco," Hideo said. "Those men—"

"—Isn't that what you hired me for?" Marco said.

"The stealing, yes."

"What did you expect me to do?" Marco said. "They would have killed us both."

But later there were more security guards, police officers in uniforms, bent over steering wheels, lying in front of cars, thrown out of windows. A truck driver with a gun in his hand, somersaulting out of his cab to sand away his skin on the road. Four street toughs with knives and clubs, propped up against the side of a bus, broken glass driven into their eyes. A woman in tight red pants with a chainsaw, electrocuted and set on fire with a severed power line. They piled up in Hideo's mind, limbs at unnatural angles, faces turned toward him, mouths open. When Marco's sentence was passed and he was taken out of the courtroom by armed escort, Hideo began to breathe in, and his lungs kept filling; his chest swelled with it, expanding until Hideo thought he might float into the air, bump against the ceiling. They would have to get him down with poles and hooks. Then the air slid out from between his lips, flowed across the room; his heart slowed, relaxed in its bed, and Hideo realized that he hadn't taken a breath like that since Johannesburg. He spent hours that night marveling at how oxygen moved through him; he was discovering continents, expanses of golden grass, deep green valleys drawn by silent rivers, unmarked by people; and that space never left him, not in the clubs of Los Angeles or on the beach with Carolyn, not even on the roof of his house with guns he didn't know how to use. In the fields outside Watsonville, as the guards swapped stories of casual torture while the dogs strained on their leashes, even then he could count on his lungs, keeping time with the surf rolling in below the dune. But there on the *Lucky Sun,* his breathing is short again, the old constriction returning; he's being pulled away from the space he found, dragged back toward the cage that circumstance built around him years ago, and he doesn't want to go in.

The sun pulls itself out of the mountains, throws its light down on the Americoids, who wake up tangled in blankets soaking with dew, sit up on their elbows and squint, munch on their morning breath, and watch Felix Purple pace in front of the bus, wonder what's got him so wigged. Felix Purple has been up for hours, impatient for Limon. As soon as most of his tribe is shambling around in the dawn, he climbs into the driver's seat and turns the key over, but the bus doesn't start; the engine clicks like an angry insect. For a few minutes he convinces himself it's because he left the lights on the night before. It was the bad mojo sitting behind him, he thinks, harshing his vibe, making him forgetful. But why didn't anyone tell him? If the lights were on when it was dark, wouldn't someone have noticed? He glances over at his tribe. Maybe not, he thinks. At last, he slides up the hood to look at the bus's guts, and sees the problem: The battery's gone. There's a square hole under the hood, two squirming alligator cables snapping for their contacts. Felix Purple wheels around, robes and hair spreading wide in groovy centrifugal motion.

"Someone has liberated our battery, compadres," he says.

The news wafts over the Americoids in a hazy cloud. Some of them think that they themselves might have made off with it, they were so messed up the day before. They berate themselves, throw down their drugs and mash them into the earth, thinking that maybe their sacrifice will return the battery to them. It doesn't. Others take it as a sign that the universe is displeased with their tribe. Still others have the idea that perhaps electricity can be drawn from another source, start hooking up a lightning rod to the engine. This thing'll jump-start as soon as the next thunderhead passes over them, they say; all they need is for lightning to strike, and then to never turn off the bus again. They could spend the rest of their lives in motion, gathering water from the windows, harvesting birds with nets, picking oranges off the trees as they drive by. They could see the country twenty times over, the fields of Ohio, the canyons of Utah, until they died in the darkness of a trailer and the other Americoids commended them to the currents of the next body of water they crossed, be it the Mississippi, the Susquehanna, or the Columbia.

"Don't you have a spare battery?" Dayneesha says.

The Americoids within earshot all stop and look at her.

"Huh," one of them says.

Perched in the floating ibis position on the roof of the bus, eyes closed, and facing into the flow of the planet's magnetic field, Doctor San Diego is unperturbed. The battery will come, he says.

"The battery will come," Keira Shamu says.

Two hours later, just as the lightning rod is being mounted, three people round the top of a slope to the north. They have the battery suspended in a stretcher between two wooden poles like a boar on a spit and are taking turns carrying it. They approach Felix Purple, address him with a holler, as if none of the other Americoids are there at all.

"We had to borrow your battery," one of them says. "Sorry if we held you up."

"And you are?" Felix Purple says.

"Gladys Petersen. My boys, Dirk and Powell. We live over there"—she points to the northeast—"about four miles or so from here. Us and a few dozen other families. We just needed a little juice to get our own vehicles going. Yours should start up fine."

"How long have you been out here?" Felix Purple says.

"One forgets. Maybe a decade?"

"You didn't come out here because of the collapse?"

Gladys Petersen gives a slow shake. "No, but we did hear something about that."

The Petersens had already been in the hills for four years when the electricity went out. They'd built their cabin within earshot of the buzzing towers of power lines arrayed in a rugged range across the valley, wires drooping between arms of metal over a bald rift cut into the woods. They could hear the wires talking at night through the pulsing din of insects and birds, were always aware of the sulfur glow of distant towns projected onto the bellies of clouds. One night Gladys woke up in near-darkness, her pupils dilating to show the contours of the cabin's insides, the guns on the wall, the fat stove with its pipe poking through the ceiling, her sleeping sons turning in their beds; and her ears caught the edge of the hole punched in the soundscape: She heard animals calling to each other and trees creaking, but no electric hum at all. She had to confirm it, put her coat on over her nightgown and walked in her bare feet over fallen needles to the cleft in the forest. Sure enough, the wires were silent, the clouds above her no longer illuminated from below, no planes thrumming overhead, no light at all save the dimness of the stars straining through the atmosphere; and Gladys Petersen felt the ground growing around her, the land opening up, the roots pushing through the dirt under her feet, the branches of the pines reaching toward each other across the empty space the power lines had left. She felt the planet turning on its imperfect axis, and she closed her eyes, turned her face toward the sky, and couldn't keep from laughing.

"You've been out of the world a long time," Felix Purple says.

"I suppose we have. But then, he'd know something about that." By he, Gladys Petersen means Marco, whom she's just noticed.

"What do you mean?" Marco says.

"You've been out of the world too," Gladys Petersen says to him. "You're still gone."

She comes in close, puts a black-nailed finger on Marco's shoulder. "You ever get tired of trying to get back in, you just come and find us, all right?" She points to the northeast again.

"I don't know what you're talking about," Marco says.

"Sure you do," Gladys Petersen says.

Marco is still thinking of her as they descend toward Denver, careening out of the mountains, sending marmots and pronghorn in waves of flight before them. He's thinking of the black nail on her finger, pointing to a round hill spiked with grass. He has this idea in his head that he's been there—a hillside, a stream, fields carved out of the woods, houses of felled pines. Scarves of smoke unfurling across the sky. Rangy livestock. Children with mud-colored skin, vegetable gardens in a corral of chicken wire, the pelts of wolves and coyotes soaked in their own blood to ward off other animals. Men with callused palms sleeping beneath piles of wool blankets. A woman smoking strips of venison for the winter. They listen to the radio as if they're receiving the last transmissions from a distant planet destroyed by a meteor five centuries ago. In the winter when the storms come, the sky is like the ocean, a roiling gray capped with white, and they're underwater, looking up into the shimmering light as the snow whips around them, turns their lips to ice. It doesn't seem so bad, that life. But Marco is a man who does things, and there's still so much to do.

From a distance, driving down from the snow-shot Rockies, Denver looks as it did before the collapse, towers of glass rising from flat earth, the smoky highway a strip of rippling mercury; but now it's people on mares, in horse-drawn buggies made from the bodies of small cars. A few people have real carriages; some they got from museums, others from someone who decided to start making them again, read books, broke into an abandoned factory to bend wood, cast metal, cut glass.

Denver has become a horse town again, a hitching post; along the streets downtown they're selling mirrors, razors, glass that looks like it came off of the office buildings. Books, piles of them, speckled by mildew and faded by the sun, the pages fried brown around the edges. Nineteen ninety-five, the numbers in the corners say, but a man with three teeth is selling them for fifty yuan, or an intact cooler with ice packs, or a set of silverware for four, and people alight from their carriages to thumb through the pages.

The Americoids take Highway 86 away from the Rockies, cross Wolf and Comanche Creeks, the West and East Bijous, until they're driving through waves of land, all brown earth and low scrub, rusting wire lining the road, snipped and rolled back to let paths meander through. A few ranches, much reduced in size, shrunken versions living in the shells of their former selves. Some of the land has been given up, and the scrub grows tall; the grass gone to seed chatters in the wind. They reach the old interstate and climb the hill into Limon, a town of houses along forested streets, a wide boulevard angling down the middle, people on horses trotting through the asphalt intersections, stopping in front of storefronts to tie the reins to parking signs. A mural of John Wayne on the side of a brick building, staring down passersby like he's expecting something. What do you have to say for yourself, pilgrim? All Felix Purple can think about is his baby and his baby; he's mad with it now. He folds the bus and trailers into the empty parking lot next to the grocery store with alarming speed, stops the engine, and before anyone can thank him for his awesome driving, man, he's gone, ambling down the street, a straw doll made from California grass in his hand; he chewed on its leg a little himself to make sure the taste was bitter and sweet. The Americoids spill into the bright Colorado sun, blink at the buildings, the road to the east, the brown hills. Then, one by one, they wander into the town with packages tied to their backs, looking for trees to sleep under, the friends they'd made who'll let them doze off on an old green couch, under a window, the cold night air sooth-ing them to sleep.

"How long will we be here?" Dayneesha says.

Keira Shamu shrugs. "A week? Two weeks? I don't know."

"Really?"

"Sure. Nobody knows how to drive the bus but Felix. We tried once. Big mistake. Of the on-the-sidewalk, off-the-wheels variety."

"Two weeks is too late," Asia Sherman says. "They'll be in Oklahoma by then."

The New Sioux, Asia Sherman says, follow a strict route, stopping along a chain of towns, camps, and posts that stretches from southern Canada to northern Texas and back again. In a week they're due in Salina, Kansas, where they'll stay for two days, load their horses with slabs of dried meat, canteens of water, boxes of bullets from Indonesia. The people of Salina, those who are left, are complicit in the secret. Three hundred and sixty-three days out of the year, the long straight streets are quiet; they say you can hear the paint peeling off the bun-galows near the crumbling grain mills. But for two days, the Sioux horses line Santa Fe Avenue; the Sioux children riot on the wide lawn behind the middle school, line up at the Cozy Inn to eat sliders by the bagful—beef, onion, pickles, ketchup, mustard—like the collapse never happened. The Sioux ride slower out of Salina than they rode in, packs full, stoves fixed, boots reshod with dried buffalo hide culled from the returning herds. For those two days, the Sioux sleep behind doors, in beds. The other side of the window, Asia Sherman likes to say. For some, the stillness, the lack of a breeze, troubles them. They churn the sheets, stare at the squares of light thrown onto the ceiling by the moon, which is reflected in water that puddles in the street. But for Robert Blackfeather Sherman, it's the best sleep he gets all year; his dreams are among the most clear. He's riding his horse at a full gallop through the alleys of a mossy city dense with skyscrapers, reins in one hand, machine gun in the other, a knife in his teeth, the cries of his people all around him.

"So we have to get to Salina soon," Marco says.

"That's the idea. Problem is, nobody'll take you," Asia Sherman says.

"Why not?" Dayneesha says.

"You'll see."

The Limon train depot behind city hall is a low stucco building slung along the curve of the tracks running from Denver and south into the plains; it was built when Limon was the Hub City, balanced at the confluence of roads and rails, when the forces of commerce, fickle gods that they are, conspired to raise a town out of the earth and abandon it. But the people stayed, turned the train station into a museum. At the time they wouldn't have said so, but now that the station is a station again, it seems obvious that the trains would come back; the rails were abiding their neglect, forgave their forgers when they crawled back to them. The station's walls are plastered with broadsheets bearing news from two weeks ago about the haps on the coast; grainy advertisements looking to hire coal men waver behind the bonfire near the split-rail fence, by the line of antique farm equipment, the remnants of the museum days. A bazaar swirls under a striped tent driven into the pale gravel, selling wide sides of salted beef, heaps of used clothing, a mountain of sneakers. When trains pull in from the north and south, throwing their shadows over the old schoolhouse, the market opens into shouts and sirens, twanging music from a set of speakers taped to the tent pole, a theater troupe in costumes of brilliant rags, a curtain hanging from a wire stretched taut around coat racks. They do modern morality plays, tales of cosmic balancing wrought upon former insurance executives, of a great leveling in the economic order of things, a new society fierce in its kindness. The actors wear papier-mâché masks, bulbous heads stiffened in cackles and grimaces; they crouch into frog and monkey shapes, jump up and sweep their arms across the stage, contort themselves into grandiloquent gestures, elbows and knees bending to the contours of withered tree limbs. Beware, they say, the day is coming soon. Sooner than you think. A bird salesman stretches out his arms, and the claws of a dozen species line up from his shoulders to his hands. They'd carry him off if they could.

People are always going east from Limon by train; they slide across the prairie on the old freight lines as fast as they can, for the plains are a hole in the world, the place where the map goes blank. They've been using steam engines, old coal furnaces. Nobody talks about what happens when the coal runs out. And the trains don't go to Salina at all anymore. The last train moving between Kanorado and Goodland found the tracks bucked off the earth, bent toward the sky. The crew spent three hours standing in the sandy red earth out there, arguing with the train's owner, who refused to believe that the rails were ruined, thought he could bend them into wholeness again through will alone, as the sunlight slanted to a near-perfect horizontal, wavered away into greens, blues, deep purples that slipped into blackness. That night, the owner snored in time to his pulse while the engineer lay awake, petrified, because he heard the howls of steam and gears far off in the night, was sure he knew what was making those sounds, and tiptoed through the gravel, turning off all the lights. The *Janis Joplin*, a rusting train of coal cars heavy with animals and crates of ammunition, the engine silver and red with portraits of the singer screaming on the sides, the phrase *Dios Bendiga* in a semicircle around her head, is about to leave Limon for Columbus; they're going up to Denver, then down through Colorado Springs and Pueblo, crossing into Kansas at Coolidge. They'll get as close as McPherson. From there it's forty miles north to Salina, and Marco and Dayneesha will have to find a way to cover it themselves; though no one recommends it, they won't say why.

"The New Sioux," Marco says.

"No," they say. "At least you can bargain with the New Sioux."

"See?" Asia Sherman says. "I told you." She likes the two of them, doesn't want Dayneesha to go, considers sleeping with her just to get her to stay, but knows it's no good: the man's eyes won't stop looking east, and the woman doesn't want to be here anymore, won't stay if he doesn't. Marco tells the engineer that McPherson'll be close enough, and the engineer shrugs like he's talking to a man who insists on jumping off the top of a crane; almost sure to kill you, but hey, it's a free country. Asia Sherman gives Marco a salute and wishes him luck. Be ready to dodge bullets, she says. Or worse. She looks into the sky, gives Dayneesha a long hug, pulls her in close, whispers in her ear: Get away from him. He's bad news.

"I'll keep it in mind," Dayneesha says, and kisses her on the cheek. "You sure I can't get you to come with us?"

"I can't go back," Asia Sherman says.

"But it's your family."

"Which is why I can't go back."

Oh, honey, Dayneesha thinks. You're just going to throw it all away? Just like that?

"Take care of yourself, now," she says.

"Always."

"And don't party too hard."

"Never," Asia Sherman says, and blows Dayneesha a kiss, pirouettes away, her feet tracing the steps her mother taught her. Asia Sherman's first memory is of her parents dancing in the kitchen, a dim light swinging on a chain, throwing its glow over sheetrock walls, a brown linoleum floor, Sam Cooke crooning through a tinny speaker, her mother's hands on her father's shoulders, his hands on her back, her head on his chest, blue eyes closed, her cousins in a circle around them. She remembers her father as a man who smiled, clicked his heels in the driveway, clinked bottles with his friends on weekends, made up stories to amuse her about the secret, sentient lives of the neighbors' dogs. His first visions came to him when she was fifteen; he came home dazed and sobbing, said nothing while he ate boxed macaroni. Later that night she could hear them talking in bed. I'm scared, he said, and she kept hushing him. Go to sleep and dream of good things, she said. Dream of your daughter. But the visions kept coming, piling onto him until he broke, and his smile left him. Her parents destroyed the radio in the kitchen when Asia was nineteen, in a fight that ended with broken dishes and glasses obscuring the linoleum, cuts on their faces and hands, tattered scrawls of blood painted across their clothes. Her mother left her father that day, took his 1989 Ford and drove out of Pine Ridge as fast as the car would let her, and Asia watched her father gain followers, people who believed in him. We will reclaim history, he said, but all she saw was violence. She came home one day to find him and five other men loading guns, stacking thirty-six of them on the couch in the living room; she was there for the parties in the road as the government went under, the packing up, the abandonment of mold-infested houses before they tore off in a swarm of jingling bridles and whining children, past the graves of their ancestors, the places where they'd been brought down. She ran away at last after a year and a half, after a battle with local militia that left thirteen Oglala dead. What was the point of that? she said. Retribution, he said. This isn't retribution, she said, it's just people dying. When she hears the stories of the New Sioux now, she shakes her head, tries to keep from crying, for her father is gone now, has become a puppet of his visions. Your father is a prophet, they say, and she doesn't reply, can't say what she's thinking: My father is a slave, a zombie, and when history has no more use for those visions, what will he do then?

The *Janis Joplin* has four machine-gun emplacements, mortars pointed sideways out of windows, what looks like a howitzer on top. Three cars are crazy with chickens, and within hours, chicken guano. Marco falls into a game of backgammon with the engineer, who's drawn a board on a stray plank of wood, uses red and black bottle caps, tells Marco to be careful not to bend them, because it took him forever to collect the set. The engineer used to work for the air force, in various unusual capacities, as he puts it. There were warehouses of machine guns that nobody but him and three other guys had the keys to, and on the last day before the fall, when the secretary of defense's tin voice whined over the loudspeaker, informing them that the armed forces was no more, that there would be no final paycheck, they played the national anthem. The engineer was at the door to the first warehouse before the bombs were bursting in air. He fumbled with the key for three seconds, then kicked the door wide, and damned if there wasn't so much as a bullet inside. The engineer laughs. Somebody outside must have had information—outside information, you might say, he says, and laughs at his own joke; outside information, ha. He never did see any of the other three guys again.

"That where you got the howitzer?" Marco says.

"Nah," the engineer says.

The train trundles through eastern Colorado, following the highway through the towns of Hugo and Kit Carson, past rows of motels in fading coats of what used to be friendly colors, the cutout silhouette of a cowboy marking what used to be a barbecue joint. The land turns red and brown with scrub and weeds. A lone silo stands by the tracks, rusting and stripped of its sheath, the machinery inside throwing a shadow that looks like a monkey slumped in a cage. The road is gauzy with dirt; a dervishing dust devil wraps itself in earth, pulls itself up into a flickering cone that the wind whips into a mimicry of flame. They pass through Cheyenne Wells, a city of trailers and feed towers near the cylinders and tarantula legs of a shambles of a grain elevator that crawls near the tracks, dropping rust onto the ground. The state ag school, the gas station on the edge of town, are all awash with dust. Just before the town ends and the ruddy earth begins again, there's a playground made of tractor trailer tires and sewer pipes, painted blue, red, yellow. A sign hangs from the jungle gym: WE LEFT. YOU SHOULD TOO.

Then the engineer tells them what happened twenty miles south and more than a hundred years ago, near where Highway 96 rockets over the ground outside of Towner and Chivington, when 133 Cheyenne men, women, and children were massacred near Sand Creek by American soldiers bleary with whiskey. Kill every Indian you find, their commander had said, and they complied, and mutilated the dead besides; even though Black Kettle waved a huge American flag over his head and had his people rally underneath it, because the Americans had said they would be safe if they did.

On the engineer's first trip to Limon from St. Louis, the train broke down for three days in Cheyenne Wells, and the engineer went to see the spot where all those people had died. He couldn't find it. There were just cracking benches under trees near where the road crossed the creek's dry bed. A few miles west, near a set of corroded rails, the state of Colorado had put up a memorial marker at a rest area, but the sign had been vandalized into illegibility. The engineer stood in the gravel, regarded the empty hills. A hawk lurched in the breeze, dangling its gangly legs in flight. Nobody passed on the road for twenty minutes; the only signs that we'd done anything at all with the land were the broken fences, the ragged telephone poles, the hollow grain silos simmering in the mirage down the road. This is what we killed them all for, the engineer thought, for this; and understood something of their anger. We had to get them off the land, the American myth said; it was about the land, our destiny, unbroken dominion of the soil between two oceans. But it wasn't about that at all, was it? We named the towns and counties in equal share after the people we'd slaughtered and those who'd done the slaughtering, and now the wind was taking the towns apart; the telephone poles and trailers were becoming dirt again. One day it would all fall over, and the names, the state borders, would exist only on maps that sat fading in the metal racks of abandoned convenience stores; and the engineer wondered if all of the first Americans—the Comanche, the Kiowa, the Onondaga and Mohegan—would shake off the long nightmare of occupation and return to the places that had once been theirs. There could be new towns in the hills and along the rivers again; they could stand in the metal and plastic ruins we left behind, and the people could name everything again, as though the world were starting over, a new cycle of reincarnation, the past just a pull at the heart, a note sounding in the brain when they passed over the ground where their ancestors had fallen.

They enter Kansas, and the ripples in the earth flatten until they can see the curve of the planet falling away far from them, the long lines of roads stretching to the horizon, marked by black crosses of telephone poles etched into the sky. There are fields full of thrashing grasses, bowed and dusty heads of dead sunflowers. Shocks of wildflowers that crept into the gigantic farms to invade the soil, still dotted with dead corn and wheat, are taking over everything now: the giant centipedal skeletons of irrigation equipment; the rusting boxes of tractors and combines; the tilted fossils of oil derricks, their hammerheads pointed to the earth, axles rusted in place. All choked with tiny yellow wildflowers. Every dozen miles, something blocks the tracks: a telephone pole, an animal carcass, an overturned car, a tree thrown there by a cyclone. Hauling them aside takes longer than it should because the train workers don't want to be out there; they draw lots with a set of marbles to figure out who has to go. The men at the machine guns tweak themselves up as the engineer scans the clouds, like he's thinking of shooting one of them down.

"You know, if someone were coming, you'd see them from miles away. Lots of time to prepare," Marco says.

"That's not what we're worried about," the engineer says.

"What are you worried about?"

The engineer seems distracted. "I seem like a rational guy to you, right?" he says.

"Sure."

"Not bonkers, off the deep end, sucking on the gas line, anything like that?"

"No."

"Because I'm going to tell you something that makes me sound like a real nut job. I'm going to start by telling you that we don't like to talk about them, because they can hear us. And I don't mean that all superstition-like—I mean that they can hear us. Their ears perk, and they know we're afraid of them. And that makes them come."

Marco leans in. "Tell me everything," he says.

When the Great Plains emptied out—when the last of the cars put the last of the gas in their tanks and shot east, west, south—the people left behind wandered down the wide main streets under the shadows of stone courthouses and municipal buildings, blank stoplights swaying on cables over empty intersections. They ate what was left off the shelves of the grocery stores: wilting produce, pickled olives out of jars, relish, ketchup, processed cheese sagging in warm, dark refrigerators with broken bulbs. They slept in hollow bungalows and factory houses; heard how the prairie was seeping into them, lifting off the clapboards, driving chisels of air underneath, soaking into the foundations and turning them to silt, marking the rooftops for lightning. Let the flames come now. They started sleeping in yards, on splintered playgrounds, in the empty streets. Then they left the towns, walked into the sea of weeds, lay down half-starved and stared at the sky, arms out, mouth open, the fires of wildflowers all around them. And the sky stared back, screaming down from its heavenly reaches and descending onto the plain to eat them; and the prairie crawled into them, under their fingernails, into their ears, behind their eyes, into their brains.

You'd have thought those people would've just died out there, but then there was Cyclone Cal and the Circus of Industrial Destruction. Story goes that Cal worked in a rendering plant outside of Arkansas City, Kansas, processing the skulls of lambs, the intestines of swine, the bones of chickens, hooves and horse heads, euthanized cats and dogs, skunks, rats, and raccoons killed on the roads and brought in by the state. He saw the mountains of the dead on the plant floor, shimmering with swarms of maggots, saw it all shredded and boiled into soup, the fat skimmed off, meat melted off the bone. He smelled that soup wherever he went. It had leached into his skin. They finally let him go on the day he ran onto the floor, dove into the stripped carcass of a steer, and curled up inside its rib cage, saying we were all the same, us and them; this is what industry did to us. It took three of them to get him out again. People saw him in Arkansas City, Winfield, Wichita, standing at the gates of factories, mills. I can smell it on you too, he told them. The stink of machines, the offal of progress. He got his picture in the paper twice for disorderly conduct. Then, right before the collapse, he wandered into the fields.

They say he wasn't out there a week before a tornado formed right around old Cal, twirled out of the clouds and lifted up the earth he was standing on, transported him skyward. Story goes that he was up there for a day on an island of land that got smaller and smaller until it crumbled away, and he fell. When he opened his eyes, the earth was a different color and the plains spoke to him in a language like a razor, cutting into him until he obeyed, until he knew what he had to do. He collected the people who remained and they moved across Kansas, stripping out the mills, the construction equipment, the oil rigs; got at last to the plant outside Arkansas City, the place where he was born, he told them. They took everything they could use—the motors, the cables, the shredders, the hooks—took all of that refuse and rebuilt it all, into machines that lurch and wander, that spit and wheeze but do no work, a mockery of what they were. Nobody knows where he got the camels, the rhinoceroses, the elephants, but they've seen the circus when it sleeps, people and animals spread on the ground around Cal in a spiral. And when he lifts his arms and speaks, they gather around him and move in a crawling clot of screeching gears and horns, machines hanging in the air, and the people who see it run. They've heard what the circus does when it comes to town. Some of them have seen it themselves, and they either won't talk about it at all or can't stop, as if they're trying to empty their heads of it. The circus is trying to undo progress, some say, trying to make it as though we were never here. I don't know about that, say others. I just know that a lot of people have died before they should have because of Cyclone Cal. And I can't find the town where I was raised anymore.

Marco looks at the howitzer bobbing at the end of the train.

"Bullshit," he says.

The engineer shrugs again.

"You ever see a town they've hit," he says, "you ever see what they do to the people they find, you'll understand why we have that thing."

The yellow and black of the fields yields to green and brown, and the land begins to ripple again. Scrub grows into trees that line the track and the creek beds, mark the old lines between farms. A wooden barn stripped of paint leans on a combine black with mold. Rows of auto repair places, motels, and minimalls. All the lights out. In the middle of a gigantic field left fallow is a red house surrounded by trees, a small field enclosed in wire, green with cornstalks and vegetables. On the edge of Lyons, laundry is strung up to a cinder block garage, a pen with two horses. A chicken shack. In the shade of a rise in the land, a man and his wife bend to the earth, killing potato bugs with their hands while their three children fly tattered kites on the roof of a mill. The train curls around a turn in the tracks, sweeps by a hill with three crosses leaning off the ridge, one of them broken, CHRIST PILOT ME laid into the hillside in white stones.

"We're almost to McPherson," the engineer says.

The squares of the land break against a line of trees at the edge of town as the *Janis Joplin* passes the silver spires of an oil station, a nest of train cars with doors blowtorched off of them to make homes for swine, though none of the pigs remain. At a railroad crossing, without explanation, the lights are still flashing, bells chime, the barricades lower to block the quiet highway. Four squad cars with shattered windows are parked along the side of the police station. A squat white building across the street has an ad painted on the side of it, a jailbird in striped jumpsuit, ball and chain around his ankle: IN JAIL, NEED BAIL? CALL STEVE. Then trees again, masking low-slung bungalows, lawns overrun with crabgrass. Buildings of bricks and stone all around the train, the twin hulks of grain elevators, awnings of corrugated metal hanging over the tracks. The train wheezes to a stop, and the engineer looks at Marco.

"Here's where you get off." He points up the road. "That'll take you all the way to Salina. I advise you move quickly. There's not much here anymore. Tornado, you see. Just a week ago."

The train squeals against the tracks and rattles east, the chickens frantic in the cars. Then, for Marco and Dayneesha, it's quieter than it's been in days. Along Main Street, there are cars left in the middle of the road, doors hanging from hinges. Shops with the doors propped open, hardware, furniture. Two blocks south, jutting piles of rubble on either side of the street, shattered timbers and masonry, a splash of broken glass. A jagged rend in the turret of the courthouse. Then they smell them, the bodies lying on the asphalt, buried under fallen buildings, tangled in the grass next to the tracks. They all deserved better. Once there were cars ambling down these streets; strollers on the sidewalks; bookstores selling paperbacks and greeting cards from wire racks; an instrument shop kicking back in the cavernous lobby of a bank building, the man inside friends with all the musicians for seventy-five miles; a restaurant near the green lawn in front of the library serving scrambles from skillets snug in planks of wood. But a storm wrote its name across this town, left nobody behind to erase it. The cyclones are the land's agents, its saboteurs. They bring down power lines, buckle roads, shudder the walls of houses so the winter can knock them down. In time, perhaps, one annihilating tempest will level everything, smooth it all over with dust and dirt; the grasses from the prairie will come in, cut the city apart blade by blade. It will take centuries to push McPherson into the earth, cover it over, for our structures are stubborn. But the land can wait.

Twenty miles away, the town of Buhler is an inferno, a shimmering pyramid of light and smoke. It has been like that for days, the flames jumping from one house to the next, from rooftop to rooftop. The houses squirm, breathe out smoke through the windows, grow arms of fire that wave above the chimneys until the structures give in and fall into the basement; push the pictures from the walls; burn up the poster bed in which five generations had slept, the lacquered green spinet piano from the living room, the white electric stove. In the fields to the north, on the heels of Buhler's refugees, the soil shakes and stones scramble across hardened dirt to the rumble of machinery and the stomping bulk of animals as the Circus of Industrial Destruction wheezes across the prairie, powered by the panting and huffing of gigantic lungs, the screech and whump of flying machines shuddering through the air.

The people of the circus are going wild, rattling the bars of the animals' cages, hooting and shouting, clambering onto the backs of elephants and jumping off again, chewing on the flesh of the citizens they slaughtered as the melody from the calliope stumbles and gasps. In the middle of it all, shaded by human pelts and plastic, Cyclone Cal himself sits in a slashed and tattered car seat, hands behind his head, eyes closed, face tilted toward the clouds, transported back to his time in the sky, when everything fell away around him; in his head, the tornados are always descending, bearing him up but leaving him within reach of the earth to do their work when they can't get close enough. He asks them if they like what his circus did in Buhler, the way it tore the town off the earth so that future maps will forget it, as though it never were; lets out a cackling laugh when he feels their blessing.

Above him, Tyrone Fly, hands and legs hogtied, swings from the belly of a mechanical vulture, seven other captives swaying on ropes around him, three of them butchered and cleaned already. He has left the present, refuses to feel what the people of the circus have done to him. It's a bad joke, a bad dream. His eyes don't see the flaying fan belts, the spitting teeth; he can't smell the stench of grease and innards; he is back in his past, in the arms of his ex at the state fair, among funnel cake and painted signs, the screams of children, the blinking lights of amusement park rides. He is in his mother's kitchen in Phoenix, a steaming tamale in his hand; he peels back the husk to reveal the warm flesh beneath, cornmeal and jalapeño peppers, the tang of chorizo. He can taste it on his tongue now, and he hangs from that memory, fingernails dug in, knuckles parched and bleeding. He'll stay there until he's free, or until the people around him finish what they've started.

CHAPTER XI.

Security grows lax; OKONOMIYAKI,
kumis, and REFUGE AMONG Swedes;
the CIRCUS comes to town.

A small cloth bag crosses into New York City over the George Washington Bridge, taped under the driver's seat of a truck carrying a load of television parts; it vibrates with the grooves in the West Side Highway until the driver reaches under, pulls it out, lobs it out the window at a square of sidewalk in the Financial District, where it's picked up and tied to the rack of a bicycle that weaves through the streets and squeals to a stop at the loading dock for the downtown jail. There, a pair of gloved hands slides the package into the bottom of a crate, covers it with cabbages. It hides in the kitchen for two days, is moved back and forth from stockpot to saucepan, until it ends up in Maria Lista Sandinista's hands when she returns her tray to the dishwasher, who gives it to her with a nod. The bag already has a line of thick white tape weaving down the side; she shoves it in her pants, sticks it to her thigh just above her knee, and conveys it back to her cell, where she waits until night to open it. Inside is a lump of plastic explosive, enough to demolish a car. She molds it to the larger block of the stuff that's stashed under her bed, figures she now has enough to open one side of her cell to daylight. If she wanted to, she could free herself this minute, herself and anyone who survived the blast. They'd scatter into the streets, swim across the river, disappear into the countryside. But she has this idea that she wouldn't survive it; and the bomb is meant for Marco, anyway, for leaving her on the pier, leaving her here after she'd given him such devotion. In the bomb's bloom, he'll see how he has wronged her. If she could, she would slow the explosion so that the boiling heat crawled through the air and gave him a few seconds to speak. There would be repentance then, pleas for forgiveness, and she would rush forward and accept them all, until the flames overtook them. In her cell, just the dream of it, the phantom blast burning the back of her neck, is enough to make her happy.

But nothing could make the Aardvark happy now. He stands before a topographical map of the United States that he stole from the corporate headquarters of a pharmaceutical company six days before a man drove his truck into the front of the building, sent the revolving doors spinning across the marble floor and into a bank of defunct elevators, causing the front of the building to swing down and chew on the truck's back, the windows above to lean over and shatter on the sidewalk. Across the street, another man took pictures of it all. He later presented it as an art project: The Collapse of Corporate America. That man is now famous among international businessmen; museums in Europe and Asia commission him to address the fall of the most recent superpower in his work, give lectures in front of harsh white screens. What was the United States, anyway? the artist asks through a microphone in Seoul. He lets the question float through galleries and halls. What is it now?

The Aardvark isn't unhappy about the man's prosperity. Once, he might have been; in his days as a crime lord, he was a collector of sculpture who despised performance art; it's public flagellation, he used to say. He had a Giacometti in the living room, a small Rodin in the bathroom. He once bludgeoned a man to death with a Picasso—a model for a monumental piece—after the man argued that sculpture had never existed as an art form until the twenty-first century. But he can't find the urge to care about art these days, because his city is coming loose around him. There are water shortages, a rumor that one of the main pipelines collapsed somewhere north of the city. People say they heard it underneath the street in Queens, a raking crash that echoed into a rumble. But it can't be confirmed; the Aardvark can't convince anyone to go down there to investigate. And the subways only go halfway into the outer boroughs now, after a series of explosions—the Aardvark has no idea what caused them—left jagged holes in the elevated platforms. No trains arrive at the sweeping Coney Island station anymore; it's become home to a colony of musicians and pigeons. Then there are the ships that draw a warping grid in the water of the harbor, gather into a floating city, the piers lit with trade. The Aardvark can't say what goes in or out, or how much money is involved. All of it is documented, the papers are piled seven feet high in an office on the floor below his screaming family, but he has no way of verifying what they tell him. Crates and containers come off the ships, into the streets; crowds flood on and off the decks. There could be plagues, armies, carnivals invading his city, and he would never know until his fingers fell off, a bullet careened toward his head, the clowns in pink and purple descended from the ceiling. They'll all find a way in.

Then there's the map in front of him. An array of broadheaded pins has been pushed into it, one for every slave camp he financed. Just a few weeks ago, the camps fanned across the country, arms of a vast spiral of commerce circling his office. He put the pins in there himself, in the days when the excitement of a new market, a new industry, held him in thrall. He imagined that it would only grow because he had rigged it to be so: The interest he charged the slaveowners on their slaves was so high that their operations must grow or perish, and people weren't getting any less desperate.

But in the last few weeks, he's been pulling pins out. First in Watsonville, Eureka; later in Nevada, in Utah. It's a disease; he can see it in front of him, chewing through red muscle. The Aardvark wants to blame the Slick Six. He recognizes Marco's havoc in the stories that came out of Watsonville. He'd seen it himself, the first dozen times he hired Marco, back when Marco had just left Red Kwon, before the Slick Six were slick. First for extortion, theft. Then assassinations, for which Marco showed unusual flair. The Aardvark tripled his fortune while Marco was working for him, extended his enterprise into Southeast Asia, China, India, for the flood of the world's money was flowing from there; they were the Tigris, the Euphrates. And he saw more of himself in Marco than he did in his own children. They'd both had a youth of bones and metal, of howling in the dark; the urge to act before thinking, to cut straight lines through the arc of the planet's surface, leave marks that could be seen from space. Before Marco's last job for him—though the Aardvark didn't know that yet—the Aardvark invited Marco to his office. Marco stood before him, awaiting orders. The Aardvark tried to get him to sit, have a drink.

"What for?" Marco said.

"Because I'd like you to work for me all the time," the Aardvark said.

"I do."

"I mean, me alone."

"Why would I do that? Can you pay me that much?"

"..."

"..."

"I see," the Aardvark said.

The Aardvark never called Marco for a job again. But he did talk to him once, after the Slick Six had taken their first few million from him and he traced where it had gone.

"Why did you do that to me?" the Aardvark said.

"The pay is excellent."

"I'll double it to get you to stop."

"Sorry," Marco said. "I work for them now."

"Ah."

"You would have done the same thing," Marco said.

"No, I wouldn't have. I never would have."

Later, on the dirt of a runway dug out of a Peruvian jungle, the Aardvark already on the plane, the propellers spinning, twenty soldiers with machine guns stationed around the aircraft to ensure a safe flight, Marco descended from the sky. Watching him at work on the soldiers, shouting *go, go* to the pilot, the Aardvark thought of folklore, like a hawk through sparrows, the wheat before the scythe. By the time the Aardvark was in the air, the runway was a dark, slick smudge of earth, fingers of shadow reaching into the air in the plane's wake. It was the same there on the California coast; he was sure of it. Spurning the loyalty he'd offered. Screwing him.

But Eureka, Nevada, Utah—these were bigger than anything one man, even Marco, could do. Men who'd never been in a fight before fighting each other. Bullets searing air, skittering on the ground, hitting the wrong people. Boards with nails in them. The blunt ends of farming tools. They say in Watsonville that the Devil rose from the sea to sweep the fields; in Provo, they say it was just a riot. The slaves are doing it all on their own. The Aardvark has warned all of the remaining camps to arm themselves, has given them advances to do it; in public, he blames the owners when the camps flutter away in screams and fire. But he knows it's not the owners or the slaves. It's him, who pushed too hard; it's history, pushing back. And he doesn't know where any of the Slick Six are, or what they're planning. He goes to his desk drawer, opens a bottle of pills, pops a bright orange amphetamine into his mouth, but his unhappiness is still profound.

Seven thousand miles away, a half-digested yellowish biscuit that was once a slug of dough squirms in Zeke's stomach, then lurches into his esophagus and pops out of his mouth, riding a fountain of orange bile. Zeke's hands shake and grip the rail.

"Just look at the horizon," Captain Bengwe Saloon says.

Zeke gives him a friendly wave. Blow me, you bastard. For three days, Zeke has been sick while Captain Saloon has been churning around the coast of Thailand, wrapping up his business with the *Mumbai Stinger*. First there was the matter of ditching its crew and passengers; he let them go in Phuket, because with three of the Slick Six as his new slaves, the captain was feeling generous. Then to Bangkok, where Saloon repainted the freighter and sold it under a different name back to its owner, a shipping conglomerate owned by a Korean loan shark; none of the people in the company had seen the vessel in years. Captain Bengwe Saloon smiled. "I found it derelict at sea," he said.

Two days later the *Lucky Sun* glides, freighterless, into Osaka Bay. It's night on the water fifty miles off the coast, but as they near the city, it's like they're sailing into the sun, the city's hundreds of towers building a wall of light that bounces off the wrinkled waves. The *Lucky Sun* passes beneath the giant arms of cranes, the bridges lancing over the Yodo; approaches piers blazing with electricity and bleary with steam, looking like noon at two in the morning. A slim car is waiting at the end of the pier, bright yellow with teeth painted on the hood, windows stained black enough to be reflective. The door swings open and a man who recognizes Hideo from the deck of the *Lucky Sun* raises his hand, though not a muscle on his face moves. Captain Saloon bows; bids farewell to his baby; walks with Zeke, Carolyn, and Hideo to the car, which slides through the streets into downtown Osaka, a canyon of electricity glittering over canals of green and gray. The streets and alleys are tangled with people, the agents of global commerce, men and women in expensive suits and raincoats speaking into cell phones, a mélange of English, Chinese, Japanese, Spanish, for there's trade to be done in Mexico City, Buenos Aires, London, Milan, Frankfurt; they bark out huge numbers that are lost and found again in the noise of trucks shifting gears, idling outside stores, blocking the roads, delivering silver and yellow fish packed between cubes filled with liquid nitrogen. Delivery boys with headlamps tied to their helmets dodge through the crowd on bicycles and mopeds outlined with glow sticks. Overhead, glued to the side of a building by suction cups, utility workers in yellow jumpsuits are fixing an antenna. They're shouting at each other because the men inside the offices are shouting at them; every second that passes, the company loses seven million yen.

They cross the corner of Americatown, where the signs blossom into katakana and English, advertising used books, pirated Hollywood movies from ten years ago, photographs of major cities and celebrities. A man in a baseball cap sells hot dogs from a cart advertising, in kanji, a brand of soap. Behind him is the James and Sons Smokehouse, a green-and-blue apartment building converted into a barbecue joint; a tall metal chimney jutting from the roof, spilling the smell of smoked ribs onto the people walking below. Mr. James himself is from Topeka, and the expats say his ribs are damn good, though not as good as what you could get at Gates in Kansas City.

Zeke hasn't been to Osaka in years, and he's forgotten what it's like, the way the light makes him think he's inside, that over him is not a sky but a ceiling, painted a flat gray and lit from behind, a moon projected onto its surface. At any moment, he thinks, the image could change; the moon could be two smiling schoolgirls flashing V-for-Victory fingers. A pink flounder. A large white pig upside down, a pomegranate in its mouth.

They approach the colossus of the Sanwa-Sumitomo complex, columns of plastic and glass tapering toward the clouds. In the side of the central tower is a small wooden door sized for a ten-year-old, stamped with the insignia of a dog's long face, two fangs curled over the lower lip. Hideo knocks with both hands, two measures of a five-on-four polyrhythm, and then stands back. Behind them, an electric bus hisses to a stop amid rising steam. A woman calls from a mochi cart, waving her hand in slow motion, as if she's getting her picture taken by a thousand photographers. The door opens to reveal a man in a long tan raincoat that doesn't conceal the gun at his waist crouching there, looking out.

"Takahashi-san," he says.

"*Hai*," Hideo says. There is a quick exchange in Japanese that Zeke can't follow, though it appears that Hideo is vouching for his, Carolyn's, and the captain's grooviness. No trouble from us, sir. The man with the gun glares at them, and steps aside. They all must bow to enter; the door shuts behind them. They're on the shore of a rock garden, shaped to mimic the coast of southern Kyushu, where Inu Kimura was raised. How the son of a restaurant owner became a yakuza lord and financier for a major bank, Hideo has never been able to figure out, and Kimura has never cared to reveal. Kimura believes that the only things worth telling about a life are how many times it turns, how sharp the turn is; even after Hideo became a confidant, when they each knew enough about what the other had done to send the other to jail for several lifetimes, Kimura talked about his past only as a series of decisions and epiphanies, his memory focused on precise moments of realization, the years between them inconsequential, unworthy of commentary. The decision to become yakuza was equated with eating barbecued beef in a restaurant near the harbor in Kobe. The understanding that he was one of the wealthiest men in Japan, and thus in the world, arose from a moment on a train speeding north from Tokyo, his hands folded over the handle of a brown briefcase. My memories of myself are just sparks in dark places, Kimura said. Yet he never seems to forget anything about anyone else.

Kimura is waiting for them in an iron pagoda rising from the middle of the rock garden. He makes an expansive gesture, and the man with the gun ushers them forward. They take off their shoes and enter.

"Hideo. Zeke. Carolyn, of course." He doesn't even register the captain. "You all look unwell. Perhaps something to eat?"

"No, Inu," Hideo says. "We are not hungry." A lie.

"The last time I heard of you was before the collapse," Kimura says. "You two had gone to Los Angeles, and you had gone to Monaco. Out of the trade, they said, forever."

"It seemed that way at the time," Carolyn says.

"So it is with final decisions," Kimura says. "They are never final. But here I am assuming that you are entering the trade again."

"We are," Zeke says.

Kimura's eyes move across each of them, and he sees everything. Zeke's quickening pulse. Carolyn's serenity. Hideo's hesitation. My disciple doesn't want this, Kimura thinks.

"I am convinced you're unwell," he says, and whistles three ascending notes.

"Inu—" Hideo says.

"—No, I insist. You will hurt my feelings if you don't eat. Now, what have you come to see me about?"

"A plan," says Hideo, "of large proportions."

"Having to do with the Aardvark and the slave trade," says Zeke.

"You want to usurp it," Kimura says.

"More like dismantle it."

Kimura laughs. "You cannot dismantle the slave trade. True, there are revolts now—haven't you heard?—but the trade will return. It exists because you have no laws against it. It exists because you have no workable laws at all."

"What if we bring back the law?" Zeke says.

". . ."

"Your plan is much bigger than I was thinking," Kimura says. "This is not a heist. This is a revolution."

"It is only a difference of scale," Hideo says.

"But you are only the Slick Six. Not an army."

"Not if we have your help."

Servants are bringing in trays of food: marinated fish, stewed vegetables, strips of sashimi and Kobe beef, plates of okonomiyaki wavering with seasoning. Hideo slips into Japanese and pulls out a scrap of yellow paper, on which he draws a very accurate silhouette of the former United States of America. A dotted line runs from California to the middle of the country. Then he dots a line from Wisconsin to Texas. Kimura leans over, nods, grunts. Hideo circles the place where the lines intersect, gesticulates with his chopsticks as Kimura takes a quick bite of squid, keeps nodding and grunting with tentacles hanging out of his mouth. Hideo draws another line, from the circle in the middle of the country to New York, makes a gesture suggesting decapitation.

"How much do you need?" Kimura says.

Carolyn says a very, very large number, and doesn't blink. She understood everything, Zeke realizes.

"*Hai,*" Hideo says.

Kimura chews. Swallows.

"Both the risk and the expense of this are ridiculous," he says. "I am surprised you think I can liquidate such money on such short notice."

"You can do it," Zeke says. "I've seen your records."

"What do I get? In return?"

"Half of the island."

Captain Saloon's eyebrows rise.

"The southern half," Kimura says.

"You'll have to—"

"—The southern half," Kimura says, and Zeke imagines him pumping their stomachs until they vomit up his food, then beating them all on the head with a pipe.

"Deal," says Zeke. The other two look at him. He looks back, and if it's possible for eyes to shrug, his do. He turns to

Kimura. "Just out of curiosity, where are you going to get six hundred billion yen?"

The Vibe enters Kimura and shows him the neatness of it all, a circle closing. He giggles like a two-year-old.

"I will get it. But I need a few days. Is that acceptable?"

"Do we have a choice?" Zeke says.

Kimura smiles.

"Eat," he says, then nods to Hideo. "Please come with me for a moment."

They walk out of the pagoda and across the rock garden to an elevator that conveys them without sound to the top of the central Sanwa-Sumitomo building. Osaka is an ocean of light that stretches to the horizon; corporate towers and the spindles of telephone antennae rise through the glow of neon and sulfur. The sky sparks with aircraft that disappear behind the underlit buildings nearby; the bellies of helicopters leave greasy red streaks of light in the air. Up here, all of the sounds of the metropolis, the voices and snippets of songs from cell phones, the screams of machinery, words intoned from loudspeakers, music blaring from convenience stores, dogs yipping and barking as men stand outside bars encouraging people to enter, girls calling across sidewalks searching for each other, the aquatic blasts from boats moving off into the night; all of this resolves into a rushing hum, the expectant static of a microphone poised before the planet's mouth, waiting for it to speak. At one corner of the roof are a table and two chairs, a bottle of sake, two cups. Inu Kimura and Hideo sit, drink, regard the strings of lights on the bridges over the river, the dark line of the bay.

"Why don't you like the plan?" Inu Kimura says in casual Japanese.

"I do like the plan," Hideo says.

"No you don't."

" . . . "

"Do you think it won't work?"

"I think it may work."

"So why don't you like it?"

"Because I don't want to return to the trade."

"Ah."

". . ."

"When you worked for me, I knew you had such talent," Inu Kimura says. "You understood so well how to move in the cracks in the world. But I always wondered if you wanted the life, the life you saw me living. When you left me, I assumed it was to do something legitimate."

"I thought about it," Hideo says.

"Instead, you created the Slick Six."

"Yes."

"You could just walk away," Inu Kimura says. "Why don't you?"

"Because I am a slave. To that captain. To the Aardvark. So the plan must be seen through before I walk away. And I want to take Kari with me."

"She is very smart. And charming. And beautiful, when she lets you remember what she looks like. I understand why you want to keep her."

". . ."

"We haven't spoken in years," Inu Kimura says. "But you know that I've always been very proud of you, the work you've done. You know that the silence between us was nothing personal. We just lost touch with each other."

"I know."

"I could sabotage the plan if you want. Kill the captain, kill the Aardvark. I could even kill Marco, I think."

"Don't. It's important that the plan work. The plan is important."

Inu Kimura laughs.

"You haven't grown a conscience, have you?" he says.

"Maybe," Hideo says. "But I also want to be able to walk away from it afterward. The plan, the Slick Six. All of it."

Inu Kimura takes a sip of sake, leaves the cup at his lips for a second.

"I understand," he says. "You made the Slick Six. So you feel, maybe, that you have to unmake it."

"Maybe."

"When do you think you'll do it?"

"The moment I can do so without jeopardizing the plan."

". . ."

"Don't worry," Hideo says. "I'll make sure the risk you're taking pays off."

Inu Kimura smiles.

"You were waiting for me to say that, weren't you?" Hideo says.

"Only in the sense that I knew you would."

At first the rest of their talk is of the details of the scheme, the dividing of assets, the movement of funds, but soon it's easy and cool, of women and men in jail, in government, people who died years ago from poison and bad luck; until the sake runs out and Hideo slips to his feet, excuses himself, for he remembers that his people must be waiting.

Inu Kimura waits until the elevator is gone, then looks over his city, starts to do the numbers, adds up the capital that brought slavery howling back to the United States plus the five to eleven percent interest strained from the slaves' blood, their lives turned into money. The Aardvark has it—Inu Kimura knows he does, has been making sure of it for months. Kimura will collect what he is owed, and when the Aardvark is deposed Kimura will take his island too. If the Aardvark survives what's coming, when he's wandering the earth in ragged robes a decade from now, his caravan of a family in tow, his imperial days will seem like a dream. I ruled New York once. A mighty country ate from my hand. But Inu Kimura is almost certain the Aardvark will not survive it, won't want to, and the world will descend upon what he leaves behind. There will be calls for laws, Kimura knows, for the balance has tipped too far toward disorder, the brutal rules of wealth and poverty; but the framers of the new regime will rig the laws to keep the spoils flowing, make sure they're downhill when they do. Property and money will flit from hand to hand; there will be rushes for empty government offices, the country reborn in a tangle of advantage and vendetta, blind and beautiful optimism, luck and circumstance. Former bureaucrats will be bureaucrats again; mayors made paupers and paupers mayors; lawyers called back to work, maybe even to the same offices, as though the legal system were just holding its breath for five years, plunging underwater just to see how long it could stay down there. For the New Sioux, the wealth will transform their lives. They'll wake after heavy revelry as new people, redeemed at last, the land beneath their feet theirs again. They'll marvel that they have so much. But it will be nothing compared to what Inu Kimura takes. Another giggle wriggles from his throat when he thinks of it, for the Sioux will be getting less than half the interest from the Aardvark's repayment of his debt. Kimura will walk away with the other half, and the principal besides; and then, as the land's value multiplies, he'll sell it off piece by piece, the largest haul anyone has seen on a real estate deal in fifty years. He'll profit from it all, the death of an empire and the pangs of a new country's birth; and it will all be done before anyone even sees what's going on. It'll be the greatest heist since the wreck of communism, the price America pays to regain its soul, and nobody will even know he did it.

In the street below, two women in business suits and pigtails accost Captain Saloon, but he doesn't even see them; he only has eyes for his honey.

"Do you think he can get the money?" Captain Saloon says.

"He says he can get it," Zeke says.

"Do you believe him?"

Carolyn watches Hideo open his mouth, and knows what

he'll say. I never believe anything. Every day that I wake up and do not find the planet breaking apart, the crust lifting off into space, is a small miracle. She puts her hand over his mouth.

"Yes," she says.

Captain Saloon smiles. "Excellent. We must proceed to New York at once, then."

"But so many things must happen first," Hideo says.

"Not really. The prices on your heads have gone up. I own three of the most valuable fugitives in the world. So I figure, we must get to New York as fast as possible. And either I get an island, or enough money from the Aardvark to keep the *Lucky Sun* running for a decade. Good plan, no?"

"How long will it take to get to New York?" Carolyn says.

"Three weeks at the most."

Marco, Zeke thinks. You'd better hurry, wherever you are.

The red-and-white sign for Dillon's Food Market on the road out of McPherson still gets power, though nobody's in the aisles. The half-empty counter at the deli reeks with rotting potato salad. Marco and Dayneesha find a box of doughnuts, three cans of Clamato, start walking the road north to Salina. The line of the highway hops from hill to hill, shoots straight across deserted fields thick with tall grass and straggling saplings with crooked branches, fringes of leaves. Telephone poles tilt at strained angles; power lines hang dead from their spars. Once this road roared with trucks on their way to Interstate 135 while people pulled grain from the fields around them; in another few years, Dayneesha thinks, the fields will be forests and meadows, the stray livestock that survived long enough to go feral will come to graze and shelter themselves in the shade. Marco and Dayneesha just happen to be here for its fallow period. The road drops in front of them for a mile, dips and bends over the crest of the next hill; a lone tree claws into the skyline, and Marco is taken back to Mongolia, before the Slick Six, after his childhood days of blood and gunfire in South America.

He had eight tattoos then, long strands of color running along his limbs, flashes of paint on his back and chest, a tendril of fire curling from his ear across his cheek. You will have to erase all of that, said Red Kwon, his mentor. It will do you no good to be memorable. I'll never get rid of them, Marco said. Red Kwon just smiled; the light that flashed off his teeth said, You angry, stupid young man. But I did not pick you for your brain, now, did I?

For as long as he can remember, Marco has always been fighting. First it was in the ring of slums around La Paz; then in a camp in the jungle near the Brazilian border. At the age of eight, he could explode an orange with a Kalashnikov at a hundred yards, couldn't see the crucial difference between fruit and people. He fought first in Bolivia against men in uniforms who hesitated before they shot at him, didn't understand that Marco wouldn't return the favor. In Peru, he killed more men in camouflage, a few in suits and ties, one of whom he met on a crowded Lima street and gutted with a bayonet. In Colombia, he razed villages, shot anyone who fought, anyone who ran. By then he was twelve years old and thought he was in the official army until his commander abandoned him in Guatemala City out of fear, because Marco was getting very good at killing people, and it was getting harder to make him stop. But he was still a twelve-year-old, and he cried like one when four teenagers tried to pry out his gold teeth with a pair of pliers while a fifth held a semiautomatic pistol to his head. He was yelping and kicking, a stray dog beaten with a stick; then a shock ran through his brain and he was standing in the middle of the street, four of the kids dead around him, the fifth dying against the stop sign on the corner, a policeman sitting on the curb screaming and clutching the remains of his legs, two other officers stumbling away, unspooling long streaks of blood behind them, begging, Please let me go, I'll do anything if you just let me go. Red Kwon stood beside him, his hand on Marco's shoulder. You are squandering your gift, he said.

In Mongolia he learned how to break horses. Master a horse, Red Kwon said, and you can master any machine. Marco laughed, and Red Kwon pulled a wooden pole from behind his back and put him on the ground with it. Listen to what I say to you, boy. The first horse bucked him off and drove its hooves into his back and legs before he could get away. He spent five months on his back under thick blankets in a yurt, drinking yak's milk and shivering with pain. After he got back on the horse, he was bucked almost every day for a month, but stayed on longer and longer; he understood then that it was anger keeping him alive, anger that healed the wounds, dulled the ache, and it was stronger than the horse, flat-eared and screaming. After another week, the horse understood this and submitted. The Mongols applauded; a few weeks later there was a party: throat-singing over horse-head fiddle and doshpuluur, vodka and kumis drunk out of bowls that smelled—like everything else—of horses, though Marco didn't notice it anymore.

"You know what broke the horse," Red Kwon said.

Marco nodded.

"Good. Now when something breaks you, you will understand that too."

But nothing broke him for years. He learned how to kill in treetops and caves, in apartments in gleaming cities; learned how to fly in India, how to become invisible in Indonesia. He brought death to gangsters in Bratislava, arms dealers in Freetown, businessmen in Dresden, ivory traders outside Abéché. By the time the Slick Six found him, he had made and given away a small fortune three times over, scattering it between a string of orphanages across Central and South America, none of whom would ever learn who their benefactor was, or what he had done. When he shook Hideo's hand, kissed Carolyn's, he was all glass and smoke. Johanna got to him first, after a night of sambuca in Hanoi, a cot in a wooden room open to the Red River, her sour lips; then the rest of them crept in without him even knowing. Then one day in Kinshasa, after a con involving defunct government bonds and a pickup truck full of gold and reactor-grade uranium, they were sitting on the sagging roof of an old colonial post office building drinking beers, and there were stars blinking through the clouds, and Marco realized that he was happy for the first time in his life. The happiness broke him, but Red Kwon was wrong: He didn't know it. He understood only that he wanted to be good, good for his new family, good enough to deserve them. That was all. He didn't see the betrayal, the way his family let him go onto the prison ship while they spread themselves over two continents, free and never needing to work again.

"How much farther to Salina, do you think?" Dayneesha says.

"Depends on how fast we walk," Marco says. "Two days?"

"Any idea what we'll do then? What if the New Sioux aren't there? What if they are there?"

"We just have to state our case."

"What if they don't buy it?"

Marco smiles. "I'll get you out of whatever we get into, Day."

". . ."

"What?"

"Nothing."

"No. What?"

"It's nothing," Dayneesha says. Flashes back to her hands against the side of the bus in Oklahoma, Robert Blackfeather Sherman whispering in her ear, We won't kill you, and Dayneesha thinking, I don't believe you. This wasn't what she agreed to when Hideo contacted her years ago. She wanted numbers, names on screens, keys clattering under her fingers. Her brother in community college, her mother in a little green house outside of Chicago's last suburbs, and her at a club, feet moving. Not this.

A line of trees appears at the edge of the land, and the fields, all at once, become fenced-in crops, the last of summer's harvest, the beginning of fall's. Peppers and tomatoes hang from bowed branches tied to trellises; squashes crawl along the ground. Three women and two men are kneeling in the dirt, pulling weeds. One of them looks up at them and waves. Dayneesha waves back. Five men approach them, riding horses at a fast trot along the side of the road, guns tied to their saddles. One of them is wearing a red wool hat, the letter L stitched in white thread. When they get closer, the horses slow to a walk, stop at what they think is a safe distance; though, in reality, they're already dead if Marco wants them to be.

"Mind if we ask what brings you out here?" the man in the hat says.

"Going to Salina," Marco says.

"Not much in Salina anymore, except maybe a hamburger or two. You two Sioux?"

"No sir," Dayneesha says.

"But we're trying to find them," Marco says.

"What for?"

"Revenge."

The men on horses look at each other. Nobody moves for their guns.

"Well, the Sioux aren't around here just yet," the man in the hat says, "because we haven't been raided yet. They're due any day now, though. We have food and a place to stay, if you'd like. First night's free; after that you have to work for it. We can always use more workers here, and between you and me, the work's not that hard. Easier than starving, anyway. Most people who find us wind up staying."

"Why?" Dayneesha says.

"You tell me."

The men on horses gallop ahead of them, and Marco and Dayneesha cross the line of trees, pass by a gas station set up with troughs of feed and water; a woman with blue hair sitting in a pink recliner against the side of the building, watching over eight tables, a pair of boots, a box of plastic bottles, an ottoman with a zebra-print cushion. Along the streets hedged with broad-leafed trees, wood siding gleams bright white and blue; fences stand taut and upright; roads have neat patches in them, the work of someone who'd never fixed a highway before, but figured it out. People clop by on horseback, clothes stitched with fishing line, baseball hats held together with tape. But there's fat on their midriffs, taken from livestock squealing in backyards, from the crops south of town; looking at them, Marco realizes he hasn't seen a healthy person since Malaysia. On Main Street, the brick cobbles are lined with stands of ruddy vegetables, flower-print clothes, silverware, firewood, a wood stove squatting underneath saddles and tackle, horseshoes looped around an iron ring. In the middle of the street, a band is ripping through Swedish fiddle music that throws out vines of happiness amid the sweet scent of pancakes and lingonberries. The banners from before the collapse still hang on every streetlight—WELCOME TO LINDSBORG—but they look a hundred years too young for what's going on below them. The people here are surviving by going back. There's talk of dismantling the electrical system, using the metal for something else. Maybe we never needed it in the first place.

They put Marco and Dayneesha up in the second floor of the toy shop on Main Street, and that night, there is dancing, to a band of trumpet, accordion, bass, drums, and saw pumping out maniacal polkas. They drink corn liquor that tastes horrible but does the trick. At the pace they're going, Dayneesha knows, half of the town will be up until the next day. She goes out to join them, and they pull her in with a collective whoop; glad you're here, glad you made it. At first she thinks it's just partying, but later, when a wind starts to pick up off the plains and the accordion works harder, the trumpet blares and blows, and the people cry back in ecstasy, she understands that it's defiance. It's a war with the prairie, a war with history and what it did to them, and it doesn't matter whether they're winning; it matters that they're fighting.

By an hour before sunrise, the accordion player has dragged his voice into a ragged yelp; his fingers play fewer notes, but his arms are still nailing the rhythm. Blood runs down the bass player's wrist, he's wrapped his fingers in leather. The drummer's in a stupor, the trumpet player passed out from the liquor an hour ago, and the saw player stands over him, wailing out his own parts and shouting out the trumpet player's lines in ripe harmony as the dancers shout and spin, stomp the groove into the bricks under their feet. Against the brightening sky, Dayneesha thinks she sees Marco on the roof, scanning the land north of them, watching for smoke. She wants to invite him down to join them, but she's beginning to understand. It's about the slaves and the Slick Six, the Aardvark and his years at sea. The bloody footprints he left as he walked across the earth. He found something and lost it, and he'd burn down the world to get it back. Down in the street, in the squeal and thump of a party that still has a few hours left in it, she pities him, and is afraid for everyone else.

Days pass in windy heat, crisp cold, the plains dark under the bowl of the sky. There is still no sign of the New Sioux. No reports from the outlying farms of raids, no men on horses galloping away with vegetables dangling from their saddles. No shooting along the highway; no disappearances of livestock. Maybe they're late, says Lindsborg's mayor, who runs a hardware store at the end of the main drag. He shrugs. I don't know what to tell you. Except that folks around here like you, and you're welcome to stay. There are signs of something else, though, clanking and chugging, the steam-forged tone of a factory whistle warping upward at the end, the trumpeting of an elephant. The refugees from Buhler heard the same sounds the night before the fires, the stampeding animals, the blood running over the cracks in the sidewalk. On the third night of Marco's and Dayneesha's stay in Lindsborg, there are reports that two cows are missing from a farm east of the town. The New Sioux, some say. But then the cows are found farther

north, under the overpass to I-135, lowing at the drizzling sky
from its the dry shadow. Their owners had left the gate open.
The refugees from Buhler are not calmed. They look up into
the hazy clouds, open their mouths, put their tongues out.
Swear they can taste diesel in the rain.

"Come on," the mayor says.

"It rained like that before Buhler too."

"That doesn't mean anything," the mayor says.

"Can you explain it?"

"Can you explain anything that's happened in the last five
years?" the mayor says. "It just happened, okay? It happened."

The mayor was born and raised in Salina, moved to Lindsborg when he was twenty-two because of his wife, a Lindsborg
native with long red hair who refused to leave the house with
her dying parents in it. They buried them and stayed, ran an
antique shop for tourists who wandered off the highways while
driving across the country, who dribbled into town for the
dwindling Swedish festival every summer. The tourists told
them about how crowded it was around New York, how you
could sit in your car and go five miles in three hours, couldn't
walk down the sidewalk in a straight line. They could see it on
television, in the movies, people hanging off of straps on screeching subways, staggering off commuter buses. And the money
was weird: stocks rocketing up and crashing down, people buying one-bedroom apartments in tenement buildings for two
million dollars, people living on two dollars a day. Cars that
cost as much as houses, only to be chewed on by the salt on
northeastern highways in the winter. People taking cars and
trains six hours a day to work and back. Penthouses, public
housing. Most expensive slice of air in the country. Poorest
congressional district. The people on television in suits and
ties shrieking about these issues as hundreds more in suits and
ties shouted at each other behind them, as though it all mattered. They looked out the window, to a brilliant sun throwing
bands of color across the horizon, to the mist rising from the

fields, to the sound of crickets, dogs, a solitary car. Silent fireworks in the sky every night. The mayor walked out onto the porch, turned back toward his wife, who sat on the stairs. Promise me we don't have to leave here.

When the collapse first began, it was just more suits and ties shouting. He didn't pay a lot of attention. But then the television showed people in the street rioting, chairs through windows, flames in the cities on the coast. A few of the television channels disappeared; the gas stations outside of town ran out of gas. Then the shelves in the supermarket started going bare; the price tags came off.

"How much for this box of matches?" he asked the cashier.

"How much you got?"

Then the dollar was gone, the banks were gone. The street became the new market, filled with haggling people. It was weird, he thought, but it didn't seem so bad. They were all playing Old West; they looked like the photographs he'd seen of Salina in the early railroad days, when it was the grain capital of the world, pictures taken from the roof of a building on Santa Fe Avenue, looking down toward the Masonic temple over a rippling surface of hats and carriage tops, horses and umbrellas, the turning flow of skirts. They were photographs you could hear: fiddles and barkers, a pump organ, the numbers for the price of wheat, announcements about when trains were leaving for the rest of the hungry world. But then they heard that the big farms west of them were closing; there was no more government money to run them, not enough people close by to buy what was left. Hundreds of miles of unharvested grain rotting in the fields. Farms black with crows, picking over the remains. A wave of people moving east, half-starved. Where are you going? he asked them. East, they said. Haven't you heard that the towns to the west are dead now? All around Goodland, there's nobody there anymore. It's got to be better to the east. But the mayor looked out over the fields again, the rising mist, the colors in the sky.

"I still don't want to leave," he told his wife.

"Me neither." And smiled. "You'll see. It'll be better than it ever was."

She was right. The town's economic development committee closed their offices, took up farming and masonry, knitting, shoe repair. There's no television out here now except what people get off satellite dishes; a little radio from a few local boys who run the station out of the attic of their parents' house when the power's on; thirty-two computers that still work after five years thanks to the tender ministrations of a dedicated geek able to resurrect the dead. Sometimes they miss the movies. The mayor wants to have Hollywood Night in the main intersection, set up some chairs and throw the picture against the side of a building, and they'll all sit in the summer air, swatting away flies while giants play out the melodrama of a country they're already forgetting the details of. He found a working projector that would do the trick, but he hasn't found any films yet. It makes him sad sometimes; but then he rides out to the farms, comes back to his house, his wife, his children, and wonders why he's so upset when the life he's living now is nothing to be afraid of.

The water in the Caribbean is turquoise, brightening in rings around islands that slope out of the water, rear up with spines of palms, deciduous trees draped in vines. The islands are like sleeping dinosaurs, Zeke thinks; he keeps expecting them to raise their heads from the water on leafy stalks, turn to appraise the *Lucky Sun* as possible prey, then swim off together in a flock, leaving swirls of sand boiling in their wakes. But the islands do not move; people fish among them from wooden boats, laying nets in the water, tying them down. One sail has a snorkel painted on it, half obscured by a mended patch of bright red, a scar from a hurricane that descended on St. Croix two years ago, when some people fled to the jungle in the interior of the island while others stayed to loot. They say that everybody seemed to be armed that day, that there were drums coming from the forest, from places that nobody had thought were inhabited. This planet, Zeke thinks, is just waiting for us to go; then there will be no more history, and the world can go about healing itself from the damage we've done.

They've been at sea for two and a half weeks, following the dots of islands through the South Pacific, the locks of Panama, during which the captain's wife stood at starboard for the entire day. Near the Caribbean coast, a man waved to her from a distant bluff, and she waved back. Captain Bengwe Saloon has become friendly with his property, tells them stories of his pirating, of oil tankers ablaze off Norway, black smoke heaving into the sky, of the time he crept aboard a Chinese cruise ship from an aluminum dinghy, of the girls he knew before he was married. So many girls, he says. His wife knows he's making most of them up, but lets him talk all the same. Hideo, Carolyn, and Zeke are friendly back, share four bottles of rum that almost send Hideo and Zeke into the ocean off of Easter Island. But if they push too far, the captain snaps, puts them back in their cell. Reminds them of who owns them if things don't work out.

Hideo has been avoiding Zeke as much as it's possible to on a fishing boat, and Zeke knows it. He's quiet in the bunks, quiet at dinner. Zeke sees Hideo and Carolyn talking to stern, approaches them and makes a joke involving the phrase "sucking the monkey." Neither of them says anything. What's going on? Zeke later asks Carolyn. She shakes her head. Hideo needs to talk to you. I'm with him, but this is his thing.

The *Lucky Sun* enters the Sargasso Sea, and the ocean slows, the wind slows, there's only the sound of the boat's cranky motor. Hideo comes on deck, walks over next to Zeke. Puts his hands on the rail.

"Soon we will be over Miami," Hideo says.

"This thing can fly?" Zeke says.

"Off of Miami," Hideo says. "You are catching Kari's condition."

"I caught it years ago," Zeke says.

"Yes. Do you remember the job in Miami?"

"Three banks and a Han dynasty sculpture."

"Yes. Did you know that Kimura still has no idea how we did that? He asked. I would not tell."

"I assume you came up here to talk about something else."

"Yes."

"Well then."

". . ."

"Well, is it about Marco?" Zeke says.

"Yes."

"Are you going to make me have this conversation by myself?"

"No. Kari is right. There are things that must be said. You and I must say them."

"I think we said a lot of them five years ago."

"We were not calm then," Hideo says. "We are calm now."

"Then say what you need to say, and be done with it."

"If we succeed in our plan," Hideo says, "I believe we should consider it the Slick Six's last job, our greatest heist yet: stealing an entire island, an entire government. Then, the Slick Six should no longer be."

"So you're just using Marco to get your freedom," Zeke says.

"We did not ask him to free us in Watsonville," Hideo says.

"That's the most pathetic thing I have ever heard you say."

"I am sorry," Hideo says. "But do you think we should return to our former lives—lives that no longer suit any of us, even you—because we owe him?"

"No. I just don't quite understand why you don't want to go back."

"You can stay with him if you want to," Hideo says. "It's your choice."

"You don't see this as a betrayal?"

"It does not matter how I see it. I do not want to go back.

Kari and I do not want to go back. We are tired. We just want to go home."

"That's all Marco wants too."

"He has to find another way to get there."

"I don't think he knows how," Zeke says. "You know this might kill him."

"It will not," Hideo says. "He survived five years in prison. He is too good a fighter to be undone by this."

"But he can't fight this," Zeke says. "Or you."

"No. He cannot."

". . ."

". . ."

"You've both decided, then?" Zeke says. "You and Carolyn? There's nothing I can say that'll change your minds?"

Hideo shakes his head.

"Why didn't you say something sooner?"

"I needed time to think. I have always needed time to think. It does not happen for me right away as it does for you."

"I know."

"Please do not judge Kari and I."

"I never have," Zeke says. "I'm in no position to do that."

"None of us are."

"What will you do instead?" Zeke says.

"We do not know," Hideo says. "That is what freedom is, is it not?"

The sky over Lindsborg is tinged with green and yellow; the clouds swirl above the town as though time is speeding up. A far-off keen rides in on a low rumble that brings people in from the fields, makes animals lie down in their pens; then it rains in torrents, hard drops that bounce off the bricks and explode into sparks until the street sizzles with liquid electricity. But even through the rain's rush, the people can hear the roar of motors, the cries of the performers working the machines. The sound continues throughout the night, and they lie in their bedrooms listening, looking out the windows at the moon's green light. After the rain stops, the refugees from Buhler meet at three in the morning in the main intersection of the town, take a good look at the clay-colored street, the bright paint on the buildings, and head off into the fields to the north. We won't go through that again, they say.

The next day, the wind sweeps across Lindsborg in a steady gust, rattling siding, sending waves of dust across the windows; and as people lean out and close their shutters, run outside to pull the laundry off the line, they can tell that the noise is getting louder, and something sinks in them. For the last few days they'd been comforting themselves with the idea that maybe the circus would pass them by; if they were just quiet enough, it would mistake Lindsborg for abandoned, go stir the ruins of McPherson instead. But no, someone left a candle in the window at night, someone kept the fire in the fireplace burning too long, and the men clinging to the backs of hippopotami lifted their heads, sniffed the wind, and veered northward. As the horde appears on the edge of the world, topping the hill south of town, the flying machines tottering in the air, the people of Lindsborg can hear the circus start to howl, and the sirens on the old fire stations wail their answer. Shotguns are pulled from walls, pistols from drawers; strings of people run from the outlying houses into the center of town until Main Street is a frantic mob of shouting and crying—some running toward the basement of the school, others seeking the safety of crowds, still others grouping together, counting weapons, horses, ammunition. The mayor organizes them fast, sets up a line of men and lumber in a barricade twenty yards from the stoplight at Main and Lincoln, asks if anyone's willing to start fighting now. Five men with horses and shotguns volunteer without saying anything, and the mayor sends them galloping out of town.

They break out of the streets and trees in forty-two seconds and are racing across the earth, the circus rearing up before them in a haze of dust and oil. They careen toward it and split to either side, put lead into trapeze artists and animals, wheel away, are about to return for a second run when forty acrobats spring from the tent at the circus's heart, roll on the ground, and sprint toward them. Two of the riders see what's coming and peel off, but the other three are going too fast to change course, so they glide into an amoeba of flesh that overwhelms them in an instant. The two that escaped look over their shoulders and see only a clot of thrashing limbs, drenched red within a second; then the amoeba pulls itself off the six corpses, regroups, and sprints after the horsemen in a rising cry. The two men turn and take down fifteen in the front, but there are just too many of them. And now the horses aren't taking any more orders; they rear and ditch their riders, leaving the two men on the ground while the mob rushes toward them. The men look at each other, the guns in their hands, then turn and empty the rest of their ammunition into the tide until it pulls them under.

On Main Street, the men behind the barricade hear the blasts from the guns, the screeches of rhinos and elephants, the undulating voices. For one moment, there is a lull in the noise that lets them hope that somehow those five riders turned the circus back; but then they see the smoke rising over the buildings, hear the machines kicking back into motion. The Circus of Industrial Destruction is starting to burn Lindsborg down. It takes only a few minutes for the sky to thicken into a boiling black wall filled with angry fires, and at last the circus emerges from it, churning toward them in a raging wave of metal, hair, and skin. The people behind the barricade start firing into the mass, raise a mist of blood from its ranks, but then a surge of humanity storms from its borders, swells over the barricade, and all discipline is lost in a blast of screams and shouting. For Dayneesha, it's as if a tornado is coming for her; she stands paralyzed, one hand on a green-painted streetlight, watches the carnage rush toward her, blanches at the stench of offal, sees one man's stomach opened up by a piece of scrap metal, three more torn apart by lions, their faces a hash of anguish and surprise. Behind it all, she sees the tent looming on the elephants' backs, bucking and swaying in the smoke. Seven clowns are running toward her now, bodies smeared with gore and trailing tattered cloth, and she has a chance to send out a message to her family, into the ether. Can you hear me? I tried to find you. I really tried.

Then, as if by magic, her attackers stumble in unison, clutch their bellies; an arm flies off of one, a head rolls off of another, and as they all tumble to the ground, Marco's hand is on her shoulder. He nods at her once, as if to remind her—he told her he'd get her out of whatever they got into, didn't he?—looks into the chaos, cocks his head as if he's doing math, then leaps, climbs hand over hand to the top of the streetlight, draws two swords, jumps, and turns invisible. For the next few seconds, she can't see the man or his limbs working, but watches a swerving line of death cut through the horde, men and animals falling away on either side of it. A cry of alarm rises from the attackers: They're trying to regroup, but it's way too late for that. Marco continues to wreak havoc across them, streaking through them like a sentient bolt of lightning, jagged and unrelenting, pulling the flying contraptions out of the air, breaking the machines, at last disappearing into the tent; it bulges like a balloon for four seconds before caving in on itself. All at once the circus is in disarray; it comes apart at the seams, and in a collective moan, the pieces slow, their denizens flee, are brought down by gunfire from the rallying towns-people. It's over fast, the circus dispersing into the fields, shedding its dead and wounded, howling into the horizon. Dayneesha looks at the people in the street, dyed red, hugging their children. There are legs on the sidewalk. A torso draped over a mailbox. Above her, two arms from two different people are hooked at the elbow over the bend of the streetlight. There's a head under the tire of a rusting yellow wheelbarrow. She can hear the blood draining into the sewers, and looks at her own hands; the palms are smeared dark red, as though she's about to leave a print on a white curtain, draw a turkey around it.

To the south, the town is still burning; they'll lose a third of it before they can get the fires to stop. All around are the wails of townspeople finding their dead, the shamble of feet moving among the corpses. An elephant lies on its side under the stoplight at the intersection of Main and Lincoln, succumbing to sixteen bullet wounds, tusks scraping against the bricks, its lungs rising and falling, a giant bellows filling with water. The mayor and six other people stand around it, talking; then the mayor puts a shotgun in the animal's mouth and unloads it into its skull. The dead circus performers lie all around them, limbs disjointed, clothes in shreds, the blood soaking the bright colors into red, purple, black. They never got a chance. Once they were farmers, mill workers, truckers. They worked gas stations in the middle of the empty land, stood under a tent of fluorescent light at night and looked out at the dark highway. Nobody ever seemed to stop. They waited tables in a family restaurant with walls still stained from the days of cigarettes, everyone smiling, everyone trying to get along. They drove fifteen miles to get a toothbrush. Their towns were withering away even before the collapse, row after row of boarded-up storefronts and empty brick thoroughfares, the curls of masonry cracking in the cold, falling into the street. A ruin at the end of the sidewalk, the sign for a local opera company from seventy-five years ago painted on the last wall standing, just about bleached away by years of sun and snow. On the gigantic farms, machines dug enormous circles onto the earth, giant spiders moving over the dirt. The horizon spiked with grain mills, power stations, tanks of natural gas. Church steeples. When the collapse came at last, they were at first no worse off, for there were no jobs to lose, no assets to liquidate. Then, when the food stopped getting out to them, they were much worse off, starving in the midst of a thousand miles of rotting grain. By the time Cal found them, they were ready for him; after the jaws of industry and commerce were done with them, they had nothing else.

The people of Lindsborg start moving their bodies to the sidewalk when a gasp gargles from the shell of a chassis nearby, a leg kicks, and four women with guns surround it, ready to shoot. But it's just a man, tied and bound, twitching and hurt, covered in gashes and scratches, semicircular wounds that one of the women realizes are bites taken out of him by someone else, by many other people. Her face wrinkles, softens, and she bends down and touches him with her free hand, just two fingers on his cheek. He flinches, stifles a shout; then his eyes open, and the woman swears she sees them flood with life.

"Am I in Cincinnati yet?" he says.

"No, honey," she says. "You're in Kansas now."

And just like that, Tyrone Fly's past spins away from him at last, swinging into the sky over the carnage and mayhem below. His stints as a slave in Eureka and Watsonville, the killing of a woman. The waiting for his ex, always waiting, thinking he would go and find her, she would come and get him, they would meet in a truck stop bathroom, the parking lot of a burned-out mall, a bridge over the Ohio River. It has all been too much, too much for him to bear, and as another woman bends down and wipes his face with the cuff of her sleeve, he lets it all go. And all at once, the gauzy clouds in the atmosphere above him, the panes of glass in the windows around him flowing out of their frames, the stretcher beneath him, carried by dirty, blood-streaked hands, are miracles to him, and he can't keep from laughing. It starts as a smile that shudders into a chuckle by the time he's suspended over the street. As they bring him into a furniture store to tend to him, he is guffawing so hard it hurts, but there's no stopping him now; he laughs for another half an hour, through the pain of the doctor's ministrations, the worrying of his wounds, until he can't take another moment of being awake, and he sleeps like he's a new father, his child slumbering in his arms.

"You saved him," Dayneesha says to Marco. "You saved them all. Everyone who's left, they owe you their lives." They're at a party in the fields south of town in Marco's honor; the people of Lindsborg drink until they're blind, make him an honorary sheriff five times over. Men and women come up to him, try to crush him in their arms. Thank you for protecting my child. If there's anything you ever need, anything I can do. Marco is already moving beyond them; Dayneesha can tell. He did it to protect her. He did it because he wanted to be good. But Dayneesha's thinking about those blurry images she saw through security cameras, back when the Slick Six were slick. About Hideo coming back from Johannesburg, how he'd just handed over the information, said nothing about what had happened. About what they're going to do in New York. They'll make it look like Main Street after the circus visited, the pieces of human beings, the smell sweet and rotten, rolling over them all. He saved this town, Dayneesha thinks, but that street is where Marco is all the time. He carries a wasteland within him, fallow soil wet with blood. It scares her. The whole thing scares her.

"I'm not going," she says to Marco in the morning.

"What do you mean?" he says.

"I mean to Salina. I can't go. You can do it yourself, right?"

" . . . "

" . . . "

"Yes," Marco says. "But what about New York? Are you coming to New York?"

" . . . "

"We need you. You need to make the calls. Move the information."

"I can do it from anywhere," Dayneesha says. "I don't need to go with you."

"And what about after New York?"

" . . . "

A few days later, reports come in from the outskirts of

Salina that the Sioux have arrived, so Marco takes the road north, sloping up from the motels and the old antique shop in the metal barn, out again into fields spiked with telephone poles. Dayneesha watches him until he's gone, hates herself for hoping that he might not come back.

The road into Salina is a four-lane strip lined with auto dealerships, malls, fast food restaurants, Chinese buffets, and their empty parking lots, signs marking the state of commerce at the time of collapse. The movie theater lists titles from five years ago, letters missing. LUNCH SPECIAL $5.99. ZERO DOWN FINANCING. CABLE TV, WEEKLY RATES. PROPANE SOLD HERE. The end of a car angles out of a burnt-out convenience store window, a casualty of the last days of cheap gasoline, when the road was empty and the Salinans ran drag races down its middle. Nothing else left to do. In the left-turn lane, a long row of horse droppings, gathering flies.

The Sioux on guard approach Marco with caution; they can tell what he is. They escort him to the steps of the Masonic temple on Santa Fe Avenue, a mammoth cube of a building with a Greek portico with six columns. To the left of the stairs stands a statue of a man wearing a fez, leaning on a crutch in his right hand, a child sitting in the nook of his right arm. On the pedestal, the relief of a scimitar, a crescent of horns, a star hanging on a metal chain. It all seems to mean something, but Marco can't decipher it; it's just another set of symbols from another age.

Through the metal doors of the temple, in a marbled lobby with a checkered floor, Robert Blackfeather Sherman sits in a red leather wingback chair before a great door. His wife, whose pregnancy swelled from invisible to mammoth in two days, is sitting on a yellow blanket, legs out in front of her at almost a ninety-degree angle. She is prone to bursts of superhuman energy, strength that humans shouldn't have; last week a horse died midtrot, toppled on its side, pinned its rider—an eleven-year-old boy—beneath it. She flipped the horse off him in a single heave, put the boy on his feet, told him he'd live.

Since they left Wisconsin, Robert Blackfeather Sherman's dreams have become epic. Two nights ago, on the Kansan plain north of Salina, amid the oceanic breathing of his people and their animals, he dreamed that his tribe had grown to swarm across the country, repopulate its dead cities; they tore down all of the buildings of concrete and plastic and replaced them with spindly towers made from cornstalks and buffalo bones. They were changing all the names, taking down the green metal signs and putting up their own, calling the streets after their ancestors. Crazy Horse Drive. Standing Bear Road. And he stood at the center of the country, not far from where he is now, the beating heart of a proud nation. So he came to Salina expecting great tidings; he isn't surprised that Marco Oliveira is before him, kneeling on the marble floor—not in homage, but out of protection, because Sherman can tell how lethal he is. Robert Blackfeather Sherman's eyebrows rise only a little at what Marco proposes. Three months ago, he would have laughed. But instead he has the guards bring Marco outside again, then sits in his wingback chair, scratching behind his ear.

"You're taking his offer seriously," she says.

"Yes," he says.

"It's insane. You know that, right?"

"Yes. But everything we've done in the last five years has been insane."

"True."

"What do you think I should do?" he says.

"Your dreams are telling you to do it."

"But you have more common sense than they do."

She pushes herself off the floor and goes to him. His eyes rise to meet hers, and they're back on the reservation, when they first met. He's standing in front of the post office, a map in his hands, water around his feet. She's in the driver's seat of a pickup truck that's older than her father. Their eyes lock for two seconds as she's driving by, and then she turns to the open window and spits. Their lives are running out ahead of them, she thinks, waving at them from the horizon. What else can they do but follow?

"Just one question," she says. "Do you trust him?"

"No," he says. "I think he knows not what he does."

"But you don't think it matters."

"No."

"Then I think we should do it." She shakes her head. "New York City."

He strides out of the temple. Marco is waiting on the steps; the two soldiers standing next to him tense up, guns pointed at his head and stomach, waiting for Sherman's word. He lowers their guns with a wave of his hand.

"We'll follow you," he says. "We leave in two days."

Marco smiles, they shake hands, and Robert Blackfeather Sherman sees it again, as he did when Marco knelt before him just a few minutes ago: The light warps around Marco Angelo Oliveira; the colors of the trees and sky stretch and smear, as if Marco is an empty place in the shape of a man and the earth and air around him are screaming to fill it.

PART THREE

★ THE BIG ★
NOW

History builds a prison for all of us, people and nations, and most of us stay in it, serving our sentences. Some of us seem to think we need to tunnel out with a spoon. Some of us look for the open window. And a few of us know there's really no prison there at all.

· DOCTOR SAN DIEGO OF THE AMERICOIDS ·

CHAPTER XII.

Revolutions.

The Colorado morning starts cold, a bite that nips the skin, talks about the coming frost. Then the sun angles horizontal across Limon, paints zebra stripes of bright pink and shadow over the roads and the Americoids' bus, which is still jackknifed in the grocery store parking lot; bursts into the windows of the houses where the Americoids sleep, in oblivion. On the bus, they slumbered through thunderstorms and swerving near-accidents, hailstones as big as a fist; a little sunlight is nothing. But Keira Shamu, snoring faceup on a couch in a sagging bungalow, wakes up after a minute of the light tickling her eyelids. She snorts, blows her nose, wonders how that happened, but then realizes it's the Vibe tickling the atmosphere around her, making her magnetic, pulling her toward the hinges of the door. Time to go. Time to move, if you want to see what's going down on the eastern shore of this dissolute nation.

She finds Doctor San Diego meditating in a handstand on the roof of the train station, greeting the beginning of the day, makes her steps quiet at first because she's afraid of startling him. But he knows she's there; he was with her when she woke up. Greetings and congratulations, for we get to live another day.

"I need to get to New York," she says.

Doctor San Diego lifts one hand off the roof. "I understand," he says, and she has the uncanny sense that he does, even though she never told him what Marco told her about his plan, in the dark near the Snake River. The theft that stops the clocks.

"We've been here for a while now," she says.

He lifts the other hand off the roof, maintains his position. "Yes."

"Do you think we could start heading east?"

"It's not for me to say," Doctor San Diego says. "You'd have to talk to Felix."

She finds Felix Purple sitting on the rotting white porch of his baby's house, eyes closed and facing the sun, a cup of coffee in his hand, curling out steam. He opens his eyes when he hears her step.

"Keira!" he says. "How goes it, my friend?"

"It goes," she says.

"Getting used to Colorado?"

"You could say that. Look, there's something we need to discuss," she says. "About getting to New York."

"You, or all of us?"

"What's the difference?"

Felix Purple thinks about that. The difference, that is. Her arms. Her mouth open in sleep, showing yellow teeth. Their boy's fat fingers. Bacon frying in a shallow pan. She's my woman and I'm her man.

"My definition of 'us' appears to have changed," Felix Purple says. "My tribe has grown smaller. More sedentary. Once we were hunters. Now we are gatherers."

"But we need you to drive."

"Someone else can drive. It's a bus, not a spaceship."

But none of the other Americoids will do it; they don't want to be held responsible, condemned to sobriety. Driving's a big job, man. I'm sure you'll find someone else to do it. Hey, let me know when we're leaving.

"Why don't you drive?" Felix Purple says.

"I don't have a license," Keira Shamu says.

"You don't need a license"—he puts quotes around the word with his fingers—"to do anything."

"I mean I don't know how to drive. At all."

"Oh," Felix Purple says. "Well, don't start now. It's a raw deal."

It's the same with all of the Americoids she finds; not right now, maybe later, why don't we wait a couple weeks, what's the hurry? What do you want to go to New York for, anyway? She tells them she's gotta tear across the country for the big thing that's happening, can't you feel it coming? But it's Zeke too, the lameness of his jokes, his detached calmness; the charge that jumped between them when the drugs were in her, the gunshots outside, the fire in the valley. She needs to know if it'll jump again without those things, though even if it does, she has no idea what she'll do. She's standing near the bus in the orange afternoon, Letty Frizzell sliding out of a house behind her, about to give up and just go herself, leave her people behind, when Asia Sherman strolls up in her jacket, hands in pockets, the words a little more faded in back after Nevada, her past that much further away, but still where she's from.

"People are saying you want to go to New York," she says. "That true?"

Keira Shamu nods, and Asia Sherman nods back. They don't even have to talk about it. Asia Sherman has been thinking about her father, the visions in Pine Ridge, the shootings up and down the Midwest, gurgling wounds, blue smoke from gun barrels. It was still violence, people dying, but maybe her father was right, maybe it was also retribution, the calling in of the debt of history. She needed to see it for herself. And there was the hope, a moth in her head, that maybe her father would return to her, the one that existed when their radio was whole, sound thrown from a distant antenna, and the world was composed of her relatives' faces, the clink of bottles, her parents' feet squeaking across the linoleum floor.

They leave on the next train heading east, crammed into a car with fifteen other people and eight crates full of pulleys and kitchenware that the train's owner swears won't shift in transit. From the roof of the station, Doctor San Diego watches her go, blesses the train with his grooviness. He follows it with his eye for longer than he has ever followed anything, keeps it in his mind when it's out of sight. He's trying to slow time, stay between the precious seconds as long as he can, for he knows what's coming. At last, the Vibe appears in front of him, reaches out its hand. I only exist to serve you, Doctor San Diego says. And you have been most faithful, the Vibe replies. The doctor stands up, takes a good look around, at the broad, bright sky hazy with thin clouds, the glint of the sun off the rails, the red hills rolling away into plains and forests, meadows and beaches, towns and cities. The country he loves, the people he loves. He doesn't know how to say good-bye to it all. The Vibe takes his hand and pulls him close, speaks into his head, the last lines of the long, dark joke of American history; and Doctor San Diego laughs, closes his eyes, and fades into the air.

The other Americoids sense his departure, drift out of Limon by train, by bicycle, walking in a line along the highway north toward the Rockies, because Denver's got to have a few parties left in it. They trudge on the shoulder by the dozen, turn around and stick out their thumbs whenever anything drives by, act surprised when nobody stops. In time, the only thing left of the Americoids in Limon is Felix Purple and the bus, its parts eroding away from salvage and casual robbery. The windows leave first, then the tires. Soon the whole caravan is up on blocks and jacks, except for the two wheels with slow leaks in them. Then the mattresses inside go, the engine, the doors. Screws, panels, rivets. At last, people start blowtorching off sections of the metal walls. Within six months, only parts of the chassis are left, and Felix Purple salutes them

every time he passes, his kid on his shoulders, his woman's
hand in his. Now and again there's a twinge, Highway 61 in
front of him, lost in the rain near Clarksdale and that famous
crossroads, the wipers moving from side to side. A sausage
cooked over a fire under a full moon, crashing waves. But it
happens less and less all the time.

In New York's harbor, the *Rosalita* is still at anchor a short
swim from the rim of the floating city, its hull covered with
graffiti in thirty-two languages, an explosion of faces, animals, buildings, the work of artists who wanted to mark the
famous vessel. The prison ship is now a sign, posted at the limits of the Aardvark's power—there's a blackened smudge near
the stern, the bruise left when the Aardvark tried to blow a
hole in the hull by driving a boat packed with explosives into
it. It should have succeeded. Everyone in the *Rosalita* was
asleep, the former prisoners, the new citizens, even Big Mother,
who should have been watching that night. But the bomb went
off early, illuminated the harbor, forced a pulse of water against
the shore. Big Mother woke from the flash, saw the flower-shaped
cloud rise above him lit from below by the sinking boat's fire,
the *Rosalita* rocking on the tide.

Maggot Boy Johnson is on watch now, though he knows it's
pointless. Nothing'll put the *Rosalita* down until it finds the
Mozambican coast and Malaysia crawls out of the hull. He's
looking over the city's cluster of towers, clear and sharp with
shadow in the early October light. Then he notices a rustling
among them, like millions of birds flying from the buildings
together, wings flashing in the sun; it's leaves turning in the
wind at the ends of limbs, growing from great trunks of maples
and oaks that push their way between the skyscrapers, rising
and thickening until they've cleared the concrete heights. They
unfurl their crowns, and the branches spread over the length
and breadth of Manhattan. Brooklyn and Queens become a
forest that sends the smell of pollen across the water. Inside the
ship, a satellite phone rings; Maggot Boy Johnson hears Big

Mother's hello, startled from sleep. A string of uh-huhs, then Big Mother's steps on the stairs to the deck.

"It's time for us to go. According to the plan," Big Mother says to Maggot Boy Johnson.

"I know," Maggot Boy Johnson says.

"You got the papers?"

"Right here." Maggot Boy Johnson pats the briefcase in his left hand.

"What kind of a name is Kuala Lumpur, anyway?"

"Capital of Malaysia," Maggot Boy Johnson says, and smiles, a big wide thing. He turns to the city. "Don't worry. We'll be back soon."

From his tower, the Aardvark watches the *Rosalita* swing its bow northward, churn its way up the river under the skeleton of the George Washington Bridge. He leaves the window, sits behind his desk, tilts back in a leather chair, places a pink sugar-coated amphetamine tablet on his tongue that slides to the back of his mouth, angles down his throat. His empire is crumbling beneath him. The slave revolts keep coming east; there are signs of unrest in Ohio already. He could swear that they're spreading faster and faster, a wave sweeping out of California; by the time it reaches New York, the Aardvark thinks, he'll only see it for a second, a glimmer of light on the New Jersey horizon; then it'll rush over him before he can run or say a word. And then there's Kimura, calling in his debt. It's not just that Kimura did it, the Aardvark thinks. He was entitled to it whenever he wanted it. The Aardvark remembers the pagoda in Osaka, how Kimura took him in, all smiles. This will be so good for both of us, Kimura said.

"I don't know how to thank you," the Aardvark said.

"Thank me by repaying me," Kimura said, "though I know I do not have to say that." He waved his hand as if swatting away a tuft of dandelion down. "The money means nothing. It is numbers on paper. Our reputations, the ground beneath our feet, are all we have."

But now the *Rosalita* is gone, and the light plays on the Hudson. Something's happening, the Aardvark thinks. Something's about to happen. Where is Marco?

A few miles southwest near the bottom end of Manhattan, Maria Lista Sandinista hasn't left her jail cell in two weeks, says she's on a hunger strike, but she's really been finishing her bomb. It lies under her bed now, complete, bars of explosive hung with wires that squirm into an electrical switch, a battery. She's amazed that such a small thing will be able to do so much harm, her orchid bulb, ready to bloom petals of fire. Sometimes at night she curls herself around the bomb, holds it against her chest, as though it were a small dog, an infant cub, closed eyes and soft claws, paws working the air. Her fingers tangle in the wires, wrap around the fuel, and she thinks: Where is Marco?

Seven hundred miles south, the Free State of Asheville is getting slaves from the west, freed by the revolts. They arrive in scores, packed into the backs of trucks meant for livestock. We heard we could be safe here, they say. We heard we could be free. The fields around the town are a thronging city of wooden beams draped with laundry and mossy blankets; they're starting to build houses from the woods nearby, dig trenches for plumbing and sewage. They've already run a few power lines into the camp, siphoning electricity off the town; when it gets dark they eat under a string of naked bulbs, turn on the radio to listen to whatever the country-music freaks are playing from their station on top of the next mountain over: the Louvin Brothers, the Delmore Brothers, Hank, Hank, Hank. They say they're starting to like it here. Johanna toured the new city yesterday, kicked up the dirt on the paths between canvases and tarps, let the steam from stews curl into her nostrils.

"You're all from the revolts?" she said.

"That's right."

"Are there a lot more of you coming?"

"Oh, yes," they said. "Many more. Unless you can make some other place free too."

She's heard the stories about how the revolts are spreading, a virus through the body of the Aardvark's domain ever since the magic happened in Watsonville. There's not a doubt in her head about who's responsible. She's seen the pictures of some of the corpses, a model of how tidy death can be. And every couple of days, just-liberated slaves show up in her office, at her house, saying they've got a message for her. The words are getting garbled because they've passed from mouth to mouth, but she can hear him speaking through every one of those strangers' throats, the baritones and sopranos, the accents that take in the ice near the Canadian border, the sand near Mexico, the mist rising off the Oklahoma fields, the trees hanging over the hollows of Kentucky. The street corners of the cities on the coast, the towns on the rivers. Am I good enough yet?

Where is Marco? she thinks. And looks at her deputies, the growing town.

"Ralph?" she says.

"Ma'am," Ralph says.

"How would you like to be mayor?"

"Do you mean for a day?"

"No. For the rest of my term. Into the next one, I suppose, if you win the election."

"Hadn't given it much thought."

"Well, think fast. I'm leaving."

"When?"

"Tomorrow. I have someone to find."

She's up before dawn, leaves the door to her house open, a sign on the table that says USE ANYTHING YOU NEED, and walks down the mountain toward the interstate, a duffel bag in her right hand, a shotgun in her left. It occurs to her while she's hitching a ride toward Tennessee that she doesn't even know where to start. But the highway she's heading toward runs north or south along the spine of the Appalachians. All she has to do is pick one, start asking the world where he's gone; sooner or later, it will have to answer.

The swinging arms of I-787, which runs along the Hudson in Albany, saw their last big trucks years ago, and for a month or two, stillness reigned upon them; they became sculptures, monuments to the industrial age. Then the first buildings were erected on them, metal garden sheds with windows cut out of them, sleek trailers with the wheels taken off; flanked by people on horses and bicycles, a few stray cars, small pickups that ran on vegetable oil. They took out the guardrails separating the road from the river; cut them into pieces; welded them into piers that grew one by one from the shore, reaching into the river's current, straight, bowed, or sagging at the mercy of the heat and cold, the wet and dry of the seasons. But it was enough. Small ships left Albany, sailed down to New York, came back again. Near the strap of land that runs from downtown Albany to the Route 7 bridge over the river is a market, rank with the products of the fields to the east and west, glimmering with machinery from the south. The old houses on cobbled streets on both sides of the river fill with the finery of the new age: furniture from Asia, fabric from Europe, paintings from the latest exhibition in Mumbai. There are women who trade with seventeen countries from a cell phone on Troy's shore. It's an old joke already that they've never had it so good since everything went to shit, but it's true. The city's heart beats now like it did centuries ago, when it fought New York City for supremacy of the state. They never forgot that they'd lost.

Albany's port is presided over by the Queen of Delmar, who floats above the river in a pink-and-purple hot-air balloon, directing the movement of ships on the water. During the day, she says, she can see as far as Poughkeepsie. Nobody believes her, but they can't explain how she knows what's coming, day or night, or how the balloon stays aloft; they've never seen it come down. The queen sees the *Rosalita* churning north, the colors flashing on its hull, and sends a signal to the *Lucky Sun*, already there, waiting. Zeke, Hideo, and Carolyn stand on the pier as the *Rosalita* docks and the gangway is lowered; two men—one gigantic, one wormy and skinny—stride toward them.

"Zeke Hezekiah and Carolyn Crowley? I'm Big Mother. This is Maggot Boy Johnson."

Zeke hands a suitcase to Big Mother.

"Your down payment," he says.

Maggot Boy Johnson hands Carolyn a briefcase with water stains on it.

"The papers to land in New York," he says.

Hideo is holding a very large suitcase that he's having trouble carrying.

"Where is Marco?" he says.

The Queen of Delmar sends a signal to the piers to make room, lots of it. The crowd parts, and the people on the pier can see a great mass moving forward from under the overpasses. Marco appears from out of nowhere, scares the crap out of everyone; shakes Big Mother's and Maggot Boy Johnson's hands, then finds a way to hug the three of the Slick Six present at once.

"You're here," Marco says. "I can't believe you're all here." I've never seen him so happy, Zeke thinks.

"Is Dayneesha with you?" Hideo says.

"She says she'll join us when this is over."

Zeke looks at Hideo, at Carolyn. You going to tell him it's over already? he says with his eyes. But they won't look at him.

"Where is our army?" Hideo says.

The sounds of horses, shambling axles, voices speaking in sharp syllables; and the war party of the New Sioux moves from the city onto the highway, all leather, calico, and rifle metal, faces hardened by wind, eyes appraising the prison ship, the small band standing in front of it. They've come a long way, through Ohio and Pennsylvania, up into New York, unused to traveling so far in such unchanging, gloomy weather, though they could feel the days shortening, the darkness coming earlier; feel, too, the shades of their people rising to watch them, the wars between tribes forgiven so they could move as one, put out their hands, touch the riders as they passed. Robert Blackfeather Sherman rides in front, his face painted for conflict, his soldiers fanned out on both sides, jackets creaking against saddles, bows and machine guns angled across their backs. The Sioux form a thick semicircle at the end of the pier, and Robert Blackfeather Sherman dismounts, strides forward. With a grunt, Hideo lifts the suitcase.

"This is yours," he says.

Robert Blackfeather Sherman shoulders it with ease. "For our trouble," he says.

"Yes."

"And land besides, if we succeed."

"Yes," Hideo says. "And land besides."

Robert Blackfeather Sherman turns around, faces his people, and a unified shout bursts from the New Sioux that volleys across the river, into the hills. From the decks of the *Rosalita*, Maggot Boy Johnson can see the city curl into the earth behind them, the Iroquois climb out of the rocks to stand along the water's edge. A wraith with white hair and gray skin, wrapped in a blanket filthy with tuberculosis and smallpox, hobbles over to Robert Blackfeather Sherman, beckons with a bony finger. This was a chief who had watched his towns and crops burned on the shores of the lakes to the west, his people driven from their country into exile or death on reservations. His descendants lingered along the interstates at night, threw rocks at the windshields of tractor trailers growling by, while farms and factories rose and fell around them, cities were built and abandoned, the canal the revolutionaries had shot across the state filled with silt. What was it all for? The Sioux chief leans over in the saddle so the old man can whisper in his ear, and his voice enters Maggot Boy Johnson's head: I'm sorry it came to this, that we couldn't stop them. I'm sorry for what they did to us, and then for what they did to you. And Robert Blackfeather Sherman puts his hand on the old man's shoulder, looks up at the *Rosalita,* sees Maggot Boy Johnson watching him, and knows that he can see it too, hear it too.

In New York City, Jeannette Winderhoek is at the window of the Aardvark's tower again, watching the sun go down over New Jersey. The sunsets are paler than they used to be, she thinks, now that so much of the pollution's gone. When both sides of the river were mobbed with cars and trucks, the sunsets used to be glorious, rich with colors the world couldn't have made on its own, except during catastrophes, eruptions. That's what we'd done to the place, she thinks—made it into the inside of a volcano exploding all around us, all the time. She supposes it's better now; but sometimes she misses those colors, the taste of fumes on her tongue. She misses candy bars, Twinkies, and Mallomars. She misses all the people. She'll be walking along a sidewalk in midtown at 5:15 on a Tuesday afternoon, and her brain will repopulate the block with people in raincoats, holding umbrellas aloft, swinging briefcases and purses, shouting into cell phones, hailing cabs, climbing onto buses with windows foggy from the crowd already inside. She wonders if there's any way she might return to that someday; if there's anything she could do to get all those people to come back. She looks down to the river; looks again to make sure.

"The *Rosalita* is back, sir," she says.

The Aardvark staggers to the window beside her, watches the ship cut a curving wake in the darkening water, heading for the 34th Street pier. At first, because he doesn't know about Mozambique, the Aardvark thinks it's going to plow into the dock, run itself aground, it's lined with explosives, a nuclear device, germs from Nairobi. He's so distracted by the thought of it that he doesn't even notice the *Lucky Sun* skirt the *Rosalita,* pirouette around the island, and dock at the 42nd Street pier near the United Nations building, even closer to where the Aardvark is now.

"Miss Winderhoek," the Aardvark says.

She picks up the phone, dials three digits. "Send police to the 34th Street pier," she says. "As soon as we can board the *Rosalita*, arrest everyone on board."

The *Rosalita* docks, lowers its gangway, and a squadron of policemen gather at the pier to greet them. Two sergeants board the ship, disappear into the bridge, then come back out with nobody in tow.

"What just happened?" the Aardvark says.

His phone rings.

"Um," says the police sergeant on the other end, "I'm a little confused."

"How's that," Jeannette Winderhoek says.

"The *Rosalita* has full permission to land."

"Given by whom?"

"Your boss."

Jeannette Winderhoek looks at the Aardvark's desk, the bottle of amphetamines. On the Queens side of the East River, Kuala Lumpur, forger and counterfeiter, is on the roof of her building, watching the *Lucky Sun* dock at 42nd Street. Her phone rings; she knows who it is immediately from the static crackling on the signal through the Kansas atmosphere.

"Check's in the mail," Dayneesha says. "Your Singapore account."

"Thanks," Kuala Lumpur says.

"You did excellent work. As always."

"I always try to do my best."

"So what are you going to do with the money?"

"I always liked Argentina."

"You taking Nerve with you?"

"He won't go. He's still waiting."

"I get that," Dayneesha says.

"Sorry, Day."

"Don't mention it," Dayneesha says. "I know we're supposed to say good-bye now, but I've stopped doing that."

"At the next good party, then," Kuala Lumpur says.

"Right. At the next good party."

The next plane for Buenos Aires via São Paulo leaves tomorrow morning. In a few hours, Kuala Lumpur will leave Nerve half of the money the Slick Six gave her, in the form of Japanese treasury bills. A note attached to the documentation: Thanks for saving my ass five years ago; now get out of here, he's not coming back. In Buenos Aires, she'll buy a three-bedroom apartment in Recoleta, spend her days drinking coffee with sugar, her evenings sipping limoncello with the owner of the French bistro at the end of the block. He'll make the liquor himself in the basement, where the stones smell of cinnamon and lemon rinds and he insists on listening to Carlos Gardel, who's the reason he came to the country in the first place. When her new neighbors learn where she's been for the last few years, they'll turn reverent, as they do for survivors of bombings in Colombia, political purges in Chile, diseases in Central Africa that killed everyone else.

"What was it like?" the restaurant owner will ask.

"You should know," she'll say. "It happens here all the time."

"Yes, but we've always bounced back."

"So can we."

"Of course," he'll say. "But the first bounce is the hardest, I think."

In his tower, the Aardvark has his palms against the window. The things that he paid Marco to do, the dirt on the runway in Peru. A hawk through sparrows.

"There's only one squadron down there, Miss Winderhoek?" he says.

"Sir—" Jeannette Winderhoek says.

"—Send more down."

The policemen's helmets are too loose, too tight, their uniforms hang where they shouldn't, but they do their best to line up. The head of the squadron is already barking the terms of arrest through a bullhorn as the *Rosalita*'s cargo doors begin to open. The policemen prepare to surge forward, but they're stopped all at once by a full-throated, ululating scream, soon joined by dozens more, the whinnying of horses, the stamp of hooves against metal. Then the first of the New Sioux race onto the pier in a tight whip of a line, loading their weapons on the fly. They trample the squadron and race down the middle of 34th Street. Two blocks from the shore, another group of policemen is more prepared for them; they form a blockade across the street and start shooting at the shapes streaking toward them in the dying light, under streetlights buzzing on one by one. Three of the Sioux are knocked from their horses, fall into a jumble of limbs; the rest steady their guns and pull out Molotov cocktails, let fly with another war cry, and the police line disappears in a cloud of blood and fire. When they reach the Empire State Building, the tower the Mohawk built, Robert Blackfeather Sherman turns his horse, points a flare gun toward the sky, and lets loose a rocket that draws a trunk of smoke high above the city, then sends off branches of green light, fronds of color that turn the glass around them into mirrors. At this signal, the Sioux planted all around the city burst out of hiding and begin to take their island back.

Charlene Duchamp is in her office in the South Bronx, her feet up on her desk, the window to the river open so she can hear the first attacks. For the last two days, she and her boys have been shuttling back and forth between Albany and New York, snaking through the city to the subway stations and sneaking the Sioux into them. Someone always saw the drops: a man with a mustache sitting in front of a deli, a woman sitting on the curb smoking a cigarette next to a green station wagon up on blocks, three kids on a fire escape playing with a rat on a twine leash. They stared at the Sioux, at their half-shaved heads, the ends of their guns peeping out from under their jackets. The Sioux stared back. Nobody ever said anything.

She picks up her phone after the second ring.

"Did it work?" she says.

"They're taking the city now," Dayneesha says. "Can you hear it?"

Charlene goes to the window, phone under her chin.

"Yeah," she says. "A little."

"What does it sound like?" Dayneesha says.

Charlene holds the phone out of the window. Across the river, an explosion blooms, then the report of another, of sirens; and then the power in northern Manhattan is out. Above the dark apartment buildings, Charlene can see the glow of midtown, of the Aardvark's tower. Shouts and screams, machine-gun fire. Isolated shots. The warbling war cries bouncing off of the brick towers of the projects. Charlene thinks of the riots, the fires leaping out of windows. People sinking in the river. Bad times. But this life she has now, flying across the country blasting Stax, always a bit of money in her pocket, always with friends nearby, always a bed to sleep in, would never have been possible without them. She puts the phone back under her chin.

"You hear all that?" Charlene says.

"No."

"It sounds like mayhem. It sounds like five years ago. Like we're all going to have to start over again."

The Aardvark's phone won't shut up. All around his tower, smoke pours into the clouds, rising from police stations, roadblocks, power stations. The stutters of machine guns ricochet up to him, tap through the glass. Even in the dark and from so far above, the Aardvark can swear he sees them, people on horseback, one hand on the reins, the other swinging a firebomb on a long rope; the rider lets it go, and it spins into a storefront, starts another blaze.

"Miss Winderhoek," the Aardvark says.

"Yes."

"You are hereby relieved of my employ. Don't say it has been a pleasure serving me. I know it hasn't. Just one thing before you go: Please make sure my family is out of the building. They don't deserve this."

Jeannette Winderhoek walks to her desk, high heels tocking against the floor. She snaps her briefcase shut, walks out, without smiling or looking at him. Presses the button to call the elevator, waits for four seconds. Looks down at her feet. Before the elevator arrives, she has headed down the stairs instead. The elevator rings, a sharp chime, and the doors slide open; then the power goes out, and the entire room, the entire island, is dark. The buildings have become their shadows, and in the Aardvark's office there's only the gray light from the last of the sun, the angry orange glow from the fires below. All across the island of Manhattan it's like that, and people huddle in their apartments, listen to the screams outside, figure they've got to stop soon, it can't go on like this much longer. In the jail downtown the darkness is almost perfect; the emergency generator, long ago eviscerated for its moving parts, doesn't kick in. Ten seconds later one of the guards is down, and six prisoners run from block to block, unlocking all the cells to shouts and giggles, clapping and cheering. A couple hundred inmates have already started a party in the cafeteria; they'll miss everything that's going on outside, assume when they emerge that it's been that way for years. But Maria Lista Sandinista is out on the blackened streets in minutes, listening to what's going down around her. She recognizes it at once: It's what her parents told her about, the disorder that had to come, needs to now and again, and she's ready. She looks uptown to the Aardvark's tower, a dark, jagged knife against the sky, and starts running toward it, cradling the bomb, her baby, to her chest.

The Slick Six are still standing on the shore of the East River, looking down the dark valley of 42nd Street at piles of flame in the street that once were cars or barricades but now illuminate the corpses nearby, helmets connected to padded shoulders at the wrong angles, a leg bent backward, a foot pointing straight up. A man tumbled where the pier meets the land, poked with bullet holes, one arm twisted back and lying underneath his torso, a look of surprise on his face. A woman curled around the post of a parking meter, her intestines unraveling around her. A bicycle tottering down the sidewalk, riderless, its tires on fire. A horse on its side near the flames, a half a block away. All around them are the shouts of police, the yelps of the Sioux, the drumrolls of guns, the racket of horses charging on concrete and asphalt, a low rumble of the moaning of the dying. This is what we were talking about in California, Zeke thinks. It's not as bad as I thought it would be. But Hideo and Carolyn are just shaking their heads.

"Let's go," Marco says, eyes only on the Aardvark's tower. "We've done buildings like this before. We just have to cover the staircases to make sure he doesn't get out—"

"Marco," Carolyn says.

"—then block off the—"

"Marco," Hideo says.

"—and then before he can—"

"Marco!" Carolyn says.

"What?"

"We're not going with you."

Marco nods. "I understand. I can take care of the Aardvark myself. Just wait here; give me two hours. If I'm not back by then—"

"—Marco," Hideo says. "We are not waiting."

"I don't understand," Marco says.

"We mean," Carolyn says, "that we don't want this."

"I still don't understand."

"This," Hideo says, and his arm makes an expansive gesture, taking in the dead around them, their open mouths and eyes, their broken horses. "This is too much."

"But it's almost over," Marco says, "and then—"

"—And then what?" Hideo says. "More of this? We do not want it."

"But this is what you've always asked me to do," Marco says.

"*You* wanted it this time," Hideo says.

"To set you free. To set us all free. To . . ."

Do some good in the world, Zeke thinks. He doesn't even have the words for it.

"I did all of this to get you back," Marco says. "To take us back to where we were, us and the world."

"But we don't want to go back there," Carolyn says. "Us or the world."

They can't see his face, but they hear him make a sound, a long sigh with a shriek coiled inside it, and it occurs to each of the three of them that they might have only a few seconds to live. I should have married her years ago, Hideo thinks. I should have called my parents, Carolyn thinks. And Zeke's mind goes to the photographs he's seen of Victoria Falls, the canyons of water, the rainbows upon rainbows. I should have gone when I had the chance. But Marco just stands there, his breathing coming fast; he wrestles it down, breaks it, forces it to slow.

"I see," Marco says. "Now I see everything."

"Marco," Zeke says.

"Don't," Marco says, and Zeke feels an arm go around him, Marco's hand on his back. "I know you must have tried." Then he's gone, and the three members of the Slick Six regard each other in the glowing light of the fires along 42nd Street. Carolyn won't say anything, won't let Zeke speak. Did we have our last conversation already? Zeke thinks. Was it today? Yesterday? What was it about? Hideo's brow has two vertical wrinkles in it. He wants to say something. They all do. They're mustering phrases that you can't take back, the words you say to end something, and as their voices rise all at once, a bell goes off in Zeke's head from a church covered in skin. Let the fights begin.

There are no fires at the doors of the Aardvark's tower, and so the thirty policemen who've been ordered to guard them are waiting in the dark. At first they were jumpy, twitching with their loaded guns toward every sound, and their fear made them hear everything: A rat scrambling in the gutter was a galloping horse; a paper hopping across the street echoed like gunfire. But now the war cries of the New Sioux seem far away, the shouts and shots recede, until the policemen are alone on a quiet street, in another country.

"Maybe they're going to wait until tomorrow to attack us," one of them says.

"Daylight. Yeah, they'll wait until daylight."

"So do we wait here or go home?"

"We can't go home. What if they attack in, like, twenty minutes?"

"What if they don't?"

"That's what I'm saying. We don't know. So we have to wait here."

Somewhere downtown is the whooshing rumble of a building collapsing, an arc of cheers.

"You hear that?"

"I'm not deaf."

". . ."

". . ."

"You ever hear the one about the bus full of ugly people?"

"No."

"Bus full of ugly people goes over the edge of a ravine and everyone in it dies."

"This is a joke?"

"Yeah, man, it's a joke."

"Well, I don't feel like hearing it."

"How about the one about the woman who walks into a sex shop looking for a—"

"Come on, man. Now is just not the time."

"Okay. A man walks into a bar and says, hey bartender, I'll

bet you five hundred dollars that between me and this guy here, we have five testicles."

"I told you, man, I don't want to hear it."

"All right, all right. Two beekeepers meet at a beekeeping convention—"

"Shut up!"

"Aw, come on, they're funny."

"I'm sure they're hilarious. That's not— You hear that?"

"What?"

For the policemen, the next thirty-two seconds are a blur of blood and bone, whistling knives, blind gunshots. A man finds his own arm on the pavement; another doesn't understand yet that he's been cut in half. The ones who are shooting don't know what they're aiming for, end up shooting each other. For Marco, it's a cleansing ritual. He'll do this thing, leave his mark on this place, then return to Hideo and Carolyn; he'll ask them again when the world is new, and they'll see it as he does, take him back. They can all move to an island off the coast of Belize, steal fruit from trees, hunt animals only to cook them over small fires. They will be beings without history. He stands before the doors of the tower, slick with blood and smelling of meat, breaks the locks on the door and walks inside, looking for the stairs; doesn't notice the woman behind him, following him in.

The Aardvark has pulled his chair out from behind his desk, dragged it over to the window, and he sits there looking over the amber glow of the city below. Empty bottles of pills roll around on the desk, tracing circles; something in the way the Aardvark is settled in the chair suggests to Marco that he doesn't intend to ever get up again.

"Miss Winderhoek! I told you to go," the Aardvark says, swivels around in the chair. "Oh. It's you."

"Hello, sir," Marco says.

The Aardvark looks him over, the gore on his clothes, the weapons in his hands. "I see you've been busy today. You've come to kill me; that's plain to see. But where are the rest of the Slick Six?"

"They're . . ."

"They left you again?"

". . ."

"Oh, Marco. Marco, I'm so sorry."

". . ."

"They never had the courage you did, did they?" He scoops up an empty bottle, takes it for a spin in his chair. "You were always what gave them their teeth. You're what made the Slick Six slick. Sick slick licks. Lick sick six." He stops the chair, gazes at the ceiling, head wavering. "That's why I concentrated on sending you to prison, you know. You never would have sold them out, but I knew at least one of them would not return the favor."

"Do you know which one?" Marco says.

"Does it matter?" the Aardvark says. "None of them deserved you in the first place. You were better than all of them put together. You still are."

"No, I'm not."

"Yes, you are. I always thought so." At once the Aardvark stares at him. "Why didn't you stay with me?"

"We talked about this a long time ago—"

"You call that talking? One little conversation after years of service?"

"It was just business, sir."

"You broke my heart." An expression seizes his face; his head jerks to the side, as if he has been shot in the back of the skull, and his left hand rises to cover his forehead. A long sigh.

"But that's the game, isn't it?" he says. "A couple of people get lucky, but most of the time, everyone always wants someone else. If we didn't, if we all just found each other, matched up two by two, three by three, four by four, all the way out"—he's smiling now, arm out, fingers fluttering in the air—"and all our desires went away, there wouldn't be much history, would there? No more. Just everlasting bliss."

" . . . "

"Sounds boring, doesn't it?"

"No, sir. It sounds all right to me."

"Please. I know you better than that. We are both men who do things, and we try not to think about them too much because that would make us crazy. Look out there." He waves toward the window at a new plume of fire rising over the rooftops. "Look what we made, you and I."

"No. You made that. I'm trying to undo it."

"Oh, Marco. Don't you see? We're history's agents and its slaves. It has made us do its bidding, made us go around the wheel again and take the whole country with us. But now it has no more use for us. Kill me. Then kill yourself. Then it's done, we go into a book somewhere, and everyone else can go on living their lives."

"I did come here to kill you. I had every intention."

"Then do it."

" . . . "

" . . . "

"No," Marco says.

"Then what are you going to do?"

"I don't know."

"I do," says Maria Lista Sandinista. She thinks of her parents, in the back of a van, in an apartment in St. Louis where water poured out of the ceiling, in the Wyoming hills. Mom, Dad, thank you so much for teaching me everything you could. Then she says, "You should have set me free too, Marco."

For an instant, the explosion from Maria Lista Sandinista's bomb is contained by the glass at the top of the Aardvark's tower, and its livid eye glares upon the city, sweeps a flash of light over the island in all directions at once. I see you. Then the glass gives way and the flames roar out, boil around the top of the tower, scatter into the sky. The metal holding up the top stories groans, and the pinnacle slides down the side of the building, tearing holes in the towers around it in its descent, until the frame of the eye is on the ground, blinded by flames and heat.

It silences Hideo, Carolyn, and Zeke, who stop fighting in midsentence, but don't close their mouths. Kuala Lumpur, who has been watching from the roof, gives a low whistle. For the police, who could see the flare of the explosion all over the island, it's a signal, a final order. He's gone. The word goes out on radios, to the boys in the park who had set up barricades along the stone walls, to the ones along the shore being forced into the water by Indians on horses, and they all put down their guns, put up their hands. They'll walk into the dark streets tonight, looking for ways to shed their uniforms, change into something else. They'll drink in bars lit by candles or running off of generators, in front of delis where there are beers on the sidewalk that they're just about giving away before they get warm. And the New Sioux will race up and down the island of Manhattan, whooping and crying; in a few hours, they'll gather around the pond at the southern end of Central Park, in the shadow of the mansions that commerce built, start one more fire, bring out drums and instruments, and sing and dance for what has been returned to them. The centuries are folding in on themselves; the next nine hours exist off the calendar, cannot be measured by clocks. It's the eternal present, the Big Now; this night will circle the Earth for decades.

CHAPTER XIII.

Reunions.

The Aardvark's tower still stands in the middle of New York City, a burnt, jagged spire stabbing the sky, but the planet is reclaiming it: The windows fall out, spin end over end to crash into the street; the floors fall in, and plants grow through the spaces they leave. Vines twine up the walls, young tree branches curl off, and at the building's shattered summit, a baby maple starts to spread its limbs. In the fall, the building will mimic the explosion that ruined it, the leaves flaming red and orange, stirring into the street below. For Robert Blackfeather Sherman, who lives with his family in a cabin at the north end of Central Park, the tower is a sign of balance, of equilibrium restored, though he can only guess at the significance. He has to read the world as he finds it now, for his visions have left him; the Vibe doesn't visit anymore. He can't remember the moment his gift disappeared, but it must have been just after he met Inu Kimura and they drew lines across Manhattan, gave Kimura the southern half, the New Sioux the northern half, cut Central Park in two. Gave a certain Captain Saloon his island. In the days before the meeting, when the New Sioux were settling into the city and Robert Blackfeather Sherman walked from one end of Manhattan to the other, the river rippled with the ghosts of his ancestors, all coming to thank him, to say good-bye; the streets blurred with the streaked trails of inhabitants past; the air above him warped with the arrivals and departures of gigantic spacecraft. Buildings rose and fell, winked out, streets turned to mud, to stone, back into streets, until it was all happening at once, a grand comedy of hope and futility, civilizations born and dying in a rainbow haze. The country was unmooring itself from its history at last, the past was the past, the past was the past, and they were all the land's new natives: the New Sioux, the rebelling slaves, the people who held on through the Aardvark's empire, bureaucrats sneaking into their old offices to fix by force what diplomacy before the collapse couldn't touch, women with briefcases flicking on fluorescent lights, traders occupying stores the Aardvark had closed years ago, new immigrants arriving by ship and plane to write their own history across the bricks and bones of the old nation. Robert Blackfeather Sherman could feel the soil swell with it all, and under his feet, the first beat of a deep pulse, a heart shocked into stillness working again, and there at the northern tip of the island, in the fields before the cliffs on the other side of the river, he knelt and cried for what had happened and what was coming, for the way he had done what the Vibe asked of him.

But after meeting Kimura, there were no visions. It took him a week to realize it; he kept expecting them to come again; they didn't. The great work of my life is over, he thinks now. I won't do anything like it again. He thinks he's content now, for it seems like more than enough to have taken New York back for his people, to have given his family a home. But when he's older, he'll miss the visions, the sense of purpose, the feeling that he was molding the clay of the world into a shape of his choosing. He'll dream of riding the green-and-gold plains again, his horse beneath him, a machine gun across his back. But he'll never go back there, never see his daughter Asia, who arrived with Keira Shamu just in time to see the last ceremonies on the steps of the federal courthouse, the deals that turned the land over. She watched her father shake hands with Kimura, with the new representatives of the city, the state. His speech was generous, there was kindness in his delivery, and when he grinned into the peals of applause, she recognized his old self returning; he was shedding his years as an agent of retribution already. He left the podium, descended into the crowd, and she fought through the masses to try to intercept him, losing and regaining sight of him, rehearsing what she wanted to tell him; found him in the arms of his wife, the unborn child big between them. His back was to her, his face resting in the crook of his wife's neck. Over his shoulder, his wife could see her husband's first daughter, her querying look, though she didn't know who the girl was. And the words left Asia Sherman's head; she waved and turned tail, deciding that her father had had enough of the past.

A week later, at a nightclub in Atlanta, Asia Sherman will meet the son of a Chinese coal magnate on the dance floor; he'll invite her to a party in Jakarta, and from there, she will fling herself into the arms of the lords of commerce. For the next three years, her life will be a shrieking chain of parties, in clubs in Santiago, Kobe, Colombo, Nairobi, Berlin; on a ship off Shanghai; at a decaying banana plantation in Ecuador; on an unnamed spur of rock a half-mile swim from the hills of St. Croix. On the arms of men in silk suits, soaked T-shirts, women in linen pants. In hotel rooms where the new cities of India draw serpents of light across the land at night. She'll have twenty-seven boyfriends and nineteen girlfriends, until her last partner, a Brazilian man who wants to marry her, finds out about her history and strands her in Cape Verde, leaves her at the airport. All at once, her party years will be over, though she won't believe it at first. The hotels and clubs will be closed to her; the airlines won't take her money. I know who you are, they'll say. So she'll stay on the island for two more years, change her name, farm sugar, learn Hindi and Bengali, go back to India and make a fortune in electronics. In time, she'll meet the Brazilian again in a restaurant on the top floor of a former monastery in Moscow, carvings on the walls of epiphanies and martyrdom, suffering and redemption.

"I know who you are," the Brazilian will say. "I know who you were years ago."

"Can't a girl change?" she'll say.

"Just like that?"

"Just like that."

Inu Kimura came to New York to examine his new piece of real estate, and hasn't left. There's too much money to be made, even with slavery outlawed again and other laws introduced, some of which Kimura resents, for they impede business, take a cut from his profits. Taxes, they call them. Graft, he says. Robbery. You call yourself a government now, but you are as much of a thief as I ever was. Nerve, now an instrument of legitimate trade, is always there at the docks with a clipboard, marking down with horrifying accuracy the movement of things into and out of the city. Every half an hour, his cell phone rings, and another agent on another pier barks at Nerve in a code that Kimura, eavesdropping, has given up trying to understand. At the end of every month, Nerve hands Kimura's secretary a piece of fruit—a pomegranate, a kiwi, for these things are valuable—and walks into Kimura's office to settle accounts. Sometimes it's all business, and the smoothness of the transaction is the only indication that the two men know each other's pasts. Other times, though, Kimura is feeling nostalgic.

"We used to screw people like us," he says.

"It's not as much fun being on this side of the law, is it?" Nerve says. "But isn't this worth it?"

The harbor teems with even more ships than before; the shoreline is a wall of rusting hulls, sails, and solar panels. The piers shimmer with light and sound, the buzz of music and commerce. The old slave block is a taquería with a ranchera band playing on the roof, amplified through the bullhorn mounted over the front door. The accordion sounds like a circus, like a train, and the streets are full of people again, from the cities of Asia and Africa. They're painting their passports brown; they speak new languages that change the meanings of things, tell stories of what it was like before, as though "before" were a distant planet.

"Maybe it's worth it," Kimura says.

But he still thinks of Osaka, the rivers of neon, the wooden door with his insignia burned into the grain. It irritates him to watch the men in black suits waiting for the fishing boats to come in; they poke through the catch with long white poles, give a nod, and men lift a prize tuna as if it's a piano and convey it to an ice-packed crate, in which it will be flown to Japan to be eaten by men for a stupefying price. Once, he was at that table, eating too; now he can't afford not to sell it. The money's too good. Four months later, after a dinner of sea urchins and sake, Inu Kimura will suffer a stroke that kills him on the spot, but before the police even know what happened, the body will be gone, the scene clear. Kimura will return to Osaka as ashes; his funeral under the Sanwa-Sumitomo building will be the biggest and most secret party the city has seen in a decade, ministers and former heads of state with their arms around counterfeiters, chief financial officers hustling across a dance floor to a fifteen-piece band composed of diplomats and opium dealers. At four in the morning on the third day, the revelers who remain will commend his ashes to the Yodo, and they will wind through the ocean of light, tour the city he loved. All over the world, he used to say, I am a feared man. But when I am in Osaka, I am still that city's child.

Nerve will hear stories of the party a few weeks afterward, stop by Kimura's old office to deliver a final pomegranate.

"Who will they get to replace him?" Nerve will say.

"Replace?" the secretary will say. "Not him. Nobody could." Two months later, Nerve will be in Vermont, standing in front of the ruined house of his lover's brother. You got that right, he'll think, and turn around and get in the car without going inside. He's seen all he needs to, wonders if Kuala Lumpur still has room for him in Buenos Aires. She does.

On the pier at East River Park, there's a noodle shop thick with steam where a woman named Ono Fidelia slings anemones soaked in butter, fried in garlic, submerged in curry. Zeke Hezekiah and Keira Shamu plan to meet there, so he's standing in the doorway on a rain-pelted afternoon, after the last ships have gone out, before the first ones come in. There are only four tables, eight chairs, and seven of them are empty; a man in a gray coat plays chess with himself in the corner, making a move, turning the board, puzzling over the pieces.

"If only you knew what your opponent was thinking," Zeke says.

The man looks up, squints at him. Looks back at his pieces. The rain becomes a torrent, and Zeke steps outside, waits under a giant multicolored umbrella that turns the water around him into a beaded curtain. Keira arrives seventeen minutes later, wearing a newspaper that she's folded into a wide hat. She smiles when she sees him, so hard that her affection for him spooks her and the thoughts scatter from her head.

They haven't seen each other since North Carolina, when he got off the bus in Asheville, but they've heard reports of each other. Of Zeke: that he went back to Monaco, to Andalucía, to South Africa. Of Keira: that Doctor San Diego had joined the cosmos at last, the bus trip was over, the Americoids were over, she was staying in New York; that she had showered, cut her hair, become a painter, given up the trade.

"It's good to see you, Zeke," she says.

For half an hour, they dodge personal questions and talk about mutual acquaintances. How Doctor San Diego's body was found in Mali, grieved over by griots. Nobody knows how it got there, but it was discovered that he was one hundred and twelve years old. How the Americoid tribe was gathering as something else now. That was the thing with those people: The names and faces changed, the combinations changed, but the vibe was the same. They pulled their family out of the ether.

"It's not as easy for some of us," Keira says.

"No," Zeke says. He got a postcard in Monaco from Hideo and Carolyn a few months ago: *Living in Osaka. Have child. Are happy now.* He hasn't heard from Dayneesha at all, not since the last phone call from Kansas while the New Sioux were setting fires in New York.

"What are we doing next?" she said.

"Day. There's no next. There's no we."

She was silent for a moment and then said, "Mr. Hezekiah, it's been real nice knowing you."

"You too."

"You know how to find me if anyone needs me," she said. But he didn't, and never will.

"Why didn't you say anything to Marco?" Keira says. "Before they did?"

"They needed to say it. And I thought that they'd just fight about it, and then—"

"They'd come together."

"Right."

" . . . "

"It could have been good, you know? Really good," Zeke says.

Zeke Hezekiah, Keira thinks. If only you knew.

"There's no way he could have gotten out, is there?" she says.

Zeke looks outside. The stripped spike of the tower, a burnt weed in the rain.

"If you had seen that explosion, Keira. Just the size of it. I don't know how anyone could escape it."

Keira thinks of the Digby pier, of engineers and Inuit. She knows.

At first, Marco thought his trick hadn't worked, for the fire was all around him, eating his clothes, biting into his flesh;

then he understood that he was riding the spire of the Aardvark's tower out of the sky, toward the ground, and for a full
second he was weightless, could have reversed his direction,
floated above all this, flown away. Then the spire crashed into
another building, opened a long gash in the side, and Marco
watched gray chairs, black metal desks, and stained plastic
walls of empty cubicles flash by. He jumped, snagged a length
of bundled cables hanging from the cauterized floor, slowed
himself down as he slid along its length. Stopped with a yard
to spare, looked up, and climbed hand over hand into the
wounded building while the spire fell away beneath him, trailing smoke.

He watched Zeke's plane take off from a boat in Jamaica
Bay, watched from the roof of a housing complex in Battery
Park while the ship carrying Hideo and Carolyn cleared the
harbor. Thought for a few days that he could wreak vengeance;
he could ruin them, destroy their lives. But it wasn't what he
wanted. He went south again, walked along the cracking roads
to Asheville, up the mountain to the leaning barn where Johanna had been. But she was gone, the sign she'd left washed
out by rain, the room shimmering with ants, spiders, small rodents making nests in cabinets. In Fort Worth, the war was at
the city limits, Dayneesha's warehouse a skeleton streaked with
ash, a hole punched in its head by a shell. In Miami, the islands
in the harbor were smaller, the waves lapping away at the
beach; the residents were building walls around the perimeter,
trying to keep the ocean out, while the ocean bided its time,
knowing it could get in whenever it wanted. He stole onto a
freighter bound for Venezuela, where the oil was almost gone
and the guns were growing around what was left. In the Ama-
zon, the tribes who'd taught him how they fought were gone. A
woman with her hands on the wheel of a pontoon boat said that
some had became loggers, some moved to Caracas, others moved
deeper into the forest. Two became criminals, lords of favelas
in Brazil. One became a pop star who lived in a yacht in the bay

off of Rio de Janeiro. At last, Marco was in Zimbabwe, where they were taking down the last of the streetlights to sell the wires, the discs of tinted glass.

"I'm looking for the Last True Chief of the Shona," he said.

"You want to see into the past?" they said.

"No. I don't want to see it anymore."

In Mongolia, they're still breaking horses, but there are fewer people, fewer horses; they've withered into the ground, leapt into the sky. We think of them sometimes, say the people who abide. In Ulaanbaatar, they haggle for tires and feed, offer blankets, promise their labor. At night they lie on the ground outside the city and look for satellites, pretend to shoot them down with arrows. That's what you get for trying to watch us. In Korea, Marco stands before Red Kwon's grave, a broken tower alone on a hillside overlooking the DMZ. Why did you make me into this? he wants to ask, but he knows how Red Kwon would answer. His eyelid would flicker, he'd show the whites of his teeth, and give Marco a pole to the ribs. You were supposed to know when you were broken. It's not my fault that you didn't. He thinks about Pulau Tengah, the colony of New Elysia, how the orange light fell into the dark ocean while the lords of global commerce on the other side of the island called an office thousands of miles away, moved 240 million euros in two seconds. He could go back there, join the oil executives in their atonement, plant himself on the beach, his toes in the water. He could lie on the shore and wait until the sea rose to take him, him and the island, the coastal cities of the world, wait for the planet to decide it had had enough of us and eat our history, then pull itself out of orbit to die in the sun.

The street in Guatemala City where he first met Red Kwon is underneath a pile of broken stones and timber, the victim to a bombing by narcotics traffickers. In the villages in Colombia, Marco can see the signs of the wars of his childhood on the fathers and mothers, the rifts in their skin, the snap in the muscles, the dull spark along the edges of their eyes. But it's not in their children. In the evenings, the kids sit on the curbs along the painted walls of plaster houses with sodas and beers, stretch their legs into the road, slump their backs, assume that the crackling chain of sound from another part of town is firecrackers, though they wouldn't be able to tell the difference.

He moves into Bolivia, to the twisted trees and dirt roads, the slanted fields, the slums that grew him, though he can't remember them. Near Quebrada del Churo, a wavering wooden building leans over the edge of a ravine, its porch in a slow slide as the beams beneath it warp, the ground shifts.

He spends a year killing and eating animals, collecting nuts and insects, while he clears a plot of land around the former schoolhouse. One square patch of earth against the fingers of the trees, he thinks at first, but then reconsiders and lets the trees take back part of the land he cleared. He doesn't need it. Soon he's growing vegetables, more than he can eat. He sells some to the people around him, knows that the world will take the rest. A papaya eviscerated by birds. A pepper plant strangled by weeds. He spends most of his nights alone in his house, looking into the ravine, while the noise of the river below moves through his head. Sometimes he walks to the nearest town to hear music, drink burning liquor, talk to the man who built the cot he sleeps on, the woman who made his blankets. They can't see the marks on him that show what he was, and he speaks the same language that they do, though to them he sounds like a child.

Right about when Marco loses track of how long he's been there, the assassin's ghost steps through the wooden door of his house while Marco is eating dinner, moves across the floor without a sound, sits across the table from him, eyeing the meal, the steam writhing from vegetables.

"What brings you here?" Marco says.

"Just passing through," the assassin says.

"Do you want something to eat?"

"No, I'm not hungry."

"So how is it? Being dead?"

"You get used to it. For me, even the dying wasn't so bad, though I know that's because you were merciful."

"Do you still see the past?"

"Yes and no. It all looks a little different from here."

"Different how?"

"It's hard to explain."

"Try."

"It's beautiful. Do you want to see?"

"Yes."

"Now?"

"I don't know."

"You could if you wanted to," the assassin says. "Come on." He stands up, holds out his hand. Marco puts down his fork, looks down at the food. A slice of pepper. A mound of rice. He doesn't want to go, but he doesn't know why he wants to stay, either.

After the rains stop, Marco paints the house in reds, oranges, blues, yellows. He brings in fruit from the field, strings it from the porch rafters to dry. Antonio Morales, who sold Marco his furniture and shared a beer with him afterward, their legs dangling into the gully, passes through his field, waves, knocks, and invites himself in. It takes Marco a while to realize that Antonio is making sure he's still alive.

Just before the rains start again, Marco hears a whistle from the field, Antonio shouting about how he's coming and bringing a visitor with him, someone from far away. Marco grabs three warm bottles from the table, moves through the house, opens the door. Johanna is standing there among the hanging fruit, the birds in the fields eating his crops. Her hands on her hips. She has been to New York and back to Asheville, Fort Worth, Miami, spent two weeks in bed in a shuttered room in Venezuela squirming from a sickness that scoured her out while a bass player thumped through the floor beneath her and dogs mated at her door. In Harare, she traded her watch for a ticket to Karachi, broke up a knife fight over the sale of a girl in Mongolia. She slept under a bed in Guatemala City as bullets flew through the open windows, singed the covers with their passage, drilled themselves into the plaster of the far wall. She took the highway all the way down the backbone of Latin America, stopping everywhere to hold out a folded photograph, a copy of Marco's mug shot almost faded into unrecognizability, always asking, have you seen this man? Do you know where he's gone? Two years, four months, twenty-seven days; she has counted every hour.

"You look even worse than you did when you got out of prison," she says.

"You don't."

"You didn't have to go so far."

"I didn't know what else to do."

For four seconds neither of them moves, and both wonder if there will be violence. She could bring the past screaming onto the porch and butcher it, the things he did, the things she did, what she told the Aardvark that cost Marco six years of freedom. They could kill each other with it, leave two corpses—one in the field, one in the ravine—the villagers reading their histories in their entrails. It almost comes out of her all at once, crawling out of her throat, trying to escape, but then Marco lunges forward, puts his hand across her mouth. Shakes his head. No more history now. No more. Then he swings the door wide and opens his arms, and she walks in.

"I'm so sorry I abandoned you," she says. "I'm so sorry I betrayed you. You didn't deserve it."

"Yes, I did," he says.

Six years pass of coffee and onions, weddings in town with brass bands whose members scowl in black suits and sneakers, making music to which Johanna dances with every man there, whirling and clapping. Their first child is born in the field in front of the house, dies of dehydration three weeks later, and they put him in the ground where she labored with him, hammer a wooden marker into the soil that a big storm carries off. A second child is born on the cement floor of the bar in town during a birthday party. She lives, speaks Spanish better at three years old than her mother ever will. When she's five, Marco takes her to La Paz to show her what a city looks like; the bus passes through the slums where Marco's sure he was raised, but looking over the cinder blocks, the metal roofs, the nests of electrical wire and open ditches, the dogs and chickens in riot, children staring at him hard as he goes by, he doesn't recognize any of it.

On the way back to Quebrada del Churo, as the sun is going down, the bus breaks down on a straight shot of road through the country. A metal part falls from the engine so twisted that nobody, not the driver nor any of the two dozen passengers, can tell what it is. It's getting dark under the trees overhanging the road, so all the passengers get off the bus to sleep with their feet in a ditch, their heads in the dust on the road's shoulder. Marco climbs to the roof with his daughter; lies down amid the bundles and packages tied down with rope, straps, and bungee cord; folds his arms across her; and the people on the ground all fall away, the bus beneath them rises into the air and bears them aloft until they're high over the landscape and they can see the road curling away, the long line of the horizon tracing the arc of the planet, the trees bowing and swaying with gravity; and there in the air he asks the world if he's free now, if he's good enough. The Vibe doesn't say a word, for it's been done with him for years; but in his daughter's breathing, the calls of birds from the vines draped over branches, the thickening sky talking about rain, the insects landing with rustles and whispers on their faces and hands, the ruts in the road that connect La Paz with his wife sleeping on the warping porch at the edge of the ravine, he thinks he hears the answer.

ACKNOWLEDGMENTS

To Steph, again. To Liz Gorinsky and Cameron McClure, for pushing. To Nathan and Dawn, for taking us to see Dr. Evermor. To the McPherson police department, for understanding. To Deanna Hoak. To Robert Legault. And to all of you too.

Laurel J. Silton

Brian Francis Slattery edits public-policy publications dealing mostly with economics and economic issues; he is also an editor of the *New Haven Review*, a literary journal. When not editing, he plays the fiddle and banjo. He also writes occasional nonfiction pieces about public policy and the arts, mostly for his local alternative weekly. He is the author of one previous novel, *Spaceman Blues*, and lives just outside of New Haven, Connecticut, with his family. He can be reached very easily at www.bfslattery.com.